CLOCKWISE TO TITAN

CLOCKWISE TO TITAN

ELON DANN

HOT
KEY
BOOKS

First published in Great Britain in 2013 by Hot Key Books
Northburgh House, 10 Northburgh Street, London EC1V 0AT

A CIP catalogue record for this book is available from the British Library.

ISBN: 978-1-4714-0095-7

1

Typeset by Palimpsest Book Production Limited, Falkirk, Stirlingshire
This book is set in 10.5pt Berling LT Std

Printed and bound by Clays Ltd, St Ives Plc

FSC

Hot Key Books supports the Forest Stewardship Council (FSC),
the leading international forest certification organisation, and is committed
to printing only on Greenpeace-approved FSC-certified paper.

www.hotkeybooks.com

Hot Key Books is part of the Bonnier Publishing Group
www.bonnierpublishing.com

To Helen, Josef, Jane
My three pylons

Contents

Chapter 1

Outside

The Moth swayed on the top of the wall, delicately positioning his feet to avoid the tangled coils of barbed wire. He wobbled as he fumbled for a handhold on the metal bars.

'Come on!' I rasped up at him through the darkness. 'They could catch us any second!' We should have had hours to spare, but things were not going to plan. We'd barely scraped through one disaster, and now we were desperately late. Moth's slowness was an agony. Was I going to have to steer him over every tree stump and hole in the ground for the entire week?

'I'm doing my best; it's not easy for me!' he whimpered. Releasing his grip on the bars that supported the wire coils, he made a sudden backwards leap, springing away from the wall and dropping more than twice his height onto the soggy ground beside me. He landed heavily in the slippery mud, but remembered to buckle his legs as he did so. He stood up, clearly winded and a little shocked at his own rashness, and leant against the wall. He raised and waggled each foot at me in turn to prove that he had managed to avoid snapping an ankle.

'That was risky, Moth,' I cautioned him, impressed all the same. Perhaps we had a slim chance. Maybe this could work;

perhaps I could take a snooty, snotty, fourteen-year-old bookworm across open country for six days and avoid capture and all the horrors that would entail. After all, we had now made it beyond the walls of the Institute, the first time anyone had done that since Topsy-Turvy had smuggled himself out in the meat skip.

We crept hurriedly along the wall in the direction of O-Wing, visible as a black slab contrasting against an overcast night sky stained orange with the glare of reflected lights. Snow was falling in soft, sticky flakes the size of coat buttons. It must have been five degrees below, but The Moth and I were already too hot in our layers of overalls and plastic wrapping. After a few minutes we reached the accommodation for female wards, where we paused for breath and scooped up handfuls of snow to pat on our crimson faces. I counted the required number of windows from the end wall, grateful that Harete lived on the ground floor. I recounted them twice more, only too aware that if I made a mistake it would be the staffroom I would be alerting to our presence. And that would spell the end of us all.

Needing no instructions, Moth hung some way back and readied himself to make a run for it. We were so far behind time by then, we didn't know if Harete would still be waiting or if she'd been discovered. The room might be empty, or it could be full of people ready to leap out and grab us. If we'd any sense, we'd leave Harete behind and just get going by ourselves, as I'd wanted to do from the very beginning.

I looked nervously over at Moth. His goggle-like spectacles shone blankly back at me, and he made a winding motion with his hand, urging me to get on with it. I shrugged and rapped on the window with my knuckles, the noise muffled by my gloves made from socks and plastic bags secured with tape.

'This is where it goes wrong,' I muttered. 'Why did I agree to bring her? I might as well have agreed to take along a bag of anvils, or a . . .' I tried to think of the most impossibly useless and cumbersome thing one could want on a long and hazardous trip. I rapped again and we waited some more. *Hurry up, you stupid girl, our lives depend on this!* Rap and wait . . . rap and wait. There was no response. She must have given up, or been captured. How much would she tell them? We'd be faster with only two, but even so, I found myself feeling grievously sorry for the girl.

The window barged opened noisily, warped wood squeaking against wood. I tensed up, preparing to flee, but relaxed when I saw a large, bulky package being shoved part way through the opening. I grabbed the end and tugged it all out. It was a cheap foam mattress wrapped up in several layers of plastic sheeting, rolled tightly into a tube and secured with lengths of electrical flex. Moth and I each had one just the same. Next, a pair of legs appeared at the opening, enlarging rapidly in a slithering motion to form the barely recognisable shape of Harete.

I shoved the window shut. The Moth came over, and he and Harete briefly clasped each other. We secured Harete's bed roll to her body and the two friends padded after me down the slope. We slipped and stumbled our way into the narrow, wooded strip that separated the Institute from the river we had next to cross. As we entered the belt

3

of copse I glanced back and saw with alarm the mess of footprints we had left behind us during our progress down the squelchy, muddy slope. I swore viciously, and hoped that the snow would very soon fall deeply enough to cover them. Everything depended on it.

The three of us bumbled and crashed our way into the scrappy wood. The light from the upper-storey windows of the Institute, above us and to our rear now, was barely sufficient to penetrate more than an arm's length into the tangle of wispy branches and snaring brambles. We had to make it to the riverbank, and quickly, but there seemed to be no way through. There was no path. The twigs and briars snared and tripped us, rasping and ripping our home-made waterproofs.

I was boiling hot, dizzy from the heat inside my bizarre outfit. At least that aspect of our plan had worked well; too well, in fact. I flailed my arms in front of me and kicked out with a leg into the dark undergrowth, but met only with more snagging thorns and whipping branches. I felt the other two hovering impatiently a step behind me, anxious to get away, not understanding why I had let them down so soon. One of them, I could not see who, bent down onto all fours and tried to force a way through a small archway of branches, but almost instantly became hooked like a fish on the thorns. Knowing that to hole our waterproofs could be fatal, I unsnagged whoever it was and they retreated.

I pulled off my improvised balaclava and let the soft, fat snowflakes cool my head as I thought. Why had this gone so wrong? Moth and I must have been missing for close to

4

half an hour by now, and we were barely out of the perimeter wall's shadow. This was worse than I had ever imagined it could be. My mind flitted back to our cell, and the awful, twitching thing that lay there, the broken spoke in the wheel of my beautiful plan. And now, these impenetrable woods. The disgrace of failing like this, after all our preparations, was insufferable.

Moth piped up. 'Let's go back!' he whispered.

My right hand rocked up to menace his chin and I had to restrain myself from making it connect. We might be within sight of its wall, but we were outside the Institute now! By escaping, we had poked out the ogre's eye, wounded and insulted him. But by bringing The Moth along, we had robbed the beast of his irreplaceable charmed amulet, mortally endangered him. That was unforgivable. We could never return.

'He means, back that way! Fewer trees, outside your cell!' Harete hissed, staring up at me angrily. My fist sprang open like a smashed clock. I forced myself to think to when I was up in my room, looking out of the barred window down at the river beyond. Harete was right, the trees *had* looked far sparser and more open there. We needed to track back along the edge of the wood until we were directly below my old cell, risk returning to the point where Moth and I had scaled the wall. Of course, if they'd noticed us missing, it would be amongst the first places the clavigers would start their search.

We set off at a fast pace, spurred by the need to make up for wasted time. To have the least chance, we simply had to be over the river before the klaxons blared and the searchlights blazed like tinned suns.

The three of us plastic-wrapped scarecrows padded back towards the main cell blocks until we were at the point where Moth had jumped down from the wall – the marks his feet had gouged in the mud were still visible. Yes, this was more like it. The short trees were thinly spread out here, the ground clear but for a carpet of leaves now disappearing under the ever-thickening snow layer. We dived into the cover of the trees and pressed on urgently through the little wood, panting heavily, trying to avoid any more damage to our strange clothes or to the bulky packs we carried. The light was terrible, the trunks and branches nothing but barely visible silhouettes. I went first, shepherding the others around obstacles that lay in their path.

'Fallen log here, then a small drop. Mind that bush to the left. Take my hand; I'll lift you over this.'

All the while I listened out, knowing that at any second the buildings behind us could blow apart like a volcano and disgorge a roiling cloud of men, men who would kick the breath from my ribs until I was four-fifths dead and think it hardly worth mentioning in their reports. *Three escapees recovered. Special-status attendee returned unharmed. One female recovered with minor facial contusions. One male, severe head and upper-body trauma. New pair standard-issue boots required, see attached requisition form. Interrogation will commence 5 a.m., no restrictions on methods. Suggest . . .*

A slight rise, a final, unwelcome barrier of scrubby, thorny undergrowth to push through and scramble over, and there it was: the river.

We huddled on the bank, staring at it. The river was high in its bed; the surface of the black waters just a step beneath us. We could see no reflections in the river; it was just a void into which the falling snow vanished. It looked utterly deadly and very, very uninviting. I no longer felt too warm, no longer felt anything at all except an undiluted, frigid dread.

Without saying a word, I unwound our home-made rope from around my shoulders and tied it in a tight loop around my chest. I took the free end and did the same to Harete, then The Moth. A decent length of the rope dangled free behind him. We were now linked together – whatever happened to one of us would happen to us all. I motioned for them to take their rolled-up foam mattresses, sealed in layers of plastic sheeting, and to hold them tightly to their chests.

'Whatever you do, don't let go. These mattresses will keep our heads above the water. They'll float like a dream, and so will we,' I reminded them. 'When we get into the river, start kicking until we're in the middle. I want us to make it to the deepest part and be carried by that fast current. It'll be icy cold, but just bear it. When I see the pylons, I'll give you a shout. That's the signal to start kicking again to get us to the other side.'

They nodded in silence, appalled at what was to come, as was I. Would we freeze to death, or drown, or be seen and shot? But I was also relieved; relieved that we were away from the horror of that prickly wood and its grasping thorns, relieved that we were again following the plan. *My* plan.

7

I sat down on the riverbank and plunged my legs into the water, then pushed myself off and into it with a splash. I was surprised at how deep it was; I was instantly floating. The short length of rope holding me to Harete meant I only bobbed a short distance into the water. It did not feel too cold; our layers of insulation were working, as were our mattress-floats. Harete followed me into the water, and The Moth was almost tugged in head first as the current took hold of Harete and me and started to drag us downstream. I quickly checked to make sure that all of us were fully in and that no one had let go of their floats.

'Go!' I said.

We kicked our legs under the black water and edged clumsily out into mid-stream, where the current was strongest. The three of us suddenly spun around, no longer in a neat line but in a twirling circle. I was staggered at the force of the current and the speed with which it started to carry us away.

We clasped our large, tubular floats tightly against our chests. Each float was as big as my torso, and wonderfully buoyant. So too, to begin with, were our clothes, stuffed as they were with packaging material to keep us warm. My legs floated up behind me, just beneath the surface. As long as we kept our grip on the floats, our heads and upper bodies would be kept completely out of the lethally cold water.

We were on our way!

'To life!' I blurted out, momentarily overcome by the improbable prospect of survival and success. Immersion in the clean, fresh water felt like a new beginning, the chill river like a liquid expressway to worlds beyond our experience.

'To j-j-justice!' came Moth's weedy voice through chattering teeth.

'To happiness!' said Harete.

We drifted and spun. Within a minute of entering the water the current had whisked us away from the Institute and the reflected orange sky-shine it had provided. Rapidly, we were in almost total darkness. We spun round and round with increasing speed, and I realised with mounting panic that I had no idea any more which riverbank was which, nor how far we had travelled. All I could see around me was a whirl of falling snow made more dizzying by our own spiralling motion.

The cold of the river, initially welcome as we stewed inside our over-insulated clothing, slowly started to grip me. I felt my legs go cool, then cold, then numb. After some minutes, I no longer knew I had legs. Far worse, water started to leak in through the dozens of gaps and rips in my clothing's outer layers where we had failed to seal them properly or where I had torn them on our way through the woods. Each new trickle of water soaked my overalls underneath and saturated the insulation, making me sink a little lower. I tried to compensate by adjusting my grip on my mattress-float, pulling myself a little higher up onto it, but it became very strenuous. Tickling needles of icy water started to make it through to the skin on my stomach and back. These were almost pleasant in the first instance, then annoying, then a torture.

For some unknowable time we drifted, twisted and bobbed. My discomfort grew, my limbs became leaden, my head drowsy. We remained like that for . . . was it minutes? Tens of minutes? An hour? I lost all gauge of time.

From somewhere in the darkness beside me came a low, despondent groan that sounded like a life leaking out into the freezing ether. The noise shocked and scared me. The fact that we were roped together began to seem like a bad idea, for if someone let go of their float and slipped under, might they not pull the others down with them?

I shook the snow from my face and stared out into the blackness, trying desperately to find something by which to orient myself. There was no sense of motion now; it was impossible to tell if we were drifting, rotating or stationary, or, if we were moving, in which direction. Nothing could be seen of either riverbank. Even the flurries of snowflakes were becoming hard to see in the dark. I tried to focus through them and onto the shore, but found my attention sucked into the vortex of flakes, infinite in number, as they fluttered, fell, rose, danced and looped. They were restful, despite their dynamic madness. And so pretty, the swirling shapes . . . so complex and yet so bewitchingly simple. Relaxing. Hypnotic. My eyelids wilted and I found that even with my eyes closed I could still see patterns like those the flakes made. Surely no harm in closing my eyes and resting for a second. Why not grab a few seconds' sleep and let the river do its work? So peaceful . . . dreamlike . . . not even cold now . . .

Suddenly, my numb legs smashed against something hard under the water, some trapped object. The pain was incredible, my shins were on fire with the pain. I detonated awake from my cold-induced trance. I knew in an instant that we were all just seconds from death. The freezing water was conveying us away, but convection was robbing us of our lives. Did we even have the strength left to paddle to the shore? Which shore? Where was the shore?

Something essential in me ignited. 'Swim!' I bellowed. We had to escape the freezing water; the river was a transport to oblivion. I thrashed with my legs, oddly re-energised by the pain from the blow they had received, and released my right hand from my float to use as a paddle, smashing it into the water and sweeping it back.

My brain flared and spluttered back into activity. I could not see where either bank was, but if we went across the river, not along it, we would eventually reach one or other shore. I could faintly make out the long, free length of the rope that tied us together trailing out over the surface of the water, and knew that must be being dragged out in a line by the current. So if we swam at right angles to that direction we would be heading to safety.

Over and over I dug my arm in, swept it back, dug it in, swept it back, deep and powerful, trying to drive us consistently in one direction. I sensed at least one of the other two was paddling as well, I could feel splashes of water on the left side of my head. Our three bodies collided, and for an instant I saw both their faces – wide-eyed, amethyst blue, stoked with terror. But alive!

'It's all right,' I was about to yell to them, but just as I opened my mouth, a dark shape divided us. Our three-in-one body jerked, I was violently yanked around and my back bashed into something. Harete screamed, and I knew at once we'd been caught.

I stopped kicking my legs. I couldn't see either The Moth or Harete any more; there was something huge and dark between us. I warily reached out and touched it. It was hard, metallic. I swivelled my head back and stared up through the snow.

We had become wrapped around the large, steel leg of an electricity pylon. I could make out its angular form, rising high above us. The Moth and Harete had passed one side of it, I had passed around the other, and the rope between us had looped around it. A pylon in the river? That made no sense . . . unless the river had flooded its banks and covered the surrounding land. In which case, it might not be deep here . . .

I took a gamble and raised my mattress-float up above my head. I sank up to my chest, but my feet settled onto soft mud. At that moment, a break in the cloud canopy appeared and the snowfall eased. Now I could see all four legs of the pylon that had snared us, and, very dimly, the next pylon along in the chain.

I waded over to the side of the metal leg where The Moth and Harete were bobbing in the water, outraged at how cold and tired I now felt. They kept hold of their floats and I strode through the water towards the more distant pylon, tugging them along behind me with the rope that still joined us. After a few dozen strides the level of the water fell enough for them to walk too.

'Be careful of what's beneath your feet. This is flooded land, there may be ditches or fences or anything at all below us,' I warned. We must have been walking up a slope, for with every step we took the water level fell – from chest height to waist height; then to knee height, then to the level of our ankles.

By the time we had reached the second pylon we were free from the water, walking on squelchy mud strewn with flood debris.

We sheltered in the right-angled fold of one of the pylon's steel legs and looked back across to the shimmering floodwater, made visible by moonlight streaming through a rip in the clouds. I understood why I had not been able to see the river's banks as I had expected when we had been adrift in the current; the river here had breached its banks and swamped the land. All I had been looking out onto was the endless, flat plain of the surrounding countryside.

Moth batted me with a stiff arm, wanting to say something. His cheeks and lips were plaster white, and he slurred his words as he spoke. It was difficult to understand him. 'Which side?' he asked. He was hardly able to stand, but he'd known the crucial question to ask, as always.

I shrugged. 'We'll wait for dawn, then we'll know. If we're still on the same side as the Institute, we'll have to go back in,' I added, seeing no value in raising false hopes.

We collapsed in a shivering huddle against the pylon's leg, delirious with exhaustion and relief at being free from the icy water. I could not yet rest; I had jobs to do. First, having removed a mitten, I patiently unpicked the knots in the rope that still bound me to Harete and Harete to The Moth. Mitten and rope were carefully placed on the ground and weighted down with stones to stop them blowing away. I was not going to let carelessness spoil our deliverance from the river.

I had just enough strength left to reach into one of the bundles strapped to my waist and pull out a small, flat tin. Inside were some pieces of broken glass. I took one in a shaking hand and used it to slice through the lengths of electrical flex that bound my float into a cylindrical shape. Freed, it uncoiled limply into its original, flat form. The foam mattress inside was covered in layers of polythene sheeting, and looked to be in good order. I motioned for The Moth and Harete to lie on the bed roll, which they did, side by side. I sat down beside them on the saturated, lumpy ground, too weary to care about its manifest discomforts, and propped myself up against the pylon.

We huddled together, all three of us soaking wet and bone-achingly cold. My brain bubbled with worries. How close behind us were they? Had our escape even been discovered yet? What had happened to . . . but I didn't want to think about *him*.

We slipped into an imitation of sleep.

This was only the start of our attempted journey to the Other country. An excursion, certainly, but an escape? Or was this all a futile charade? The doubts and vinegary injustice of it all nagged at me as I dozed, as impossible to ignore as a mouthful of broken glass.

And to think I'd once believed knowing The Moth was going to make my life easier.

Chapter 2

Inside

Looking back, I ache at my stupidity.

I thought being friends with The Moth would let me slip out of the clutches of my enemies like a bar of soap grasped by wet hands; I thought it would be my route to a trouble-free nine months before parole on my sixteenth birthday. But, as with just about everything else, I was wrong. Turns out, befriending The Moth was like scrambling for a chair next to a radiator in the canteen. Sure, you'd gain a few seconds of toasty warmth to thaw out your fingers. But in the Institute, warmth and friendship are tradable commodities, and owning anything desirable marks you out.

'A word . . .' said Atom, on some day like any other.

'Which one? So many to choose from, so few to describe how ugly you are!' I laughed back. Moth was daydreaming beside me, paying no attention. I was safe in The Moth's exclusion zone, hunched up against the autumn cold in a drab corridor underneath a barred window.

Atom snarled, but he respected the invisible sphere. 'Sticky wants you to introduce him to your pal,' rumbled the hulking teenage robber, one of the Swingers, Sticky's clan. The clan name was a distortion of 'C-Wingers', and most of its members came from the Institute's C-Wing, a gloomy concrete ingot of male dormitories that stood across the courtyard from my own B-Wing. C-Wing had a distinction for housing internees with disturbing records of violence.

'W-what?' I spluttered.

Atom delivered the rest of his message. 'Sticky wants to be friends with him. Best friends. Fix it, or else!' *Him* was The Moth, as Atom's thumb signalled. He went on. 'You pay no premiums –'

'How can I? I receive no visitors and get no parcels from outside!' I pointed out, almost proudly. Owning nothing and caring for no one were my two best protections from the clans, The Moth aside.

Atom nodded. He couldn't have been much older than me, but the clansman had stubble you could have used to scrape the asphalt from roads. 'So you do this for Sticky instead! No friends, no eyelids. Hunderstand?' Then he marched away, up an iron spiral staircase. I sprinted after him, setting the steps clanking noisily as I skidded over the rivets.

'I can't just . . . Moth's different! He won't *like* Sticky!' I shouted.

I'd strayed from the zone. One of Atom's hands clamped onto my face. From the other hand, crusty, brown-tinged fingers that reeked of negligent hygiene and suspect habits shot out and pinched one of my eyelids, then stretched it out much farther than I realised it could go. 'Everyone pays Sticky, one way or another!' Atom growled. I writhed as Atom opened his mouth to say more, but the creaking steps had attracted attention.

'You! Cease! Behaviour code infraction!' shrilled a voice

16

from below us. Jelly! We both ran, and gained the exit before he reached the top of the curving stairs, leaving him fuming but ignorant of our identities. Jelly blew his whistle and summoned other clavigers to chase us, but Atom and I soon gave them all the slip. After all, we were both old hands – although I at least occasionally washed mine.

Atom wasn't his real name, of course. Everyone in the Institute had a nickname; there's not a kid I knew who was ever called by his or her real name. Same with our baton-twirling clavigers. Mind, if you ask me, their job title itself is a nickname. 'Claviger' means 'one who carries the keys', or, as The Moth pointed out, it can also mean 'one who carries a club'. A very appropriate title indeed once you understand its meaning – which very few people do. But they are only called 'clavigers' because the bigwigs above them never like to call things by their proper names. It's a compulsion with people like that, people in charge of the more unpleasant things in life like sewers, prisons, executions. If their bosses were honest, the clavigers would be called 'guards', or 'warders'. And the Institute wouldn't be called 'the Institute'. Above the main gate it would instead say, 'Detention centre for young people we don't know what else to do with'.

That run-in with Atom marked the point when Sticky started to be my greatest problem, and when many lives started to come unstuck.

Unstuck . . . not as in 'became free'.

As in 'fell apart'.

Shaken, I made my way over to Moth's cell and kept an eye open for Harete. You might think it a little odd that girls and boys were allowed to mix freely, and that internees like me and innocent wards like Harete were permitted to mingle. But during the day, when we weren't on work shifts, the clavigers would open up the doors which linked together the different wings and blocks of the Institute, the male and female sections, and people were relatively free to roam.

I didn't know Harete's true name, either. Even her nickname was wrong; it should have been 'Arete'. That's a pretty classy nickname, and she had The Moth to thank for it, because he gave her the name and it stuck, despite the fact that no one but he knew what it meant. I guess people just liked the sound of it: 'ah re tay'. The name is something from ancient Greece, because The Moth was very into that sort of stuff – myths and legends from ancient times – and just about every other sort of stuff too. But the people in that area of the country, being lax-lipped, slug-tongued peasants for the most part, can't say anything properly in that accent of theirs, and they have an urge to shove an 'H' onto words that begin with a vowel. Hidiots, heach hand hevery one of them.

Still, as I say, even with that stupid extra 'H', Harete was a decent name to live with. You may not think so, but when I tell you that I knew people called Gut Gas, Stains, Two Spoons, Trembles and Nipple Slits, you may gain a new perspective on the matter.

Harete wasn't an internee; she was a 'ward'. But that's just another disguised word – in the Institute, it meant 'orphan'. Almost everyone who wasn't an internee was a ward. By my own reckoning, I'm an orphan too. Except that Dad is certainly still alive, although I haven't seen him for years. We reckon on balance that Mum's no longer wearing out the lino. The Moth says that on that basis I should class myself as *semi-orphanic*.

However, since Dad and I haven't passed so much as a swearword between us since he confirmed my identity to the marshals after they'd found me in a stranger's car when I was twelve, it hardly seems to me that he counts as a living parent either. My father was a delivery man – I think – but I didn't spend a lot of time with him when I was growing up. He preferred to leave me alone in the various tatty flats we lodged in, and when he found even that too much effort I was placed for months at a time in the care of 'closed schools' and 'special foundations'. These were much like the Institute except with colouring-in books and a milk ration. Of course, when I say 'placed in the care', I mean it in the same sense that maybe your family places its refuse in the care of the kerbstone once a week.

As for Mum, I don't remember her at all, and I'm not sure Dad can do much better. I don't think she was very capable. She was terribly thirsty though. Dad said she left me with him when I was still in nappies in order to pursue a life less vertical, and he had no idea if she's still dead drunk or just plain dead.

They convicted me of trying to steal that car. How can you steal one when you're asleep on the back seat? That's why I'm called an internee, a criminal.

Spotting Harete as she trundled over from her own wing, I tagged along and told her about my new problem, how Sticky wanted me to arrange for him to be friends with Moth. There was no possible advice Harete could give, nothing she could teach me. I was one of the oldest, one of the biggest, I knew every trick and dodge and scam and skive. But she was still good company.

'Worth a try?' she suggested. Even she looked doubtful.

'You're joking!' I gasped. 'Sticky and Moth? It took me long enough to get to know him, and I'm not sure he likes me even now.'

'Oh, Mo! You know he does!' Harete reassured me. 'He hates his name though, did you know that?' There was a pair of clavigers just behind us, striding rapidly in the same direction, but they swerved off to the right. We made it to Moth's cell. A year younger than Harete, and he had his own cell! Normally at that age he would have been in one of the male dormitories with around twenty other kids; you didn't get a cell until you were fifteen and even then you had to share it with at least one other boy. We shut the door just as the corridor exploded into chaos.

'Why don't you like your nickname, Moth?' I asked him. I pressed my ear against his cell door whilst he scribbled away at his desk in a notebook. I could hear the mayhem booming on the landing beyond; Jelly was ripping apart the other cells on the wing looking for a stash of cigarette butts (I heard him screaming about that), and to judge from the cries, giving the inhabitants of the cells an intensive pummelling to boot. Jelly was new, the youngest and keenest claviger by far, and easily the most loathed of all our guards. He was a yapping, bragging hyena whose inexhaustible ardour for discipline and punishment made his brother clavigers resemble a brood of drowsy, tetchy crocodiles.

Moth's cell should have been off limits even to Jelly, but nothing was ever certain with that man.

'A moth is an insect. It's not very flattering,' said Moth. He showed no sign of worrying about the mayhem in the corridor, or even of hearing it.

'Maybe not flattering . . . but definitely fluttering!' I replied, proud of my little joke under the circumstances. 'Well, it could be worse. It could have been an insect people don't like . . . a dung beetle, a cockroach, a spider . . .'

'Spiders aren't insects. An insect has six legs and wings. Spiders have eight legs and no wings,' Moth pointed out.

'Yes, yes, thank you, professor. Suppose you could have chosen your own nickname, Moth, what would you have gone for?' I asked, suspecting that Harete and I were about to receive a lecture.

A tip-off – Sticky, I guessed, simultaneously appraising events outside as I chatted with The Moth. Who else? I guessed that the kids on the wing hadn't paid him enough premiums that week. The cell search and beatings would be his revenge. Why have your clansmen graze their knuckles when a judicious whisper will get the clavigers to do it for you? He was clever like that.

'My preferred name would have been Ki-ron,' Moth interrupted after a moment's thought. At least, that's what it sounded like. He moved over to the door, brandishing his notebook and pointed to a picture he had drawn and at a word underneath it. The word was:

CHIRON

'You say it like Ki-ron,' Moth informed me. 'He was a

21

centaur, a great teacher. In ancient Greek mythology, you know. He was skilful and wise and taught many of the heroes, like Jason and Theseus.'

'What's a centaur?' I asked.

'That is,' said Moth, pointing at the picture.

'That's a man standing behind a horse.'

'No, it's a centaur. In mythology, they were half human, half horse. Sometimes they were drawn with wings, too.'

I saw a rare chance to get one over on my friend. 'Ah . . . wait, Moth. You're doomed. Look – it has six limbs and wings. It's still an insect!'

We got on all right, Moth and me, even though he and I had nothing in common, even though he was ignorant of and immune to all the dangers that kept my mind busier than a flea-infested juggler on a tightrope. He was something from another world, a world of ancient myths. And moths.

The Moth might not be pleased with his nickname, but there was nothing he could do about it. He became The Moth within about a month of his incarceration in the Institute. What's more, the nickname had something of the whiff of official approval about it, since it was given to him by one of the clavigers, a rare honour. It came about because he loved books, loved reading. But you can't read without light, and in his first days there it was noticed that he would always home in on any source of available light, book in hand. It was a dingy place, the Institute; light was at a premium. The grimy, grey walls soaked up light like the grimy, grey canteen bread soaked up the grimy, grey soup. We had no control over the lights in the dormitories

22

and cells of course; they were all turned on and off according to the time of day. So poor old Moth was forever hunting out skylights, windows, security lights, anything which gave out enough light to read by, and his addiction to illumination earned him his nickname.

After a couple of months he was allowed a reading lamp in his cell, one he could actually turn on and off by himself, whenever he wanted. Can you believe that? A lamp with a glass bulb . . . on and off, at his own convenience. Incredible.

Harete told Moth of the pressure Sticky was applying, but Moth looked blankly back at us. We couldn't really expect him to understand, his life in the Institute was completely different from ours. He had extra food rations, was excused all compulsory exercise, did no work, had his own reading lamp, his own cell.

All this luxury was due to his unique status. Moth was neither a ward nor an internee but something else altogether, an 'attendee': a person who is present. How's that for a disguised meaning? Of course he was present. Anyone could see that. What this verbal camouflage meant was that he was compelled by the government to be kept under lock, key and peephole at their special and most considered request. Indefinitely.

Not because he had done anything wrong, and not because he had no one to care for him, for he had two loving parents, both alive; in fact, Moth's situation was entirely due to them. Unforgivably, his parents had decided that it might be a good idea if things were called by their proper names, and if people talked about events that had actually happened, rather than just those it was thought polite and healthy to talk about. What's worse, they had not just thought these things, they had said them as well.

Had they been people like you or me or a claviger, no one would have given two sniffs of a tramp's pants what they had said. But since The Moth's mother was a professor, and his father was an important judge, people tended to listen to them. Or at least, did so until his father went abroad and was told he couldn't come back into the country, and his mother found that she wasn't allowed to leave the house any more, or speak to anyone on the telephone, or receive visitors. 'House arrest' they call it.

Just in case Moth's parents hadn't understood that the government really, really did not wish them to continue their stimulating line of discussion, their only son was invited to become a member of the Institute. Months before, not long after he'd arrived, The Moth had told me the invitation came when he was walking home from school and without warning found himself being lifted from the pavement and squeezed into a car between two marshals. 'They were very nice about it all,' he told me, 'they'd even been home and packed some of my things for me – some notebooks and pencils, my spare glasses. I did my homework in the car and we stopped to let me show them the occultation of Jupiter when it got dark, using their binoculars.'

'The what? Dabbling in the occult were you, Moth?' I teased him. 'Seeing if you could free yourself by slaughtering a chicken at midnight and dancing a tango over its insides, that sort of thing?'

'The occultation of Jupiter! It means the planet Jupiter passed behind the moon,' he went on. And on . . . easier to rugby-tackle a rockslide than to dam the frothing Moth-mouth. 'Jupiter's the protector of the solar system – it captures comets that might otherwise smash into the Earth! For an hour we watched it hide behind that cold stone before gliding back into view. Something majestic obscured by something familiar . . . don't you find that stirring? It's a very rare event!'

'You're a rare event, Moth! There you were, the filling in a thug sandwich, and you were worried about doing homework for a school you never went back to and the alignment of the planets?'

'I told you before. Mum and I knew it was going to happen; we were prepared for it. There was no point fighting them,' he replied.

Moreover, The Moth had immortality, or a close second to it. For despite all his special privileges, despite being a four-eyed weakling, despite being the son of a judge and a professor, despite, in other words, all the fine and just reasons that would normally have condemned a boy to a life of being tripped up, spat on or pushed down stairs, he was never, ever bullied. The clavigers did not isolate him from us, they did not even need to keep an especially close eye on him. It had simply been understood from his first day in the Institute that he was not to be troubled by anyone, ever, for any reason, and that whoever broke this rule would be hacked to a pulp. His regal treatment was because of his parents, of course. If they, his father in particular, had learned that their son was being bullied, they might have

25

had fewer inhibitions about speaking those considerable and troublesome minds of theirs.

Little wonder that The Moth loved his ancient legends. He was up there with the gods; he was immortal. Plus, he had a supplementary biscuit allowance.

Incidentally, I should say that the government of my home country, of the Institute's country, is not the sort of government that actually kills people who disagree with it, or that sends them to work in radioactive mines with only a teaspoon to dig with. Not nowadays. Maybe in the past it was like that, if you listened to what some people had to say, but not by our time. No, you can say what you like, pretty much. But if you're important, like The Moth's parents, and kick up a fuss, you can expect to be . . . inconvenienced. Maybe you might lose your job, or find your friends all cross the road to avoid you. Perhaps your telephone will be disconnected or you'll have to move to a remote dump of a town in a backwards part of the country where the yokels stick an 'H' onto the beginning of words. Things like that.

It's the same thing with the Institute. I don't want to give you the wrong impression of what life there was like. It wasn't too harsh. Well . . . not normally. The clavigers and the Director didn't really care enough to be brutal towards the youths they were charged with guarding. They were, in the main, simply indifferent to us. We were like pots of yoghurt or car parts, moving along a conveyor belt in a factory. They didn't care about us, but since it was their job to keep things trundling along in an orderly fashion, they had no passion for damaging us.

On the other hand . . . oh, curious phrase! Reminds me of Zinc Fingers, who lost his real digits but gained his slipshod replacements and a new nickname when a claviger slammed his hand in a cell door. Ten times. I say 'a claviger', like it was any of them, but it was Jelly. Two nicknames were born of that finger-crushing detonation, now that I think about it, because Jelly's came into being that day too. Some said it came from 'gelignite', on account of his explosive nature; but others who'd witnessed the event, and many similar ones that followed, reckoned the name sprang from a funny sort of jittery wobble he exhibited just before he lost control. Along with the nickname there arose a song, shouted out behind his back by those swift enough to run away before he recognised them. It went:

> *Face is purple, face is white,*
> *This claviger is gelignite!*

> *Wibble wobble on a plate,*
> *When will Jelly detonate?*

Zinc Fingers' misfortune was an exception though. A once or twice a month sort of exception.

When the shrieking and the banging in the corridor died down, I left Harete with The Moth and threaded my way back to my own cell. Sounds easy, but even a short trip like that could be surprisingly worrisome in the Institute.

Left, down the stairs, past rusting pipes exposed by cracked tiles and eroded mortar, the Institute's varicose veins. Avoid that dorm, it's full of jabbers and snorters . . . see that skeletal wreck with the nettle-green skin, there by the buckled window grille? He's their insensible sentinel, skull-full of inedible chemicals. A diet of tile polish . . . lovely teeth it gives you, mind.

Something had become lodged in the treads of my Institute-issue shoe; it was a tooth. 'Nice work, Sticky,' I muttered.

Sticky was an internee too, but he really was an accomplished crook, and a clan chief. Once, he had been just a minor block-baron, a thief and a bully, one amongst dozens, reigning over nothing more than a couple of dormitories and a handful of cells, and only then by dint of licence from Eye Inside. Now, just as Jelly had bubbled up like a warm fart in a cold bath to become brigade leader and deputy Director (at least according to Slate Tooth, nearing retirement and as indiscreet as he was jealous), so Sticky's warped star had waxed high to the point where his greed and power were almost unconstrained. Eye Inside's influence had waned to practically nothing.

Claviger! Which one? Bent Neck, as old as salt and largely harmless. Hobbies are spitting, swearing and hurting people; no different to most of the kids, really . . . straighten up, look like you're on an errand and move on. Dark here, the barbed wire's coiled so thickly outside the window almost no light gets through. Institute ivy, I call it.

It had been to shield myself from people like Sticky that I'd made such an effort to cultivate a relationship with The Moth; anyone who had a brain in their head – about one quarter of us there, at a generous estimate – would think that a smart move. Immortality of Moth's variety is mildly contagious; everyone, clavigers included, made sure that no rough stuff happened within a circle of ill-defined yet universally observed radius centred on Moth, as if he were a priceless ornament on a shelf in a museum. Entry to the sanctuary was strictly at Moth's bidding. Best of all would have been to share a cell with him, for that would be to live in a bubble of almost round-the-clock safety for yourself and your gear, but that was beyond the reach of my ambition. I'd settle for friendship.

But it was not as easy as that, for The Moth was a silent type, and had no desire to be friends with most of the other boys. He was never rude, but it simply was not possible for the average kid in the Institute to find common ground with him. The Moth wanted to learn and to read and to teach. He wanted to talk about, say, Mercury the messenger and Mercury the planet and mercury the metal, about geography, geology, geometry, genealogy, genes, geniuses and genies. Few boys could understand one word he spoke, nor could he understand their obsessions: fighting, gambling, contraband gum and cigarettes.

Consequently, The Moth was left alone. The would-be friends who had hoped to smooch their way into his supplementary food rations and his zone of invulnerability just drifted away once they realised that they were not only not his friends, they were in danger of annoying him and therefore risking a claviger's hoof to their soft and dangly parts.

Take the back route. Who's that crying? Big crowd of them all at it, no one I know, don't get involved. These buildings trap sadness like a honeycomb holds honey.

This corridor, right, then right again. No, it's a maze all right, but not a hive. Bees can come and go as they wish. Bees work together. Even the cockroaches get along with each other better than we do.

I had observed the failed attempts to get matey with The Moth, and figured I could do better. The times I'd spent as a youngster being left alone in empty flats had not been entirely wasted. My dad may have been a drifter and a deadbeat, but he was not a dunce. He always left me in the company of books he bought for pennies from the market, and cheap encyclopaedias given away free in weekly sections with newspapers. Self-schooled, that's what I am. I hoped my schooling was enough to make some impact with The Mighty Moth.

Unfortunately, Harete beat me to it, which is why I initially disliked her.

Worse still, she didn't even befriend The Moth to gain any advantage for herself, something which was incredible and unforgivable to me. It showed a lacking in survival instinct bordering on the reckless. The Moth evidently liked Harete for who she was, rather than how useful she was to him. It was he who gave her the name 'Arete', after all. She wasn't even anything special to look at, but then again, no one in the Institute was. All of us – male and female, internee, ward and attendee – wore the same dark blue overalls. The boys had their hair shaved off every month, the girls were allowed to grow theirs to their shoulders but it was always tied up.

We all had skin the colour of bacon rind, a sort of dirty, greasy, off-grey. Well, apart from me and a few others, I'm quite a bit darker. Our waxy complexions and flaking fingernails were the fault of the food; the Institute cooks were strangers to minerals and vitamins, or at least had never been properly introduced. We were all issued with toothbrushes and toothpaste, but the former were used as weapons and the latter as snack food. I never saw a tooth which wasn't as yellow as the margarine.

Harete was of medium height, whey-pale and sparrow-thin, with rat brown hair, not too dissimilar in many ways from The Moth. Unlike him, her plain, friendly face did not cower behind large, thick-lensed glasses. Regardless of her thin limbs and slender fingers she exuded a certain physical confidence, even toughness, whereas The Moth's clumsy and fumbling movements betrayed a lack of both. Moth was a little taller than average, though still a lot shorter than myself. He was round-shouldered, soft-voiced, spotty and so thin that I reckon he must have needed to move around in the shower to get wet.

Here comes the tough bit, sprinting past the doors of B1 annex, home of the Beta Blockers. It's a minor clan, chieftain is Pharaoh. Most dangerous thing about him is his skin condition, but some of his team are shrewd bruisers. Pharaoh is doing a two-er for . . . best not go into that.

Eventually I did manage to infiltrate my way into the affections of The Moth and Harete. They appreciated my knowledge of the Institute and my instincts for how life was led there; they learned I could join in their conversations and even better their wits. My plan to benefit by being friends with The Moth was a success! It was just a bonus that I rapidly grew to like the scrawny, walking encyclopaedia, embarrassing as it is to admit that.

Harete was another matter. Once The Moth and I were

friendly, she was neither threat nor use to me, so I tolerated her company. Sorry if that sounds harsh. You survive places like the Institute and the Establishment by making useful friends, and if they are not useful, well, they can be a bit of a nuisance. You can end up taking risks for them when there is nothing to be gained. Harete was nice enough, but I reckoned her naive, lacking in resilience, not a wily survivor with two years' graft and craft behind her, like me. She'd go under soon, my instincts told me, and once down, she'd stay below. The Institute gorged on chovies – that's *anchovies*, our slang for the kids who never wised up, who never learned it was kill or be krill. Harete was fodder.

Done it! They must all still be on a work rota, would have expected at least a token rattle. I've nothing to take and they know it, but they have to put on a show.

More clavigers now, Ball Bag and Three Much. They're busy doling out boot-borne woe to some young 'uns, easy to slip past them. Across the hallway . . . odd, the canteen doors are open – explains why everything stinks of the slurry they call hash. The kitchens here are the only place I know where garbage men deliver.

I still couldn't understand Sticky's intentions. Like Moth's drawing of Chiron, the one I had thought to be a sketch of a man and a horse, I could see the parts but not the whole. Sticky did not need Moth's protection! Sticky was one of those we needed protecting from! Atom's attentions announced that avoiding Sticky situations was about to advance even higher up my list of preoccupations. That, and sidestepping *the squeeze*.

The squeeze? That was my name for what you always

had to be alert for. It only took a little brains to keep out of the way of the clavigers, and there were plenty of bad, bad kids you needed to steer clear of too – fast legs or quick talking were usually enough to save you. But the squeeze was what happened when you were dumb enough to get trapped between two such forces, for instance between the implacable stupidity and unpredictable tempers of the clavigers and the prowling, exuberant cruelty of *them*. *Them* – the kids too damaged and random even to gain admittance to the clans, the kids who feasted on violence and destruction, the ones who sucked it in, stewed and thickened it, and sprayed it back at everything around them.

Bad luck was when you sat down in the wrong spot in the canteen and the kid opposite you gobbed a greenie into your rice and told you that it was his now, and you'd better slide it over to him. And one look in his pinched, lye-eyed face would tell you that he meant it, that he'd bite off your lips if you crossed him. But the situation became a *squeeze* if a claviger plodded up behind you and told you to eat up your rice, with a cautionary crack on the skull with his club to hint what would happen if you disobeyed, and then stayed put to make sure you did. We all experienced bad luck, life in the Institute was full of it, but it took lots of experience to avoid the squeeze. If you did get caught . . . well, only a bolt from above or the intervention of an angel could help you.

In the Institute, surviving is all about the gaps; you live and breathe in the little spaces that open up between the forces that threaten to choke you.

Doesn't look like I'm being followed, but I'll dash out into the yard and mingle with the crowd before doubling back, just to be safe. I'll stick close to Semi-Precious. A very hobscure and hintelligent name, as he puts it himself. He's got two hammer fists, see?

Nine more months, that's all I had to get through. Nine more months of the stench of disinfectant and puke, of thin soup and thick ears, of the knee-bleeding tedium of polishing floors, hustling for food and finding somewhere warm to hunker down and avoid the fighting.

Or rather, nine more months and my parole hearing. That was when I'd have to satisfy a committee of visiting busybodies that I would not be using strangers' cars as temporary accommodation after my release. But it was not certain that I would pass. If I failed to behave, got into trouble or just annoyed too many clavigers, I would instead find that my sixteenth birthday present was a transfer to the Establishment.

Back inside. Up the stairs, one flight, two flights . . . Nearly home now, an easy run this time. Stay cagey though . . .

The Establishment was an adult version of the Institute. We knew little about it, save that it was a lot tougher than the Institute. Cudgel Drudge, who claimed to have previously worked as a guard there, used to growl that it was full of men who'd slit us up just for making too much noise when we slurped our rain-flavoured soup.

For some, like Sticky, a move to the Establishment was not only assured but desired; it was their university, their ticket to the big time and the gangs who, they claimed, were secretly responsible for running at least half the country. My feelings were different. Graduating to the Establishment was something I was very, very keen to avoid.

My landing! My corridor! A dash, a swerve, three cells along, made it! Careful with the heavy door . . . no, no one's hiding behind it. No one under the bunks either, just my cellie Granny sleeping under the covers on his bed, must be back from the hosp—

My hands made it in front of my face just before the jug of boiling water sloshed over me, at least I had that to be thankful for. Who had been hiding under the blanket I never knew, nor from where they had managed to obtain such scalding hot water. Not from the showers, that was for sure. From the way the boiling water clung to my skin and refused to be wiped off I could tell they must have stirred heaps of sugar into it first, typical clan malice. I plunged my hands into the cell's toilet bucket, so great was my need for something to cool them with.

'Remember Wingnuts!' my attacker shouted, so I knew it was a C-Wing kid on an errand. Remember Wingnuts? We weren't likely to forget, were we? Not even the pain of burned hands could make me forget him. Lovely kid, and that was a bad start. Mad about aeroplanes he was, and he made the most fantastic models from wood scraps. They were brilliant! He knew how to make glue from milk and vinegar and baking soda to hold them together. He actually had a decent chance of joining the air force when he was released because he was only doing six months for graffiti. So he had all these wonderful models, and then some of *them* visited him. They knew that he cared about something, and that was enough.

In the Institute, you can't show that you love something. That's the greatest weakness of all. *They* will sniff that weakness on the wind and hunt you like jackals. Not for profit, for thrills.

Wingnuts was a massive kid with concrete hands and I-beams for bones, so they had to be clever. But they are. They goaded him into testing one of his planes, tricked him into throwing one out of the window to see if it would glide, and it did; it glided right into a claviger patrolling outside. The guard summoned him down, kept him talking for ages, made him apologise, gave him a whack and then, for good measure, crunched the model plane under his boot. But Wingnuts was in the squeeze by then. All the time he was outside, *they* were busy, joyfully smashing and shredding and pulverising all his other models. When Wingnuts returned to his end of the dorm, he faced not only the wreckage of all his beloved craftwork but a second ranting claviger who sentenced him to a week in confinement on account of the mess. Wingnuts looped the loop. He punched the claviger out cold. Hurting a claviger . . . that's the worst thing you can do.

Wingnuts lost an eye in the ensuing fight and the empty socket went septic, but it was never treated. I don't know the details. I remember watching through the canteen windows when his folks came to collect the body though.

Evil is rarely random. Look hard enough and you'll find a pattern that gives it form, a cobweb underneath the dead flies and dewdrops.

Before Wingnuts, Sticky was small-time. By arousing *them*, telling them what hilarious fun it would be, timing matters so that a claviger would be outside the window and another one present when Wingnuts returned to find

36

his handiwork trashed, Sticky conducted the whole thing. That marked the start of his ascendency, for the death of Wingnuts (cleverly arrived at with no risk to his then tiny band of clansmen) gave Sticky the best advertisement possible for his grand idea, the collection of premiums. You could pay with your food or stuff or labour or favours. Pay up . . . or suffer, perhaps even die. Everyone paid.

After that, Sticky flourished. *They* destroyed or hurt for pleasure, same as before, and now Sticky's clan hunted for profit, and smashed or stole or beat to make examples of poor payers. And the rest of us cowered in between.

I dangled my seared hands out of the cell window in the hope that the sleeting rain would soothe them; what was in the bucket was too warm. Must have been from the kid who attacked me. Nice. I cried a lot that afternoon – those hands *hurt*.

Do you see? Nothing in the Institute was called by its true name. Our guards didn't protect us; we paid premiums to retain what was ours anyway; and friendship brought not security, but menace. By becoming mates with Moth, I achieved not the immunity I had sought, but a state of heightened danger – I owned something desirable I could not give up even if I wanted to.

Still, Sticky, clans, burns and bruises, it was all routine stuff. I was only being pushed from one side, and I knew how to bend and roll. Nothing was getting at me from the other direction, it wasn't yet a squeeze. And the clavigers were not overly cruel, provided we didn't attack them, get a girl pregnant or kill each other. Ah . . . sore point. Maybe I shouldn't have said that. I'll get on to that later.

Chapter 3
Under Way

That first morning of our escape I awoke under my plastic sheet with a mouthful of wet mud. The slime in my mouth and the feel of my own frozen breath on the plastic around me snapped me instantly to my senses. I was in a field, under a pylon, on the out and on the run.

My mud-caked eyes cracked open, I turned slowly onto my back and gazed outwards. There was hardly any light yet, just a slight brightening of the sky on the horizon and a tint of rust where the cloud base caught the rising sun.

But the light brought with it a hope far exceeding its feeble luminance. Its pallid rays stirred my torpid brain.

The winter sun rises in the south and east, now to my right . . . therefore that way, straight along the line of pylons is north . . . so we are on the north side of the river, which is behind me. I jerked upright from my muddy bed and double-checked my reasoning. There was no doubt about it. We'd done it! Yes, by accident, but all the same; there was no need to risk death by crossing the river again.

The realisation was like a sugar rush; it was almost enough to compensate for my appalling aches and feelings of tiredness and cold. For some minutes I stood shivering and staring into the dawn glow, enjoying the sight of the orange clouds wreathing the far-off pylons. Every part of my body throbbed and twinged with pain; it had not been a good idea to sleep directly on the rough ground. But still – we'd made it over!

Our solitary triumph briefly beguiled me. We were back on course, unbounded by wall or wire, free and alone!

Then why . . . my hair was shaved so short it couldn't really stand on end, but I felt it wanted to.

Something didn't fit.

The unidentified error needled me, and at once I could sense anew the burnished gaze of long lenses being twisted into focus and taste the hatred hosing out of them.

I swiftly clambered onto one of the lower cross-struts of the pylon under whose ferrous arms we had spent the night, suddenly desperate to confirm what my research in the Institute had told me.

By now the sun had wound its way above the horizon and was punching cold, comfortless beams of light through the clouds and across the countryside around us. The landscape in all directions was as flat as a becalmed sea. To our immediate south lay the river, spilled over its levees in a wide, irregular stain. Even in the low light it was dazzlingly bright and difficult to look at. Squinting, I could make out floating branches and in the middle distance, a mass of shifting grey shapes, a flock of herons or some sort of wading bird, I reckoned, the only signs of life.

Elsewhere, nothing could be seen but large, regularly shaped fields. Not farms, just huge, machine-tilled fields. The fields were frozen and empty at this time of year, the iron-hard soil ploughed into knee-deep furrows. The ground undulated gently, but there was nothing higher than the pylons as far as the horizon. Snow covered the fields in thin layers, filling the valleys of the ploughed ruts and drifting away in wispy strands from the ridges. The brown-and-white-striped landscape was doubtless fertile, valuable agricultural land, but it looked to me then like a desert.

What I had read was correct, this was a region populated by no more than a few hundred people thinly spread between a handful of hamlets and mechanised farms. It was a landscape fabricated for elephantine farm machinery to roam and graze over, not a land for people to live or play in. Nothing lived here but what was permitted to exist according to some agricultural master plan. It was a colossal factory floor.

All was as it should have been, but the prickling feeling did not abate.

I jumped down from the pylon, dispirited by the bleakness of the countryside and still itching with suspicion. *Paranoia*, that's what it was, I told myself. My vision was faulty, trained for a world encircled in barbed wire and unaccustomed to open vistas. Or to freedom – we really, really needed to get moving. What was I waiting for? An order from a claviger?

I yanked the rustling plastic sheet off the sleeping Harete and Moth and started to shake the moisture and snow from it. Exposed to the cold wind, The Moth woke up.

'Moth, get up! We're across the river!' I told him. The good news did not seem to excite him. He sat upright on the foam mattress, removed his glasses to wipe his face with a gloved hand and stared at me with a look of absolute contempt.

'What? Oh, yes. That. I don't care. I want to sleep. I want to go back,' he croaked. He sat stock-still, head bowed. Was he crying? Had he fallen asleep? I retrieved my glove and the rope from where I had put them the previous night.

'Moth! We must start walking!' I said firmly. Again, no response. I kicked him. 'Now!'

The Moth lifted his head. Even in the dim quarter-light I could see his face underneath his balaclava glowing cherry-red with anger. 'Are you mad?' he spat at me. 'Have you gone round the twist? You want us to walk on? You almost kill us with your insane escapade, your stupid ruddy river, then you leave us to die of exposure in a field, and you think we're going to carry on with you? You . . . you barbarous lunatic! I hate you, and I am not going one step farther!'

The Moth's tantrum stunned me. I'd never seen him like that before, never heard him raise his voice or lose his temper. Normally, back home – I mean, back in the Institute – The Moth just stopped talking to you if he was annoyed. When he needed to demonstrate that you were being particularly irritating, he'd blow a deep sigh and tap the bridge of his glasses with his pencil.

For a moment I did not know what to say. Mutiny had not been something I had anticipated. I rocked on my heels and made a goldfish mouth as I formed my response.

'Moth . . . I never said this was going to be easy. In fact, I told you it was going to be difficult and dangerous. But the worst is over! All we have to do is walk! We crossed the river and found the pylons,' I explained.

41

The Moth's face crumpled into tears and he blubbered into cupped hands, 'I'm not coming. I'm staying here. You can go on without me, leave me here and I'll wait to be picked up. They won't harm me!'

I charged over to his side. 'No, but they'll most definitely harm *me* if we get caught, especially after how things turned out in the cell last night! Learn this, you little brat: I don't care if you have to be pulled along by the ears, but you are coming along with me, both of you! We are going to walk all the way to the border, or die in the attempt!' I snarled into his ear. Was all my work, all my planning, the preparations, the training, the making of all our gear to be jeopardised by this pampered, mummy's boy book-maggot?

'Yes, I think I've learned just how prepared you are for the possibility of us dying,' came his answer. 'In fact, why not just make certain of it and kill me here? You don't want me to stay because you're afraid that if they find me, it'll lead the way to you. You don't give a damn if I actually live or die, just so long as my body doesn't lead them to you!'

I reeled. This was something of an emergency. I needed The Moth. Without him, my escape was pointless. Harete's presence was superfluous, but The Moth had to make it with me to the distant border. So in that respect, he was completely wrong, I cared very much that he lived. And against all my personal rules about not making friends for friendship's sake, I liked The Moth.

All the time we squabbled, I was aware we were haemorrhaging time. My anxieties mushroomed. I broke off from the argument to scan edgily about us. The sun had clicked a little higher, snow had started to fall in tiny mote-like flakes, and a fog as thin and grey and as full of holes as a slice of Institute bread was drifting in on the wind.

Nothing looked obviously amiss, but my feet itched. They wanted me to put air under them. My eyes had tipped them a clue that had bypassed my limp brain, something that pulsed like a beacon: you are not safe, you are not alone.

Institute instincts, I reassured myself again, *they don't apply out here.*

I squatted next to my friend and painted on a smile. 'How can you say these things, Moth? It's because of you that we're doing this! This is to get you back together with your father . . . you know . . . the whole, um, politics thing,' I said, painfully aware that my voice lacked conviction.

'Pah! All about me? This is about you wanting to escape; it has nothing to do with me!' came the scornful retort.

'Yeah? Then why did I bring you?' I shouted, springing up again. 'Think about it, Moth, you're the one who's supposed to have the brains. It would've been far easier for me to escape on my own. You're just baggage, a hindrance. Name one step of the plan where I needed you – go on, name one!'

The Moth could only manage a grumpy, sniffling silence and a shuffling, squirming motion, like he had something unpleasant in his pants.

He had made a rare mistake in his reasoning. I wasn't being dishonest either, just not totally truthful. I really did want The Moth to get back with his dad. Not that I really cared one way or another about allowing his parents to be free to speak their minds, that wasn't of any interest to me, but a bright kid like The Moth should be living with his family. Harete deserved better too. We all did.

The other reason, the one which meant that The Moth absolutely had to make it with me to the frontier, I'd long ago figured not to tell him about. Especially now. This episode made it clear to me how right my intuition had been not to confess to him about the . . . incident.

The incident. That was why we were all there. In my mind, the Institute became an advent calendar – not *my* scene, even as a kid, but I'd seen them in shops – and behind each paper door lay a cell with a lie or disaster behind it, most of my making. Behind the really big one in the middle was the incident, and a ghostly, choking voice that called me a . . . a what? A killer? Almost as prominent was the one for last night, another writhing body calling out and accusing me.

'I'm just so tired. So tired and cold,' Moth said, breaking into my useless introspection.

The rumpled shape of Harete next to him on the mattress stirred into life. *Here comes another nagging bag of trouble*, I thought, despairing of ever making a prompt getaway, or even of departing at all. Harete always stood up for The Moth. Those two were closer than the two halves of a clothes peg.

By then, I was so wound up I was beginning to fear what I might do. Far away over the river, powerful people were being shaken awake to a Moth-less morning, and here we were, still bickering in the grass.

The reptilian midst of my mind began to spawn. *Ditch them both!* Impossible, I rebuked it, The Moth was my passport. *Use the glass blades! Threaten them!* My hand snaked to the tin that held the jagged shards and I silently popped the lid.

'We're all tired, Moth,' Harete said in a quiet voice. 'We're all freezing and uncomfortable. But we can't stay here. I don't want ever to go back to that place. We'd be punished so much if we got caught! We'd be sent to the Establishment even if we are underage!'

She's wrong there, I reflected dourly. If recaptured, the Establishment would be far better than anything I could hope for. My fingers probed into the tin. Could I do it?

'They can't touch you, you're too valuable,' Harete continued, 'but we're not. Anyway, if this plan works, they won't look for us here, so if you stayed put you'd die alone. And if they do come looking for us here, we'll be caught soon anyway, so you may as well come with us and we'll all get taken back together.'

I blinked with astonishment. First Moth's tantrum, now Harete agreeing with me? We all knew Harete was the source of sense, but somehow I had not thought this would extend beyond the dank corridors of the Institute. Of the three of us, Harete had the least to gain from this adventure. Until this point, I had assumed that she'd come along only because she was ignorant of the true risks.

'That's right, Harete, you are so, so right. We've burned our boots now, Moth, so buck up and let's push off,' I declared, delighted with my unexpected ally. I clicked shut my tin and tucked it back into my overalls.

'Boats, not boots. We've burned our boats. Or bridges,' Moth snivelled.

Ah, this is more like it, I thought, *give him an opportunity to show off his knowledge!* I smiled, an idea forming, a ruse to get The Moth up and walking.

Mistakes like the one I made with 'boats' and 'boots' were meat and drink to The Moth; he'd swim oceans and climb mountains to pick someone up on factual mistakes or points of grammar. He couldn't let an error go uncorrected. A vision came to me of him crawling on all fours over sun-seared dunes, his tongue black with thirst, in pursuit of some ragged, skeletal figure. 'It's "could have", not "could of",' he'd whisper to his quarry, before both collapsed and died.

'Boats, boots, bridges, fridges, we've bunged the lot into the furnace,' I said. My brow furrowed as I tried to remember and then deliberately misremember a phrase he had taught me, a snippet of half-learning from his favourite subject. 'We've crossed the Ruby . . . the Ruby Come.'

'I think you mean "Rubicon". That's quite apt actually,' Moth corrected me. He stood up stiffly, and helped Harete to her feet.

'About time!' I cried. 'Let's pack, let's shift!'

The two of them stood and watched passively as I folded the foam mattress they had been resting on, rolled it up in the sheets we had slept under, and secured the whole uncooperative mass into a bulky cylinder using the electrical flex.

As I busied myself with these tasks I ruminated on Harete's perceptiveness. She had been correct when she had reminded The Moth that, if things worked as I intended, no one would look for us here.

46

The genius of my escape plan was the supreme stupidity of the thing. No one who broke out of the Institute would ever go the way we had gone, north. Firstly, there was the matter of the river, fast and cold and wide. Any claviger or marshal who stood on its banks and looked across it would never believe for one minute that even three adults could get across it without a boat, let alone us: three grotty juvenile runaways. That's the thing about clavigers and their sort, about adults in general really: they assumed we were all ignorant and lazy and incapable of doing anything they themselves couldn't. To them, we were just useless kids.

Secondly, and more importantly, no escapee who had any sense would go north because there was nothing there. No towns. No villages. No railway stations, hardly any roads, almost no people. There was nothing to eat, nowhere to shelter, no means of transport.

That was the logic I was relying on our pursuers using. I imagined them now, poring over maps, dogs tugging on leads, helicopters idling noisily in the background, walkie-talkies hissing and burping. South, they would have to think, they must have gone south! Good roads, the nearby town, plenty of means of getting out of the vicinity. That's where we'll search.

As long as the authorities did not think too much about the distant border with the Other country, as long as they considered that to be an impossibly distant target, unachievable by three youths on foot, then my plan was sound. Of course, there was the matter of what had happened in the cell, the buckled spoke in the wheel. But I thought I'd fixed even that, spun it to our advantage.

So much for reason. The bristling and itching argued differently, claiming something was champing at our backs.

'Problem?' asked Harete, doubtless noticing the concentration on my face.

'No, everything is perfect,' I lied. 'No one will come looking for us here. Plus, we have these,' I added, and slapped the pylon's leg with the flat of my hand. 'These are the ones I read about, Moth, I'm certain of it.'

The Moth did not look convinced. 'You can't know that for sure. How far do you think we drifted downstream?'

'Umm . . . rather lost track of time when we were in the water,' I admitted. 'We must have come quite a way though.' To forestall any more awkward questions, I decided to galvanise my troops with a pep talk. 'Listen. We've got to walk every minute of daylight, from dawn until dark. We've only food for seven days, remember. I don't care how uncomfortable you get, I don't care how wet or cold or hungry you are or how much your shoes pinch or your clothes chafe, we walk. The pylons will show us the way; they're like signposts to the border. We don't need a map or compass –'

'Just as well, we haven't got either,' interrupted The Moth.

'We don't need them. We just follow the pylons in a line northwards. If we get disoriented, remember that the sun rise must be to our right,' I rolled the 'r's for emphasis, 'and sun set is to our left,' I said, exaggerating the 'e' sounds. 'We can't get lost. Stay close together as we walk. No talking, unless it's an emergency. Oh, and listen out for dogs too,' I cautioned.

'Dogs? What dogs?' Harete asked.

'Tracker dogs. The marshals are bound to use them. Tulips told me about them; his uncle was a dog handler in the marshalry before he was done for fraud.'

Tulips had been an older internee who had been released just three weeks previously. He was incredibly short, incredibly freckly and liked to speak very, very softly and almost entirely in obscenities. Stashed in the repulsive housebreaker's small skull was a bulging repertoire of smutty songs and boundless knowledge about anything to do with the marshals. Every member of his family was a career criminal, a marshal, or both. He had told me about two sorts of tracker dogs, 'Ones wot follow odours on ver soil and ones wot sniff ver air.' According to him, nothing you did in the way of crossing your tracks or staying downwind could do much to help. 'Buy you a little time, but ver dogs'll get yer, venshlly,' he always concluded.

Tulips knew about more than dogs. 'Course, yer manhunting's a job for a speshlist. Local troops, but led by an expert. Like Orion. He's ver best, a legend!'

'Orion?' The name sounded funny. 'Is that foreign? Irish?'

'Do what? No, a code name! Capo-Colonel Orion. Course, he has his little ways!'

I'm not repeating what Tulips told me. If true, then when Capo-Colonel Orion found his quarry, he did something to them with a length of harp wire that ensured they'd never be the subject of one of Tulips' filthy ballads. Recaptured women faced a different *little way* of equal depravity. Worse, even.

Only edited highlights of my learning had I passed on to Moth and Harete. Besides, my planning had accounted for dogs. I told her, 'We should be safe from dogs. We travelled a long way along that river; dogs can't track smell in water.'

Harete and The Moth did not reply. Had I persuaded them? They stood huddled together, looking miserable and droopy. And we'd still to move one step.

'Any more questions? Or are we finally ready?' I cried. We'd descended into one of my own dreams, I thought, one where I was trapped in treacle as freaks fermented in the sump of my soul closed in around me. I'd done too good a job of convincing them of my plan's brilliance, I realised; they felt safe.

With a jolt, I remembered one essential job had been overlooked. 'Quick, give me your bottles,' I said. The Moth and Harete dug into their overalls and pulled out two large plastic bottles that had been deliberately squashed flat. I retrieved mine from where it had been stuffed down the front of my own overalls. I then splashed back along the direction we had come the previous night until the floodwater was halfway up my shins. The water there looked fresh and clear, the grass visible underneath. I popped and massaged the plastic bottles back into shape and immersed them to fill with the river water.

Behind me, I heard Harete say something to Moth about bad weather to come, reciting that old rhyme about red skies and shepherds. I squinted across the shimmering surface of the flood, re-examining the watery scene that had been obscured by glare when I was high up on the pylon, fascinated by the way it merged seamlessly into the sky.

The lying sky.

The orange-tinted cloud around the rising sun was wrong. How could it swirl about those pylons like that? How could there be grey clouds and mist *behind* it?

Because it wasn't a cloud. It was smoke, coloured smoke from a signal flare.

That was the error I'd seen but not perceived. I rubbed my sleep-hazed eyes to look again, and my throat turned to sandpaper.

Tiredness, fog and the dim, oddly slanting light had deceived me. Perspective was playing to different rules. The grey creatures I had seen before were not nearby birds, but far-off people, dozens and dozens of people wading into the river. And the floating objects weren't drifting branches, they were boats.

They were coming straight for us.

We were as good as in the bag.

I grabbed the bottles and splashed my way back to the pylon.

'Grab those packs and let's GO!' I commanded. The last fleck of confidence vanished down my throat like a loose tooth accidentally swallowed. My dismay was complete, and fear and shame pooled like solder in my bowels.

Without waiting for a reply I picked up my mattress roll and pounded out from under our pylon in the direction of the next one in the chain. I could see another three or four in the distance, the snow-thickened air stealing the others from my sight. The Moth and Harete followed me, some way behind, side by side.

We had to run parallel to the deep furrows, balancing on their raised sides. It was rough, hard going, and the mud was studded with big stones. Large areas of the field were poorly drained and lay under standing water. We sloshed and squelched through these as best we could, trying to maintain our balance as we were unable to see the deep ruts that lay underneath the cloudy puddles. Every few seconds I glanced backwards, over the heads of the others, looking, listening, fearing.

As we slogged along, I fretted silently. Survival was all down to me, the only adult, the only one with the determination and cunning to survive.

'Slow down, I've got a stitch!' came a voice from behind.

I spun around. 'You'll have a split lip to go with it, too! Keep quiet!' I barked. *Chovies!*

Eventually, we reached the second pylon. We were all hot and out of breath. 'A few seconds' rest, no more,' I panted. 'We must keep moving. Men, behind us!' The others looked at me grimly and shrunk into their balaclavas.

'Hey, Moth, now you really are a stick-in-the-mud,' I joked, hoping to lighten the mood, my own in particular. I pointed at the huge balls of gummy loam that had accumulated around his shoes.

At that moment, we heard the sound of a dog barking. We stood still and strained our ears. More barking, and another, buzzing, whining noise – an engine? An aeroplane?

'And you've got feet of clay,' muttered The Moth.

I understood, but said nothing. I turned away from him and set off at a fast pace for the next pylon, thinking about life back in the Institute, the world we'd left behind, the world we seemed destined to be dragged back to.

Chapter 4

Under Lock and Key

To really understand the Institute you'd have to sample the stink of the place, especially in the mornings when the steaming air was curdled with the ammoniacal tang of hundreds of soiled blankets.

The place was full of bed-wetters. What can you expect? Twelve hundred boys and girls, some as young as eleven, removed from homes and parents (or from the streets in many cases), forced to live together under the uncaring gaze of the clavigers. We had nutcases, headcases, damage cases, hard cases, sad cases and special cases. We had thumb-suckers and blanket-huggers mixing it with chain-smokers and wrist-slashers. We had orphans and arsonists, the soppy and the psycho, the dreamy and the druggy, street urchins with fleas and country bumpkins with lice. We had kids who ate from toilets and kids who swallowed pencils, kids who wrote on the walls of their cell and kids who spoke to the voices in their heads.

Some coped, some didn't. Some new starters never recovered from the shock of their first few days in the Institute. Sometimes they'd break down at the marrow-jarring clang of a claviger's club on the bedstead during their first morning wake-up. Or perhaps they'd crinkle at their first sight of the food, or the experience of the induction-day head-shave, or the new uniform issue. The ones who folded early usually stayed folded. They spent their days cowering in paper overalls, rocking backwards and forwards in one of the special units.

Most of us found some way to live. For the smart ones like me, who'd known the Institute and all its brother organisations for most of our lives, settling into the Institute was like putting on a pair of new shoes. There was a bit of pain at first, but after a few weeks you'd forgotten it had ever been any different. We knew how life was lived and needed no other person to help us.

Some inmates joined a clan. Sticky's Swingers wasn't the only one, there were perhaps a dozen in the male section alone, and as many amongst the girls. Even Eye Inside still had a small band of followers from the psych unit, the Unitarians. When not scrapping, most clan members spent their days huddled in sullen bunches, exchanging insults with surly gatherings from other clans. Members tried to give themselves tattoos using sewing needles and ink from ballpoint pens. These crummy tribal marks were usually invisible underneath the field of bruises, cuts and black eyes that were the true badges of clan membership. Clans were generally for meatheads, although there were some exceptions.

'What's that?' I asked Retread, a member of the Swingers. Despite this, Retread was a decent sort of lad. He had been born with a harelip, and a foreign charity had paid for his face to be surgically reconstructed in the recent past, from which fact his mocking name arose. Maybe this act of generosity was responsible for Retread having an unusually approachable nature.

'That, old pal, is my new tat. A badge of honour,' he replied, visibly proud. 'Took nine hours.'

'But what is it meant to be?' I asked again, looking at the smudgy, blotchy splodge on his forearm. It resembled a very bad tracing of a chicken clutching a fish in its beak surrounded by wobbly, childishly drawn letters.

'It's an eagle. With a dagger in its mouth. And underneath it says, "Non me tenet clavis." That's Latin for "keys cannot imprison me",' he answered, keen to show off this knowledge.

'Did you say Latin, Retread? Since when did the C-Wing mob have an interest in dead languages?' I suspected I knew the answer already. The wording on this tattoo was a cut above the normal choice of "Mum", or obscenities, or some combination of the two.

'Your mate, Butterfly,' Retread replied.

'You mean Moth!' I chuckled. The name seemed to jog Retread's memory. He backed away a fraction and placed a not-unfriendly hand against my chest. Business. 'Reminds me! Sticky wants to know what you're doing for him. Getting Butterfly to be his friend. He means it, mate. Soon!'

I groaned. *That* nonsense again. 'I don't understand, Retread. Sticky doesn't need protection by hanging with Moth. He's even got most of the clavigers in his pocket!' I said.

'Not all. Not Jelly. And only here.'

'Eh?'

'Not in the Establishment. Eight months, and that's where Sticky will be. He's looking forward to it, wants to make contacts. But being friends with Butterfly will do him very nicely when he's settling in; he'll be a handy screen.'

This was true. Sticky would be transferred to the Establishment, no doubt about it, and for him it was a case of advancing his professional development. It was rumoured that some of the gangs there were as rich as senators. But I was still baffled. 'Sticky might be moving up. But Moth won't, he's only fourteen and a half!'

Retread grinned and revealed two rows of filed teeth. 'Right! But when he's fifteen he can ask to be transferred!'

Lunatics, I thought, *it's pathetic.* 'And why would he do a stupid thing like that?'

'If Sticky was his friend, he would. He'd want to be there then, wouldn't he, to help protect his new best pal? He'd still be untouchable in the Estabo!'

I bashed my fist on the stone wall, frustrated with this ongoing, inane delusion. 'Noooo way! Moth will never be friends with Sticky. He's got privileges enough of his own and he'd hate him. He's very, ah, principled,' I exclaimed. Couldn't they understand?

Retread's reaction surprised me. His face sagged and the hand moved up to squeeze my shoulder. 'Yeah, he does act like he's royalty. But shame, shame for you,' he said, looking genuinely saddened.

'Why? Why, Retread?' I asked, almost wishing I hadn't. My heart started banging. A shame for my face? For my ribs?

Retread strode away, rolling his shoulders and hips for added swagger. He wasn't very convincing. He gave up after a dozen steps, flapped his arms, turned and spoke, his voice cracking a little. ''Cos if Butterfly ain't friends with Sticky, Sticky will have to get *you* moved to the big "E". That way, you'll all go together. You'll all be mates there,' he blurted.

I ran. A claviger yelled out for me to stop, but I ignored him and just fled to the far side of the exercise yard, my new understanding ringing in my skull like a migraine. *So that was the full picture.* Sticky would take Moth with him to the Establishment, use him as an umbrella. And if Moth didn't want to go – he'd get me there, trusting Moth to volunteer to follow to lend me his protective influence. They'd be bound to put all us juniors in the same cell and on the same work shifts. Compared to the hardened denizens of the big 'E', even Sticky would look like reasonable or at least familiar company. Moth's prestige and protective sphere would envelop Sticky whether Moth intended it to or not.

There'd be another twist, there always was with Sticky, for he won whichever side up the coin landed. Moth had told me his exiled pop had more than one close friend whose features appeared (or would, when they died) on a stamp or banknote. The details were beyond me, but it spewed on the shoes of belief to think that Sticky did not plan to use this knowledge to enrich himself when acting as The Moth's Establishment gatekeeper.

It was all devious and brilliant, I had to say, and very easily achieved. All Sticky needed to do was trick me into committing a serious breach of the rules and have me put on report. Instead of a parole hearing, I'd be measured up for a new uniform.

Hours later, morose and drained, I cautioned The Moth

not to offer the same service to other clan members as he had to Retread. 'You don't want to get involved with them. If you provide a classy motto for one, you'll have a queue of them outside your cell wanting the same,' I advised him. 'Leave the clans alone. Let them forget you.'

'He seemed genuinely interested,' Moth told me. 'He came to me for advice on writing. He'd copied what he wanted from one of his friend's tattoos. I think he meant to have "C-Wing crew bad boys", but he must have been reading it upside down. And even then, some of his letters were back to front or upside down or missing or wrong. He'd actually written "shop pap marc buM-C". Do you know,' Moth lowered his voice and leant close towards me, 'I'm not sure Retread can actually read or write.'

'I think you're probably right there, Mothy,' I replied. Moth's naivety never failed to amuse me. My guess is that more than half the population of the Institute could not read or write, and that included the clavigers.

Away from Moth, I tried to work out a new strategy to get by. Drop The Moth? Then I'd have no protection, and would incur Sticky's anger. Try the impossible, sell The Moth on Sticky's good points? I couldn't think of any. Lacking a new angle, I resolved to put my faith in routine, be extra-alert for tricks, and hope Sticky grew bored or became distracted by more lucrative openings.

I soaked myself into the Institute.

Mornings started predictably enough with everyone being roused from bed by the clavigers. That is, if you had not already got out of it on account of wetting it, or a weak-bladdered bunkmate doing the job for you. After washing, we queued in the canteen for breakfast. We ate in silence using wooden cutlery and drank water from enamelled mugs.

After breakfast came schooling, or physical exercises on alternate days. Few kids paid much attention to the classes. It's not like we were going to get to take any exams or gain any qualifications. We just sat, arms folded, and listened as we were lectured in being better citizens, the history of our country and its glorious leaders. A claviger was always present in every lesson to maintain discipline. He'd grind up and down the aisle between the desks in his squeaking shoes and creaking belt, even more bored than we were.

There was only a single noteworthy lesson in all my time at the Institute. Not long before my life sprouted complications, a set of scruffy geography textbooks was handed out. They all bore rubber stamps that showed them to have been withdrawn for disposal by some outside school as being too out of date. The teacher was burbling on about our nation's road and railway networks – fat lot of interest that was to us – and I took to idly flicking through my copy. I found a chapter all about the backwater region which was home to the Institute. There were lots of pictures of farms and charts showing the amount of cereals and vegetables grown locally. There was a paragraph about the local town, only a few minutes' drive from the Institute and home to most of its staff, but no mention of the Institute itself, a fact I noted with a smile. There was also a small map. This showed the town, the nearby river I had already glimpsed from certain windows, and a huge expanse of farmland devoid of towns or cities stretching to the north.

Right at the top of the map was a dashed line that curved up and down as it weaved across the page from left to right. Above this, the map changed colour. The line and the blue shade above it were not described in the map's key, but I knew what they represented. Using the interval from my thumb knuckle to the tip of my thumb, I measured the distance from the town to the dashed line, and compared it to the map's scale. I filed the resulting figure away in my memory, even then finding it an intriguing one. Some distance to the left of the town was a faint black line running vertically down the whole length of the map. The unlabelled line was very hard to make out and was studded with regular, small cross marks. I faked a noisy coughing fit and tore out a handful of pages.

When the books were passed back to the teacher I stuffed the stolen pages into my sock. Information was always to be treasured.

After lunch in the canteen, and another hour outside, came time for work. Work was allocated to different dormitories and wings in rotation. There was canteen work (peeling, scrubbing, washing-up); laundry work (loading clothes into washers, working the stream presses); outside work (sweeping, painting); and general inside work (washing walls, polishing floors, cleaning windows and latrines). Despite the hundreds of boys and girls pressed daily into this brushing, scouring, buffing, swabbing, laundering, disinfecting and rinsing, everything about the Institute had a permanently dirty, grimy look to it, as did all the inmates.

'Herculean, wouldn't you call it, Moth?' I asked, never

missing an opportunity to curry favour with my friend and his love of old stuff. 'All this cleaning work?'

'Sisyphean,' quoth The Moth.

'A sissy what? You're in no position to insult me, you're excused all work, you weed. Or is poor diddums all tired out today after having to sharpen a pencil?' I snapped back, jabbing him with his own ruler.

'I'm not calling you a sissy. And even I'm not allowed a pencil sharpener – counts as a bladed tool, strictly banned. What I said was "Sisyphean", after the myth of Sisyphus,' he calmly rejoined. 'He was a king who was punished by the god Zeus. He had to roll a huge boulder up a hill every day, for all eternity. At the end of the day the boulder would roll back down and he'd have to start all over again.'

That was The Moth. You learned something whether you wanted to or not. 'Zeus . . . he was the powerful one who disguised himself as a sick cuckoo, wasn't he?'

Moth looked as pleased as cheese. 'You remembered! Yes, so that Hera would take pity and hold it to her breast. Then he changed back and attacked her!'

'Naturally! Why do you waste your life on this bog-wash, Moth? Ever thought about learning something practical?' I guffawed. Moth's stories irked me. I hated the way the people in them were set out like dominoes by grotesque deities lolling in luxury on mountain tops or skulking in the chilly intestines of the earth. The humans were only there to be shuffled around and kicked over. The so-called adventures were no better, like the one Moth insisted on boring me with, the nautical geezer with the golden fleas; those yarns were always one damn problem after another,

61

foe following fiend following fight. *That's nothing like my world*, I thought. Putting aside the clavigers, I was very much in charge of my own life, and my enemies were tediously constant, varying only in the relative measures of their maliciousness.

In the late afternoon we had free association time. That could be dangerous – a time when clans fought, when bets were laid and debts were paid, when odds were set and kids got even. It was when *they* went hunting for trouble. Then came dinner, followed by another free association slot. After that it was lights out, lock-up, bed.

I spent as much time as I could with The Moth, safe in his hassle-free zone. Every second I was not with him, I was compelled to assess my surroundings for trouble and trickery. Institute life was the background beat, but vigilance was the refrain. You know how it went . . . *check my cell for intruders, and this time look IN the bunk as well as under it; who's that kid lurking over there? Why's Wizard looking at me like that?* It was tiring. *Will it be a cup of floor cleaner in the face? Can Sticky risk hurting me too much without putting off Moth?*

Days passed. I grew bored.

The melody faded, drowned out by the beat.

Lulled by the rhythm of daily life and its parade of woes and foes, I relaxed and allowed myself to savour the occasional distraction that arose. You never knew what surprises even a place as controlled as the Institute could throw up, things like that map in the schoolbook.

Pebble Dash waved to me from behind a pyramid of rubbish bags at the rear of the boiler house. It was dusk, raining lightly, and at five minutes to lock up, everyone else was inside. 'Yay! Come see!' he called out.

'What's new?' I replied, ambling over. Pebble Dash was no threat, his name a reminder of nothing more sinister than a reputation for shocking spontaneous regurgitation.

'Ever hear of Topsy-Turvy?'

'A claviger?'

'An internee! More, an escapee!'

I was staggered. We had heard hints of rumours of only one escape from the Institute, years before, but never a name.

'Look!' whispered Pebble Dash. From a slit inside a bin bag at his feet, the gangling boy pulled out a tattered blue folder. Only the top two-thirds were existent, the bottom third was a tangled mass of paper ribbons.

'Shredded. Well, partly. I've been taking a shufty; these bags are all full of papers from the admin block, waiting to be incinerated. This one was poking out. Begging to be read, it was!'

'Well? What's it say?' I said, looking around me. No one. The rain fell harder.

Pebble Dash summarised. 'There really was an escape! The kid's Institute name was Topsy-Turvy. He got onto the roof. He leapt from there, five storeys up, into a waste skip for food scraps parked outside the kitchens. The slops provided a soft landing and the bin was wheeled onto a truck and driven off before it was noticed he was missing.'

I was agog. 'What happened to him?'

'Too damaged to read much, but it says something about "docks" and "Canada" on the final page.'

Pebble Dash thrust the folder towards me. 'Got to go! Takes me three minutes to get to D-Wing! Read it yourself!'

'Out-bloody-rageous!' I giggled, taking it from him as he vanished and flipping it open for a sneaky peek before the light faded. Gold dust! What a find! What were the chances of that report just –

Clunk! A set-up.

I dropped the report like it was a flaming wasps' nest. By luck, it slipped into the gap between two black rubbish bags.

'Eight six five! Eight six five! Stop! That is an order!' screamed Jelly. He strutted over to me in double-quick time, from what hiding place I could not fathom, holding his stick straight out in front of him at shoulder height, aiming it at me like a rapier. 'What have you got in your hand, eight six five?'

I held out my hands to show him. Empty, of course. Jelly glared at me then started to hack with his club at the bags nearest my feet, looking for any sign of what I had dropped. He poked too energetically, and a bag split, sending papers and shreds spilling out and further obscuring the folder.

Jelly was half the age of his colleagues and already their superior. He was hardly taller than I was, his face was angular, bird-like, and he moved with bobbing, dipping, darting jabs of his head and limbs. His compact body itched and stirred with a peculiar kinetic urgency, like a dancer waiting in the wings, awaiting her cue. His uniform was immaculate, his chin was close shaved, his boots shone like black sapphires. Most unusually, he had no truck with our nicknames and always called us by our numbers, displayed on our shoulder patches.

'These bags contain official Institute documents,' he squawked, ramming his sharp face up so close to mine that the tips of our noses briefly made contact. 'They are state property. This is conspiracy! This is espionage!'

Jelly ranted at me for several more minutes, bawling every spittle-flecked word into my face at point-blank range and jet-engine volume. He radiated fury. I was to be tried for treason at a military tribunal. I was to be shot. No, that was too good for a traitor; I was to be partially hanged, then shot. I was a saboteur, I . . . Jelly jerked his club above his head as if he were about to smash out my brains, then halted. His stiff legs pivoted gently about his heels and all colour deserted his face, as if escaping to a place of safety. His eyes bulged, his lips quivered, but the engine of his anger had stalled. I cowered beneath the raised baton and brought up my arms to protect my head, much more intimidated by this display than by any of the farcical accusations he had sprayed me with. Jelly stayed in place for a moment, exactly as he was. Raindrops splashed from his face and he rocked in the breeze. I shut my eyes.

Jelly swallowed, his colour returned, and he gradually piloted his rage back to ground level. He was mad, but he was a prisoner of his own love of regulations. There was no evidence against me. I was let off with a solid beating that left me with welts you could have used for speed bumps, and a week's extra duties for missing the lock-up bell. When we departed, Jelly walked off like a drunkard, I like someone saved from the firing squad.

Lucky doesn't begin to describe it. Had the report been in my hands, it would have been well within the rules to have me charged with any number of crimes. Illegal possession of Institute materials was a very serious offence.

I could never know to what extent Pebble Dash had been a willing participant, but as a demonstration of Sticky's powers, it was awesome. How had he known Jelly would be there? Had the report been genuine? Whatever. It was enough to prove to me that Sticky had not forgotten his plan, and that he had now moved in earnest to phase two; he had given up on becoming friends with The Moth and was set on ensuring that I, and Moth as well, would be in the Establishment with him.

I'd like to tell you that I was a noble boy, that I scuppered Sticky's plan by telling The Moth that no matter where I was sent, he was never to ask for a transfer to the Establishment. But I didn't. If I did have to go to that dreadful place, I wanted him with me.

My week's extra duties comprised a variety of chores, one of which was polishing boots in the claviger's locker room. The clavigers all ignored me. Only Slate Tooth spoke, although what he said brought me as much comfort as a dose of the flu.

Slate Tooth was a spiritless guard with a face as creased as a worn leather sofa and sickeningly grey dentures. He was to retire in a few weeks, and cared little about concealing his low opinion of just about everything and everyone, Jelly in particular. One evening, he paused by the door to the locker room and looked at me as if he'd found a slug in his tea mug.

'*Boy*. He's waiting. You'd all better watch out.'

'Sir?'

'Him. He's waiting.' Slate Tooth wrinkled his nose and flicked his eyes upwards. Someone above him . . . his commander, Jelly?

'For me, sir?' I asked, momentarily panicked.

'One more blunder, just one big one, and he'll be in the Director's seat. That's all it'll take. He'll have this place run his way then.'

'Sir?'

'He'll treat you lot like cattle in a slaughter yard,' said Slate Tooth, and he slouched off.

That was about as much of a conversation as we ever had with the clavigers. Our guards, our key-twirling, club-happy, blockheaded guardians were a prickly and taciturn bunch. Their choicest dialogue was always reserved for their boots and sticks.

And yet I knew exactly what Slate Tooth meant.

Above all the clavigers floated the bloated, rumbling figure of the Director, our ultimate guardian. He hovered menacingly over the entire Institute like a July thundercloud. Or, as The Moth preferred it, like a constipated turkey. None of us had any dealings with the Director, save Moth, and he had to report only that the man was addicted to placing bets on horseracing and taking bribes.

Moth's dealings with him came about because every so often he had to report to the Director's office to be read the letters sent by his mother and to dictate his replies. Moth was very quiet about the entire process. He seemed to find it all intensely embarrassing. When he returned from the office he was always in a funny mood, brittle and withdrawn, and had about him the affronted look of someone who'd been forced to eat tripe off the floor of a morgue. Harete once asked him if anything *funny* went on during the meetings, but The Moth said no, it was just the effect that such proximity to the Director had on him. The first thing he always did after these sessions was to wash those dainty hands of his. Then he'd stash the edible goodies his mother had sent him away in a cupboard, untouched.

The only time the stony invulnerability of the Director or the clavigers had come even close to being chipped was after the business with Wingnuts. Days after his death, a bus load of inspectors arrived from the Authority. Stooping men with spectacles thick enough to deflect a tank shell and jute-skinned women with hairy chins beetled around with clipboards, sniffing and probing into the Institute's recesses and fissures. For a week, the clavigers were on edge. But the only result was a purge of all personal belongings. A clear-out and a bonfire saw to that, and the clavigers breathed easily again, all wrongdoing concealed by the smoke.

Wingnuts's death must have been the first blunder. From Slate Tooth I now knew that it would need only one additional embarrassment for the high-ups to retire the Director and let Jelly take control of the Institute.

I took hold of the next pair of boots and started to rub them with my rag, numbering my misfortunes.

Sticky was after me.

Jelly had me in his sights. A clash with him was like contracting malaria, it was something you'd never shake off.

A squeeze was forming around me.

To unwind, I contemplated the report I had almost been caught with. Had it been genuine? Had a boy called Topsy-Turvy really made a successful break-out?

No, it must have been a fabrication. In any case, it made little odds to me whether Topsy-Turvy had ever really existed or not. I was content to leave him to his place in the hall of legends, alongside The Moth's mates Chiron and Sisyphus and Zeus. Escaping held no lure for me. What would be the point? Life in the Institute was definitely tough and getting tougher, but as Harete used to tell me, we had meals and beds and *most* people got out alive and with all their limbs intact.

My week's punishments complete, I slotted myself like a cracked cog back into the Institute's grinding gears. As soon as possible, I located Moth. Making up for lost time, we did what we always did best together: we had a pointless conversation.

'You are seriously telling me that you never heard about my father's exile before we met?' he asked me.

This was the day it all started.

'Duh! Moth! Your family might be the talk of the town on the outside, but in here, no one's heard of 'em. When do we ever get to hear the news?' I laughed.

'Well, I must say! When he was forced from the government it was in all the newspapers. It was even in our newspapers, not just the foreign ones.'

'Oooh! Big deal! Listen, you know how closed off we are here. Your father could have been the president, the prime minister, we wouldn't know, or care. You're not from our world.'

69

'But my world is your world. My parents are very concerned about you ordinary people, as am I,' he said pompously.

'Moth, Moth, you orbit a different star entirely. Your parents not only had a car, they had a driver. Knowing your background, even he probably had his own driver. My dad *was* a driver. Only he didn't drive bigwigs around, he drove vans full of pet food. Your dad had a seat in the government. We didn't even have a seat on our toilet! What did you get on your last birthday?' I challenged him.

'My parents paid for me to learn to ride.'

'A bike?'

'A horse.'

I hooted hysterically, clutching my sides. 'And you think that's ordinary?' I cried, incredulous.

'No, I am well aware that my background is privileged. I did not claim that my background was ordinary; I said that my parents cared about ordinary people. My mum's under house arrest and my dad's in exile precisely because of that,' he answered seriously.

'I thought you told me that they got into trouble because they wanted the authorities to be open about the past?' I said.

'Partly, yes.'

'Well, we ordinary people would not give you the hairs on a dog's bum for the past,' I told him. 'Mouldy marble and tumbledown temples do nothing for us!'

'You're wrong. Anyway, I'm not talking about ancient history, I'm talking about the recent past. There are plenty of people whose relatives vanished not so very long ago, and I bet they'd like to know about the past. You can't live with an incomplete or tainted history.'

'You most definitely can, Mothballs. My mum vanished; my past has more taint in it than you can waggle your dad's gavel at.'

At that point the bell rang and we leapt up to file to the canteen for dinner. Moth's parents were dense, to my way of thinking. Our country was not so bad, you just had to live by the same unwritten rules as in the Institute. If they'd not shown they cared about something, if they'd just shut up and cared in private, they could all still be living together as a family. There was no hope for people that stupid.

The girls ate before the boys, so by the time we'd finished and had returned our trays and stacked up our chairs, Harete was waiting for us outside in the main courtyard.

That evening, she was not alone but in a huddle with several other girls. This was very unusual. Harete was not a loner, but she was the sort of person who liked the company of a select few friends rather than a large crowd. We ambled over to see what was holding the girls' attention. Pushing into the crowd, we saw Harete holding her cupped hands out in front of her. Inside the chalice of her hands was a tiny bird, cheeping noisily.

'Is it a baby?' asked someone.

'No, young, but not a fledgling. It's an adult,' said Harete.

'Why doesn't it fly away, then?'

'I think its wing's deformed. I found it stuck in an air vent in the shower room last week. I've been keeping it in an old box and feeding it scraps. The matrons all love him, they don't mind,' she answered.

In the female wards' accommodation, the rules were a little different. The female clavigers encouraged the girls to call them 'matrons', and security was less strict. This was why wards were allowed into the main unit, but we internees were not allowed into their block.

The girls, The Moth and I all looked at the little bird singing away, snug in Harete's hands. 'He's ever so nice; he's really sweet, really pretty,' said The Moth.

My skin erupted in sweat, and I started to shudder. I felt waves of sickness pulse up and down my shaking body.

I broke away from the group and ran away, pelted across to the other side of the yard and skidded breathlessly to a halt in a brick alcove. 'I know how this ends, I know how it ends,' I gasped, and leant against the wall, my eyes closed. Vomit rose in my throat and I had to breathe in short, sharp gasps to suppress it.

The little bird would get stomped.

Of course it would. I'd seen it before when kids adopted pet mice or beetles. It was always the same. They'd get attached to it, they'd show the creature around, or someone would get to hear about it. And then someone would stomp it. For a joke. For a laugh. Places like the Institute, they're full of kids who just aren't right.

Them.

They hate anything that isn't part of their mean, lousy, limited lives. They hate anything different or fine or kind or gentle. They were the ones who'd rip up your picture if you drew one and thought it was good enough to stick to your dorm wall above your bed, the ones who'd burst the football we'd once had, the ones who'd tear up letters and photos and smash presents sent to other kids because they themselves hadn't received any.

And if *they* didn't get to the bird first, Harete would be pressured to pay a premium to the Swingers, or an allied female clan, to prevent it from being killed.

But she had nothing to pay with, so they'd kill it anyway. The clans worked on the ruthless logic of profit rather than instinctive, squirming hatred, but what difference did it make in the end?

Them, or the clans. Another squeeze.

I stumbled inside to get a drink of water. Whilst she had that pet, I could not see Harete. She and The Moth were out of bounds for me for as long as they were anywhere near that doomed bird.

'Problem?' grated a throaty voice from the dark. I looked around, but saw no one. Then a figure pressed forwards from a dark corner under a burned-out light bulb.

Eye Inside!

Eye Inside was a spent legend. Once the top dog amongst the inmates, he had run an empire funded by gambling but had lost all ground to Sticky once that boy had struck pay dirt with the premiums, so ably assisted by the sorry example of Wingnuts. He had, it seemed, accepted the loss of his prestige with the detachment of a true high roller, claiming that it was just an extended run of bad luck.

Eye Inside had been born sighted but was blind by the age of ten. Before I was even in the Institute he had achieved infamy by gouging out his two useless organs with a sharpened spoon and swallowing them, an act that so repelled and impressed his contemporaries he was elected at once to be chieftain of the Unitarians. There were only about three of them left, the last of his believers.

'No problem, Eye Inside,' I whispered.

You couldn't lie to Eye Inside. 'Tell me! Is it the lickle birdy?' he asked. His eyelids were sewn shut over empty caves, and two tattoos of staring eyes drawn on the lids were pointed straight at me. Not Institute tattoos, real class jobs.

'Yes, a bird. Some lame girl has it as a pet.'

'Not just a girl, your friend, I think. A good friend . . . more, perhaps . . . You know it will be killed, don't you? And you weaken at the thought?' His dragging vowels and chopped consonants fluttered as ensigns of his otherness. In the seedy cinemas my dad used to take me to, it was the accent adopted by actors playing eastern lagoon raiders and fen-dwelling diabolists from centuries ago.

You couldn't lie to Eye Inside. He was plugged into the nervous system of the Institute, plumbed into its arteries; he sensed its most miniscule vibration, tapped into every rumour, received and retained every secret. It was how he'd prospered as a bookmaker.

'It's got less chance of surviving than an ostrich egg on a rifle range. Less chance than an ice cream on a bonfire,' I said. 'Worse odds than a kitten in a car crusher.'

'And you feel bad about that?'

'Of course I do! What harm has it done to anyone? What harm has she done?' I yelled at the blind boy. 'It deserves to live and be free, just like we do!'

Eye Inside said nothing for a long minute. He curled and uncurled his fingers in a flurry of rapid movements, like they were beads on an abacus and he was performing a computation. 'Dead by the end of the week, you'd say?'

'I'll bet. I've got to go . . . goodbye,' I said, and I tore myself away from the bizarre boy, feeling even more profoundly ill than before.

When it happened, as I knew it would, I'd lose another part of me. Even if I were not around to witness it, just knowing it had happened, knowing what Harete had seen and how she would feel would be enough.

In the Institute, we were all like beads of water on a hotplate. Have you ever dripped water into a dry, hot saucepan? You can make the water drops dance and skitter around. Make the drops too big, and they just blob out into a flat puddle and rapidly evaporate away. Too small, and they spit and fizzle into oblivion in an instant. But get the size right, and they jitter about and stay intact for ages. Moth explained it to me after I described the effect I'd observed when gobbing onto an iron in the laundry room: the right-size drops survive because they sacrifice a bit of themselves. The outer layers of the drops turn to steam, but the steam keeps the rest of the drop away from the hot surface. They whiz around protected from the lethal heat by a thin layer of vapour made from themselves. Eventually, of course, they give up too much and vanish.

That was us, of course. We survived the Institute by giving up a part of ourselves to the heat and the horror, floating free above it, insulated from it. But stay too long and you gave up too much and boiled away.

Later, I told The Moth my fears. I begged him to make Harete set the bird free, or to give it to one of the matrons or to a girl who was leaving, and to never, ever show it off again in the courtyard. I told him what would happen.

'She won't get rid of it; she's hooked on it. She loves the little chap,' he replied.

Stupid, stupid, stupid. Chovies like The Moth and Harete and others, they just don't understand. They can't sense what I sense, the unthinking, hollow hatred thrumming through places like the Institute. You couldn't get attached to things in the Institute, nor to people . . . you had to keep only what was useful to you. What use was a small, soft, warm bird?

I'm right. I know I am.

But I was only half right about what would happen to the bird. And nowhere near to guessing what the consequences would be.

Chapter 5

Under the Pylons

The sound was an anguished, mournful drone that cycled in pitch and spread itself like poison gas over the land. When we first heard it, we were clutching our stitch-sore sides and spitting on the ground, shattered from the chase between the pylons.

'What's that? What are they up to now?' wailed Harete.

'A siren,' I wheezed. 'Perhaps we've been spotted.'

'What's their game?'

'Chess,' said Moth. We lumbered onto pylon five, the terror behind us hidden in the freezing, ground-hugging cloud. 'We move forwards one pylon-square at a time, like pawns!'

He was wrong. You can only move to an empty square in chess, and each of ours already had a castle on it, a tower made of metal struts.

'Hide-and-seek,' panted Harete. Wrong again, I thought, stumbling over the muddy corrugations and trying to ignore the cold air that cut my lungs, for in that game you take turns. Our game was one I'd seen played when I was a child, staying in the slum apartment of a distant aunt. A plump cockroach was scurrying over the floor, resisting every attempt by my aunt to trap it under a cup. So she

77

lifted up an edge of the carpet and started to laboriously roll it up. Soon, the cockroach was trapped in a narrow gap between the advancing tube of rolled rug and the wall. Next, my aunt ran a coal shovel sideways along the gap, until the cockroach was hemmed into a corner. Then she dropped a flat iron on it.

We were the cockroach. The marshals were rolling up the countryside behind us. They didn't even need to catch us, I realised, that would just be an added bonus for them; all they needed to do was to prevent us from doubling back, and force us up against the wall to await the falling iron. We were in the biggest squeeze of all.

'Come on, faster!' I implored my companions.

The lumpy, sticky soil was nightmarish to run over. We had to keep peeling head-sized clods of earth from our shoes else it became impossible to progress. Harete and I soon copied The Moth's idea of finding a chunk of flat limestone to act as a scraper and keeping it with us.

Every time we reached a pylon, we rested, breathless, for a count of ten. Snow fell, propelled by an icy, stinging wind that lashed our faces like a flail. Each mini blizzard lasted a few minutes, leaving us half blind and gasping for air, then the wind would drop and the snow pitter-pattered down in lazy slivers. Our hands and faces and feet became raw with cold. Our mood darkened with the sky, and the unseen siren wailed on.

The droning noise abruptly stopped and the instrument began to dispense crackly, brassy words, audible whenever the wind eased.

Give up! Turn back! Give up! Turn back!

The volume rose as the wind changed direction. We fought on, but couldn't help listening to the toxic bombast. The words butchered hope.

Evasion is impossible! Survival is impossible!

They were right about that. The plan had been to walk undetected to the border, not flee at full tilt. We'd never make it. I slowed down.

We guarantee punishment will be minimal if you surrender now!

My pace faltered. Could that really be true?

You will receive hot food and medical attention!

Hot food! Imagine that! We had only old, cold fat scraped from pans!

Give up! Turn back! Give up! Turn back!

Ahead of me, Harete and Moth stopped. Harete turned about, bent down, stood up again. Predictable, I thought; the weakest had given up first.

It's nice and warm inside! We can see you! We can seeeeee you!

That voice sounded almost like – *Ow!* Harete tore off my balaclava and whacked a hand hard over my left ear.

'Squash it in! Block out the sound!' she yelled, before I could react. Then she punched my other ear with equal force, and I felt her press something wet inside it.

'They can't see us, not in this murk and snow. It's all lies, words to weaken and confuse us,' she hollered. I could hardly hear her, the soft mud she'd poked in my ears deadened all sound. She did the same to The Moth, then shoved me from behind to set me moving again. I set my eyes on the most distant pylon I could see and slogged on, released from the spell of the gangrenous propaganda, appalled I had given it any credence. By the time the mud dried and fell out, the loudspeaker had stopped. If they used it again, we never heard it.

At pylon number twelve we all looked wrecked, so I suggested we eat. We slumped down and probed inside our clothes for our food bags. 'Break off today's ration, then split that into two,' I instructed. 'Save one half for tonight, and take a good bite of the other half. We'll snack on the rest as we walk.'

We each unwrapped our food blocks, which had been carefully measured and scored by us into eight even portions – one for each of the seven days we'd expected to be walking, plus one spare in case of delay. I grasped the greasy slab in both hands and slowly bent it along the first cut mark. It yielded a little, then tore messily. The torn-off lump I tugged roughly into two equal pieces, each about the size of a chocolate bar. One, I pocketed for the night's dinner. I bit down into the other waxy lump and chewed slowly, holding my breath in order to lessen the taste. The others followed suit. 'Blurrrrgghhhh,' I shuddered as I swallowed. 'Nasty. But nutritious. Moth, your recipe is a success.' My appetite was not assisted by the sight of the long mucus pendant that dangled from Moth's nose.

'Yes, it's not too bad. Fat, grains and sugar . . . it's like gritty lard,' commented Harete. 'Gritty dripping. That's what we'll call it!' she enthused.

'Good name, Harete. How are you doing, Moth?' He was still chewing, not having dared to swallow. He ignored me. Perhaps he thought it was rude to speak with his mouth full. After several more gyrations of his jaw I saw him scrunch his eyes and flinch as he committed the food to his stomach.

'How many more pylons do we have to do today?' he asked me.

'I've tried counting the paces between them. Presuming they're evenly spaced, I think we have to do about fifty a day.'

'And we've done . . . eleven?'

'This one we're eating under is number twelve, Moth.'

'Yes . . . but that's only eleven pylon-to-pylon distances we've covered. So we've done one fifth of the distance, on the first day of seven, or one thirty-fifth of the total distance.' Moth's voice cracked slightly as he made his dispiriting calculation and he slumped farther down. I felt a little angry towards him for mentioning this. What he said was true, but it was not helpful.

I opened my water bottle and took a deep swig, aghast at how thirsty I was and how refreshing the river water tasted. I passed the bottle to the others, and they too drank deeply from it. When it came back to me, it was all but empty. I tried to scoop some snow out of a furrow into the bottle, but hardly any went in through the narrow opening.

When we had stowed away the bottles and food, we picked up our mattress rolls and continued briskly walking. Our hurried break had lasted for no more than a couple of minutes. I hoped that the battalion on our heels would stop much longer to eat, for every moment we rested they gained on us.

Pylon number thirteen loomed ahead, the metal barely

discernible against the tin sky. Now another problem halted us, one for which my plan had made no provision.

So far, all the pylons we had travelled between had been standing in just two enormous fields separated by a narrow ditch we had effortlessly stepped over. But the next pylon's field was separated from our own by a substantial hedge. The hedge was taller than me, as wide as I was tall, and dense with spiky brown and green foliage. The hedge vanished into the murky distance to the left and to the right. We looked at each other. Harete crouched and scanned along the base of the hedge where the foliage seemed sparser, but there was not a gap large enough to force even an arm through.

'We'll have to go along and hope there's a break in it,' I mumbled. Nothing in either direction hinted at the presence of a gap. I shrugged and set off to the left, away from the pylons. Every step in this direction was a step across the path of our pursuers, rather than a step ahead of them, but what choice had we? I reckoned them to be not more than a few minutes behind us. Only the fog and the size of our band were in our favour, since small groups can always act quicker than large ones.

We scurried along for perhaps a quarter of an hour before we found an opportunity to cross the huge barrier. Even then it was not really a gap, just a stretch where the hedge had lost its shape somewhat and had degenerated into a low, broad mass of compact greenery. I sort of climbed into the hedge, standing half in and half on it, my feet breaking through the surface layers until they became jammed in the woody maze of branches and brambles below. I stretched out a hand and hoisted Harete up to where I was, then propelled her over as much of the other side as I could. She landed heavily, but recovered and rolled onto the field beyond, all without complaint. Moth followed, after dithering for ages, and when he came he whinged and moaned and unleashed his entire arsenal of infantile insults against me. With great difficulty I disentangled myself, fought my way out of the hedge's scratchy embrace and stamped to where The Moth stood quaking behind Harete.

'Moth . . . grow up!' was all I could think to rage at him. I stormed off across the field, too cross even to worry about giving away our position.

That was only the first of dozens of hedges we met.

The next hedge we reached was smaller than the first, and I was able to vault clumsily onto it, then drag the others up and over. The one after that was even bigger than the first and took an age to get around, the third was a scruffy, straggly affair we traversed with only minor discomfort. At the crossing of every thorny barricade, Moth griped and grizzled. In my boiling anger and resentment I quite enjoyed his suffering. All this pain and effort, and he just didn't get it; he could not bring himself to stop whining and commit himself to the matter at hand.

After hours of hedge-hopping, we came upon a large drainage ditch separating one flat, stony field from the next. The ditch was deeper and wider than any others we had seen so far that day. At the bottom of it lay a fractured, thigh-wide plank of ice, but beneath the ice I could see liquid water running. I felt inconceivably weary. I sat on the bank of the ditch and waited for the others to catch up, dreading the seemingly inevitable arguments with The Moth. Why did it have to be like this? He was my best friend. I had been prepared for the journey to be tough, but putting up with an uncooperative Moth was much more exhausting.

My companions caught up with me. 'Sit down and rest,' I said. 'I'll refill my water bottle; we'll all have a drink.'

I scrambled down into the ditch, smashed a hole in the ice with my shoe, filled the bottle and passed it back up. We took it in turns to guzzle and I refilled the bottle once more. Then we ate from our 'walking' ration. Mine did not taste so good this time. I stayed down in the ditch, the other two sat above me.

'Look,' I groaned. 'We have to stay friends. I'm sorry. I'm sorry I've been so angry with you.'

The Moth shrugged.

'You're a fish out of water, Moth. You're a boy of books and learning, not walking and scrambling though hedges. You're happiest indoors, in cities – you're an Urban Moth. I know this is hard for you; it's hard for us all. We have to stay friends,' I said again, exasperated. What could I say to make this better? 'It will be for the best.'

'You sound just like a claviger,' said The Moth. He adopted a leering, sing-song voice, 'It's for your own good!'

I let this jibe pass and we sat for more minutes in tense silence. I had no idea now how long we'd been walking. The dawn seemed a very long time ago, that was for sure.

'Where are the pylons?' asked Harete.

I realised with a gut-thumping jolt that I had no idea. We'd lost sight of them in the gloomy light and thick, snowy air. During our march across the fields the mist had thickened, and we'd had to change direction several times in the course of negotiating the hedges.

I hauled myself out of the ditch.

'We've lost them,' grumped The Moth. 'That's just great.'

'Do we need them?' asked Harete.

'Yes. The path the pylons take is the shortest route to the border, north. If we stray, we might have days more walking until we reach it. And in this weather, we can't see the sun well enough to steer by. We might end up going badly off course, particularly if we have to keep following hedges for gaps,' I reminded her.

'The pylons are the true path,' Moth added with sarcastic solemnity. 'Amen.'

I spat on the ground to clear my mouth. 'Yes, well, they are. We need to get back on track. And fast – before those men catch us.'

We had to find the pylons and I needed to devise a way to cross those hideous hedges. My mind was empty. Why did I have to do all the thinking?

Harete interrupted my sulking.

'I bet the pylons are over there,' she said, pointing along the ditch to her right.

'Why?'

'Look at the crows. They seem to come from over there when they fly into the fields, and when they've pecked at the ground for a bit, they fly back in that direction.'

'So? What are you saying? Are crows electric? Do they need to recharge?' I did not understand her. It was true though; there was a constant stream of large, black birds emerging from the mist, alighting in the fields, and then returning the same way.

'Now who's being stupid? Didn't you notice, when we were under the pylons? The crows roost on the cables between them. Hundreds of them.'

The Moth and I sat up and looked at each other.

'You're right, Harete. That's brilliant,' he said.

I laughed, hardly able to believe the marvellous observation. 'Yes, yes it is brilliant, it's utterly, totally fantastic! Let's go, together this time. We walk as the crow flies!'

We scrambled to our feet and started off along the birds' bearing, parallel to the ditch. It was remarkable how our energy and mood were at once renewed. I felt cheered, yet also annoyed and a little diminished by the excellence of the girl's thinking.

An unforgiving, freezing cold wind sprang up, roaring into us like an enraged wolf. The wind stripped the dry snow and loose soil from the ground and flung it at us, scouring our already sore faces. We had to lean into the wind to stay upright. Every step forwards took a huge effort, the noise of the wind deafening, the stinging cold on our exposed faces intolerable.

'This is hell, this is hell, this is hell,' grizzled The Moth, barely audible, and this time I had to agree with him.

'Let's get into the ditch!' I yelped.

All three of us jumped down into the deep ditch to our left. Instantly we were out of the wind and the noise dropped to nothing. We giggled and guffawed with relief, the contrast was almost too great to believe. It felt warm by comparison down between the straggly, grassy banks, warm and wondrously silent. We trudged along the ditch, placing one foot either side of the crust of ice snaking along the bottom.

Pleased with my idea, I tried to grow another. It was my job, after all, as leader of the expedition, to care for the others and to command them. My pride and confidence returned. We needed a better way to cross those large boundary hedges; they were each as big an obstacle as the river had been, and hugely time-consuming to get over or around. Might the rope be useful? I still had it, wound over my shoulder, but could not picture how it could be of value. We'd crossed the river using our bulky, rolled-up foam mattresses to keep ourselves afloat. *Pity we can't float across the hedges.* Gradually, a plan started to assemble in my mind. *I can do it*, I told myself, *this can work.* I vowed there that I'd never give up. Hedges, hunters, hunger, I'd beat them all. Maybe our escape had been half-throttled at birth, then turfed out of its cradle, but it could still succeed. We had only to walk fast and stay out of reach of the men behind us. What more could go wrong now?

I heard the twang and snap, but did not stop walking until The Moth shouted at me. Spinning about, I saw Harete bent double, clutching her left leg, her face wound tight with pain.

'What is it now? Sprained your ankle?' I said brusquely, but the words died on my tongue. Harete's leg was locked between two rusty metal hoops. Thinking she'd stepped on nothing worse than a piece of scrap metal, I sprinted back along the ditch to her side, and only then saw that she was caught in a trap, a hideous, spring-jaw mechanism big enough to bring down a bear. The two iron hoops were viciously serrated, the inward-pointing teeth now embedded in Harete's calf.

'A mantrap!' I said, unable to believe that such a thing could exist. It looked old, a forgotten relic, but even before I tried to do so I knew I would not be able to wrench the jaws apart. Where it had seized Harete's leg, her plastic waterproofs were punctured and I could see a dark red patch growing slowly under her overalls.

'That's not a problem then,' gasped Harete, her eyes screwed shut, puffing her words out in short, rasping breaths. 'I'm a girl, aren't I?'

Moth and I looked over the device. 'They have sown the dragon's teeth, and they have sprung upon us,' he said quietly, his face grim. Had the trap not been so rusted, I am certain it would have broken Harete's leg.

'We need a lever,' I said, and I clambered out of the ditch to search for a length of wood, although I knew it to be a hopeless task in that treeless landscape. As I reached the top, the bullying wind set about me with all its petulance. For a handful of seconds, the fog and sleet were shunted to one side and I was able to see right across the fields in the direction we had come. An irregular row of bobbing red dots caught my eye, bright against the gloom. The fog thinned more, and I could see they were the lighted ends of cigarettes clamped between the lips of men, a straggly line of hundreds of men clumping towards us through the mist, swinging long clubs at their sides. I slid at once back into the ditch, unable to swallow the scale of the emergency. Despair and panic diffused out from every cell in my body, but only for a moment; my own dragons pounced and fed on them.

'We need to get you out,' I said calmly to Harete, aware how redundant my words sounded. I gestured for Moth to keep lookout above the ditch. 'Tell me when they're almost on us,' I whispered to him. 'If we can't get her under cover before they reach us, they're bound to see her!'

Squatting on my haunches at the bottom of the frozen ditch, I quickly ripped out the weeds that had grown over the base of the trap and fumbled around with the rusty mechanism, trying to see how it worked. 'How's it hurting?' I asked. I couldn't shake away the image of the approaching men, but I was determined not to give Harete up until the last second.

Harete's pale face was placid, controlled, her breaths fast and short. 'Beautifully, thanks,' she replied, muttering through teeth clenched together tighter than the trap's iron fangs.

'I've nothing for the pain,' I admitted. There! I found the ratchet, a toothed wheel and springy metal catch that locked the jaws into place.

'Talk to me!' said Harete, sounding like a bad ventriloquist as she grated out words through the barrier of her teeth.

'What about?'

'Anything! Make up a story, you dumb jerk, say something to take my mind off the pain!' she rasped, her whole body quivering.

'What sort of story?'

'Any! Distract me! Give me hope!'

89

'Moth!' I said. 'Help!'

'About four hundred paces away now,' he hissed down, misunderstanding what I wanted from him, 'coming in fast!'

Why not a story? If lies sprayed from metal horns could bamboozle and weaken us, might not different words lend strength? My story would be Harete's anaesthetic as I operated. But what could it be about . . . my mind filled with pictures of gnawing fangs, crows, animals in flight.

Working fast as I thought, I pulled off a generous mass of gritty dripping from my food block and liberally slathered the greasy stuff over the heavily corroded, toothed ratchet wheel and the hinge where the jaws pivoted. I knew we'd miss the food later on, but there was no choice.

I pulled off my gloves and with frozen fingers tried to ease the catch away from the gear wheel, at the same time pushing with a foot against one of the iron loops that had bitten into Harete's leg. The catch was incredibly tight; it bent only a minute distance before my fingers let it slip.

'My story is set in outer space, not like all his dreary legends,' I began, speaking softly but quickly, jabbing my free foot towards Moth. 'Space, with rockets and stuff. A very, very long way away –'

'How far?' moaned Harete.

'About three hundred and fifty paces!' Moth called out, listening to us as he craned his neck over the edge of the ditch, monitoring the men's progress.

'No, much farther! Thousands of light years and many, many dark years too! There was a large planet.' All the time I spoke, I fumbled with the catch, but still it refused to budge. My aching fingers were greasy with the lard I'd used

90

to lubricate it; I wiped them on the grass and tried again.

'More!' winced Harete. 'A planet, yes, now what?'

My mind had a question for me, a question I could not ignore. If the men got to us before I'd freed her, should Moth and I run or stay? Was this why Harete really wanted the story, to stop me coming up with an answer to that?

'Go on! The story!' said Harete. 'Please!'

'Three hundred paces! Oh! There are loads of them!' gasped Moth.

'Anyway, there was a very large planet that orbited a very small sun,' I carried on, still grappling with the catch. 'Actually, it was a major argument on the planet as to whether the planet orbited the sun or the sun orbited the planet.'

Lift . . . snap . . . lift . . . snap. Every attempt failed, the catch held fast; I couldn't raise it high enough to allow the toothed wheel to move.

'They orbit a common centre of gravity, in fact,' interrupted Moth. I told you, he just couldn't let an error go unmentioned.

'Yeah, well, whatever, but they didn't know that. Shut up, Moth, I've lost my train of thought again now . . . I'm only making this up as I go along, you know,' I said, pausing to shake the soreness out of my stiff, cold fingers.

'Yes, shut up, Moth,' squealed Harete. She groaned and squirmed against the crushing grip of the trap on her leg. Looking up, I could see the effort she was making to hold back the pain. Her wind-reddened face looked ageless, pickled in agony. She could have been a young child or a grandmother.

'Keep still!' I snapped. Over and over I tried again to prise up the catch, and again and again it slipped from my freezing fingers. 'Wait . . . yes, and on this planet there lived a . . . a pilot. The pilot was very brave and able, an air-ace. One day, whilst flying solo –'

'How low?' Harete butted in.

'So low that the ground racing past the cockpit window was almost within reach – the pilot saw a huge . . . flock of birds . . . called . . . um . . . Naw-Naws. They were flying straight at the aeroplane,' I continued. *How is this stupid thing going to end?* I thought frantically. My pinched, freezing fingers were covered in blood from where the cruel catch nipped the skin every time it snapped back into place.

'One hundred paces! I can see them clearly! They're all smoking as well!' Moth butted in, his voice tinted with disdain.

'Naw-Naws are very graceful, silent birds and the pilot knew that if they struck the plane they would all be killed,' I said, speaking fast. Moth had thrown me a clue.

'Fifty paces!' screamed Moth. How was he judging the distance? I briefly wondered what Moth-od he was using. He slid back down into the bottom of the ditch and looked at me, wide-eyed behind his thick spectacles. *'What do we do?'* his expression asked, begging me for an answer.

I knew the ending, I'd worked it out. I pulled out my tobacco tin, the one containing the glass shards, and removed the lid. 'So rather than risk destroying the birds, she deliberately crashed her plane into a lake and swam ashore!' I concluded at a gabble.

'She! I wasn't expecting that! Go on!' prompted Harete.

She smiled down at me through her tears. 'I won't tell them I was with you!' she cried. 'I'll say you two left me behind at the Institute, that we went different ways!'

I tugged one last time at the tricky, slippy catch, and managed to raise it ever so, ever so slightly, only this time I hooked the corner of the metal tin lid underneath it. Pressing with my legs on the hoop, bracing my back against the wall of the ditch, I pulled on the lid.

'They're here!' squealed Moth. But we knew anyway, for by then we could all clearly hear the men's shouts and coughs and feel the tramping of their feet. They had voices like boots, hard and leathery and studded with iron.

The tin lid finally caught under the catch, the catch lifted, the ratchet wheel spun. With a mighty push, I straightened out my legs and the jaws yawned wide. Harete fell out, and landed on top of me, clutching her bloodied leg. She bit her own arm to stifle a scream. The three of us scrambled madly together, flattening ourselves close against the muddy embankment as the first of the men reached the ditch. We held our breath, and each other, as a small army marched over our heads. Each man traversed the ditch, the taller ones taking it in a single stride, the shorter ones needing a leap. We saw their flapping rain cloaks, the ends of the staves they held and the undersides of their boots. I recognised those boots – not clavigers' footwear, but marshals'. I'd been on the underside of enough pairs in my time.

For a minute or more they marched over the tops of their prey, never bothering to look down into the ice-locked drain they vaulted over. Once, one of the dogs they had with them saw us, but we held still and it was jerked away by its handler, its barks of protest unheeded. Clods of mud and the smouldering ends of spent cigarettes and profanity-laden sentences showered down on us as the searchers crossed over.

We waited for a long time before daring to speak again. 'Amateurs!' I sneered contemptuously. 'Even their dogs were useless!'

'We're wearing all our clothes,' Moth said, guessing aloud, 'so they've nothing with our scent on back at the Institute, nothing to train the dogs to follow.'

I asked him why he thought the trap had been there, but he said he didn't know. His best guess was that farmers found them when ploughing and just threw them into the ditch. Harete rolled up the layers of her clothing to look at her leg, wincing as she did so. It was savagely bruised, and ringed with cuts where the trap's teeth had dug in, but it was not broken, and the cuts were only skin-deep. Together, Moth and I bathed it in icy water and tore off lengths of tape to act as sticking plasters. She tested the leg, and found she could walk on it, much to our collective relief. We resumed plodding and hobbling along the ditch, keeping sharp eyes out for buried traps, but found no more, only the occasional rusty rivet or spring to show where others had once lain.

'Look,' Harete said after some minutes, pointing upwards, 'wires!'

Directly overhead, high above us, were sets of thick cables in pairs. I checked about us for marshals, and we climbed out of the ditch. A pylon stood a short distance to the left, and another one farther away to the right. Those giant metal frames with their 'T' cross-shapes never looked as welcoming as they did then. I noticed that the cables and the pylons were all dotted with black crows, exactly as Harete had described – the rooks on the castles! The Moth and I both slapped her cheerfully on the back, and we all grinned with relief. We had regained the pylons, freed Harete, and now we were behind our pursuers, safe for the moment – until they doubled back, or sent another wave.

'Which way now?' asked The Moth.

'Have you no sense of direction? That way!' I told him, pointing to the pylon that had been to the left of the ditch as we had struggled along it, justifying my choice with a patch of lighter cloud that showed the sun was to the west.

As I made my demonstration I was shocked at how low the sun was in the sky. We probably had only two hours' more walking time before dark and we had no idea now how many pylons we had passed. I explained again the necessity of getting as much walking done as possible before nightfall, and this time my words met with no protest or sarcasm. We shuffled off, each taking another bite of our rations as we walked. Of our pursuers, now ahead of us, and away to one side, nothing could be seen. *They won't be the last*, I reminded myself, *they'll send more*. I stopped briefly and reconsidered my own fears. *Orion will send more.* They'd hire the best for The Moth.

After a few minutes we passed straight under the next pylon. Moth stopped and started to circle it, looking carefully up and down each iron leg and peering up at the zizzag cross-beams.

'Aha! I thought as much. Look, you two. These pylons are not nameless,' he declared, a note of smug victory in his voice.

He pointed up at a square white plaque mounted on a cross-beam. The plaque had a series of numbers and letters on it:

K331-L-RN-16/0

'I thought the engineers who repair these things must have a way of identifying each pylon, something like a car number plate. This is it,' enthused Moth. 'We'll note these digits and compare them with the ones on the next few pylons. With luck, we should be able to work out a pattern and use this to help us count them.'

Harete and I nodded. 'Good idea, Moth,' we chorused, content to leave the job to him. 'Should keep him happy,' I muttered to Harete.

The remainder of that first afternoon passed by in a gloomy daze. Under darkening skies we plodded on from pylon to pylon. We met no more hedges, which was a relief but also a slight disappointment to me because I had now formulated what I hoped would be a way to defeat them. We slogged ahead across the monotonous, drab, empty fields, myself in the lead, Harete and The Moth trailing some distance behind, she leaning on him to take the weight off her damaged leg.

Every time we passed under a pylon Moth looked for its identification plaque, not always with success. The temperature and the wind dropped, and the snow started to make a real effort at settling.

96

One pylon was marked in a different way. It was by the side of another of the big drainage ditches that cut across our path. Suspended from a cross-beam was a scarecrow, a parody of a human figure made from sticks and stuffed sacks. It twisted and jiggled in the wind, dangling from its neck by a length of twine. We stared at it in pained distress. Painted on the sacking chest in red letters were words, or parts of them.

EAT   TO   P IES

'Eat two pies?' I laughed. 'Why put . . . no, wait . . .' I filled in the gaps and guessed again. 'Death to . . .' This was not funny.

'Spies?' suggested Harete.

'Can't be, the spacing's wrong,' I grumbled, and I tugged angrily at its leg. Turning one of our homely pylons into a gibbet felt like a desecration, with or without the peculiar slogan.

'Don't ask, I don't understand!' wailed The Moth.

'It's been hung facing east,' he commented a minute later. 'Or do I mean *hanged*? The same direction these drains run.'

'What's there? What's to the east?' asked Harete, white and shaking.

Moth shrugged. 'Nothing for a long way. The coast, ultimately,' he said after a moment's thought. We swallowed our revulsion and moved on, our spirits chilled.

Later, we reached a pylon with a visible name plate. Moth studied it, screwing his eyes up through his wet and dirty glasses. 'I can't make it all out, but I think it's K-three-zero-nine-dash-A-dash-letter-letter. Can't read the rest, but that's good though. The number after the first letter is the pylon number, so we've walked from number three-three-one to three-zero-nine, that's twenty-two pylon distances covered.'

'Less than half our daily total,' I said, my heart sinking.

'Yes, but we only started noting the numbers after we got out of that ditch. We've got to add on the distance we covered before then,' he reminded me. 'We've been walking for a long time, since dawn in fact. We must have done at least that same distance before then. Anyway,' he added sniffily, 'I'm not walking any more today. You can threaten me all you like, but I'm through until tomorrow.'

Harete murmured her agreement, citing the pain in her injured leg as an additional reason to stop, and I realised that I, too, was totally exhausted.

'Let's eat the other half of the day's ration, then make camp,' I suggested.

We chose the pylon leg that seemed to offer the best protection from the falling snow and sat cross-legged in a close-huddled circle against it. With no great enthusiasm we finished off whatever greasy crumbs remained of the first half of the day's ration and started on the second half, the evening-meal portion. The rations were very short because of what I had used up lubricating the trap, and I reckoned we'd need to go to half-rations for the next couple of days.

'I'll say one thing for the gritty dripping, no matter how hungry you are, it never really appeals. We won't be fighting the temptation to eat too much,' commented Harete. We had to force ourselves to chew the stuff. The fat was vile; its dirty taste spoke to me of the Institute. The gritty grains inside it ground unpleasantly between our teeth. We drained one of the plastic water bottles to wash away the taste.

The plastic bags covering my mittens were thickly coated in streaks of white fat. I pulled off my balaclava and wiped the mittens all over my face, getting as much grease as possible on my cheeks, nose and forehead. The other two looked at me open-mouthed.

'The grease will reduce chafing from the wind and keep my skin from getting chapped,' I explained.

'Will it really work?' asked Harete.

I shrugged and said, 'Ask me tomorrow night.'

After this, we began the uncertain process of making our first proper camp, not the hasty affair of the previous night. We arranged the three foam mattresses, protected from mud and water in their plastic wrappings, and placed them together on the flattest patch of ground we could find under the pylon, then covered them in more sheets of plastic to make a ramshackle bivouac. The Moth's and Harete's bed rolls included their worn, grey blankets from the Institute; mine was lost. These blankets seemed like an inconceivable luxury to us at that point. Upon seeing hers, Harete cried out as if finding a long-lost favourite toy. She pressed her blanket to her face and sniffed it deeply. She and Moth climbed into the plastic cocoon and lay on their backs between the plastic top-sheets and the plastic-covered mattresses. I handed them their blankets, which they spread out over themselves.

Before crawling in to join them I scanned the landscape. Only the bloodied scalp of the sun remained above the horizon so there was hardly any light left. The impending darkness did not bother me, in fact it was a reassurance. Our little harbour seemed awfully exposed and vulnerable whilst there was any light to see by, so the darkness and the snow which fell steadily from low clouds felt very protective.

I lifted up a loose corner of plastic and slid in beside the other two. We shuffled our bodies close together for warmth. Although I felt completely drained and ached all over, I found that I could not get to sleep. The bivouac was very uncomfortable, and besides, I was too scared and too excited by our bizarre adventure to relax properly. The twisting and rustling sounds from my companions told me that they were finding it equally difficult to sleep, especially Harete, who kept sitting up to rub her leg.

'Who wants to hear the rest of my story?' I asked on a whim.

'Your story?' asked Harete, sounding as shocked as if I'd made an improper suggestion.

'The one I told you earlier. I can't sleep. I'll make up some more,' I replied.

'Oh yes! The pilot, and the . . . what did you call them? Naw-Naw birds,' said Harete. 'It was good. It helped me to bear the pain, it really did.'

'Where had I got to?' I mumbled, collecting my thoughts. 'Ah, yes . . . the pilot crashed the plane to save the birds and was drummed out of the air force. Being of low rank, she was drummed out to the sound of a triangle.'

'What is the sound of a triangle?' asked Moth.

'Very clangy – it was a right-jangled triangle. So the pilot had to return to the monotony of civilian life. She married badly and soon fell pregnant.

'At exactly the moment she realised she was pregnant, astronomers detected a new planet, much like their own but shrouded in dense cloud. As the pilot grew larger and larger in pregnancy, so the strange new planet grew larger and larger in the sky. At the very moment she gave birth, the new planet entered into orbit around their home world.

'This caused an uproar. Scientists were worried that the presence of the planet would cause massive tides and earthquakes, or even that their own world might be ejected from the solar system.'

Moth broke in again. 'Yes, the three body problem!' he babbled. 'Impossible to predict precisely where three interacting bodies will end up! And with gravitational forces there would be profound effects on the entire system, depending on their relative masses.'

'If you say so, Moth. But it was the masses of relatives that mattered most to the pilot. No sooner had she given birth than they descended upon her and her husband in huge droves. The ones who could drive arrived in droves, the ones who could swim came in swarms, the ones who could fly came in floods. Of tears. This was too much for the pilot, and she handed her baby to one of her relations and vanished out of the hospital. She was found dead in a cave a week later.

'The pilot's son was an odd child. When he grew up, he was like the Naw-Naw birds: silent and very graceful.'

'And the son's name was . . . ?' asked Harete.

'A mistake. The drifter father did not really want to take responsibility for his son. When an official asked him who was going to look after the child now that its mother had vanished, all he could do was stutter, "Oh, hell! I am. Why? You are? I . . . " A passing registrar took that to be the child's name, and the boy was legally recorded as being Olim, Yuri. So he took the name Yuri, which he thought was fitting for the son of a pilot.

'Yuri followed in his mother's footsteps and became a flyer, a truly excellent one. So good in fact that he was asked to captain the first spaceship to investigate the new planet. It hung very large in the sky but its surface could not be seen through the thick cloud layers. They had named the new planet "Future" because, like the future, everyone knew it existed but no one could say anything about it with any certainty.

'Yuri agreed to the mission, but insisted on taking his best friend as his co-pilot, and his co-pilot insisted on taking his new wife.

'Once they had blasted off from their home world, they had to cross a huge expanse of empty space. They ran low on everything and started to argue. Just when things looked like they could not get any worse, they ran into a terrible obstacle. Future was surrounded by rings made up of zillions of chunks of rock and ice. However, it was not all bad news. They were able to obtain water and air from some of the rocks to replenish their stocks, and, incredibly, they discovered some of the larger ones to be inhabited.'

Moth, again. 'What was their ship called? All ships have a name.'

'Who cares! I don't know! It was named after . . . um . . . the co-pilot's aunt. Her name was . . .' I stuck my head out of the bivouac and looked up at the pylon above us. Twisting around I could see that the legible part of the name plate was

K309-A-RN-

'Karen,' I grunted, 'the spaceship's name was *The Aunty Karen*. So they spent many weeks flitting about between the larger lumps of rock that made up the rings, bathing in strange energies like infra-dead and ultra-violent radiation.

On one rock, they found a tree and a young prince who gave them a map showing a safe passage through the belts. He did this because his own father had been a famous pilot who had died young and he felt sympathy for the struggling crew.

'Unfortunately, luck disowned them. The co-pilot's wife was shot from the ship by a faulty ejector seat, and she spiralled away into a bleak hole.'

'A *black* hole,' said Moth. 'Where all light and matter are crushed to a single point and nothing can escape.'

'That's what I said. Next, Yuri found he'd taken the wrong piece of paper from the prince, and instead of a map he had the first draft of a drama about llamas, a dromedary comedy. Inevitably then, Yuri erred. *The Aunty Karen* was caught between two massive rocks, which smashed together with great force, destroying the spaceship. Yuri set the vessel on a crash-landing course, but he knew from his calculations that the ship was a tiny fraction too heavy to survive the impact. He rapidly pulled on a spacesuit and jumped out of the airlock into deep space. He was never heard from again.

'Thanks to Yuri's bravery, his co-pilot managed to crash-land on Future. Under a swirling green sky, he set off to explore the new world. Nowhere did he find any signs of life. Yet, when he returned to the wreckage of the ship many years later, he found all the land around covered by an immense, sprawling tree. Gagging for fresh food after years of living on dehydrated soup from the ship's supplies, he plucked a piece of fruit from the tree and, little caring whether or not it was poisonous, bit into it. He was staggered to discover that as he ate the fruit he could hear his wife's voice. "I live! I am this tree!" said the voice.'

Harete stirred. 'That's pushing things a bit far! Back from the dead, and as a tree?'

Moth disagreed. 'He never actually said she was dead, just that she fell into a black hole. The laws of nature have no jurisdiction there. Right at the point when everything is extinguished, there's always scope for marvels.'

'Eh, thanks, Moth!' I said, surprised at his support. 'Now, the co-pilot spent the rest of his life living on Future under the shade of his wife's tree, eating the weird fruit she grew and talking to her. When he lay down to die amongst her boughs, the tree asked him, "What have you learned?" And he replied, "All plans fail, all ambition is futile. The universe is too strange for man's schemes."

'The end.'

Harete brooded over the story for a while before saying, 'I thought it was an interesting tale, but why did you make it end so sadly?'

'It wasn't sad. It was realistic. Everything does end in failure ultimately, because we die, and that's the end of that. Moth tells me that even the sun will die one day, after it's expanded and frazzled the earth, so everything that anyone has ever done will be crisped up and forgotten.'

'Well, that's an inspirational note to end the day on,' she grumbled.

'Too many word tricks for me, if I'm honest,' was Moth's opinion, and I had to plead guilty. Anyone nurtured by the Institute knows that names and words are double-crossers, plastic and doughy. You need to stretch them and snap them or fold them over on themselves to tease out chance pleasures and latent intents. 'What I did like about it was that it had mythic elements. You made out it was going to be a science fiction story, but I think you've been learning from me.' In the darkness I could imagine the smug grin on Moth's face.

'Hate to admit it, but maybe I have. Your lousy stories are all I've heard for months on end; thought I'd try to beat you at your own game. Still, load of rubbish really, these legends. You can put anything you like in them, since nothing has to make sense or be possible. Talking trees! I can spin this dreck out like a spider spins silk.'

'No, no. There's always truth in stories. Always things which ripple and echo,' Moth argued. 'Every time you make up a story, it changes what happens in real life, and everything that happens to you in real life affects your stories. You can't separate the two.'

'So, if that's right, our escape – our plan – is going to fail? We're going to get caught, or die?' said Harete, sounding upset.

'Forget it, forget what Moth says. It was just a story, fiction, nothing to do with reality. And I'm tired now,' I said, annoyed with Moth for spoiling everything. Or maybe it was my fault for not finishing the story properly, but I hadn't known how to do that. So Moth was right, the story was like life, both ending in failure and doubt . . . I worried about it for few minutes more until I let go and invited sleep to enshroud me.

It was our first proper opportunity to rest for two nights. The mattresses did a good job of protecting us from the cold and lumpy ground, and our clothes and the plastic layers seemed to retain enough of our body heat to keep us tolerably warm. In my many waking moments, I thought groggily about the day to come. How could I stop The Moth from having those tantrums? The story seemed to help . . . Harete had proved hardy though, cool-headed too, that was a revelation . . . a real battler . . .

Sleep teased me, first sending a warm current to draw me from the shore of confused wakefulness, then rolling me back up onto its slippery shelf. Once, deep in the night, I came fully to. We were all coated in a thick film of our own condensed breath, but I knew that underneath its greasy paint my own face was also wet with tears.

Chapter 6

The Incident

This is what happened in the Institute which finally set me – us – on the path to escape.

For a week I had avoided Harete and her pet, and Moth too. The bird was still alive, much to my surprise. Some very heavy-duty types kept close by whenever Harete brought it with her into the courtyard, but they'd made no moves. If anything they seemed to deter others from trying.

On the day it happened, I was folding up old cardboard boxes in a basement store room, just me and a couple of lads watched over by a bored claviger. I'd volunteered for extra duties during free time, a privilege older kids could do to earn an increased food allowance. We heard an explosion of shouting from the yard, heard running feet, jeers, cheers and scuffles.

I dropped my work and raced outside.

There was a huge circle of about a hundred boys and girls, all shouting and yelling madly. A circle inside the circle as well, an empty zone around The Moth, who was hugging Harete close to him. At the centre of the main circus ring was Sticky, holding something aloft in one fist.

'Come on! You want it? You want it? Come and get it then!' Sticky was shouting, jigging around as he did so.

Grasped in his raised hand I could just see the protruding head and beak of the little bird. I looked over to The Moth; he was holding Harete back, but only just. Harete was struggling against him like an angry dog on a short leash, and swearing like a paratrooper.

'Keep her there! Moth, don't let her go!' I bawled at him. I forced my way through the crowds and faced Sticky directly. The crowds parted easily; I sensed I was expected. I saw clansmen everywhere, keeping the whooping crowds away from the star turn.

'Give it back!'

'Make me!' Sticky taunted. He was short, plumpish, red-faced, smirking. In control. We were honoured to see him; he usually lived in his grotto of a cell surrounded by his swag. Clavigers brought him his meals, and he never worked.

'Give it!' I thundered. My fierceness staggered even me. I was much bigger than Sticky. His belly might cushion the blows, but he'd go down.

'Make me! If ya dare!' came his answer. His smarmy smile widened. I saw two clavigers racing over the yard towards us, batons drawn.

What's his angle? I thought.

'Five!' shouted Sticky. He tightened his grip and the bird's beak popped open.

He wants me to fight him. Wants me to be caught brawling in front of the clavigers, have me done for inciting a riot!

'Four!'

'I won't fight you!' I shouted, and the crowd roared and booed. Cries of: 'Save the bird!' and, 'Coward!' and, 'Kill it!' erupted from the throng. 'Stomp! Stomp! Stomp!' chanted some.

'Three!'

More, this is too simple for Sticky. He has to win whatever the outcome. Another twist . . . I spotted Eye Inside in the crowd. He was drowning in the surging mob, flailing his arms, and finally his gravelly voice cut through to me. 'Don't let him kill it! The bet! I'll lose everything!' he was saying, but much else was lost.

Bet?

'Two!'

Sticky's complete plan came to me. Entice me to fight him, get put on a charge, get sent to the Establishment. I knew that part. *The bet!* Eye Inside must have set a wager with Sticky, a bet on who would kill the bird, a last gasp at restoring his power! The blind boy's cronies must have been protecting the bird until now, but Sticky had broken through to claim the prize in person.

'One!'

Sticky gave me a final, contemptuous glare. 'Last chance. It's your choice. You can easily take it from me.'

I shook my head. He held the bird out in front of him. I gave another shake, of my whole body this time.

Eye Inside's lone voice called out again, 'Don't let him! The bet! What's happening?'

My opponent peeled back his lips to show me an exaggerated, sarcastic grin. Just as the claviers reached the outermost line of spectators, Sticky gripped the bird's head in his other hand and twisted it sharply right around, like he was unscrewing a stubborn bottle top. *Click.*

The crowd stopped shouting. Total silence.

He let the bird fall. It dropped vertically like a stone to the ground. Sticky raised his foot and stamped it down.

I heard it crunch, then pop and burst under his shoe like a balloon.

A claviger barged through, kids fell forwards, roars pummelled my ears and Harete's scream skewered me through my vitals. Her howl obliterated even the black, raucous laughter that belched from the throats of Sticky and his crew.

Clavigers thrashed and raged and the crowd scattered. I was left alone, looking down at the ground. A red smear, some feathers, a minute brown lump . . . and by my shoe, tiny yet unmistakable, a shattered fragment of the bird's beak.

Not entirely alone. Eye Inside was there too. I didn't know you could cry if you had no eyes.

'The bet, the bet!' he groaned.

'What was it?' I murmured, amazed that I still had a voice. The blind could cry and the dead could speak, apparently.

Eye Inside aimed his cartoon eyes at me. 'I bet Sticky everything I own for a quarter of what he owns. *That you'd fight to save the bird!*' he hissed. 'You coward! You fool!'

The walls of the cell blocks loomed upwards and cupped themselves around me, spinning as they did so. I remember a great heat like that of a blow lamp playing over my skin, the yellow splatter of yesterday's food on the concrete, but after that, nothing.

* * *

After two days I was well again, and I welcomed the cold resolve that had coagulated in me.

When Harete joined us in Moth's cell, I told her of my intent.

'I'm going to get back at Sticky,' I said, and I brushed a huge tube of sweets from Moth's desk into my pocket, a present from his mother.

'No! It's not worth the trouble it would cause. You've told us enough times, don't mess with the clans,' she replied, red-eyed from crying. 'You were right, I should have let little Icarus go. He'd have been better off taking his chances with the local cats,' she said, 'but that's no reason to get yourself half killed too. I don't blame you, you know that!'

'He needs to be taught a lesson!' I snapped. Both of them knew about Sticky's designs on me and Moth, but I'm not sure they'd made the association with Icarus's demise. Sticky had again failed to entrap me, but he'd never stop, he'd escalate the pressure. I couldn't take another scene like the one with the bird. Pain I could suffer, but not something that could corrode and liquefy me from the inside and turn me into someone like *them*.

Harete was unmoved. 'I forbid you to get revenge. If you harm him, you're no friend of mine,' she said.

'I'm not going to beat him. Couldn't even if I wanted to. Going to get rid of him!' I said, clenching and unclenching my fists.

The Moth frowned and asked, 'What are you going to do? Complain to the Director? Doubt he'd be interested.'

'I've thought it all through. I'm going to make sure he

111

goes away from here and never comes back. His clan will fall apart without him,' I informed them both matter-of-factly.

Harete fumed and fretted to a degree that surprised me, but I would not be persuaded to change my mind. Nor would I be hurried. At nights, I lay on my bunk and stirred through a soup of ideas.

This is why I'm an adult. Kids are always plotting revenge for something or other, a beating, a theft, an insult, or they make plans to avoid their work shift, or to get transferred to the lazarette – that was the Institute's little hospital – or escape, even. But their plans are always nonsense, just empty, angry words. As soon as they start to tell you their plan, you can see a dozen reasons why it wouldn't work. And if you tell the kid, he'll get all huffy and you can see he wasn't serious at all, it was just childish play.

You have to do these things properly. Thoroughly. You have to think about every single step. You have to prepare for every eventuality. You need to think about what could go wrong and to have a way around it. That's what I'm good at, and that's what I did. That's what being an adult is all about. You see a problem, you think deeply about it – deeply and calmly – you come up with a plan and then you put it into action. You execute it.

A plan grew in me like a tumour. To make it work, information was required, and only one person could supply it. When I came to him in his windowless basement cell in the Unit, with cork walls and a tiled floor that sloped to a drain in the corner, he was naked. The wager must have included even his overalls.

'Sorry,' I said.

'No need,' he croaked back. 'When a bet goes wrong I never blame the dog, the dice or the deck. After what you said to me . . . I miscalculated. I thought you'd do the noble thing and try to rescue the bird. I overestimated you.'

His words stung me, but I hovered my ear over his mouth. Eye Inside did not need to ask what it was that I desired to know.

'Cell C-three-eight. He's alone during the afternoon work shift; he pays someone else to do his work for him. He sleeps and will be unguarded. Keeps a beaker of juice by his bedside.' He cranked out a laugh as deep as a bassoon playing at the bottom of a mineshaft. 'Play your hand well!'

I passed him a blanket I'd stolen from an unguarded dorm, a week's bread ration and the tube of sweets from Moth's desk. He gasped when he felt those.

'You didn't need to do that,' he said. His voice carried with it a note of irritation, as if he resented being in my debt.

'Figured you needed a break,' I said. 'Seeing – I mean, being – as how you've got nothing left.'

'Listen! To sacrifice a power is to gain a strength. That's why I had Mother blind me.' He sat upright and pointed to his tattooed eyelids. 'On your way home, my tribe will find and help you,' he said. He lay back and was silent.

I slinked away back to my cell, spooked and confused. No one found me, although skirting the perimeter of D-Wing, I did collide with Retread. Strong though he was, he could hardly manage to raise his eyes to meet mine.

'Mate! Sort it out! Make everything crisp with Sticky, he'll never give up,' he beseeched, scuffing his shoes.

'I know,' I mumbled.

'Sorry about what happened to that bird. But he had the bet with that blinder, and you weren't playing ball . . . made me want to cry a bit. My brother keeps budgies on the out; I like them.'

'Thanks.'

Retread was all right. There weren't many kids who would have shown sympathy like that. Guess you have to be hard to get away with showing weakness.

My cell was a two-berth, and officially my cell mate was Granny. Granny was hardly ever there, though, because he was always ill, laid up in the lazarette for weeks at a time. The cell overlooked the main courtyard, three floors below. From the barred window I could look out over the wide yard to the main security wall, topped with hoops of barbed wire, which ran all the way around the Institute's secure units. Beyond the wall the ground must have sloped away, because nothing could be seen of it. But slightly farther away there was a strip of trees, and through and beyond them I could just see the river. I knew the river ran parallel to the main wall for some distance. In the summer, you could glimpse off-duty clavigers fishing in it.

Directly beneath my cell's window was not the courtyard itself, but a walled compound, a square of land set within the courtyard but separate from it. Three sides of the compound were high walls, the fourth wall was the wall of my cell block, the wall my window was in.

The compound was used to hold rubbish: big, wheeled

waste bins, stacked-up crates, piles of flattened boxes. A pair of hefty wooden double doors large enough to let garbage trucks enter was set into the far wall. The area was also accessed through wide doors at the rear of the kitchens.

I could move my table from its normal place opposite my bunk and slide it under the window. If I stood on the table I could poke my head through the bars, open the top section of the window and stick my head through the gap. Then, looking straight down, I would be staring into the compound, three floors below, and all the useful-looking trash that it held.

Some days after Harete's warning, I took from my pocket a coin-sized lump of lead. I'd found this in the courtyard months ago; it must have been a piece of flashing from the roof that had broken off and rolled down. I tied this to a long, string-like strip of rubbery plastic. The rubber was the outer insulating covering from some electrical cable, split open to remove the copper wire and then peeled lengthways into two thin, flexible strips. The cable was another find, an off-cut left behind by electricians who had been around some weeks before, installing lights.

Just above where I tied the lump of lead to the 'string', I wrapped around some layers of toilet paper. These I bound together loosely with some strands of the wire itself. The other end of the string I tied to a short wooden ruler, one of The Moth's. Then, I went fishing.

Standing on my table, with my head and one arm out of the opened top section of window, I dropped the weighted string down into the compound. I had chosen that day precisely for the reason that directly below my window was a haphazard stack of yellow plastic crates, and in those crates were empty glass bottles.

The bottles must have come from the clavigers, because we were never allowed glass of any kind. The windows were glass, of course, but they were always behind bars or grilles and it was always the sort of glass that was strengthened with threads of wire. There were light bulbs, but these were always under screwed-down covers. Apart from the one in The Moth's reading lamp, but that was a special concession and it was checked regularly.

We had no clocks or watches (other than the large clock mounted high up on the canteen wall), partly because they would normally have glass covers. Some kids, like The Moth, wore spectacles, but the clavigers regularly inspected them to make sure no one had removed a lens. They would do this by dabbing each lens with a fingertip, an action that drove The Moth to distraction.

We had no glass because glass can be made into weapons – a broken shard would be a highly prized thing, capable of doing terrible damage to an enemy's face. The Institute also had many kids who would slash their own wrists, given even half a chance. Most metal objects were similarly banned.

Patiently, I lowered the string and bobbed it about, trying to get it into the neck of a glass bottle. It was before the morning wake-up call, so there was no one about outside. A claviger might have looked in through the peephole in my locked cell door, but the chances were slim. If he had done so, I would have just said I was getting some fresh air.

For half an hour I dibbled and bobbled with the weighted string. It was a frustrating task. I had to lift the string, get the lead weight over where I thought I could see an upright bottle, and drop it down sharply, hoping its weight would force it into the bottle's open neck. The string drifted annoyingly in the breeze and the weight oscillated from side to side. Several times I could hear and feel the weight chinking against the side of a bottle, but could not manoeuvre it into the small opening hole. Once, a bottle toppled over, and I was certain it was going to fall from the crate onto the ground and smash, but fortunately it rolled harmlessly onto another crate and wedged itself there.

Finally, I had my catch. The lead bob plonked down plumb into the slender neck of a large green bottle. I lowered the string more. I needed the small wedge of tissue paper above the bob to soak up any leftover dregs in the bottom of the bottle. Once soaked, the tissue would swell, and prevent the bob from being pulled out of the bottle. After a minute, I dared to haul in my bounty. Gently, I wound up the string. The swollen paper did its work, the bob could no longer pass through the opening, and the bottle rose up. I looked around to make sure there was no one in the courtyard and quickly reeled the bottle up the wall to my open window. I grabbed it, and hopped back into bed.

I hid the bottle, and the lead and the string, in my cell. There were few hiding places in a cell, the best you could do was to wrap any forbidden items in some dirty laundry or stuff it under your bed. Fortunately, cell inspections were very rare occurrences. If you did not give the clavigers reason to search your cell, they did not generally do so.

Exactly a day later, I wrapped the bottle up in a spare pillowcase and blanket I had taken from the laundry. When the wake-up bell rang – the longest bell of the day – I placed the bundle on the hard floor and stamped down hard on it with my shoes on. It took four attempts to smash the bottle, but the wake-up bell rings for a count of sixty, so I had ample time. I ground the glass bottle up good and proper. The way the glass crunched like small bones brought me up green and pukish.

Another morning, I sorted though the pieces of broken glass. I removed all the sharpest shards and wedged them behind my cell's wooden corner cabinet. Some slivers were the length of my hand and looked to be lethally sharp. Smaller, useful looking fragments I placed in an old tobacco tin, which I hid under my pillow. These were all for future plans or for bartering with. I chose one medium-sized chunk of glass and placed it in my desk drawer.

During all this time, I said nothing to Harete, nothing to The Moth. Our lives returned to normal, and we never spoke of Harete's pet or his horrible ending beneath Sticky's foot. Harete probably assumed I had forgotten my vow to get rid of Sticky. That's just like kids – they can't plan for the long term.

But by night, my work continued. I had an old pair of shoes in my cell, ones I had grown out of but failed to hand back when I was issued with my new pair. I took the single piece of broken glass from my drawer and placed it in the heel of one of these. Using a large, smooth pebble I had loosened by hand and prised from a patch of crumbly concrete in a distant corner of the courtyard, I started to grind the chunk of glass, breaking it down into smaller and smaller pieces. My pebble-pestle and shoe-mortar worked superbly. After just one night's work I had a crunchy, abrasive powder made of ground glass. The hard, sharp grains glistened and glittered in the moonlight filtering in though my barred cell window.

Ground glass could be used as a nasty, cruel poison. 'Not really a poison, it doesn't actually react chemically at all,' Moth had told me many weeks previously. We'd been talking about ways of killing people, not in any serious way, just in general, just boys' talk. Moth's favourite poison was something that came from a plant called hemlock, used by one of his ancient heroes to commit suicide. 'Socrates was made to drink it. He refused to believe in the official gods, the gods the government demanded everyone believe in,' Moth said.

He wrote the name on a scrap of paper for me.

Socrates

'Sew-crates,' I read.

Moth smiled. 'It's pronounced "sock-ra-tees".'

'But if he was forced to drink it, it wasn't really a suicide – it was an execution. Another of your legends from long ago?' I asked.

'No, no, Socrates was real. He lived, he was a philosopher, a lover of knowledge,' he had corrected me. 'He could probably have chosen exile, but he refused.'

'Perhaps he should have chosen to love common sense over knowledge,' I said. Silently, I wondered if Moth's father had chosen exile over hemlock.

From this, we had progressed to talking about other

poisons. It was he who had first mentioned ground glass. 'It causes damage just by being sharp, cutting the throat, stomach and intestines when swallowed, but it's not technically a poison.'

'Well, you can add it to someone's food and it'll kill 'em if they eat it, so it's a poison in my book,' I joked.

'Unlikely. If the pieces were coarse enough to do damage, no one would eat them. They'd notice it as soon as they took a mouthful of the food. They might get cuts to the mouth and tongue, but they'd immediately spit it out. Even a tiny piece of glass in food would be instantly detectable,' Moth reasoned.

'What if it was ground much finer, into a powder?' I asked.

'Then it would be too fine to do fatal damage if swallowed. Painful bleeding from the mouth and bottom probably, but otherwise no serious injury. Very distressing though.'

'So if it's ground fine enough to swallow, it's too fine to cause real harm. And if it's rough enough to kill, it would be too rough to swallow?' I said.

'Precisely. Pretty useless,' confirmed Moth.

The conversation had stayed with me. My plan was to trick Sticky into swallowing some finely powdered glass. It would not kill him, it would just bring him some discomfort. But better, if there was bleeding from either end of that odious mobster, he would be whisked away to hospital and forced into a long stay there. Not just the Institute's lazarette, but the proper hospital in the town. The clavigers were always alert to anyone who coughed or passed blood, for they were terrified of an outbreak of tuberculosis.

My strong suspicion was that with Sticky shut up in hospital even for a few days whilst the doctors ran tests, his stash of goods would be plundered and his clan would break up as its members fought amongst themselves for the spoils. I chuckled at the thought of him having his stomach pumped, helpless, and unable to prevent his hoarded loot being dispersed. Upon his return, he'd be sickly, broken and have no clan to boss around or follow his orders.

And now, everything was ready.

Two days after the glass was prepared I bunked off a few minutes early from my afternoon's work – sweeping up leaves from the courtyard – and sneaked into C-Wing. No one would miss me; we had raked all the leaves into bags and were just hanging around waiting for the bell, shuffling our feet and blowing into our hands. We were gathered right outside C-Wing; all it took was to wait until the clavigers' backs were turned and then a quick dash to the door.

I stole my way through C-Wing, up the steps and onto the third floor. There was no one around, although I could hear a claviger whistling in the distance, probably in the staffroom. Once on the third floor, I scuttled to cell C38 and knocked timidly on the metal door, which stood ajar. There was no answer, so I pushed the door open and cautiously peered in.

Exactly as the sightless oracle had told me, Sticky was having his afternoon nap. He lay on the bottom bunk on his back, snoring softly. Sticky was slightly chubbier than the norm, mainly on account of all the food he received in tribute: portions of kids' meals were the most common forms of payment. In sleep, his shirt open and one hand thrust down the front of his trousers, he did not look remotely impressive. Nor was his personal security up to scratch – to my surprise and annoyance I saw Retread face down in slumber on the upper bunk, his well-muscled arm with the Latin tattoo hanging down. Eye Inside had not predicted *that*, I thought ruefully.

What was impressive however was the sheer amount of stuff crammed into the cell. On and under the desk and all over floor were boxes, bags and piles of *things*. Things that belonged to other inmates in the main, some stolen, most paid as premiums, although I also saw a fire hose and, fabulously, a claviger's peaked cap in amongst the gear. I'd never troubled myself with the derivation of Sticky's name before, but his cell made it clear: picture someone smothered in glue moving around the Institute, picking up everything that was not actually cemented into place.

A row of pillowcases crammed with booty and knotted at the top stood in a row against the wall under the window. I remembered what some of the other kids told me about their winter festival . . . this place was like a perverted version of Santa's workshop. Sticky, the anti-Santa.

My heart thumping rapidly, I looked around the cell for the promised beaker of juice, half-hoping not to see it, but I soon located it on a small table. Juice! Who amongst us in the Institute ever had juice? Sticky stirred in his sleep and his head flopped limply on his pillows. His jaw sagged open to let his snores burble out loudly. He oozed smugness.

In my pocket I had a slip of paper containing a

palm-sized pile of crushed glass. My hand folded around it and gently squeezed it. Was it too finely ground? Or not fine enough? Would my plan work? What if Sticky shared his juice with Retread? What if the glass fragments just sank to the bottom of the cup? Was it worth it at all?

Sticky mumbled something. Behind me, the whistling grew louder. The claviger was patrolling in my direction.

No, it wasn't worth it. Harete was right. I was as guilty as those kids who concocted daft fantasies of escape or revenge. This idea of mine was totally moronic! My heart rate relaxed and I breathed out a long, deep sigh as the tension ebbed away. Sticky could do his worst; I'd survive! And all this because of a stupid, dead bird!

I darted into the cell and my hand was out of my pocket, holding the fold of paper. I glanced across at Retread to make sure his eyes were closed and I tipped the contents of the paper straight into Sticky's gaping mouth. Then the empty paper was back in my pocket, I was out of the cell and zipping along the corridor and down the stairs. I reached the door to the outside, pushed it open a crack and squeezed through, back into the courtyard. As the door clonked shut behind me, I thought I heard something, perhaps a stifled scream or a howl, or maybe it was just a door creaking.

My absence did not seem to have been noticed. I nipped along the wall and resumed mingling with the other boys. My legs were trembling and my body jittered and juddered. The bell rang and we trooped back under escort towards the main building and B-Wing. I calmed down. It was a success! I'd acted on instinct, a little rashly perhaps, but I'd really just made the best use of the perfect opportunity.

My plan to spike his juice had been too risky, but seeing Sticky lying there like that, mouth open and unguarded, what a fantastic chance that had been! I'd seized the moment, like a champion sportsman who'd spotted a moment of weakness in his opponent's play. Sticky himself could not have done it any better.

Sticky was gone! At least for a while, long enough for my purposes!

My troubles were over!

I was free!

'Something's up,' said Moth to me when we met after dinner. 'The Director was reading a letter to me when his phone rang and he stood up so fast he almost pushed his desk over. He sent me away without even finishing the letter. Looked to be in a considerable state.'

'Yeah?' I replied. 'Probably told he was getting a pay cut.'

'No, I don't think so. Also –' Moth began, but was cut off by the bell. We looked at each other. That bell was wrong. Evening free time was never less than an hour and a half, and we'd had barely fifteen minutes.

'Told you,' said Moth, 'something is very assuredly up!'

That evening we had an emergency lock-up. The clavigers stormed throughout the Institute, roaring orders for us to return to our cells and dormitories, telling us that free time was cancelled. Some of us tried to ask the reason why, but our quartz-faced guards lashed at us with their sticks and we learned nothing.

Rumours ricocheted and careened around the Institute over the next few days. We had many extended lock-ups, but it did not stop genuine information and total guesswork from being shouted cell to cell and dorm to dorm. Each day added weight to my plunging spirits. I'd expected some reaction, but this . . . I'd gone too far. All that time spent devising the mechanism of my revenge, and I'd scarcely considered the outcome. Progressively it dawned on me that *that* was precisely why I was in the Institute.

I fretted and sweated alone in my room, convinced I was going to be hauled away at any second, dreading the merciless kicking I was surely about to receive from the clavigers.

And then what? Trial? For murder?

Gradually the inhabitants of the Institute learned that Sticky had been taken to hospital; that he had been assaulted or poisoned – opinion was divided – and that, following a screwed-up blood transfusion, he now lay in a coma, unable to move or speak.

And we learned that Retread had been arrested, Retread had received a royal thrashing from the clavigers, Retread had been taken into town and put on remand, charges unknown.

This last piece of news brought me to my knees. By now, I felt like I had been passed through a mangle. I was in the clear – at least, for the moment. But Retread, innocent Retread, was in a new universe of trouble, and all because of me.

More worryingly, I discovered that Retread's arrest, deeply problematic though it doubtless was for him, did not even provide me with a watertight refuge from accusations.

'Were you involved with this?' asked Harete, a scowl on her face.

'No! No, Harete, honest!' I protested. 'They say Retread did it; he wanted to take over the Swingers.'

'If I find it was you, I shall never forgive you,' she said sternly. 'If you know anything that might help Retread, you must tell.'

It was not only Harete who had suspicions. The boys who'd been with me clearing leaves from the courtyard had not been as unobservant as I had hoped, or as silent. There were whispers. Amongst the population of the Institute, anger at Retread's arrest outweighed joy at Sticky's departure. Kids shunned me, spat at me, tripped me up. Respite from paying premiums looked to be short-lived too, for a new clan was already starting to muscle in on that game. Or rather, an old clan – the Unitarians, who had renamed the payments *tithes*. Eye Inside had not miscalculated, and he'd definitely not overestimated me. He'd played me, used me to remove Sticky, and I didn't even have the wits to work out when exactly his game had begun.

Dreams provided no solace. One night, I saw Sticky grasping at his lacerated throat, sicking up blood. Sticky morphed into Retread, a noose wound around his neck. A hatch beneath his feet opened and Retread dropped like a stone, like a dead bird, turned back into choking Sticky. As Sticky fell, the hangman's rope rattled over a pulley wheel. On the other end of the rope, rocketing upwards as Sticky plunged into darkness was . . .

Jelly.

I woke up, gasping for air. Projected onto my cell wall, the dawn's light was divided into three rectangles by the window's two bars. Each pale slab stood as a glowing monument to my downfall.

The boy who murdered Sticky.

The boy who framed Retread.

The boy who helped Jelly become Director.

The squeeze was around me like a python.

Without the leadership and gifts of Sticky, the C-Wingers clan did indeed start to fray, although not disintegrate entirely. Sticky and Retread's cell had been out of bounds whilst it was combed for evidence, and without the supply of goods to reward them, many of the clan's members drifted away. C-Wing was now relatively safe to wander through, so a couple of weeks after the . . . *incident* . . . I went for a stroll there during free time. A boy I did not know grabbed me.

'Come and have a look, it's amazing!' he shouted, and he ran up the stairs.

I followed him to the corridor on the third floor. The clavigers were struggling to empty Sticky's cell. A large knot of boys watched in amused wonderment as boxes and bags of plunder were dragged out and stacked up in the corridor. The clavigers were plainly embarrassed at just how much material there was to confiscate. They must have been turning a blind eye to the racketeer's activities for years, and now their complicity was being exposed in front of many of his victims.

I pushed my way to the front. I had to pretend that the sight of the loot was new to me too, but it was good entertainment to see the clavigers' obvious discomfort.

'Out the way, you lot! Clear this area!' shouted one of

them, swinging his club. As he did so, his elbow sent a cardboard box crashing to the floor, dumping out its contents. A loud cheer went up from the watching mob, and before the clavigers could wade in to disperse them, dozens of hands reached out to grab the items that bounced and rattled along the floor. Two kids scuffled over a liberated comb and accidentally kicked something in my direction. I bent down, grabbed it and ran off, along with several other boys who had managed to rescue a souvenir. I stuffed the object – it was a book, I could see that now – under my shirt and skipped back to B-Wing.

'Present for you, Moth,' I said on reaching The Moth's cell, and I tossed the book onto his bed.

'Hmm! *Geology and Mineralogy*,' read The Moth, 'Where on earth did you get it?'

I explained about the unexpected bonus I had received.

'He must have stolen it from the school rooms. Odd choice. Hullo . . . what's this?' said Moth, noticing something tucked down the inside of the book's spine.

I grabbed the book back and tried to shake the object out. It shifted slightly, but my fingers were too large to get a hold of it.

'Let me try,' said Moth. Shaking the book hard, he dislodged the thing far enough for him to take one end between his slender finger and thumb and pull it out.

It was a hacksaw blade. A glossy black hacksaw blade, the length of my forearm.

We stared at each other, utterly dumbfounded.

'Excalibur,' The Moth said.

He handed the blade to me, suddenly bored with the object. 'You want it?'

I nodded, too shocked to speak.

In my mind, a new idea blinked into existence, an idea as black and sharp and shiny as the blade.

Chapter 7

The Judge

We'd overslept.

I opened my eyes, aware that dawn was hours gone. We were all clammy with moisture from the bivouac. Sticky. Memories and dreams blended together, thinning and breaking apart like wet tissue.

I peeled back a corner of the plastic sheet and was just about to yawn loudly when I saw a black bucket resting by my face. Huge, like a coal scuttle . . . or a very big boot.

Two enormous boots shuffled by my face, the wearer standing virtually on top of me. Over by the pylon's nearest leg ambled another man in a rain cloak. I let out a long, gurgling moan, certain these would be amongst the last pain-free seconds of my short existence. Black, bilious disappointment foamed on my dry tongue; to have fallen to them simply by sleeping too long, how despicable was that? Even more degrading was the casual reaction of the marshals to our seizure.

'Huh? What d'ya say?' rumbled the one nearest me. He was the size of a telephone kiosk. So help me, I almost answered him, but before I did, the second man grunted. I heard a zip, then a familiar splashing sound that endured for ages. The steaming, wet mess trickled away from the pylon leg and puddled in a hollow under my nose.

'I said, it's hamazing how you get rubbish even hout here in the country,' came the guttural reply. The boot by my face moved a step backwards and caught my fingers under its heel. I screwed up my face and took a big bite of plastic sheet. The pain was nothing to the knowledge that if he made one tiny shuffle of those boots to the left he would be trampling on The Moth, and if Moth made so much as a sigh then the game would be up.

'What a waste of time. They'll not be this far east. Just our luck if we found them right now; I've forgotten my handcuffs.'

Zip . . . then, 'So what? I've got mine. We'll honly need one pair.'

The two men stamped away.

Held rigid by a half-grasped realisation of our preposterous luck, I spied on them for as long as it was possible by moving only my eyes, listening until I could no longer hear their voices. I wondered if they were discussing the reward money, sharing gleeful fantasies of gin-stoked high jinks, nights of plum rum and plump girls.

When I emerged from my catatonia I woke up Harete and The Moth. We quaked together, and it was tough to resist the calling to run madly off or dig a pit and bury ourselves. With stiff, recalcitrant limbs we hastily rolled up the bedding and the bedraggled, mud-smothered sheets, grateful that they did indeed so much resemble agricultural refuse.

We crouched under the pylon and, when the wind

131

obliged and barged away the tea-thick mist, peered into the distance. Clumps of men were scattered like grains of rice strewn over a tablecloth. They were no longer in the regular line they had held when they had marched over the top as we cowered in the ditch the day before, but clustered into squads of about half-a-dozen men each, probably obliged to fragment by the hedges. The atmosphere reduced the men to blue-black smudges, but we could see sunlight glinting off their cap badges. Marshals – ramping up the squeeze. Most were still to the south, we observed, but it was little consolation.

'I'll hand it to you, Moth,' I murmured, 'you're popular. They miss you.'

'So much for them not working out about us coming this way,' was his only comment. My absolute failure in this regard rankled deeply with me, and puzzled me too. Total disaster I could have understood, if we had been captured at the Institute's wall for example, but this was a scenario I had not anticipated.

We set off, keeping low and quiet. At least now I had confirmation of my and Harete's intended fates – one that did not require handcuffs. That recapture would be traumatic, I had never doubted; that it might be instantly terminal had not occurred to me even in my most cynical moments. I had always thought Harete would be spared, and that whatever was left of me would endure a form of trial, that there would be a chance to plead for leniency. Orion's sick trick with the tin-snips was evidently sport of short duration. Swiftly after would follow summary execution in a wintry no-man's-land.

132

'Remember the pylon number, Moth,' I told him. What difference did it make? We'd always been prepared to drown or freeze or starve.

'Three-zero-nine,' he replied.

'Fifty to go then. Move!' I croaked, and we slinked away.

In a strange way I welcomed our spectral army of stalkers. The infuriating, sluggardly lethargy of the previous days had gone; Moth and Harete could see the danger of dawdling. We had a tangible enemy, and that kept them moving, even Harete with her sore leg.

The weather was the same as it had been the day before. The temperature was probably a little above freezing, light snow fell intermittently, sometimes settling, sometimes not. The soil beneath our sore feet varied from unyielding, frozen clods to gloopy quagmire. A ferocious east wind took it in turns with a sly northerly wind to harry us, the one bringing sleet like hypodermic needles, the other stealing our warmth. At times I thought I could detect a smell like burned meat blowing in on the wind, but I concluded it was either our own unwashed bodies or our rotting food and gave it no more consideration.

'A lazy wind,' Harete called it once, as we rested, puffing, underneath the tenth pylon of the day.

I stared blankly at her.

'Can't be bothered to go around you, so goes through you,' she explained.

'Very good – now, move!' I replied, interested only and always in our progress, darting from pylon to pylon and surveying the landscape from their relative safety.

Soon after that we met our first large hedge of the day.

This was a monstrous example, much taller than any of us and thick enough to stop a charging elephant. I'd already described my idea for mastering these living walls to the others, and we moved rapidly and without fuss into our places. I opened up my bed roll, letting it uncoil into an uncooperative slab, which flapped around in the wind. I tied one end of our rope around this, the other end I fixed around my waist. That was to stop it blowing away in a strong gust. I held the mattress vertically in front of me, grasped its sides tightly and positioned myself in front of the hedge. With a grunt and a leap, I tossed it up so that it landed at an angle on top of the hedge.

Quickly, before the wind could catch it, Harete and The Moth faced each other and linked hands to make a step for me. I put one foot into this and sprang up as they raised their arms to boost me. I landed on the mattress atop the hedge. The plastic-shrouded foam gave me a reasonably solid surface to operate from and stopped me from crashing down into the prickly vegetation. I lay on my stomach to spread out my weight and reached down with my arm to haul up first The Moth, with Harete shoving him from underneath, then Harete herself. Once they had in turn slid along the mattress and dropped off the other side, all that remained was for me to struggle down, pulling the mattress after me.

This was the most awkward step, since the hedge had punctured the plastic sheeting and was reluctant to let go. Nevertheless, we had crossed the barrier in no more than five minutes, a considerable improvement over traipsing along its bulk to find a break. Furthermore, our technique enabled us to cross hedges, whereas the marshals were still obliged to make extensive detours. For once, we had the upper hand!

For the first time in two days, I saw grins on my companions' faces. We soldiered on towards the next pylon in the chain, conquering all hedges in our path.

The pylons became our friends. They were now the milestones in our new life of mud and drudgery. Each grey tower with its lattice-work body and stubby arms was like an oasis in the siltscape, a station on our monotonous, grinding, journey.

The square space beneath the four legs of most pylons was fairly barren. Their cross-beams were placed too low to allow farm machinery to pass underneath them, so the plots they stood on were unploughed and unseeded. Consequently, most stood in nothing more than a small square of scrubby grass and weeds. But some pylons had verdant allotments sprouting up underneath their feet, thick with long, yellowing grass and spiky green bushes. We sought these out when taking our brief rests, appreciating the protection from the wind and the superior concealment they provided.

Moth was still complaining. He seemed to think that his pains were unique, or perhaps that speaking about them would lessen them. 'Every part of me hurts. The skin is peeling from my face, my feet are ulcerated, my clothes are soaked, I ache all over!' he grouched.

His fragile temperament worried me. Fearing he was about to start bellyaching again, I decided to apply what I had learned the day before.

'We're all going to tell stories,' I said as we walked briskly on, chewing on the day's half-ration of gritty dripping, 'ones we make up ourselves, like I did last night. Our own propaganda.'

The Moth and Harete flashed each other irritated looks.

'Whatever for?' enquired Harete, wincing as she limped along. 'Haven't we got more important things to worry about?'

'To keep morale up, and to keep our minds off our situation. We'll go mad otherwise. We need some diversion, something to lift our spirits and occupy our minds,' I explained. 'Moth goes first,' I added. 'You've until this evening's camp to think one up, and you tell it to us then.'

'Else?' said Harete.

'Else I kick your backsides. And make you set the camp up,' was my reply. The second part of this was a fair threat. Making and breaking the bivouac took a great deal of effort, and so far it had all been done by me with no help from either of the others.

To my surprise Moth said, 'All right. A story. I'll do it.'

'A story, mind – not a lecture,' I said firmly. I'd watched Moth perusing the pylons' scrambled angles and overlapping triangles, and I didn't fancy a geometry lesson in mild steel.

Shortly afterwards, we thought we were about to experience some much longed-for variety in our surroundings. We saw the tidy lines of trees from a distance: short, stumpy specimens but a welcome sight for all that, as much as we could glimpse them through the fog, the thickest we had yet encountered. To reach them, we had to cross an unexpected and very long and sturdy wire fence that cut across the line of the pylons. We used the same method to tackle it as we had for the hedges, although the barbed-wire crown made a terrible mess of the mattress we placed across it. 'This will buy us even more time,' I told the others as we dropped to the far side, nursing and cursing our cuts, 'the marshals will have to take the long way around.'

'Must be an orchard; the trees are all planted in long rows,' Harete mused, as we trudged closer to the bare, stunted trees. 'Funny place for one. And why the fence?'

'I guess nations make farms that resemble themselves,' I told her. 'In ours, even the fruit trees are made to stand in line behind wire, and are given very short haircuts too!'

'Coppiced,' Moth corrected me. 'No fruit at this time of year, sadly. What is that perfectly dreadful stink?'

When the wind changed to blow from the north, we all caught the smell. The stench was that of industrialised slaughter, for as we approached the first plantation we realised that what we had taken to be small trees were in fact the stiff legs of hundreds of upturned, dead cattle, dumped into pits, their hooves waggling pathetically in the wind.

Row upon row of long barrows had been dug. Some – thankfully the minority – held the swelling, fresh corpses of cows, the majority were filled either with charcoaled bones where they had been cremated, or with mounds of soil where the burned fragments had been covered over. The death-stench was rendered tolerable only because it was masked by an even more overpowering odour of gasoline, and before long we noticed a lone figure spraying

137

a pit of newly culled cows with a hosepipe. Far beyond him, a yellow digger scooped cattle corpses from the back of a large lorry and dropped them into a newly dug grave. The grisly tableau repeated itself in all directions as far as we could see.

Sick to our stomachs, gagging from the smells and sights, we darted behind a parallel row of dead animals and spurred ourselves on, trying to hasten from the hellish compound and its ghoulish attendants.

Parked up ahead of us, a small, covered truck blocked our progress. It bore no insignia, and looked surprisingly clean for something in that place. We pasted ourselves to the ground and prepared to slip around it and into an adjacent gap between the pits, but as Moth and Harete padded away, I noticed something and hung back. No driver was visible, no other crewmember seemed to be around, and, best of all, the cab and rear doors were open, creaking on grease-thirsty hinges where the wind pushed against them. Chancing everything, and sucked in by a possibility too great to ignore, I crawled forwards and craned my neck around the open door to peer in.

The keys had been left in the ignition!

I saw them dangling temptingly from the steering column. I could drive. Well, more or less; years before, Dad had let me take his works delivery van up and down the runway of a disused airfield, and I'd knocked about with enough joyriders to have picked up a few tips. Could we . . . think of the time it would save! And who would be looking for us in a truck?

With a quick look around me to make doubly sure no

138

abattoir worker was near, I jumped into the driver's seat. Taking the truck did seem a little far-fetched, but, even so, it was a prodigious storehouse! One brush of my hand against its catch and the glove compartment exploded open, showering the passenger seat with chunky chocolate bars and boxes of matches and packets of sandwiches and maps and fur-lined gloves and a torch and a log book. The fantastic goodies even smelled glorious! I sniffed again, and worked out the true source of the perfume was a plastic air freshener in the shape of a tree studded with fruit suspended from the rear-view mirror.

I bent forwards to inhale from it deeply, savouring the sweet, synthetic odours, so welcome against the external reek. In doing so, I inadvertently obtained a view of what lay behind me in the truck's load bay.

It was not what I saw there that made me spin around and stare over the seat backs; it was what was *not* there. Much as a footprint is a void, yet defines completely the foot and the figure that made it, and may even reveal to a skilled eye if he was a killer or a victim, so the few objects I saw there informed me about what the truck had recently held, and much more besides.

Firstly, there were the long, brownish, parallel streaks along the metal floor, leading out through the open rear doorway; then, six crumpled pieces of cloth, like small bags, each the ideal size to fit over a head; and, lastly, six cords that dangled from a rail running along the truck's roof in just the right place to tie up a person's hands.

I knew at once why the truck was empty, and why all the doors had been left open; for although the stench of gasoline-drenched cattle corpses stacked immediately behind the truck was foul beyond belief, it was preferable to the smell of hopeless terror that still pervaded that enclosed volume. *The driver was trying to air the vehicle*. I instantly rejected my own conclusion as too paranoid; surely this was the vehicle awaiting Harete, The Moth and myself, the one we were to be escorted back to the Institute in! No, I thought again. Six sacks, six cords? This truck was not collecting – it was making deliveries. My insides filled with ice, my limbs became stalactites.

Beyond the truck's cargo-bay doors lay the burial trench. Limbs hailed me, some terminating in hooves, some in toes.

Pinching the very tips of its corners between my finger and thumb, I flipped open the log book that had dropped from the glovebox. I could not decipher much of what I saw inside, but the tally marks and 'm' and 'f' symbols I saw convinced me that the van's journey to this place was routine and regular, that it was a scheduled trip, not chartered. My head spun one way, my guts the other; my discovery threatened to unscrew me. 'My country and me,' I said to myself, aware of the kinship we shared.

Two things only I took with me. The first was a ring, jammed into the narrow space between the roof and the rail from which the cords dangled, an object I took at first glance to be a rivet or a washer, so dull did it look. Glimpsing its muted sparkle in the dark interior, I snatched it out and squirrelled it away. I thought for a second about whoever had slipped it from the finger of their bound hand and concealed it there, and the waiting fate that had left them desperate to leave some trace of themselves. Taking the souvenir seemed not to be a crime but the greatest possible act of defiance. The second theft came when I heard footsteps tramping towards the truck, and a man humming badly out of tune.

With seconds to spare, I madly crammed back in everything that had spilled from the glove compartment and snapped shut the hatch. No sooner was it closed than it flopped open and emptied out its contents again. I had to scrabble about in the footwell to pick everything up and try again. And again . . . the man was two strides away, pausing to pat down his pockets as he looked for his keys, keys that were already in the vehicle. Again . . . I spotted an orange that had rolled under the seat, and had to shove that in too.

It took three more loud slams before the glovebox hatch finally stayed closed. Pouring myself out from the driver's seat, I dislodged something from a cubbyhole set into the door; it fell onto the ground with me, but I did not know from where exactly, so I grabbed it as I rolled away, figuring that a missing thing is always less suspicious than a misplaced thing. I watched the truck sink on its springs as the man climbed in the far side. Sneaking my way back to my friends, I passed a dozen bales of clothes done up with twine.

'Where the hell were you?' Harete hissed at me when I caught up with her and The Moth again, creeping past more aisles of swollen cadavers stinking of petroleum.

'Getting something,' I replied. I looked at my second treasure – an aerosol spray can of de-icer, used to clear frost from windscreens.

'Very useful,' sighed Harete, rolling her eyes. I did not tell her of the new wisdom I had also come by, not wholly believing it myself.

The far fence came into view soon enough, but between it and us was a great stockade filled with living animals, and more men. The animals all wobbled about drunkenly on splayed-out legs, tottering pathetically. Despite the size of the assembled herd, there was almost no noise from the doomed beasts, only the rattling sound of their breathing and the squelching of their hooves in the mud. All the animals were sickly, needle-thin and shivering.

'Diseased. You were so right, what you said before,' murmured Moth, who always saw the bigger picture. The sight of so much death seemed to affect him very little; he assayed the wilting animals with an air of scientific detachment. Harete was in tears. I was stupefied, numbed by what we beheld and ashamed that it tormented and terrified me even more than what I had witnessed moments beforehand.

Moth took over. 'Follow me,' he said, and he slid under the stockade fence in amongst the silent, swaying cows. We did likewise, and copied him as he scuttled along, low to the ground, sometimes even tucking himself right underneath a listless cow, pausing and then moving on. Squeezing through the throng of blundering, teetering animals was terrifying as they lumbered around, colliding with each other.

Around us, we listened as men started to corral the animals through a gate. We were at the fence by then, and I set about frantically slicing a hole in the wire mesh with the hacksaw blade.

Then, anarchy erupted. A gigantic, lanky stockman wearing an eyepatch climbed a short gantry not far from where we were hidden. He carefully wiped his hands on his smeary plastic apron then raised a rifle to his shoulder and took aim. With a series of immense bangs he loosed off round after round into the docile herd. The gun boomed, and targeted cows crashed to the ground like demolished chimney stacks. The startled, half-dead cattle around us started to panic and hurl themselves against the fence, flinging dung and mud everywhere, and lowing piteously. More bullets were fired; one of them ricocheted from a fence post and whistled close by my head, the noise at once familiar to me from old TV movies where marshals did battle with enemy spies and saboteurs.

'Hurry up, or we'll be flattened!' shouted Harete. She and The Moth tore madly at the fence links as I sawed. Like incandescent wasps, more bullets zinged overhead, and a flailing hoof struck me across my shoulders. With excruciating slowness a passable hole formed, and I bundled my two friends through, only then squeezing my own larger body after them. They pulled me through from their side, and we rolled away from the carnage and cacophony down a stony slope. Bullets followed us overhead, I was sure we'd been marked, but the aim was too wayward and I knew then they had just scattered from other targets.

We raced over a wide strip of smooth-tilled soil towards the asylum of the pylons. Part of me wondered about the funny metal prongs I could see sticking up through the earth, looking like the tops of metallic turnips. Harete must have been curious too, for she stretched out a foot and made to tread on one, but I instinctively kicked at her ankle and deflected it, almost treading on another set of prongs in the process.

'Mines!' The Moth called out. 'They're landmines!' His spectacles may have been covered in mud, but his mind was clear. The wind had blown away the dry top soil, and we could see many more sets of protruding metal tines.

The mines themselves, or at least the exposed ones, were sparsely planted and easy to avoid, but within a dozen paces we discerned the real danger: a web of fine, almost invisibly thin wires traced over the ground at ankle height, and we were certain that to disturb these would have set off the bombs as effectively as stepping directly on them. The wires were devilishly hard to spot and we could not predict where they lay. With the stockyard fence still in sight whenever the fog parted, we were reduced to shuffling forwards, bent double and feeling for the wires with our fingers. We progressed slower than an oak grows. All it needed was one abattoir worker to stare hard in our direction when the air cleared and it would be our clothes done up in neat parcels. Who did they give them to?

'Evil is never random,' I reminded myself. Manoeuvring myself to the front, I took out the aerosol spray and squirted it from side to side just above the ground. Beads of fluid settled on the whisker-thin cables and showed me where they ran. Like musical staves, they'd been strung out in long lines of five, then a gap, then another set of five, with the mines they were designed to trigger dotted between them in zigzag patterns, the notes of explosive arpeggios. We walked forwards as I sprayed, checking the soil where we daintily put our feet. An hour creaked by, and the sounds of the stockyard remained in earshot.

'I'm caught!' Moth said. The heel of his shoe had clipped a wire and dragged it forwards. He was balancing on one leg, flamingo-style.

'They can't be that sensitive, Moth,' Harete said, freezing her own movement. 'Else the wind and the birds would set them off.'

'Maybe they do!' he cried back. 'All plans end in failure, that's what you believe, isn't it?' That was directed at me. 'Well, here's where it all ends for us. Undone by my heel!'

'A story! Stop believing in stories!' I replied. Moth's wobbling was unsettling me more than his snagged foot; his flamingo looked like it had been on the beer. If he fell . . .

'Moth, just move your foot slowly,' Harete tried again. 'There must be rabbits and foxes here about but I see no craters where the mines have exploded.'

Moth didn't seem convinced. I toyed with the idea of digging out a stone and propping it against the wire, but the wind took the decisive action. A sharp gust sent Moth stumbling forwards and his foot snapped free of the wire. It made a slight 'ping' sound as it returned. I didn't even have time to duck.

'Achilles!' burst out Moth.

'Bless you!' Harete returned.

We crept onwards through the deadly cat's cradle for about another hour.

A leap across a ditch, and the return of ploughed furrows told us we were out of the minefield. Harete dry-retched,

Moth said words I did not suppose he knew the meaning of, I nursed my lip where I had bitten into it and drawn blood.

Turning around, we saw a distant pyre burning, thrusting up a monstrous column of white smoke that swirled around and mingled with the fog, bearing away its obscene secrets as it spiralled upwards.

The rest of the day's march was wearying in the extreme. We crossed more hedges, jumped ditches, navigated our way around flooded fields and pressed ourselves into the baleful winds for hour after hour after hour, never resting for more than a few minutes at a time, each of us trying hard to eradicate the memory of the sights, sounds and smells of the stockade. Somewhere inside my overalls, the ring jostled about, feeling cold where it touched bare skin, fiercely protesting my strenuous efforts at forgetting and denying. *Forget*, I ordered myself. *Forget, or go mad!*

The boredom of the walk became intense. Snow, hail, wind, mud, furrow, pylon, grey sky, grey steel, this was the sum of the world. 'Faster! Walk faster!' I exhorted my friends, but my words were hollow. I granted myself the perverse luxury of dwelling on our chief huntsman, Orion, and his *little ways*. A daydream sprang up of a thick-set man in khaki prodding markers across a map table in an underground control centre. Would he wear a moustache? A beret? What would be on his belt? A holstered pistol . . . a skein of wire . . . and handcuffs – one pair only. Orion wouldn't rise for me; I couldn't establish an image of him. I needed a face to soak up my hate, denying me one felt underhand. A different figure materialised, one that came already infused with my loathing. *Surely not?* I told myself. I spat on the ground and the disquieting dream popped.

Our slimy food seemed barely capable of sustaining us, and we were all painfully aware of how little of it we now had, following the greasing of the trap. 'You should have used less,' Moth griped when he looked at his meagre evening portion.

'If I'd used less, Harete might still be stuck,' I said. I forgave Moth, ascribing his irritability to hunger. I glumly wondered what sort of fat our lard was made from, and the thought made me feel even queasier. Later, I threw up most of what I'd eaten.

Our biggest problem started to be lack of water, not nourishment. Despite the cold, we sweated greatly, and by late afternoon were down to half a bottle of water between us. Almost all the ditches we crossed were completely dry. Whenever I found a hollow in the ground or a deep furrow filled with drifted snow I tried to scoop and pack it into my drinking bottle. But even when the bottle was filled with snow, by the time it had melted against my warm body it had reduced to one tenth the volume.

We stuck out our tongues when it snowed in the hope of catching flakes, but it brought no relief. The best source of water we found that day was a clutch of icicles clinging to the north-facing beam of a pylon. We harvested these and wiped them clean. The narrower ones we crammed into our water bottles, the wider ones we held on to and lapped the moisture from our plastic-covered mittens as they melted in the warmth of our hands.

We declared the day's walk over at pylon number

two-six-zero. Machine-like, whimpering with tiredness, I assembled our bivouac, and we ate.

As we lay side by side inside our damp, crinkling tent, I began to feel almost relaxed. Simply not having to walk or face the wind any more felt like the greatest luxury in the world. I no longer had the energy to care about our chasers or what we'd been through.

'Tell us a story, Moth,' I said. I was expecting him to be too tired, and was quite prepared to wait until we were on the next day's march before hearing it, but he obediently cleared his throat.

'Once upon a time . . .' he began, and Harete and I groaned.

'It's not meant to be a fairy tale, Moth,' we chimed.

'Once upon a time,' Moth continued, 'there was a king.'

'A king? Why it is always kings and queens in stories?' Harete said.

'Can I please tell my story?' Moth asked, annoyed. 'Very well. I'll start again. At some unspecified time in the past, there was a committee. Happy now?'

I laughed. 'Spoken like the son of a bureaucrat!'

'A committee of kings. But chief of these was the king of kings. He had trouble waking up in the morning, so he sought advice from a witch. She recommended that he hang a sprig of a certain herb above his bed. The aroma would drift down to his nose and wake him when he smelled it. This he did, and he was delighted one day when he awoke nice and early.

'"One's up! Honour thyme!" he said.

'He busied himself with ruling his kingdom, helped by

148

his under-kings. He was a kindly but not terribly efficient or effective ruler. He preferred to offer guidance but not to intervene in the life of his subjects too much. His advice was sound, but rather vague. This often led to squabbling between his subjects as they decided what his proposals meant.

"'Majesty," asked his under-king for agriculture, "the harvest was poor again, the people are hungry. What shall we do?"

"'Ah, yes, well. We must investigate the reasons for the poor harvest. And we must think of new crops we can sow, and above all share out our existing stocks of food more fairly. You and your fellow under-kings must decide how you can cut down on what you eat and distribute what you don't need to the poorer peasants. That sort of thing."

"'Is that the best advice you've got?" groaned the under-king for agriculture.

"'Well, what do you expect? I can't wave a magic wand!" replied the king, dismissing his adviser.

'*I'll never get the other under-kings to agree to share their food*, thought the under-king, so instead he told them that the king of kings had ordered the nation to declare war on their neighbouring countries and steal their food. This they duly did. But the war was a disaster, with huge losses on all sides. By the time the war was over the people were hungrier than ever, their houses lay smashed to pieces and all their farm machinery had been melted down to make tanks and guns.

'The former under-king for agriculture, who was now under-king for war, was very unpopular.

'"Don't blame me," he told the people when they gathered outside his palace, "it was the king of kings who made up the plan. I was only following his instructions."

'The people now started to riot and burn down palaces and government buildings. The under-king for war appealed to them.

'"Make me your new king of kings. That old duffer was no use at all. He never gave us useful advice, only waffle. Plus, the war was his idea. Elect me and we'll soon be eating cream cakes and steak every day, instead of shoe leather and daffodil bulbs."

'The people, half-crazy with hunger, thought this was a terrific idea, so they chased the old king of kings out of the country and made the under-king the new king of kings. To save time, they decided to call him simply "leader", although his official title was Pry Minister.

'"Hooray for the leader," they all shouted. Some who did not were shot.

'But the new leader was not a nice man, or even a particularly good leader. He had no ideas for feeding the people, so he secretly arranged for all the people who still liked the old king of kings to be rounded up and imprisoned. They were forced to work very hard on the farms for no pay, and killed if they refused to work or tried to escape.

'Slowly, life did improve. With fewer people left alive and many people working very hard under fear of death, there was more food to go around.'

In the dark tent, I slapped a hand down hard over Moth's mouth and looked out of the flap, my ears alerted by a rhythmic chopping sound. A helicopter was flying very low, tracking slowly northwards, keeping a course parallel to the pylons at the height of the cables slung between them. The wind must have carried its beating sound away from us. We watched the helicopter stop for half a minute beside each pylon before moving to the next. To our intense dismay, a door was open in its side, and, illuminated by a square of yellow light, we could see a man sitting with his legs dangling over the edge, holding a device to his face at eye level.

I stared, then cried, 'Binoculars, at night?'

'A heat-seeking camera!' moaned Moth. 'We're done for!'

'Snow!' shouted Harete. She tumbled from the tent and started to shovel snow and ice on top of the plastic sheets. I joined her, heaping more snow on top from where it lay in piles against the pylon legs and in the furrows. We crawled back in, the machine only two pylons away, its noise insufferable and made worse by the crazy flapping of loose folds of our plastic sheets. I was too scared to poke my face out to look at it, scared I'd see the cooling, camouflaging snow being blasted away by the down-force, scared to see men abseiling down on ropes to grab us.

My ear next to Moth's mouth, I heard him shout, 'A harpy!'

The snow must have worked; it must have chilled and stilled the lips of our tell-tale body heat, for the helicopter progressed to the adjacent pylon and moved on down the sequence.

Peace slowly returned as the machine flew on. Harete and I cajoled a trembling Moth to continue with his story, for none of us could sleep. He sniffled, composed himself, and resumed the tale.

'Much later, a judge came to see the leader. He was a very important judge, though still fairly young, and was said by some to be the person who would take over from the leader when he was too old to rule. His name was Duke Marmaduke Marduk, Chief Justice.

'"What do you want to see me about, Justice Marduk?" asked the leader.

'"I've been looking again at some of the things that went on when you took over from the old king. We broke lots of our own laws. Many people were killed or imprisoned unjustly. I think we should admit exactly what happened to those people and pardon them."

'"Most certainly not!" said the leader, looking very indignant. "Times were hard then. We'd just lost a terrible war and were starving. We had to do what needed to be done."

'"Yes . . . the war was actually your idea, wasn't it?" said the judge. "I found some paperwork which proves that."

'The leader went very red and huffed a lot, but carried on. The judge was a trusted friend, and he did not want to fall out with him.

'"We can't tell everyone the truth about those times. It would cause a lot of bad feeling. People would stop working and start thinking about all their lost friends and relatives. We need everyone to work together."

'The judge said, "I think the citizens of our country would be happier if they knew we cared about the people we've treated badly in the past and apologised to them."

'"Pah! If we start to admit we've made mistakes in the past, people will never trust us again," said the leader. "I need everyone to be thinking about the present and working hard. Besides, we're the government. We were chosen by the people and we make the laws. So whatever we do is the law."

"'You weren't chosen by the people, were you?" sneered the leader, as an afterthought. "You were just promoted into your job. When you started your career you were settling disputes over parking tickets."

"'All that is true," conceded the judge. "But . . . there's something else. I think we have too many laws. People should be able to choose how to live and do their jobs, not have us tell them how to do every little thing."

'The debate continued for some weeks. The leader grew scared of the judge, and decided he was after his throne. He asked all his most senior advisers to vote on whether or not they thought that he, the leader, was still fit to govern. But before he did so, to make sure he received the answer he hoped for, he had their wives – or husbands – and children placed under armed guard, "for their own protection". The advisers were worried that he was planning to have them shot, so they obediently voted in favour of the leader.

"'So much for your ideas!" he said to the judge, whom he now thoroughly detested. But the judge wisely decided to leave the country, and he never came back. The end.'

Harete and I mulled over the story. 'I quite liked it,' yawned Harete. 'Although it was a bit talky for my liking. Actually, nothing really happened at all. And the end was a disappointment because, well, it just stopped.'

'That was a lecture after all, wasn't it, Moth? Your dad's situation, disguised as a story,' I commented.

153

'Stories can be based on historic events. What did you expect? *The Arabian Nights?*' he mumbled sleepily.

'Fair enough. Still, no offence to your old man, Moth, but I can't really enjoy a story which has a judge as the hero. It's because of a judge that I'm in this mess,' I said.

'I don't think we need judges. We should judge ourselves,' said Harete.

The Moth snorted indignantly. 'That might work for good people like you, Harete, but not for many others.'

I had more criticisms. 'Also, I wasn't sure who the baddie was. That judge was a bit up himself, and the leader, well . . . he'd made a few mistakes in the past, told a few lies, but he *was* working to make things better. That's what matters most, isn't it?'

No more was said after that. I stuck my head out from under the plastic sheets and turned onto my front to survey the evening. I could see the pylon's legs silhouetted around us, like a huge four-poster bed. The sun was almost below the horizon, with just a tiny spot of light left visible in the west. I lay and waited for it to sink and the darkness to become absolute.

But the little spot of light did not sink. Rather, it grew in size. I rubbed the sleet and sleep from my eyes and stared harder, unable to believe what I saw. The spot grew into a disc of white light, then resolved itself into two discs, then four, then more. The discs travelled slowly from west to east, low along the ground. The wind blew from the east so no sound reached me from the luminous apparitions. I held my breath and stretched a palm onto the ground outside the bivouac, away from the cushioning foam on which we rested. Almost imperceptibly I could sense the ground rumbling. The lights continued to crawl across the sky, but came no nearer. The rumbling spoke of something unspeakably powerful and dangerous. Was it the helicopter again, sweeping out from side to side, low over the ground? A posse of men in vehicles?

I thought of the bitter old leader from The Moth's story, and wondered what lengths he would go to, what forces he would muster in order to recover the only child of his most dangerous rival. Dread sluicing through me, I drew back into the bivouac and shuddered.

Chapter 8
The Plan

The hacksaw blade we'd found hidden in Sticky's book was what started me thinking about escape. Maybe also that story about Topsy-Turvy, not that I believed in stories.

Alone in my cell I looked over the blade, astonished that even The Moth had yielded it to me so willingly. Typical of him, typical of the kids who weren't savvy, to give away something so valuable without even a second thought. For an item like this I'd have paid almost anything. The blade was the most forbidden thing I had ever seen in the Institute – it was the key to the universe.

The key brought with it a real possibility of escaping. The business over Sticky and Retread still hung very heavily upon me. The whispers about my unexplained disappearance from the leaf-sweeping gang and into C-Wing on that day had in no way abated, and these murmurings nibbled away at the ground on which I stood like drips of acid. Getting away from the Institute before the truth was discovered suddenly appealed to me like never before.

Sticky's poisoning had brought me only grief, but to one person in the Institute it had delivered a huge boost. Jelly was suddenly everywhere, and he was supercharged, aroused by the tantalising scent of promotion. He'd never lacked in zeal beforehand, but now the man was hopping around the place like he already ran it, sniffing and snooping and prying and spying and dishing out punishments for the smallest wrongdoing. Slate Tooth's words splashed in my head like drips from a leaking tap; a new scandal would unseat the current Director and propel Jelly to the top. Since Jelly remained deputy for the moment, I took it that attempted murder was not quite embarrassing enough. Jelly required Sticky's death.

Harete was revolted. 'He's like a vulture! Circling and waiting!' she had said. She was right. What he was circling in the main was *me*. He must have heard the rumours, for he began to keep tabs on me in a way he had never done before.

'Watching you, eight six five!' said Jelly, standing on guard by the canteen doors.

Another day, another encounter. 'Eight six five! Oh, Eight six five! Strip search!' he trilled.

My nocturnal brain juggled with the arithmetic of survival. If Sticky recovered, returned and reclaimed his empire, then he'd take revenge on me. That was an army of 'r's that spelled nothing but trouble; if he died, then Retread would be put on trial and I'd face another quandary: whether to confess and hang, or see my friend hanged. Yes, they hang murderers here, even juvenile ones. Squeezes within squeezes . . . I *had* to escape, and do it whilst Sticky languished in the limbo of his coma. For me, the coma became a taut, bulging membrane dividing Sticky's living form from his cadaver, and two very different ideas I had of myself and who I was. My escape might even help

Retread, I decided. I could leave behind a confession . . . or maybe send a message from safety! My knuckles bled as I chewed on them.

But escape to where? I climbed onto my table and stared out of my cell window, finding no comfort or inspiration in the bleak, unforgiving world outside. The local town and freedom lay to the south, on the opposite side of the Institute to my window. The view I had contained nothing beyond the perimeter wall except a few trees, the river, and empty countryside.

I ambled idly to my pillow and pulled out the tobacco tin that held the incriminating glass fragments from the broken bottle, with the intention of chucking them out of the window. Upon opening the tin I saw that the fragments lay on a folded piece of paper. It was one of the pages I had torn from that schoolbook, the map of the local region. I unfolded it and looked again. There was so little marked on the map: the town, the river, the huge expanse of emptiness to the north, the weaving dotted line and the blue region at the top, the odd black line running vertically to one side. I tucked the map into my shoe.

The blue region above the dotted line was another nation, I knew that. I knew that the Other country was a place that had once, many years ago, been at war with our country. We were no longer at war with them, but our two nations were not on friendly terms. Believe what our government said and the people in that land were jealous of our successes and harboured plans to invade, tried to infiltrate spies over the border. I recalled my thumb measurement of the distance from the river to the border, a value which I had reckoned to be about seven days' walk.

The next day, I sought out The Moth.

'Moth,' I asked, 'you know . . . the Other country, to the north of here?'

'Hmmm?'

'What's it like? To live there, I mean.'

Moth blinked unemotionally at me from behind his glasses. 'Well, I've never been there. Much the same as here, I suppose. The climate and flora and fauna will be effectively the same, perhaps a little colder and drier,' he began.

'No, I mean, is it . . . a friendly place? Would you like to go there, if you had the chance?' I struggled to put my thoughts into words.

'Guess so. Maybe. I've never really thought about it.' Moth resumed reading his book. Without prompting he added, 'My father went there, when he was exiled.'

'Your father lives there?' I gasped.

'No, not now. He did for a while, when he first left this country. He's moved on since then,' Moth said, matter-of-factly.

'But this is fantastic! So, Moth, if you were to turn up at the gates of the Other country, they'd know who you were? The people in authority, I mean. They'd welcome you?' I blurted out questions now, my arms flapping with excitement at the possibilities this news brought.

'Yes, I suppose so. The government there is very critical of our government. They were very supportive of my father's criticisms . . .' Moth burbled on. I understood little of what he said, but gained the impression that the people

159

in charge there would welcome Moth and the liberty it would afford his famous father to criticise our own leaders. I staunched the flow which poured from my friend's overactive mouth.

'Moth, Moth, enough! But what about your mum? Even if you went to your father, surely he'd still be unwilling to speak out because your mum is under house arrest back here?' I asked.

'No. My parents always agreed. Once I was safe, they would speak out whatever the consequences to themselves,' he informed me.

I could dimly imagine those consequences. I did not want The Moth to do likewise. Wasting no time, I changed the subject.

'Moth . . . what about me? If I turned up there, in the Other country, would they let a nobody like me in?' I asked.

Moth shrugged. 'They certainly wouldn't be obliged to return you. It would be up to them, I suppose, whether to let you stay or make you go back.'

Encouraged by what he had told me, I sat down next to Moth on his bed and breathed out a long sigh. Leaning so close to him that I was almost kissing his ear, I whispered, 'How would you fancy escaping with me, and going to the Other country? And then on to meet up with your old man?'

Anyone else would have laughed at such a suggestion or got angry with me for promoting tempting but ridiculous fantasies, but not The Moth. He did not react visibly at all, he simply sat in studious contemplation and thought for several excruciating minutes. I paced his cell, hopping impatiently from foot to foot, saying nothing, but hoping passionately he would decide in favour of an escape.

To my way of thinking, I could escape on my own, in many ways that would be much easier. But were I to flee to the Other country, and just be booted out again . . . that would be too much. Escape had to be final and irreversible, and The Moth would make all the difference. Being friends with the son of a well-known exile, being the one who had liberated him and so advanced the cause of . . . whatever it was, Moth's blah-de-blah.

How could they refuse me? Even if I was a convicted car thief; even if I was . . . but with luck we could be there before Sticky made that decision for me. Outside, as in the Institute, proximity to the golden Moth would bring me safety; my misdeeds would be washed away, overlooked or forgiven. Sticky's game, my game, but – well – Moth was my friend. And I would be helping him.

By now, Moth was wrinkling his nose and fumbling with his glasses, neither of them promising signs. Spying a packet of cookies in his cupboard, I snatched them out and began to eat them, almost smashing them into my mouth in my haste to consume them before Moth could protest that I had not asked first. Moth watched me, his eyes fixed on my slavering chops. I pinged the empty packet out of the window.

'Prove to me you have an effective plan, and I'll come,' said Moth suddenly.

'Yes! I will! Not now, Moth, I haven't thought it all through yet, but soon, very soon,' I promised, clasping his hands and squeezing them tightly.

'And this is all because of . . . the hacksaw?' he coolly asked. 'No other reason?'

'What? Yes, absolutely. That tool is what makes it all possible!' I assured him, and I dashed out of the cell and returned to my own. The Moth I trusted to flutter above the tales of my transgressions.

For some days after Moth's agreement I kept away from him and Harete, indeed I avoided all company whenever possible. In work, in lessons, in the canteen, I withdrew from all distractions and devoted my mind to thinking and planning. All the other boys shunned me anyway, and that suited me just fine.

During the long nights any claviger who leered through the peephole in my door would have seen me lying on my back, arms by my sides outside the blankets (as was strictly required by the rules), eyes sealed. But he would not have seen that my brain was thrashing, computing, plotting, scheming, that I was picturing every step of a candidate plan, seeing each potential fault, reworking it like a blacksmith working a lump of iron, pounding it out and folding it over on itself and hammering it again until it was perfect, annealed in the kiln of my mind.

Those days were spent in a haze. I had to imagine not just myself and The Moth as each trial plan was examined in minute detail, but had also to step outside myself and picture the actions and thoughts of everyone else, too: the clavigers and the Director, our fellow inmates. I studied walls and bars and clothes and people's routines, dredged my memory for facts, assembled a catalogue of useful excuses and plausible explanations. Like I said before, you

162

have to do these things properly. You have to be adult, be professional, have to give yourself up entirely to the business in hand. Few adults – clavigers, teachers, parents – can ever imagine that someone much younger than them, someone like me, is capable of doing anything *big*. That was something I was relying on.

My complete escape plan solidified. I examined it inside my head, going over it like an artist might look at her painting. I stood back and contemplated it as a whole, admiring its composition and colour, and I stepped forwards and floated my gaze closely over the canvas, looking at the brushstrokes and minute corrections.

One day, I presented my plan to The Moth. We sat side by side on his bed and I softly described each phase, patiently answering his many questions.

When we were through, The Moth nodded.

'When?' he asked.

'On or soon after the first snowfall of winter,' I instantly replied.

'Reason?'

'We don't want to escape when there's deep snow already on the ground – it would show our footprints and be hard to walk through. Rather, we want it to be snowing, and to snow for several more days, so that any footprints we make outside will get covered up,' I told him. 'So it's better to go in early winter than spring, when the wet mud would show our prints.' Spring might have been too late for me, Sticky might have died or recovered by then, but I couldn't tell Moth that.

I slithered to the door and checked that we were not

being spied upon as we plotted. My neck ached from my habit of constantly looking behind me for Jelly. Day and night I heard – or thought I heard – his voice calling out, 'Watching you, eight six five.' His ambition smelled like static electricity; you could feel its charge sour the air and tug at the hairs on your arms. I scanned, listened, sniffed. No spies.

'So we have . . . about six weeks?' Moth asked.

'Yes, the snowfall here is reliable,' I answered. 'Have you any chocolate, biscuits, any goodies like that?' I next asked him, knowing very well that he received a generous quantity of such treats from his mother, sent via the Director. Moth himself dipped into these only very occasionally, always claiming they tasted 'off'. I've seen canteen brawls where bones were busted over disputes about a single slimy cutlet or a portion of undercooked rice as digestible as swarf, so Moth's snootiness towards his sweet bullion was incomprehensible to me. But I never made an issue of it; it just meant there was more for Harete and me.

'Some . . . I suppose you want to build up a stock for the escape?' he replied, moving to show me his supplies.

'Yes, but not yet. For the moment I need them as payment,' I said. Anticipating his next question, I queasily continued. 'Moth . . . eh, you know that my plan requires us to escape at night, and from my cell? You didn't ask how it was that you would be in my cell after lock-up.'

'You need to bribe someone to arrange this?'

'More or less. Listen, Moth, something is going to happen to you soon. Something unpleasant. Can't say when, but it'll take place within the next few days. All I want you to

164

know is this: whatever passes, you didn't see who it was. No idea, not a clue, nothing. That's really important.'

His face blanched.

'I'm sorry, Moth. You know that we cannot do the escape from your cell, it's on the wrong side of the building. We have to get you moved into mine,' I explained. I stuffed into my overalls the three large chocolate bars he had fetched out from his cupboard and crept away.

Work on the plan began immediately. Boredom and listlessness were endemic in the Institute, fuelling endless fights and the clans' love of gambling. But I was above it all, in fact from that point onwards I was probably the busiest person in the entire Institute.

Directly after seeing Moth, I hurried to locate Cheesegrater and Sphinx, who were always to be found together. Cheesegrater's name was on account of his acne-scarred and pockmarked complexion; Sphinx pretended to be deaf and mute but was in fact neither. His deaf-dumb act was performed with extraordinary authenticity and conviction when in the presence of the clavigers, so much so that they almost universally held him to be genuinely handicapped. The two boys were troublemakers who sought out violence as a compass needle seeks out the north. They were prime examples of *them*. They readily took two chocolate bars from me and agreed to my scheme with gleeful enthusiasm. My new status as a leper was no hindrance to my deal; bribes overcame all reservations on that front.

Next, I swapped one remaining bar of chocolate for a needle and some reels of thread, the deal being done out in the courtyard with some members of the girl clan 'Venus

Vendetta'. The valuable needle was a loan item, and I had to spit and shake on the terms: if the needle was not returned after one month, another would be forced through my cheeks.

Following this, I requested with the appropriate claviger that I be transferred to laundry-room duties for the next month. Working in the laundry room was not popular because it was regarded as the most arduous work there was, and, unlike most jobs, had actually to be done properly and on time. Because of this, the claviger was only too happy to have a volunteer to supplement his press-ganged workers. I told him that I was suffering from a persistent cold and was hoping the steamy atmosphere in the laundry room would help clear my head.

And all the time, from that moment on, I was snaffling up every plastic bag that came my way. Fortunately, plastic bags were everywhere in the Institute. Visiting relatives brought gifts wrapped in them, we used them to put dirty clothes in en route to the laundry, kids lucky enough to have food gifts used a bag hung outside the dorm or cell windows as a sort of poor-man's fridge to keep the food cool. We used bags in our cells to cover up and line the toilet buckets, in the canteen we scraped food waste into bins lined with plastic bags. Torn bags littered the courtyard and hung in tattered shreds from the branches of the bushes and trees and the barbed wire along the tops of the walls. At every available opportunity I harvested these and any other bag, intact or broken, I could find.

I crammed them into my clothes, up my sleeves and inside my shirt, before emptying them out into a single, large black bin liner under my bunk. The laundry room was an even better fount of plastic bags, including superb, capacious black specimens, as all the laundry was sorted into different fabric types and colours and stored in them. I helped myself to length after length of these from the rolls. The clavigers did not mind; plastic bags were not items that were in any way restricted. The worst harm you could do with them was suffocate yourself, I suppose.

Along with the bags, I stole dozens of socks and a few pillowcases. These required a little more ingenuity as the number of items of clothing and bedding which left the laundry was tallied against the number received, and only small discrepancies were tolerated.

In the early mornings before first bell, and late at night after lock-up, I began to process the bags I had collected. My technique did not come instinctively, nor was it obvious. Rather, it took many frustrating hours of trial and error during free times and when locked in my cell.

Weak things become strong when combined, was my inspiration. Not a very elegant saying, but one I had arrived at over time from looking at my world. The clans were feared, yet many of their members were laughably pathetic individuals. Or, to take another example, the copper wire I had liberated from the waste bin was similarly quite strong – although not strong enough for my purpose, I had tested that – but each strand of wire inside was terribly easy to break. Yet twisted together, the fine wires made something much more than themselves.

The Moth put it differently. 'The whole is greater than the sum of its parts,' he said. He attributed that saying to yet another decomposed genius called Aristotle, a name he wrote down for me but which I could at least pronounce immediately, unlike Sew-crates.

By that time, The Moth was with me in my cell. Not just visiting, but permanently sharing with me, and sharing his crucial immunity from cell searches and raids by other boys. Had he not been, I'd never have dared to make the rope.

He was with me because Sphinx and Cheesegrater had done what I had paid them to do. They had waited until Moth was alone in his cell, then walked in and closed the door. Moth had offered no resistance, he just nodded to them and removed his glasses. That was the signal I had told them to expect to show that this was prearranged and that none of the dire consequences promised by the clavigers for touching The Moth would apply. With all the skill of their kind, they worked him over with fists and feet and helped themselves to his biscuits, placed where I had told them they'd be.

As planned, a great brouhaha then ensued. Moth was taken to the lazarette and patched up. He claimed when questioned that he had been attacked from behind, knocked out with a heavy blow to his head, and consequently had seen nothing. Visiting him, I suggested to the nurse and clavigers that The Moth be moved from his own cell into mine, in order that I, his trusted friend, could look after him whilst he convalesced and to protect him in future. The claviger in charge of cell allocations had looked a little doubtful. It would mean paperwork.

I played my ace. 'He's started to wet the bed, sir. Needs a little company now.'

'Fine, fine,' grumbled the claviger, 'I'll have you moved to Moth's cell this afternoon.'

That, of course, would have been a disaster. My plan required that we share my cell, not his. His cell at the rear of the block overlooked a closed quadrangle, bounded on all sides by more buildings. Naturally, I had been prepared for this eventuality.

'Sir, Moth would prefer my cell. He says his cell has too many bad memories for him now, after the attack, and he can't sleep in it any more,' I pleaded, looking as concerned as I could.

Clavigers rarely changed their minds, but The Moth was their most valuable inmate and they would not risk causing him more trauma. And so, upon his discharge from the lazarette, I had carried all his gear from his old cell to mine, including his lamp. The first thing Moth did when he moved in was test the lamp. Next, he stuck his drawing of the centaur to the wall.

The Moth, although understanding the role that his drubbing played in the grand scheme, was quite naturally not at all happy. He was bruised all over, his face was swollen and sore, his ribs ached terribly, or so he said. My reassurances that there had been no other way to get us together did not entirely convince him. He brooded, and I began to worry that his resentment would scupper his participation in the escape.

To take his mind off events, I showed him how to process the bags.

'Take one,' I began my instruction, holding one of our huge collection of carrier bags. 'Find the seam which runs down the sides under the handles, and rip the bag along the seams on both sides, like so. That turns the bag into a sort of hoop. Do this to a number of bags.

'Take two of the bags you've just prepared. Put them on the floor, with the bottom of one bag next to the top of the other. Put one bag underneath the other, like so . . . then pull it up and through itself, so that it sort of knots around the other bag, and pull tight,' I continued, demonstrating the action several times as I linked together a chain of several bags.

I put three such chains on the floor, parallel with each other but offset slightly, bunched them up and knotted them together. After this, I began to braid the three chains of knotted bags into a single cord, knotting new bags onto each individual chain end as the free lengths shortened.

After an hour's work, I had a length of triple-strand braided bag-rope as long as myself. To demonstrate its strength, I tied one end around the metal window bars, and pulled with all my force. The rope held.

'Do you see, Moth? See how the weak plastic bags can be braided into a rope strong enough to hold my weight? I've heard it can even be done with toilet paper.'

'*E pluribus, unum*,' was Moth's sullen response. 'Out of many, one.'

I found the braiding very restful, and whilst Moth kept an eye at the door for snoopers or clavigers I was happy to spend hours crossing and twisting the three ever-lengthening strands into one tight, taut plastic cable.

Within a week, we had a rope that I estimated was long enough to reach from our cell window to the ground outside twice over. I looked at the rope, immensely proud of it. A pile of torn carrier bags had been turned into something strong enough to hold the weight of a grown man.

Only once the rope was complete did The Moth extract his price for the beating he had suffered. He waited until we were both lying in our bunks after lock-up.

'Harete comes too,' he said.

I ignored him. Surely he had not really said that?

'Did you hear me? Harete comes too,' he repeated.

'We don't need another person. It adds risk, it will slow us down. I've not prepared for three.'

'She comes, or I stay,' he said, his voice calm. He was not trying to bargain.

'But why, Moth? She doesn't need to come. She's a ward, an orphan. She has an easier life here than even you; she'll be out for sure in a year,' I said.

'She told me she doesn't want to end up like most of the girls who get released from here,' he replied. 'She told me most of them work the streets.'

That made me feel queasy. Did Moth understand what Harete meant? I wondered.

'Harete deserves to be more than a road sweeper,' he added.

No, he didn't. I fell silent. Many minutes passed by, and I thought about Harete and I thought about my mum.

'We can't get Harete in the cell as well, Moth. It makes things very complicated. She'll have to get out by herself and then we'll need to meet up with her,' I pointed out.

'Fine. I'm sure you'll think of something, you always

seem to. I'll tell her tomorrow,' Moth replied, and I heard his bunk creak as he turned over and fell asleep.

I groaned. This was how great plans fell apart, this was how poles went unconquered and battles were lost. There should be no place for childish sentimentality and emotions. I was steaming angry, but there was nothing to be done about it. My dreams that night were a confusion of plastic bags and twisting rope. I saw a vision of myself and The Moth being twisted around each other by gigantic hands, then stretched out by some force, elongating, thinning and breaking. Time and again we were stretched and broken, found weak and wanting. Harete blurred in; she became entangled with us. The giant's hands folded the three of us over and under, over and under, braiding three cords now, not two. Again, the pulling force tested us, but this time we held. On waking, I found I had twisted my blanket into a tight, suffocating spiral around myself.

And so we had to draw Harete into the scheme, swear her to secrecy, and I had to go over the plan in fine detail once more. Again, I had to give the reason for going north, and talk about the need for snow; explain how we would feed ourselves, what we would wear and take; and tell them how we would cross the river, but only once we had gained time and evaded our pursuers by floating down it for some distance.

Harete studied the creased map torn from the schoolbook as I explained everything. I pointed out the crucial features on the map: the town, the space where the Institute should have been but wasn't, the river, the empty countryside – all seven days' walk of it – and the distant border.

She ran a bitten fingernail along the black vertical line on the right-hand side of the map. 'What's this?' she asked.

'That's the line of pylons. We'll get out of the river when we see them and follow them. They go due north; they'll be excellent markers.'

'Why are they there? You say there are no towns, only little villages and hamlets . . . so why the pylons?'

This was an excellent question, and one even Moth had not thought to ask. 'The book explained that,' I answered. 'There's a huge power station somewhere way south of here. It makes more electricity than we in this country can use, especially at night. So we sell the electricity to the Other country, at a cheap rate. They built an aluminium smelter near the border to use the cheap power, and they sell us back the processed metal at a discount. The pylons take the electricity to the smelter over the border.'

'I thought our two countries didn't get on?' she said, sounding puzzled.

'Money overcomes all disagreements,' Moth pointed out.

There was little Harete could do to assist me in my preparations for the time being, so I resigned myself to having to acquire half as much again of the various things I needed and continued with my preparations. The Moth was not a great deal of use, either. He was not a practical boy, and one particular incident cemented forever in my mind the extent to which this was true. The bulb in his precious adjustable reading lamp had blown, and he had been issued with a replacement. The dud one would have to be returned intact to the clavigers, lest it be broken and the glass used for wicked purposes. I was busy trying to

173

solve a problem related to the food we would need for our journey, Moth was trying to screw in the replacement bulb.

'Oh! How does this thing go in?' he asked crossly. 'Every time I try it just pops out again.'

I looked up, annoyed at being disturbed.

'What? The bulb's got a screw fixing, hasn't it? Same as any screw, then. Same as a bottle top.'

He tried again, and the bulb plopped from the lamp and rolled onto the floor, luckily not breaking.

'Careful!' I shouted. 'Break that one and you won't get another! What are you doing? Show me!'

I watched him push the bulb into the lamp's threaded fitting and rotate it, the wrong way.

'Other way! Like putting in a screw!' I said, exasperated by the boy's lack of adroitness.

He did the job correctly and I resumed my ponderings.

'Clockwise to tighten, always,' I said.

A minute passed by.

'Why do you say that? What's that place got to do with anything?' asked Moth, sounding thoroughly puzzled.

'What place?' I snapped, annoyed at being disrupted again.

'The sixth moon of Saturn,' he said, bafflingly.

I stared at him. 'Moth, what are you dribbling about? Has that kicking affected your mind? Moons of Saturn?'

'The sixth moon of Saturn is Titan,' he explained, and wrote the name with his finger in dust on the desktop. 'You said, "Clockwise to Titan." Is it a saying? What does it mean?'

My mouth fell open. 'I meant, you turn screws and bolts and bottle tops clockwise to tighten them . . . and anticlockwise to loosen them.'

174

We cracked up and rolled on the floor, laughing hysterically. From that time on, 'Project Titan' became our private code for working on the escape.

Moth may not have been much use on the practical preparations, but his knowledge came in useful in other areas. After we had ceased our laughter, I enlisted his brain to help in working out how much food we would need. Originally I had intended that we would feed ourselves exclusively on the chocolates and biscuits that The Moth received from his mother. But I learned that his stocks were in fact very limited and would probably all be used up in buying things we needed from other kids. What was required was some very dense, easy-to-carry foodstuff that would keep us alive for seven days of hiking across open country.

'Fat. Lard,' advised The Moth. 'It's the most compact form of food energy there is. That's why our bodies store energy as fat.'

'Could we live on just fat?' I asked, somewhat doubtful.

'For a short time, I'm sure we could. It wouldn't be very nice. We could try to improve its taste and make it more nutritious by adding something else, but fat is energy; it would keep us alive and walking and warm,' he said.

'How much would we need? Can you do the maths, Moth? The Mothematics?'

Moth could. 'Let's think. We'll be walking, and it will be cold . . .' he started. He talked about daily calorific needs and the specific energy content and density of fat, plucking the data from the encyclopaedia of his mind before asking, 'Can you picture a soft drinks can, like you may have bought on the outside?'

'Of course! Fizzy tooth rot was like mother's milk to me!' I joked.

'Imagine one of those cans filled with lard. We'll each need that much a day,' he informed me. Intuitively, the figure seemed about right, a large fist-sized block of yummy lard.

Harete now became an asset, as I had to grudgingly allow, because she was slated to work in the kitchens for most of the following month. Kitchen work was popular because it was indoors, warm, and gave the finest opportunities of all jobs for stealing food. But this was not easy – clavigers were always on the lookout. Besides, inmates were not involved in preparing the food, nor were we allowed anywhere near the storerooms or refrigerated lockers. Kitchen work was restricted to cleaning and washing-up. Having done the shift many times I knew that scraping out and washing up the heavy, scratched aluminium cooking pans was hard work, much less desirable than collecting plates and scraping the leftovers into the bins – or into pockets and tucked-away bags if the clavigers were looking away. It was the leftovers that were sought after by anyone hoping to find something even remotely edible, so plate-collecting duty was the plum job. That suited us – it meant Harete could volunteer for the despised task of washing-up, and that in turn would allow her access to the oven trays and grill pans and big saucepans, which would be encrusted with cooking fat and the drippings from cooked meats.

Harete started to bring back her bounty from the kitchens. She had a week or so to perfect a technique for scraping out the valuable muck and hiding it about her person, and we used what she brought back to see whether the stuff was actually going to be edible.

'Are you sure about this, boys?' she asked as she emptied out a plastic bag full of grey, semi-solid fat onto a sheet of paper on the desk in our cell. 'I almost threw up prising that out of an oven; the smell inside the cooker was gross.'

We looked at the icky mess. It was speckled with black bits. 'Tuck in,' goaded The Moth, so I used a pencil to lift up a lump of the muck and ate it. I screwed up my face and had to fight the need to gag.

'Vile,' I said, spitting the taste from my lips. This was bad news. Without a supply of non-perishable food we could not possibly escape.

Harete tried again. She learned to identify the pans used to cook the staff's richer and meatier meals, a much more valuable source of meat drippings. She found paper wrappers from cooking lard packets, still with lumps and smears of unused fat on them. She smuggled these out and we cut the used fat with this more palatable stuff. When cleaning tables she sought out trays of cups used by the clavigers and catering staff themselves, from which she would rescue small fragments of undissolved sugar in the bottoms of the cups and on the spoons. On washing-up rota, Harete would use a spoon to chisel lumps of dried porridge off the sides of breakfast bowls, a food totally ignored by the more discerning. These, too, were added to the mix. 'Porridge oats and cereals will be a valuable dietary supplement,' Moth had told us.

We mixed up the sugar and the oats and the fat in our cell by night. We used the heat from Moth's reading lamp to soften the fat and sprinkled in the other ingredients. Once we had mixed the ingredients, we pressed the adulterated fat into rough blocks and hung these in carrier bags on the outside of the window. This was a common and permitted practice, so attracted no risk unless someone chose to inspect the bag's contents. The weather was growing colder day by day, which was a bonus because it acted as a fridge, then a freezer, to preserve our stash of stolen food.

Our final coup was the discovery of a bird feeder dangling from a tree in the Director's little garden, a sad affair comprising a patch of grass and a few shrubs outside the administrative offices. Sifting through the material I was able to raid from it, Moth identified pumpkin seeds as being definitely edible, and we decided on balance to throw the whole lot in.

Slowly, our supplies mounted. Also, our troubles.

'Watching you, eight six five!'

Jelly was tediously true to his word, and a huge nuisance to us. He would stop me as I moved about the Institute; he would fish me out of lessons or meals for fingertip inspections of my clothes and shoes. He started nosing around our cell, and I am certain that it was only the clavigers' orders not to harass The Moth that stopped him from conducting daily cell searches. (How much pressure that prohibition could withstand I could not tell; clavigers itched to inspect our room. To discourage them, Moth spent every hour he could inside, emerging only occasionally to wash.)

I became a quivering Jelly-magnet. The walls of the

Institute seemed porous to his vision, the corridors funnelled his voice to me wherever I went. The intrusions passed beyond the physical. His thin-lipped face congealed from my mashed potato, the contours of my bedding, the clouds: cumulo-Jelly, strato-Jelly, Jelly-nimbus.

'Eight six five! I hear tales about you-ooo! *Scandalous* rumours about you and nine five two, recently departed from these shores with a dicky tummy,' he teased me, crystallising out of the billowing steam as I showered. Melting back into vapour before I was able to react, his parting news drained away the marginal warmth grudgingly loaned me by the hissing shower. 'If there's no change in his condition by the end of the month, they'll withdraw feeding and let him die, eight six five!'

'Then *they'll* be the killers!' I protested to The Moth later. 'Not one of us!'

Moth knew differently. 'Legally, he's right,' he told me. 'It's the original crime that counts. It'll be recorded as murder. What does it matter to you?'

Some lawyer! We had only until the month's end before Jelly ruled, a fortnight before some bewigged buffoon harrumphed and declared that someone needed to drop through the trapdoor for Sticky.

Fourteen days!

From then on, we worked on my plan every free hour, day and night.

As we assembled our supplies I started to work on our clothing. We needed clothes that would keep us warm and dry for seven days out in the open, and which would allow us to float down the river without getting soaking wet.

The first step was to steal a second pair of overalls for each of us. That was a cinch. One of the great things about my entire plan was that it relied only on us acquiring things that were of no value to other people – plastic bags, cooking fat, old socks, spare overalls. Everyone was issued with overalls, so what was the value in stealing a pair? Laundry bags supplied me with three sets, each two sizes bigger than the ones we normally wore, and bribes with Moth's biscuits stopped onlookers' flapping tongues.

Thirteen days!

The shopping list then required layers of plastic sheeting, to roll our thin, foam mattresses in and thereby transform them into floatation aids. Also, I intended us to sleep under these sheets when on the run. Again, rubbish like this was abundant in the Institute. During my next laundry shift a new dryer was delivered to replace a broken one, and to my delight the huge cardboard box was swaddled in layers of hardy plastic wrapping. The clavigers helped the delivery men open the box, and I pretended to tidy away the plastic. Once it was folded up, I announced that I was taking it to the waste bins. In fact, I took the plastic sheets up to my cell. Had I been stopped and questioned, there was a prepared lie I had ready for deployment: the plastic was to line The Moth's bed with, he having developed a bed-wetting problem since his beating.

That was how we had to play things – anticipate every question a claviger might have, prepare a lie, make sure the lie stood up to detailed examination. Everything needed to be thought through.

Back in the laundry room, I watched the broken dryer being manhandled into the now empty box, ready to be taken away. My magpie eyes noted the rolls of strong, fabric-backed tape being used to seal up the box. The tape looked wide, tough and waterproof. I decided we needed it. My hands whisked away the tape roll and stashed it in the crotch of my overalls – I was deliberately wearing my recently stolen, over-sized pair precisely because their bagginess allowed me to hide stolen items inside. The entire switch was done like a perfectly executed karate move.

Not everything went smoothly. My unpopularity with the clans had not abated, and truces with many boys endured no longer than the duration of a deal we had struck. Moreover, our activities and the sugary bribes we were paying out fomented new suspicions. The word was that Moth and I were up to something, that we possessed something of value, and this made our lives even more precarious.

A clan reject called Toffee (like the confectionery, he had a tendency to remove your teeth) became agitated by the stories that we were concealing something special. For days on end he pestered me for information, becoming more enraged with every encounter. My surprise was limited then when, as I passed by the latrines one day, three boys grabbed me and bundled me inside one of the squalid cubicles. My head was shoved down the un-flushed, cracked lavatory pan by two of them and Toffee sat across my back.

'Why do they call you Mo, Mo?' he asked.

'Do they, Toffee? Some do, some have other names for

me,' I replied, trying to hold my breath and keep my skin away from the smeared porcelain.

I felt his hands pat me over my body, up my legs, down my arms, over my sides. I tried to raise my head but the other two boys pushed down on it even harder.

'But why "Mo", Mo?'

'I dunno!' I squawked. How had he known I was carrying it? Had Moth let something slip? Had Toffee been looking through our cell door? 'Perhaps it's because I like to cut the grass!' I joked, but the joke went unappreciated. Toffee found what he'd been looking for, something suspicious against my side. Toffee's helpers tore open my overalls and ripped away the wide strip of tape from where I'd stuck it to my bare skin. The hacksaw blade tumbled out and fell ringing onto the floor.

'Ahhhh!' crowed Toffee. My head was pulled back, the saw blade held against my throat. Toffee gently rubbed it from side to side, playing me like a violin. I felt the sharp serrations scratch over my skin.

'We like cutting grasses too, don't we, boys?' he chuckled. But I got off lightly that time, a medium-grade kicking from all three of them, no cutting. The blade was lost, though, and there weren't enough biscuits in the entire world to buy back something that valuable.

'You lost the blade!' yelped Moth when I let him know of my misfortune, instantly clapping a hand over his own mouth. 'The whole project is dead! Trust you to mess it up!'

'Yes, trust me,' I replied, patching up my injuries. 'We'll manage. You'll see.'

Eleven days!

182

We continued to steal and to collect refuse. Each item we stole was useful in obtaining the next one on our shopping list. My 'fishing rod' was used to grab two metal cans – one thin, crushable aluminium one like a drinks can, one sturdy steel one like a soup tin – from the waste compound under my cell window, in much the same way that I had fished out the glass bottle many weeks before. Next, I used one of my glass shards to slice open the thin aluminium can and score and cut out a narrow strip of metal. The strip's ends were sharpened into points, then it was bent into a proper hook shape and tied to the end of the 'fishing line'. This in turn was used on several more early morning fishing trips to haul up from a skip in the compound length after length of torn packaging material, plastic sheets with loads of little air bubbles inside.

I also used a glass shard to cut out three very special utensils from the flattened aluminium can. These resembled rectangles with a triangular protrusion jutting out from one edge, each slightly different in size and shape.

Nine days!

With just over a week to go, our preparations were nearing their end. Our food supplies were building up nicely and I had only the waterproof outer clothes left to make. Our two enemies were time and Jelly. It was agonising to have the quick-strutting, laser-eyed, pernicious fanatic hounding me. Such was the risk of him finding me smuggling something in my clothes or stealing something, I was able to do less and less work on Project Titan, and we began to slip behind schedule.

'This is getting intolerable,' I said to Moth after lock-up.

'Must be how it is for my mother,' replied Moth. 'She tells me she gets hounded by the security police every day.'

'How does she tell you that? I thought the Director censored her letters, surprised he lets that get through.'

'We have a code. If she talks about the weather, then she's really talking about the problems she's having from the marshals. She lives a long way from here, so it doesn't strike the Director as odd that she's talking about rain when it's been dry here for ages, or vice versa,' he explained.

'How does she bear up? I could do with some tips,' I said.

'She tries to be as friendly as possible to them. Never gets angry. Never shows they are getting her down. If they're sitting in their car outside the house to watch her, she comes out with cakes for them,' Moth whispered back. 'She goes out of her way to be kind to whoever is being cruel to her.'

'Does she get visitors?' I asked, picking the dirt from under my nails, then my nose.

'None,' he answered.

'Must be lonely for –'

'Enough about her!' Moth exploded. With this, his face turned so red I thought his hair was about to catch fire. 'Shut your hole! Never mention my mother again!' he lashed out, then he huffed and puffed and covered his head with his pillow and turned to face the wall. *Touchy little mother's boy*, I thought, *what's his problem?* Was me even daring to think of his saintly mama like watching sooty-fingered drunks pawing an alabaster statue; is that how he thought?

184

Lying in bed, I determined to learn from what little he had told me of her. And from Sticky too – the way he'd lured me with that report, the way he goaded *them* and tricked the clavigers into doing his work for him. Could I buy us more time, make Jelly think me his ally, save Retread and myself? Could one big lie serve all these ends?

Our next encounter was the following morning. 'Stand still, eight six five! Clothing violation!' bawled Jelly, performing his tiresome trick of streaking into view like a jet fighter from some disguised vantage point.

'Yes, sir! Sorry, sir!' I said, standing very stiffly in my best imitation of a soldier on parade, shoulders thrown back, chest out, barely resisting the urge to salute him. He remained where he was, staring me out, scanning my face for any hint of insubordination or sarcasm. We stood like this for an age.

'I really respect you, sir,' I stammered, deadpan. Jelly continued to glare silently into my face, his viperous eyes radiating with mesmerising brilliance. I lifted my eyes to his and stared back into them, finding them irresistible. Jelly seemed suddenly to be something different, something at once inhuman, majestic and preposterous. A nervous shudder coursed through me and half-involuntarily I allowed it to tease my mouth and eyes into a hint of a smile.

Now came the gamble. 'I hope you are made Director, sir. I'd like to help you.'

Jelly's eyes narrowed. He licked his oddly red lips, lips that tested out the shapes of words but found none that would fit.

'Sir, I've got . . . information!' I breathed the word slowly and let the bait dangle. A pause for effect, a deep breath . . . then, I wheeled out my freshly brewed super-lie, one lie to solve all problems, and let it fly. 'No one poisoned Sticky, sir! He did it himself, to get moved to the hospital. His family were going to spring him from there! Only, he dosed himself wrong, sir. Eye Inside told me. And –'

The force of Jelly's hand across my face turned my cheek into a field of fire and almost twisted my head from my neck.

'Don't try to play me, you streak of grease! I need him not just dead but murdered,' he said, pouring the boiling words from his mouth into my ear with no gap between them. 'When that yob dies and goes up the smokestack, I'll be Director. I have connections, you know. With *higher powers*. And the very first thing I'll do when I'm in charge is to beat a confession from you!'

He swivelled on his heels and marched off, almost goose-stepping. My legs turned to water and I trickled onto the ground, dabbing my face to test for blood. I felt wretched. Like Sticky before him, Jelly seemed to have weaved me into his own career plan. What better way to prove the correctness of his appointment than to force a confession to murder?

I repeated everything verbatim to my co-conspirators. The rumours had by that time pierced the crust around The Moth; I had nothing to lose.

'Why didn't he believe me?' I moaned to Harete. 'My lie was plausible!'

'But not desirable,' she replied. 'It wasn't a story that fed his fantasy.' Harete wasn't done. 'You weren't involved, were you?'

'No,' I said, 'I promise.'

Harete smiled.

'We've got be gone before eight days. Whatever the weather,' I told the pair of them.

Moth frowned. 'What's the hurry? I thought we were waiting for snow?'

'Eight days is DJ-day,' I reminded him. 'Sticky dead, unplugged like a duff kettle. Director Jelly, carried aloft on a wave of official scandal. The Constipated Turkey pensioned off.'

'Good riddance!' snarled Moth.

'And on his first day, Jelly wants to beat a confession from me,' I reminded them. 'A false confession,' I added hurriedly.

Moth looked unconcerned. 'With no witnesses or evidence, you've nothing to worry about. It won't stand up. Rumours don't matter.'

'Fat comfort that is!' I squawked, omitting to mention that the comfort thinned to the point of emaciation given that there were witnesses, and might be evidence.

Putting the misfire of my lie to Jelly behind me, I began work on our waterproofs. To float down the river we would need buoyancy – that would come from our rolled-up foam mattresses, sheathed in plastic – but we would also need to be absolutely protected from the freezing cold river water. Working extra shifts in the laundry I took on the job of ironing. Into my basket of clothes to be pressed I mixed in a set of large, black plastic bin liners. When no one was looking, I would take out a bin liner and place it over the end of the ironing board, pulling it taut. Then I would pull

187

another one over the top of that, then another, maybe even a fourth or fifth. I'd then place a towel or shirt over the top of the layered bags, both to hide them and to protect the iron's hotplate. Then I pressed down hard with the iron and repeatedly worked over the complete surface of the bags, twisting them round over the end of the ironing board as each strip was completed, always making sure I ironed through the cloth layer.

The combined effect of the iron's heat and my pressing melted and fused the layers of plastic together. The end result was the same shape and size as a single black bin liner, but with the thickness of several bags: a tough, thick plastic material. Smaller carrier bags could be layered and fused in the same way, and I prepared several of these in addition to many sets of bin liners.

'*E pluribus unum*,' I said to Moth, showing him the resulting 'cloth' that my ironing had created. He fingered the bags, impressed with the result. Harete and I now worked secretly in our free times to turn the fused bin liners into three sets of waterproof coveralls. We used my sharp glass fragments to cut some of the bags into tubes for our arms. These we sewed, using the borrowed needle and the thread, onto other fused bags with arm and head holes cut into them. We waterproofed the stitching by dabbing on melted plastic made by heating more carrier bags on Moth's reading lamp.

We made waterproof trousers in the same way, stitching tubes for our legs onto bags with leg holes cut out. A complete coverall was in two halves, one for our bodies and arms, and one for our legs and lower bodies. I demonstrated how to climb into the lower half, then pull the upper part over the head and arms, and explained that we would make a waterproof seal between the two sections using the adhesive tape I had stolen.

Our preparations continued; Harete made us balaclavas from pillowcases and fused carrier bags. We could fix these tightly over our heads using drawstrings made from strips of material cut from cleaning rags. Mittens were easy: two or three pairs of old socks, covered with more carrier bags, sealed onto the rest of the coveralls with more tape.

Footwear took a little more thought. We traipsed down to the stores to be issued with shoes slightly bigger than the ones we normally wore, claiming we had grown out of our current ones. This was so that on the outside we could comfortably wear three pairs of socks inside them, for warmth. I showed Harete and Moth how we would make our shoes and lower legs waterproof by wrapping them in yet more bags and sealing these to our leggings with the ever-useful tape.

We took the various strips and squares of bubble-plastic wrapping material and meticulously cut, stitched and melted these into more limb-sized tubes, and additional large pieces for wrapping around our chests. These would be worn over our underclothes. The little air pockets would provide excellent insulation against the winter cold as well as additional lift when in the river, and perhaps also some cushioning when sleeping rough.

Five days!

My clumsy attempt to woo Jelly and get him on our side had been a catastrophe, but the earlier incident in the courtyard did transform the threat he posed, although it did not lessen it.

'Eight six five!' barked Jelly, intercepting me as I scuttled back to my cell with the arms and legs of my overalls packed with plastic bags. 'Come into my office!' he said, his tone less sharp than usual, beckoning me into a room I knew to be nothing more than a disused closet.

Hesitantly, I stepped into the dusty storeroom. Jelly kicked shut the door behind him. The tiny room was full of broken furniture; there was barely room for the two us to stand upright together.

Jelly took hold of my lapels with his fists. His manner was fidgety and sulky; he looked tired and frustrated. His hat was askew. 'Nothing's happening, eight six five!' he announced after an awkward pause. 'Nothing! It's all slipping away from me,' he whined.

I nodded, trying to look sympathetic. *He only needs to wait five more days!* I thought. *How impatient is he?* Perhaps circumstances were moving in my direction. Had a beep and a blip on a bedside monitor showed Sticky to be recovering?

'You said you'd help me!' he cried, and he shook me. 'You said you had information.'

My expression must have told him I had nothing. Jelly shook me harder. His complexion darkened.

Face is purple, face is white . . .

What could I say? There had never been any 'information', except the convoluted contrivance he'd already dismissed. I had no new ideas.

190

'Was it all just lies? Were you lying to me?' he thundered. 'Were you?'

This claviger is gelignite!

The shaking increased. 'Tell me! What have you got for me! I need something!' he shouted, his teeth clenched, the veins on his forehead standing out and pulsating.

'I . . . I . . .'

Wibble wobble on a plate . . .

I could think only of Zinc Fingers, and the remains of his pulped hand adhering to the door frame! Jelly was shaking me so forcefully now that the back of my skull was bashing repeatedly against a stack of tables.

'Tell me! You liar! YOU! FILTHY! COMMON! LIAR!'

My head whipped painfully backwards and forwards; I was close to blacking out.

When will Jelly detonate?

'Sir! Sir!' I screamed. 'There is . . . something!' The shaking stopped, my head snapping painfully to a standstill. My vision was a sandstorm of red blotches. 'I . . . I know there are some boys with a blade – a big one – over in H-Wing!' I gabbled.

I'm no snitch; I didn't mention Toffee's name. It was a poor offering, but it was just enough to derail Jelly. He let go of my lapels as he assimilated my news.

'Hmm, a knife?' he said unenthusiastically after a minute's twitching. 'A stabbing, a fatal wounding . . . that *might* be enough to get the old goat kicked out, I suppose, after all that's happened. Find out everything you can!' he yapped. Then he sneered, 'You're no good, eight six five!'

'No, sir,' I replied weakly. I supposed he was bemoaning my lack of effort in helping him work himself into a frenzy rather than the quality of my information.

He licked his lips. 'Why do you want me to be Director?'

Overcoming the sickness I felt from my shaking, I adopted my smarmiest manner. 'Gosh, sir. This place would be so much safer with you in charge. You'd tackle the clans, I'm sure, and . . . ah . . .'

Jelly frowned. 'Yes, yes, *obviously* I'd build up and support the clans, they're the only true source of discipline in this place! What else?'

'Sir, you're a . . .' I struggled, urgently trying to divine the word that would most please him, ' . . . professional. That's it. I respect your professional, military attitude!' I was virtually drowning in my own sweat.

Jelly showed no reaction. Without emotion he said, 'Was never in the military. Before this, I used to work in a car parts factory. I wanted to join up, but Grandma Caesar stopped me.'

Moth interrupted me as I related my latest creepy encounter with Jelly. 'Whom did he say stopped him from joining?'

'Grandma Caesar,' I repeated. 'That's what he said, Moth! I think so, anyway. My ears were still ringing from the shaking.'

'Interesting,' mused Moth. 'Interesting.' He leaned over and fiddled with his reading lamp, twiddling the bulb in its fitting and making it flicker. 'Go on, what happened after that?' he said.

* * *

Minutes ticked by in itchy silence as Jelly stared at me, never once removing his gaze. Then he said, 'I hope you're not going to leave me, eight six five?'

Did he know about the escape? How? 'No, sir. Got a few months left to go in here,' I replied with a shaky smile.

'I wonder. I wonder,' he said. 'When you get out,' he continued, 'perhaps you'd like to call round to my flat for a beer, or something?'

'Yes, that would be great. I'd like that very much. That's very kind,' I said, dry-mouthed.

'If you've not been hanged, that is,' he added casually as an afterthought. He straightened his cap, and opened the door. I edged myself past him and out to the corridor, breaking into a run as soon as I was out of his sight.

As always with that volatile and erratic man, it was not possible to predict the outcome of our meeting. Something about our dismal encounter seemed to have made him look upon me differently though, for as the last few days to the end of the month trickled by, Jelly began to seek me out and drag me into bizarre, rambling conversations that lasted hours at a time. Surviving each one was like defusing a bomb blindfolded. He made no more references to the matter of the knife, so I deduced that whatever improvement in Sticky's condition had prompted his brief panic had not proved permanent. Maybe the blip on the monitor screen had just been a greenfly. Maybe he was dead already. Maybe . . . the not-knowing was grinding me to paste.

Our time ebbed away, gobbled up by Jelly's interference.
Four days!
Three days!

'Two days, Moth. Two days and we absolutely have to go!' I groaned.

Moth proved stubborn. 'No, we'll wait for snow. Your original logic was sound. So what if Jelly does become Director? He'll have less time for us then!'

That floored me. 'But . . .'

'Listen!' Moth counselled. 'Even if what Jelly said is true, nothing happens overnight in official circles. Reports, inquiries, committees, it'll all take weeks. Days at least. And anyway, we're not ready. You know it.'

'But . . .' But I knew he was right. Jelly's attentions had seen to that.

'The weather is very cold now. The snow can't be far off,' Moth reassured me. 'We have the rope, the two sets of overalls each, the packaging material, the mittens, the balaclavas, the food, the plastic water bottles, the cutting glass . . .'

'The shoes, the socks, my little helpers,' I continued, thinking about the odd shapes I had cut from the aluminium can, 'our mattresses, blankets and the plastic sheets to wrap them with, the cord to tie them up with, the sticky . . . the adhesive tape.'

The empty plastic bottles were for our drinking water when on the march. These had been purchased with more of Moth's snacks. We had all these incriminating things stashed under the bunk, behind piles of Moth's books, underneath old clothes.

'All that's left is to cut the bars over the window –'

'What with? Toffee's got the blade now!' Moth reminded me. 'Thanks to you!'

'– and to carry on with our showers,' I said.

The Moth had told us that, even with our special clothes, plunging into the icy river might send us into shock and kill us instantly. He also said it was possible to train the body to withstand low temperatures by taking a cold shower every day. On this basis, we were forcing ourselves to endure a freezing shower each morning and gradually increasing the time we spent under it.

I got out of bed and put my ear to the cell door. A claviger's boots creaked by outside. Jelly's?

'Snow. For pity's sakes, snow!' I thought.

One day!

Zero days!

DJ-Day!

Chapter 9

The Giantess

On the third day, we rose at dawn, ate, and broke camp. I kept silent about the lights and the trembling ground of the night before. Even they were not my greatest immediate worry. That was a set of dainty shoe prints that ran in circles through the snow and mud around our bivouac. 'Not mine,' said Harete, and they were indeed too small to belong to any of us.

Odder yet, a chunk of Moth's food had been taken from his food bag, where he had dropped it outside the tent. We found the lump of food on the other side of the tent to the bag, untouched. 'Whoever it was, they've got standards,' Harete sniffed.

We coaxed our bodies into a laboured trot. We did not see the marshals that morning, and I hoped they had been dispersed and delayed by the hedges and the corpse orchard, but by then experience had schooled me to price my hopes cheaply.

'Pylon two-one-zero is our target,' I told the others, 'and Harete has to think of today's story.' The footprints bothered me, reminding me again of the botch-up we had made of our escape. Was the faceless Orion deliberately pulling his punches to extend our agony? The man was a sadist, if

Tulips' report was correct; it would be consistent with that. Were the prints made by a clumsy stagehand then, someone who'd strayed from behind the scenery and almost collided with the actors performing the farce?

I noticed that I was swaying slightly from side to side as I jogged along, more even than Harete with her wounded leg. Before we reached the first of the day's pylons my kidneys ached, my tongue burned and my head rang bright with a pitiless pain. By pylon three, after we had lumbered over a hedge using our mattress-and-rope technique, I was as giddy as one of the diseased cows.

'You need water,' said The Moth when we next rested. He handed me his bottle, the only one with anything left in it. I batted it away. 'Dehydration affects the brain,' he pointed out, 'affects decision making.'

'Oh, shut up, you scraggy delinquent!' I snapped.

'It is not I who am a delinquent,' he pointed out airily. 'I am most definitely linquent; my linquency has never once been questioned.'

When I tried to rise, the pains in my kidneys started to roast me from the inside and I fell back. This time, I accepted The Moth's water, and my eyes apologised for me.

Harete and The Moth laughed. 'Come on, chovie-chops!' Harete said, and to my shame I accepted her hand and we ambled along together, both limping. I felt much better for my drink, but we were now completely out of water and I knew we could not walk for much longer unless we found fresh supplies. Today there seemed to be no snow deep enough to collect and all the ditches were devoid of ice and water.

The helicopter from the night before was in flight again, criss-crossing the sky, visible as just a small, dark dot. Like a hornet drawn to the jam around a toddler's mouth, the machine would not let us alone. We concluded that it had not seen us, else it would surely have landed or directed people on the ground towards us, but every time the cloud thinned we were forced to shelter under the nearest pylon, each of us squeezing ourselves into the right-angled fold of a metal leg. Sometimes it flew low, the buzzing becoming a brain-peeling scream from the engines and a deeper, chest-thumping *whap-whap-whap* sound as its rotors flayed the air. Once, the aircraft hovered directly above the pylon we were quaking under, its black underside resembling the sole of a giant's boot about to stomp down and mash us, pylon and all.

'Run!' shouted Harete, struggling to her feet under the pressure of the downdraught and preparing to flee.

'No!' Moth waved to her. 'Stay, Harete! It can't get too near the pylons; it can't risk crashing into them!' he bellowed above the racket. The machine lifted and moved away, but continued to pester us at a distance for hours more.

During a lull in our aerial harassment came a new upset of a very different sort. Harete was off to one side, bad-temperedly pulling stones and thorns from her footwear, and Moth and I were lying low a short distance away. To relieve the pressure swelling inside me, I heaped onto Moth my secret about the death-wagon from the day before. News of the truck's cargo incited little outward reaction from Moth other than an outbreak of scratching. He either

198

did not believe me, did not care, or he already knew about it. The ring was another matter. I'd been wearing it for all the time the helicopter buzzed above us, foolishly imagining that it might act as a lucky charm and render us invisible. The silvery ring was very dirty, but clearly an object of substantial value, and was decorated with tiny pictures around its circumference. For proof of my claims, I took it off and showed it to him.

Moth blinked and recoiled as soon as I opened my hand. From the expression on his pasty face I might as well have been showing him a half-chewed rat's head on a string. He looked thoroughly discomforted, swallowing repeatedly and sweating.

'Huh! *That's* a ring that tells a story,' he sneered insincerely after some minutes. 'Not *such* a coincidence that it should turn up like that though, now that I think about it.'

'A ring that tells a story! What story?' I asked.

'The story of another ring, the Ring of Gyges,' he yawned, 'from Plato!' The yawn looked feigned.

'Play toe? Is that like thumb wrestling, Moth?'

'No! It's . . . never mind. Looks very much like my father's ring.'

'Your dad bought one like this, Moth?' I asked, disorientated by the twists of our strange conversation.

'He didn't buy it, no.'

'He stole it?' I laughed, profoundly perplexed. 'A judge on the rob?'

'Stupid! He had it made to commission. It was unique. He gave it to my mother to wear just before he was exiled.

Yes, I'm sure that's the exact same ring,' he said, studiously avoiding looking at me or the object in my palm.

I gawped. 'This ring . . . is your mother's?' I croaked.

Moth's face creased into a deep scowl. He looked fit to cry. 'Don't go on about it!' he snapped. 'I've told you before; I don't want anyone to talk about her!'

My shocks did not end there.

'At least it's all over now, the whole sordid business. Take that ring away, I never want to see it again!' he barked, his final statement.

I flopped at his side, open-mouthed. The Moth's reaction to news of his own mother's extermination left me baffled. He'd dismissed her death like it was a cheap, dirty secret accidentally exposed. She'd died because of us, because of his decision to escape! He must really believe he was one of the divine characters in his stories, aloof from normal human feelings.

'Well . . .' Moth started to speak again, but I rolled away from him and waited for Harete on my own, quaking with disgust and confusion. Any more talk on the matter would be likely to cause him to blow up again, like he had that night in the cell, and I didn't want us to be distracted by a fight. I was afraid I might lose my rag and really do him some harm.

It's true what they say, I thought bitterly. *You never really know your friends until you go travelling with them.* I threw stones at The Moth's back until Harete came over, and he never once said a word.

Soon, we were all walking again. The light snow turned to persistent sleet interspersed with shotgun blasts of hailstones. The milky fog returned, welcomed by us for the camouflage it provided, but hated for the heat it wicked away from us as its price. The fog sucked away colour and noise, made walking dreamlike.

Dogs.

We must have been dozing on our feet not to hear them. Three stocky black and yellow animals with heads like boxing gloves came bounding out of the mist to our rear. They homed in, growling and snarling, one well in advance of the others. We leapt over a large drainage ditch, but so did they. A bark boomed like a gravestone being dropped down a stairwell. Harete was the slowest, and the lead dog found her first. It opened wide its jaws and launched itself at her windmilling arm.

'Use this!' I shouted at Harete, and I threw her the can of de-icer. She caught it, and as the dog jumped she sprayed it in the eyes. It howled with pain and its teeth chomped down on nothing but air, then it skewed off to one side.

By chance, we were immediately under a pylon when the dogs began their next charge. I sprang up to grasp a cross-beam and wrapped my legs around it, then swung over to the top side. Harete gave Moth a leg-up into the framework, and started to haul herself up vertically after him, with me pulling Harete by her arms from above.

Hand over hand we ascended the metal tree. The dogs raised themselves onto their rear legs, scratching with their front paws at the metal and baying, leaving us to stare down the pink, ridged tunnels of their throats. The fog was so dense even the base of the pylon was invisible. From where we clung, it looked like there was only a single squirming

201

body from which any one of three sabre-filled heads would rise up and puncture the wet air, barking dementedly at being thwarted. Moth and I cringed and cried out with every bark; only Harete fought back. Holding onto a strut, she leant outwards and squirted blasts of the pungent spray down each salivating throat and into the dogs' faces.

'Haway!' she roared. 'Die, you tan dragons! Die!'

The dogs clearly detested the spray, and began to hesitate between attacks. The can was running dry by now though; Harete had to shake it between squirts.

'I'll force the tin down one of their throats!' she shouted across at me, oblivious to my petrified state. 'That'll choke one to death. Get your blade!' Her copper eyes glinted like a pair of polished bullets, her voice was level and commanding; if she'd ordered the pylon to jump it would have obeyed.

What a warrior! I thought. *How has it taken me so long to see? Something majestic hidden by something familiar . . .* Suddenly flustered, I tried to remember where the hacksaw blade was, grieved I'd not thought to use it myself.

'I'm slipping!' cried Moth. His grip was weak, he had only the edge of a vertical strut to grasp and his muddy shoes were skating along the horizontal girder he stood on. He stumbled into me and I lost my footing, then I bashed into Harete and she dropped the spray can. We barely managed to steady ourselves, and even Harete looked panicked.

Giving up on finding the blade, I readied myself to drop, preferring the hounds to the hunters. The dogs at least would not judge me.

From the unseen drainage ditch came a sound, a sound on the far limit of hearing, one that tickled the ear and scratched the brain. A new thing moved. Black, like the dogs, but otherwise different, sinuous and fluid. My mind clutched for a single word, a word that tried to frame the motion, but it returned with one that made no sense. *A seal*, it said. The half-poisoned dogs ceased barking, bewitched. They lunged after the moving shape as if it had been a cartload of prime steak, and scampered down into the ditch. *Snap-twang! Snap-twang!* Then, a horrible squeal, a whimper, and a gurgling sound. A third *snap-twang*, and more whimpering. We remembered the sound. Harete's leg remembered the sound.

Nothing happened for a while. Like autumn leaves, we dropped from the steel tree. Our awareness of the certain proximity of the dog's handlers overpowered our desire to seek out an explanation in the ditch, and we ran on, wailing with confusion, never once looking backwards. I thought back to my saying about what you needed to rescue you from a squeeze: a bolt from above – or an angel. The riddle provoked no debate amongst us, for discussion was subservient to our impulse to flee, and we each knew that none understood any better than the others.

We stopped under another pylon. On the run over, I'd returned to thinking about our increasingly urgent need for water. I freed one of the plastic sheets that covered my mattress roll. 'Take a corner, Harete – you too, Moth – and walk out into the open,' I told them. We stretched the sheet out between us and collected marble-sized hailstones in it, then poured them into a bottle. We filled half a bottle in this way, and immediately drank it all. The Moth then discovered he could make a decent bowl shape by holding his arms out in a circle in front of him and having Harete poke the plastic sheet into it. He then walked crab-like underneath the four lowest beams of the pylon, whilst Harete and I brushed all the droplets of water off them and into the bowl. This made another quarter bottle of clean, if rather metallic-tasting water. 'The pylons provide!' I laughed, pleased at our small triumph.

We walked on, of course. Despite the refreshment of the water and a bite of the nauseating, chewy fat, despite also our reprieve from the dogs, I still felt a caustic malaise gnawing at me. My muscles felt fine, even my feet were not too sore, so perhaps our bodies were growing hardened to the labour of walking over the rutted desolation. But I was flagging.

The sucking mud was draining my spirit, pulling me back to the Institute. As we walked between brown earth and white sky my mind was continually forced back to that place and our blighted lives there. Instead of keeping my eyes and ears open for the men to our rear I could think of nothing but the non-names of my enemies and allies: Jelly, Sticky, Tulips, Sphinx, Toffee and Retread . . . especially poor Retread. I would never be free. I was a clod briefly flung from its bulk and soon to be reabsorbed into the nameless, shapeless mass. I was from the Institute and was of it also; I carried not just its taint but its pith.

The hard lump of the ring pressed against me from inside my overalls and I thought again also of The Moth's mother. When they had learned of our escape, her government watchers must have become her killers, I reasoned, not wishing to risk her hearing of her son's freedom and spilling any secrets. I tried to imagine what sort of men could drag a woman from her home, chain her in that awful truck and drive her to a secret camp, there to slaughter her and torch her body.

But I could not empathise with them in any way, no more than I could with a stone, a pylon . . . or The Moth. He must have understood that my finding the ring meant his mother was dead! Yet he had shed no tears, only rankled at the dishonour of her unbecoming end and found relief that it was over. An idea dangled in front of me like the curled-up body of a dead spider: The Moth was just another fanatic, as callous and cruel as the people who currently ran our benighted country, as indifferent to the suffering of his own family as he had been to that of the cows. He cared only for the cracked bones of the past and some book-learned notion of justice. Was it worth Harete and me risking our lives to help him?

I heaped the idea up with my other worries, but did not forget it.

Whatever it was that affected me did not seem to trouble The Moth and Harete. I could barely keep ahead of them, even though Harete was dragging her bad leg. Although the overall lie of the land was still flat, the fields we were lumbering over dipped up and down steeply. On the long upward slopes it was Harete and The Moth who took the lead. Ridiculously, I felt angered and undermined by this. Previously, I had been incensed by their lack of urgency and the way in which they lagged behind me. Now, I began to worry what would happen if I became the laggard. Did The Moth even really need me? Would he sacrifice me to buy himself time? He hadn't minded his mother's death; mine would scarcely register. *Watch The Moth*, I warned myself.

Harete spoke, perhaps sensing my morose mood. 'Maybe now is a good time for my story. Let me tell it now, rather than when we make camp,' she suggested.

I consented, but only on the condition that we walked all the time. A brief scan through the heavy air confirmed we were not in immediate danger. I pictured the hindrance introduced to our hunters when some forward platoon discovered the dogs' bodies, but could not decide what change in their tactics it might induce.

Besides, no dogs or men or any other force could lessen our craving for the diversion the stories provided; they had become as vital to us as food. Our fears and worries were as constant as the mud, but true terror came only in brief snaps. The rest of the time we experienced only monotony and pain, and the stories were a salve for both complaints.

Harete started. 'A long, long time ago . . .' She stopped when she heard me and Moth tutting. 'Well, actually, it was yesterday. Yesterday, there was a little girl. Only, she wasn't little. She was big. In fact, she was a giantess, the only one in the land.

'But because she was still young, she was little in one sense. Hers was not a happy life. She had no friends, and not even a real name. Everyone just called her "Giantess". When she complained that it was not a proper name people said, "What does it matter? You are the only giantess around, so the word we use identifies you uniquely. A name has no other purpose." The giantess found this to be a very unsatisfactory answer.

'She was not an orphan, in case you were wondering. Her mother was an ogress who had far too many children to look after properly, and she had not one but two fathers, both of normal size.

'"I am so unhappy," she told her two fathers. "Because I am a giantess, everyone thinks I am oafish. Even though they have to crane their necks to speak to me, still they talk down to me. No one looks up to me, even though they all look up at me."

'Her two fathers discussed their daughter's unhappiness and decided to take her on a journey to the Land of the Giants, certain that she would be happier amongst people of her own size.

The giantess loved her fathers. One of them was very clever – he knew just about everything there was to know – but he could be a bit absent-minded. The other father was a very cunning and able man, and brave too. Once he killed a man—'

I stumbled, almost falling over. 'I never killed anyone!' I protested.

'Shhh! Don't interrupt my story!' said Harete. 'Once he killed a man-eating lion that was preying on the town where they lived.

'The three of them set off on their trek. The giantess walked, Clever Father rode on a mule and Cunning Father rode on a camel.

'Soon they came upon an enchanted valley. The walls of

the valley were impossibly high and sheer. As they proceeded along it, a warlock appeared. He made all the normal, tedious threats about how they were not allowed to pass unless they did his bidding, and seeing how otherwise impassable the valley was they reluctantly agreed to submit themselves to his conditions.

'The warlock produced a chess set. "To pass, you must beat me," he cackled. Clever Father dismounted from his mule and strode confidently across to take his seat opposite the wizard. "I shall accept the challenge on behalf of my family," he declaimed.

'But the warlock's moves confused Clever Father. He tried to play his best game, but the warlock kept capturing his pieces in peculiar ways.

'"You can't do that move in chess!" shouted Clever Father, "you're cheating!"

'"We're not playing chess. We're playing draughts," replied the warlock.

'"But . . . those are chess pieces," said Clever Father, aghast.

'"True, but the board is also a draughts board. I never said we were playing chess, you just assumed. And by falsely accusing me of cheating, you forfeit the game!" he laughed.

'"That's a bit unfair!" protested the giantess and the two fathers.

'"What isn't?" grumbled the warlock, looking a bit unhappy himself. "You think it's a great life being stuck in a valley, playing tricks on passers-by? I wanted to work in a zoo!"

'The warlock shuffled his feet and said, "However, I admit that was a bit sneaky, even by my standards. But it goes to show, no matter how clever you are it always pays to challenge your own assumptions. Tell you what: you two –" he pointed to the giantess and Cunning Father – "can pass, provided the gentleman who played me remains behind. His punishment will be to stay here for twelve years to teach my thirty-nine grandchildren how to tell the difference between left and right, right and wrong, and beauty and ugliness, using only pure algebra and the anatomy of the kraken for examples."

'"You are ill in your brain," said Clever Father. "That cannot possibly be done."

'"True! But think how much they will learn in the process!" gurgled the warlock. Having little choice, the party of travellers accepted the sorcerer's terms and moved on, leaving Clever Father and his mule behind.

'Rather glumly now, the two of them and the camel carried on for many more weeks. They came at last to a deep, sheer-sided ravine that stretched for many months' travel in either direction. A single bridge was slung across the ravine, and a shaman guarded the bridge.

'Cunning Father whispered to the giantess, "You know what happens next. He'll demand we pass some farcical test before he lets us across the bridge, but he'll trick us and I'll end up stuck here as his slave for a dozen years. Let's beat him at his own game."

'The giantess agreed. Using her strength, she piled boulders into the path of a nearby river and cut a channel to divert it into the ravine. The two then built a raft out of logs, and when the ravine was full of water they set the raft upon it and rowed across to the other side.

'"Ooh, you cheats!" shouted the shaman. But there was nothing he could do about it.

'As they passed alongside the bridge, Cunning Father spoke to the shaman. "Just out of interest, if we had wanted to cross by your rotten bridge, what task would you have set us?" he asked.

'"I would have asked you four riddles told me by the Potentate of the Pylons," replied the shaman. "Firstly, what sort of current would it be dangerous to eat?" the shaman challenged.

'"An electric current," answered Cunning Father.

'"Correct! Secondly, what sport would an electrician excel at?"

'Cunning Father thought hard. "The pole volt!" he shouted.

'"Also correct! Thirdly, what did the electrician's mother say to him when he did not return to his house until after midnight?"

'Both the giantess and Cunning Father pondered this. The giantess clicked her fingers and ventured, "Wire you insulate?"

'"Excellent!" said the shaman. "Your final question: what does the opposite of its name to save a life?"

'"A fuse!" said Cunning Father. "For to 'fuse' means to join, but the device actually breaks in order to protect!"

'"Right again!" said the shaman. "You see, there was no need to swindle me at all! Think of all the work you would have saved yourselves! Too cunning for your own good, that's what you are!"

'Cunning Father and the giantess ignored him. When

they reached the other side of the ravine they abandoned the raft and climbed up the rocky slope. But tragedy struck: the camel kicked a rock which tumbled down the mountainside and this started an avalanche that swept Cunning Father away. He was horribly smashed by the bouncing rocks and died instantly.

'The giantess was very sad. She and the camel walked on, still hoping to find the Land of the Giants. The shaman turned out to be a complete stinker because he sent a series of foes to attack them. Firstly, he sent a huge lizard, as big as a bus, to chase them. The lizard was like a chameleon, forever changing colour to blend into its surroundings. The camel soon fell prey to the lizard and was eaten up. The giantess fled into the cold mountains, the lizard chasing her all the while. She spotted a cave set into a glacier and an idea came to her. "I am weak," she thought. "And my enemy is strong. So he must be undone not by my powers, but by his own." Entering the cave, she used her hands to polish smooth the cavern's icy walls and floor and roof. She called to the lizard to come and eat her, and the vast beast lumbered greedily forwards, its tongue flickering in and out. When it entered the cave, it stopped. All it could see in the polished ice around itself was its own reflection. It tried to change colour to match itself, but soon got into a terrible muddle. Each time it changed colour, so did its reflection. The lizard stood still and its skin pulsated through every colour of the rainbow. Eventually, it overheated and died.

'The giantess next had to contend with a huge lyrebird which the shaman dispatched to torment her. The bird was vast, and a superb mimic. Every time the giantess shouted at the bird and told it to stop pecking at her, it copied her voice perfectly and taunted her with it endlessly. Maddened by the ceaseless mimicking, the giantess ran into the scrublands. She found a huge, solid cliff and took refuge at the foot of it. When the bird came into range, she shouted at it, "Go away!"

'"Go away!" repeated the lyrebird, much louder. The cliff wall echoed back the lyrebird's voice. The bird was compelled to copy the voice it heard, and so it echoed the echoes. Soon, it was trapped at the foot of the cliff, endlessly repeating its own echoes. In the end, the constant noise caused the cliff to resonate and shake, and a boulder toppled from its lip and crushed the bird into a pulp.

'The shaman then sent a vulture and an eagle to hunt the giantess. The eagle was a supremely good hunter with terrifyingly good vision. Being a hunter of live prey it attacked only things that moved, so the giantess had to stay completely still to avoid being ripped by the bird's talons. However, the vulture also had excellent vision. Eating only carrion, it was attracted to any creature that remained still, so the giantess had to keep moving in order to be safe from its sharp beak. This meant she was attacked day and night, whether she ran or rested.

'The giantess was hugely vexed by these two foes, but she kept faith with her earlier idea. She lay still on the ground and jerked her limbs around. This attracted both birds, for she was still enough to make the vulture think she was a dying animal, and moving enough for the eagle to think she was still alive. When both birds were within reach, she leapt up and tied a strap from the dead camel's harness to one foot of each bird.

'The two birds could not now separate. When the eagle flew off, it saw the vulture move too as it was dragged into the air and, obeying instinct, attacked it. When the eagle rested from the battle, the vulture saw it as a still, dead creature and attempted to eat it. The two birds soon clawed and bit each other to death, and the giantess was free to travel on.

'Months later, she saw other giants and giantesses working and living in the farms around her. She asked them if they knew the way to the Land of the Giants, but they all scratched their heads and denied knowledge of such a place. The giantess soon realised why. To test out her theory, she asked them if they knew the way to the Land of the Midgets, and they all pointed back in the direction she had come from, some years before. She settled down in the Land of the Giants, or the Land of the People as she had to learn to call it, and was made a citizen.

'Now grown up, the giantess – which is how she still thought of herself – decided to seek out a mate. She journeyed a short distance to the Land of the Pylons, ruled by the legendary Potentate and his son, the Pasha. In accordance with the custom of this land, she went out into the countryside where the Pylon men lived. She found them, standing in a long line which stretched from horizon to horizon.

'The men all stood perfectly still with their arms stretched out wide either side of them, each one just touching his neighbours' outstretched fingertips. She went along the line for many days, seeing how fertile and verdant the ground was beneath each Pylon man's legs, as this was an indication of the man's suitability as a husband. On the seventh day, she found a Pylon that had long, lush grass and an abundance of thistles underneath his feet and many birds roosting on his strong body. The Pylon man said nothing, he just went on humming the same song as all the other men in his line. She curled up and went to sleep in the prickly grass, which was the custom for getting married in that peculiar place. The end.'

Moth and I looked at each other in awe as we trudged in step, side by side.

'Great story, Harete! I loved it!' I exclaimed. 'Moth, it knocked your dull old tale out of the window. No judges, for one thing!' I added.

'Yes, I concede defeat. Your story was very good, Harete. The best of all three,' he said.

'How come you know so much about electricity, Harete? You know, those riddles?' I asked.

'My mum was an electrician, before she died,' Harete explained.

'How did she die?'

'She was electrocuted. Not her fault – she was working on a ship. Someone had put in inferior equipment and it didn't work and she got killed. Probably someone high up had been given the money to buy the proper gear, but they had ordered cheap rubbish and pocketed the difference. My mum said it used to happen all the time.'

'Oh. I'm sorry,' I mumbled. We broke march for a rest, and crumpled under the next pylon, still savouring Harete's story.

'Why do threats always come in threes in stories? You

214

know, the lizard, the lyrebird, the eagle and the vulture,' I wondered out loud.

'That's four, not three,' corrected Moth.

'No, three, the last two were really the same threat. I don't know. I do wish real life was as predictable though,' Harete said.

'It was a bit rude towards the end, I thought,' I said, blushing slightly.

Harete laughed. 'You dummy! I am nearly old enough to have children myself.'

To make her blush in return, I told her what a hero she'd been with the dogs, and how stupendously glad I was that she was with us, and how, despite the best efforts of her ragged overalls and her crook leg to obscure it, I'd noticed a captivating, lithe character to her movements. And that I'd only just then noticed that I'd noticed. For good measure, I threw in that when she looked at me, the way the flesh of her face, sallow and travel-ravaged though it was, dressed the bones beneath, the pylon inside her . . . well, it . . . it intrigued me.

Absolutely all these things I said, but not out loud. I squashed the words under my tongue and they dissolved in my bloodstream like nitrogen.

I wanted to have another go, but Moth asked Harete about her father. Harete told us how he'd tried to organise their tenement against the Lollipop Men barking brown-out powder and sleep-leaf opposite the school gates, and how he'd been in a phone booth and they'd rolled a car against the door so he couldn't get out and poured petrol into the booth and set it alight. She'd watched it all happen, unable to help, had seen the crisped skin lifting from his ballooning hands as he pounded the kiosk windows, remembered his shoes melting in the heat and the way the fat and plastic oozed out through the gap under the door.

This news Harete delivered with complete calmness, and I am certain that whilst the words had been gone over many times to winnow from them all bitterness and to leave the truth stark and imposing, no one had heard them before. Hers was the statement of a witness forever denied a hearing. Burned alive . . . little wonder the kerosene-drenched cattle had upset her so much. I didn't trouble to ask what had happened afterwards. The Lollipop Men and the Dinner Ladies and all the other street-cliques are tendrils of the Guilds; they'd have paid off the marshals and carried on as before.

Harete stopped walking, put her hands on The Moth's shoulders and said, 'It won't be like that in the Other country, will it? You've told us enough times how much better everything is there.'

'Have faith in that!' Moth replied, taking a deep, lecture-threatening breath. 'The quality of jurisprudence –'

'Prudence be damned, it's us three I care about,' laughed Harete. She shone her eyes above our heads for a long moment as if they were tapping into a force that ran along the blue horizon. 'Think of it, boys,' she began, 'a fighting chance for a true life at last. We're going to a place where peace and opportunity are as plentiful as mint and sugar. Maybe soon it will be *our* turn to play amongst the lawns and lakes, wanting for nothing but the willows' shade.'

Moth's features gathered around the bridge of his nose

like someone had yanked on a drawstring. 'Steady on, Harete. I never said we'd be living in luxury,' he cautioned her. 'Or even that it would be warm.'

'Oh, Mothy,' Harete said, still chuckling, but serious with it. 'I meant only that . . . that our youth won't be frittered away. When sweet spring finally comes, we'll be free to fold her into our hearts and rejoice like all young people should. Never again will we be forced to scratch about in filth and misery until ground down by sharp-heeled hatred!' Harete's face glowed as she spoke so exultantly, and her laugh came with a wide smile that was directed, I am positive, at me alone.

That sunburst smile catalysed in me an audacious hope: *Harete wanted me to be her pylon, the one in whose arms she would rest!* Up until then, the Other country had meant nothing more to me than a place of probable safety for myself and somewhere Moth – insensitive, masonry-hearted Moth, as I had learned that morning – could yak legend and law until his tonsils rebelled and unscrewed his tongue from his mouth. After Harete's fine talk of spring, I was overcome with an unfamiliar turbulence that emanated from within. Something perfectly wonderful lay awaiting me over the frozen horizon, I realised, not merely an end to the mud and cold, but something sublime and burgeoning with life.

And with Harete beside us on the journey, we had every chance of success. Tough as a terrapin! Brave as a whale! Wild as a wolverine! Our three-strand braid was unbreakable, and she was its titanium core. And once in that far place, she and I . . . the smile's spark landed amidst the dry bracken of my imagination. Busy with being gallant in my fantasy, I put off informing Harete of her leading role in my affections.

We resumed the walk, my mood transformed. The mud's crumbling tentacles still tugged at me with every laboured stride, but I felt able to pull free and set my mind fully to the task in hand. Not only were we almost out of drinking water, we now faced another problem: what little food remained was becoming inedible.

'It's all melted,' I said, holding up my food bag. Our neatly scored blocks of fat had degenerated into a gloopy mass, much like the mud we travelled through. We'd been in the habit of storing the food bags tucked inside our overalls to prevent them from freezing, but we had not reckoned on just how warm this was making them.

The liquefied food made us even thirstier, and as we set off on the final leg of the day's hike we were all well aware of the urgent need for more water. There was only a slight drizzle, not enough to collect in a sheet like we had done before, and a fresh breeze dried all the droplets off the pylons.

At pylon two-one-two we wearily vaulted across a drainage ditch that had a trickle of dark brown water running along the bottom. In the fading light, we decided to take a chance on it. Harete dipped her empty plastic bottle into the ditch and filled it up. The water was dark brown in colour and full of bits of plant debris.

'Wait,' I said. From my overalls I produced my own empty bottle, and a spare, dry sock.

'Let's filter it,' I suggested. I poked the sock into the

neck of my bottle, and proceeded to tip the water from Harete's bottle into the sock. Slowly, I filled up the part of the sock that protruded into my bottle, let the water run through the material, then refilled it. Every three fills I pulled the sock out, flicked away the bits of twigs and mud, and poked a fresh bit of sock in. After many minutes, we had about two-thirds of a bottle of light-brown water. We passed the bottle around and drained it, but it tasted earthy and sharp.

The final pylon of the day lay before us in the dusk, at the crest of a slight slope. My throat burned with thirst. Catching my breath, I paused just before starting up the final slope. There was more dirty water in a large puddle at my feet. I stared into the water, wondering if it was better to drink from puddles than from ditches. The lack of food I could accept, but to be running short of water in this wet, soggy landscape – that was ridiculous!

Ripples broke the puddles' surface. *Rain!* I thought, and craned my broiling head up to catch some cooling droplets. But no drops fell. I looked again at the rippling puddle, not understanding. I gestured to the others. 'Quiet! Stand still!' I demanded.

A deep, rumbling sound rose from the somewhere in the distance, a sound like a regiment of soldiers all clearing their throats at once. The puddle shimmied again, and this time we could all feel the ground jounce. Another huge, distant cough and now a grating, clanking sound with it.

Together we dashed to the crest of the rise and ducked behind the pylon's leg. I looked to the south and saw the evening sky there sliced through with searchlight beams.

'They're here,' I said hoarsely. 'They've almost found us. They've given up on the infantry and sent in the tanks!'

The three of us hurriedly pushed our way into the damp grass underneath the pylon and lay down flat on our stomachs. Fortunately, this was a pylon with a good growth beneath its feet. I clenched my teeth and hoped it would make as good a haven for us as it would have a husband for the giantess. The mechanical growling grew, subsided, grew again. We craned our necks but could not identify the cause of the noise. Beams of light thrust vertically into the sky then shone horizontally, almost straight at us. I peered through my fingers towards them and thought I saw someone backlit by the dazzle, a figure flitting across their path, but when I looked again it was gone. My stagehand?

'Still some distance . . . not quite here yet,' I said. I pulled out the plastic sheet and covered us in it. We wriggled our bodies together under it, trying to make ourselves as small as possible. 'We can't risk making camp. Lie as still as you can and try to sleep. If they come, I'll hold them off and you two make a break for it. Split up and run in opposite directions,' I instructed. I took out the largest glass shard and placed it where I could grab it easily. I tried to imagine how I could wrestle a dog, grab it by its head and slash its throat. A man's, too?

'How can you fight against men with guns! Don't be such a brainless dolt!' hissed Harete.

'Look at us! We all look the same, in these filthy plastic rags and overalls. They won't shoot because they daren't risk killing Moth,' I told her. Her insult didn't prick; this was a new chance to prove my metal to her.

My heart revved. Everything was good now, simple and clear. The dragging mud of the morning was gone; my mind was as tense and live as the power cables straining in the breeze above our heads.

The noises and lights came closer. There were four, maybe five clusters of them. 'Five groups of marshals . . . each with a truck or maybe a tank, something big anyway, searching in this direction, sweeping from left to right,' I mouthed. 'Sleep, or at least rest. I'll keep first watch and we'll swap later on. On my signal, you run,' I said.

Chapter 10

The Escape

The month ended, a new one began. Nothing happened, or at least, nothing we were aware of. No announcements came about Sticky or Jelly. We were on borrowed time; the countdown went negative.

'It could all happen any day now; we'll never know!' I said angrily to Moth. Life beyond the deadline was more nerve-strangling than the days leading up to it had been. I felt I was being hanged already, dangling by my neck from a rope jointly held by Jelly and Sticky.

Tick-tock, tick-tock; even with no timepieces available to us, I was constantly aware of the passing of the days and the hours, constantly clockwise.

'Please relax!' Moth replied, his answer to everything during these anxious days. But he was wringing his hands all the time too, as badly bitten by stage fright as I was.

We carried on with the work. My first job was to saw through the hinge struts of the opening upper section of our cell window. That was to allow the narrow window to open much wider than it was designed to do. I retrieved the snapped-off half of the hacksaw blade from where I had hidden it, inside a slit made in my mattress. That had been my plan all along, to deliberately sacrifice half the blade in order to neutralise the rumours that Moth and I were up to something. Ever since his well-broadcast success in taking the blade from me, it had been Toffee who had been hounded and attacked for that valuable artefact, not us. Keeping all this secret even from Moth had been a necessary precaution.

The thin steel struts yielded easily with just a few strokes. Once cut, the top part of the window could be pushed right out, slightly beyond the horizontal.

Our confidence boosted by the ease of that job, we set about the much tougher one of sawing through the two hefty, vertical steel bars which lay between us and the window. Some test strokes made with the blade against the bars at night told me that this would not be a trivial task. The blade would penetrate the bars, but it made a very distinctive noise: the sound of metal being sawed! Looking closely, I could see that the blade itself vibrated during the cutting action, and that those vibrations were responsible for the noise. In an effort to dampen these vibrations I made two handles for the hacksaw blade by wrapping layers of the sticky tape around either end. I found that if I held the blade firmly at both ends using the 'handles' and kept it taut, pressed hard but dragged it slowly across the bar, then the noise was considerably reduced.

Whilst I sawed, Moth kept watch at the cell door through the peephole, the external cover of which I had managed to snap off. From the inside, the field of view through the slit was very limited and Moth had instead to rely on his hearing to tell if a claviger was nearby. The clavigers' squeaky leather boots on the hard, polished floors assisted greatly in this, as did their various habits of jangling keys, whistling or yawning. At night, one claviger patrolled all the cells on three floors in our wing, but they did not do so continually. In the main, they sat at a wooden desk and read newspapers. At the first indication of a claviger walking along our corridor we would both leap back into our bunks and pull the blankets over ourselves. In this painstaking way I managed to cut about half the way through one end of one bar every night. At the end of each night's work, I had to disguise the cut I had made. For this, I made a mixture of toothpaste, the metal filings from the cut itself and either shoe-polish or ink from one of Moth's pens. I mixed up the black goo and packed it into the cut in the bar using my finger. Unless you looked very closely, it was impossible to tell that the steel had been damaged at all. The paste was easily scraped out again at the start of the next night's sawing.

As always, I had thought deeply about every step. Rather than making the cuts horizontal, which would have meant cutting through the smallest amount of metal, I made the cuts to each bar at an angle. The cut at the top of the bar sloped down towards the cell door, the cut at the bottom of the bar sloped down towards the window. This was so that when at last I had cut a bar free, I could jam it back into place (aided by the paste) and it would just sit there. Had the cuts been flat, it may have wobbled out, and certainly would have come free if tugged. Because of the way I had angled my incisions, the cut bars could actually be pulled forwards with some force and show no indication of being loose. If a claviger ever did test a window bar for looseness, that was the way he did it: by pulling it towards him.

Eight days into the new month, I finished work and pasted back into place the right-hand bar, now free top and bottom, as was its neighbour. My arms ached, and now my fear ramped up several more notches. So far, it had all been playing: making silly costumes, stealing rubbish, hoarding food scraps. Now, we had a cell with removable bars and a window that opened wide enough to get a boy out, and a rope to lower him to the ground. My body tingled with excitement, and sleep was impossible.

At the same time, Harete was having to make her own preparations. The need to co-ordinate her escape with ours was a substantial and unwelcome complication to my plans, and since I had no access to her quarters it was left to her to work out how to manage this. Fortunately, security for the wards was much slacker than for The Moth and me. After all, in theory they were in the Institute because they had nowhere else to go, so there was less need to ensure that they remained under lock and key.

Harete had kept us informed of her progress. The dormitory she slept in was on the other side of the Institute to ours, and its windows did not open wide enough to slip through. Careful reconnaissance had shown her that the best window to escape from was that of a small room used by the janitors to store bottles of disinfectant and mops. This window was on the ground floor, opened wide (she had seen it open) and faced the correct way. It was accessed via a door leading from the lavatories in her wing, a door that was always locked up with a padlock.

To overcome this, I taught Harete the use of my special little items, those odd rectangular shapes I had cut from a flattened-out aluminium drinks can. Based on her description of the padlock's dimensions, I selected what I judged to be the most appropriate of the three objects I had made. 'Take the metal strip and bend it around the shackle, on the side which goes in and out of the padlock body,' I began.

'The shackle?' asked Harete.

'That's the U-shaped bit of metal,' I explained. Then, 'Make sure the triangle is pointing downwards. Now, pulling the metal strip tightly so that it hugs the shackle, work the triangle down so that it goes into the hole where the shackle enters the body. Work it down, twist it about. With patience, you should feel a "click" and the padlock can be pulled open.'

Harete managed to use the technique and on her third go – not bad for a beginner, I was impressed – she had the padlock open. She greased the inside of the padlock with a little bit of our lardy food to lubricate it, and over the course of a week made sure she could reliably pop the lock open with just half a minute's work. Then, on several successive days, she crept to the toilets, opened the lock, and stashed in the storeroom most of her own escape equipment, that is to say her waterproofs, a spare mattress stolen from the bed of a girl who had recently left, a second set of overalls, mittens, balaclava and food bag.

More trips to the storeroom were needed in order for her to remove a metal grille screwed over the inside of the window frame. I loaned her the hacksaw blade and she was able to use the rounded end of this as a primitive screwdriver, loosening the screws sufficiently that they could be removed by hand. All this took time, and most of The Moth's final parcel of chocolate bars and biscuits too, these being used by Harete to bribe other girls to acts as lookouts for her.

'Clever! You've the guile and guts of a bank robber!' I laughed when she breathlessly reported all this to me the next day, the day I had finished cutting our cell window bars.

Together, we discussed the tricky matter of timing our final escape. We held a long conference in my and The Moth's cell after dinner.

Harete described her plan. 'I can only be away from my bed at night for thirty minutes – that's the longest we're allowed to be in the toilets without them checking up,' Harete told us. 'What I'll do is wrap my overalls around my waist, hang my shoes around my neck on a length of cord, and wrap myself in my blanket. I'll shuffle out and ask to go to the toilet – it's usual for us girls to wrap up like that if we have to go in the night. I can probably get away with a few more minutes if I tell the matron on duty I've got pains down below.'

'Down below what?' asked The Moth, but I silenced him with a glare.

I posed the key question of the meeting. 'The problem is: how do we know when to leave? I mean, on whatever night we choose, Moth and I have to leave the cell at such a time that we can be outside that storeroom window of yours when you are there, dressed and ready to leave. But how do we know when that is?'

This was the problem. With no watches or clocks – Moth

and me in our cell, Harete in her dorm – we had no way of synchronising our activities, no way of signalling to each other.

'We'll have to use the early morning shift change,' I said. At some time in the early hours of the morning, I would guess about two o'clock, the clavigers changed shifts. The ones who had been on duty handed over to a new team. If we kept our ears to the door we could tell when this happened because there was always a lot of key jangling, footsteps and some audible banter as the tired claviger chatted with the new one before bicycling home. Harete confirmed that her clavigers, or matrons as she called them, also swapped over a while after midnight.

'But we don't know that your matrons and our clavigers swap over at the same time,' pointed out Moth. 'If they work different shifts, there could be an hour or more between them.'

That would be death to our plans.

'I have an idea,' Moth said. He had me cut two strips of cardboard, each about as long as my forearm. 'Your dormitory faces south, Harete, since it's on the other side of the Institute from ours. You can see the moon from your window?' he asked.

'Yes . . . yes, sometimes,' she said.

'Good. Tonight, as soon as the shift change happens, get out of bed, go to a window and do this. Hold the cardboard out at arm's length and close one eye. Place the strip upright so that the bottom of it rests, or looks like it rests, on the top of the perimeter wall. Not on the barbed wire, but the stone. Slide your thumb up until the bottom of your thumbnail just touches the bottom of the moon. Put a little tear in the cardboard at exactly that point. The moon is almost full now, and it looks like it will be a cloudless night. Then return the cardboard to me.'

He coloured one end of the cardboard as being the 'wall end' and handed it to a perplexed Harete.

The Moth and I then sought out someone from our block whose cell faced south. One of the neighbours of Moth's original cell was prepared to oblige us for the cost of two more biscuits. We made sure that his arms were the same length as Harete's, repeated the instructions to him, and handed him the second cardboard strip. 'It's for a science experiment,' Moth explained to the boy.

The next morning, we collected the two strips. Moth placed them side by side and noted that the nicks made were at approximately the same distance from the bottom of each strip.

'Not very precise, but it's an indication.'

'Of what?' I asked. This latest piece of Mothery was a mystery to me.

'Both Harete and Wambo have arms the same length. If they carried out my instructions properly – and Wambo is a boy of some diligence – they have each measured the apparent distance from the top of the perimeter wall to the bottom of the moon at the shift-change time. The wall is of even height, runs along flat ground, and is about the same distance from our block and Harete's block. Since the marks they made are at about the same place, we know that each of them saw the moon in the same place relative to the top of the wall. And since the moon travels in an arc, from east to west, its height above the horizon changing as it does so, that means that Harete's matrons and our clavigers must have changed shift at about the same time. *Quod erat demonstrandum!*'

'I'll take your word for it,' I said. When I thought about it a little later it did begin to make sense to me, especially once I drew a little picture.

All this having been done, we needed only to choose a day to make our break. It couldn't come soon enough for me.

The weather had turned truly cold, the skies were overcast almost every day and grains of snow buzzed in the air when we gathered outside for work or free association. But this was not enough. I needed a night when it was going to snow heavily.

I needed the snow to cover our footprints between the wall and the river. Everything in my plan relied upon the authorities believing we had somehow travelled south, and a trail of footprints going through the woods and to the river would wreck that. But how could we tell when it was due to snow? We had no access to the weather forecasts. I briefed my team on clues to look out for.

Then it happened. Harete scooted towards us in the courtyard one afternoon. 'I've seen it, I've seen it!' she panted. Moth was with me, on a rare excursion from our cell to get some fresh air and assess the weather.

'Tell me exactly what you've seen,' I said, holding her steady. This was important, I needed a precise report.

'Working in kitchens . . . two clavigers . . . came to the

dry goods lock-up . . . took out bags of salt, three, maybe more,' she gasped.

'What size bags?'

'Big. Sacks. You know, bigger than a pillow.'

'And they took them where?'

'I don't know! Out! Also . . . there are no bikes by the gate house,' she gulped, fully aware of the significance of that final report.

That was the clincher, the clue I'd been seeking. Most clavigers bicycled between the town and the Institute. No bikes meant that the forecast had been for heavy snow. On those days, I knew from overheard conversations between our guards, fleets of buses were put on to ferry the staff to and fro. The salt must have been taken out to grit the paths and courtyard, something I had seen before on icy days.

'Tonight!' I said.

'Tonight!' said Moth.

'Tonight!' Harete acknowledged, and ran back to her block.

'Tonight? What's tonight?' said Jelly. We spun round. There he was again, my uniformed shadow, my blue curse. How did he move so silently?

'Oh, hullo, sir . . . yes, tonight, we think it's going to snow. Do you think it will snow, sir?' I said.

Jelly fixed his face on mine and slowly turned his head from side to side. It meant nothing, I knew that by now. The man's body language was as contradictory as his monologues.

'Doing your B-Wing tonight, eight six five. Be able to keep my eye on you!' he said with glee. My heart crashed to my boots. That was all we needed. When Jelly was patrolling at nights he always kept looking in on us – or rather, on me – through the peephole. This was beyond a disaster, it was a catastrophe. Much worse, there was no way I could cancel the plan now, Harete had already gone back to her dorm. We could not possibly get a message to her. If she made herself ready for the break and we failed to meet with her because Jelly was stationed outside our door, she'd be caught for sure!

'Oh, that's nice, sir,' I lied. 'First or second shift?'

Jelly bridled. 'That would be an operational matter, eight six five! You know perfectly well that we do not discuss such matters with the likes of you. Learned that habit from the army!'

Despite having told me before that his only previous job was in a factory, Jelly's claims to have served in the armed forces had since escalated. Sometimes he had stories of his time in the army, sometimes the navy, and on occasion he boasted of flying jets. The transparency of his lies never bothered him in the least.

'Although, as it happens, I shall be doing a double shift tonight,' he said airily. He turned and marched off. Moth, understanding how bad the situation was for Harete, let out a long, low moan.

'A double shift! That means that even if he isn't watching us all the time, we won't know when shift change is!' he cried. 'We can't go tonight! But we can't stop Harete!'

Jelly had completely killed all our enthusiasm for the escape. We were doomed. I felt sick. My throat was tight and I tasted vomit.

Far worse was to come. As soon as we began walking back to our cell for the night, fretting over Jelly, a group of young kids hared past us from the direction of our block shouting, 'Cell out! Cell out!' We broke into a run, and it was as bad as we feared. Along every corridor in the block clavigers were emptying out cells, throwing the contents into the landing and removing anything that was not strictly permitted. It was pandemonium, with kids arguing with clavigers, clavigers hitting out at kids, and piles of stuff everywhere underfoot. Some clavigers were busily scooping up armfuls of whatever had been confiscated and were stuffing it into sacks marked 'incinerator'. I saw grubby soft toys, books, handmade chess sets, clothes, letters from home, food, family photographs, favourite blankets (crusty where boys had been sucking the corners), dirty magazines and collections of cigarette ends – the treasured, personal possessions of boys, hoarded and hidden from bullies and Sticky – all condemned to the flames.

We raced up the iron stairway to our own floor, and saw that our cell, along with its neighbours, was receiving the same treatment. Our time had run out; Moth's brief absence from our cell had been all the excuse they'd needed.

Two clavigers – Uncle Bludgeon and The Sniff – were pulling out all our gear from under our beds and from inside the corner cupboard and roughly sorting through it. 'Chuck! Chuck! Chuck!' The Sniff droned, flicking dismissively with his club through our waterproofs, our bags of food. Moth appealed, playing on his special status, but his pleas had no effect. The only break we had was that the clavigers did not think to look behind a row of books on Moth's shelf, so the rope and a few other items were saved. The confiscated material was dragged off, we were herded into our cell and the door locked for the start of what should have been our last night in the Institute.

The crushing disappointment was a small thing besides the danger we were now in. If we did not break out that night, Harete, waiting in the storeroom, was certain to be caught. Her own equipment would betray her intentions, and it would be obvious to even the most sludge-brained claviger that she'd been expecting the arrival of accomplices. I fumed to myself, for I had never forgiven Moth for involving Harete, and now his sentimentality had endangered both her and us. We conducted a hurried inventory and learned that our stocks of equipment were depleted to a ludicrous degree. We had our two sets of overalls (because we were wearing them), our rope, our mattresses, the empty soup can, two lengths of electrical flex and the plastic sheets we'd pretended were needed in case Moth wet the bed. No bubble-plastic for insulation, no mittens, no balaclavas, no waterproofs, no spare socks, no drinking bottles. No food. Even my tobacco tin was lost.

'That's that, then. That's *that*!' I said, angrily slinging the rope under my bunk. 'We either stay and Harete gets the chop, or we rescue her and freeze or starve to death!' I said and waited, making sure Moth understood the choice that faced us. 'Which is it to be, Moth?'

'Freeze and starve,' he said immediately. 'A chance is a chance, and maybe one of us will live.'

I patted him on his shoulder. Suicide is not my thing, but I felt so fused and primed with hate for the clavigers and

234

the Institute that night that the idea held a novel appeal. To die trying, it seemed to me then, would constitute a fitting protest and a noble victory.

We calmed down and lay quietly on our bunks. I quarried my memories in a search for anything else I'd ever done that bore a glaze of nobility, but I came up empty-handed. From my shoe I pulled the crumpled page that showed the map of the lands to the north. Moth took down from the wall his drawing of a centaur, his favourite sketch, and we each idly studied our personal obsessions for the final time, then nodded off.

Hours later, half-awake, I heard the claviger on duty moving along the corridor, locking each cell door in turn. Without even looking I knew from the squeak of the boots that it was Jelly.

'Good evening, eight six five,' he said, with disgusting cheerfulness, as he poked his head round our cell door. 'I've saved you till last!' he breezed. Then, rather than just pulling the door shut and locking it, he came into our cell and sat down on my bunk next to me. At once, I was more alert than if a ravenous panther had been admitted to the room. I noticed the map was still on my bed. I swept it off with my leg and it fluttered to the ground, landing upside down.

Moth sat bolt upright on his upper bunk, dropping his own picture. There we were, with the bars to our window cut and just resting in place, our rope barely concealed under the bunk, and we had a claviger in our cell trying to make small talk.

'Yes . . . thought I'd come for a chat. No hurry, nothing to do now all evening.' He smirked.

I grunted. I knew being uncommunicative was the thing Jelly liked least, but I despised him so much at that moment I did not care about angering him.

He started on one of his monologues, one I had heard almost verbatim on at least two occasions before. On and on he droned about the importance of physical exercise and a regular training regime, about how we'd all be doing them every day, all day when he was in charge. As to the likelihood of that event occurring, he made no comment.

The conversation lurched from the tedious to the horrific when he made me try some press-ups on the cell floor. I managed five.

'Rubbish!' shouted Jelly. He rolled up his sleeves and moved to get down on the floor and show me how press-ups should be done. That was the moment of absolute crisis – if he got onto the cell floor he absolutely could not fail to see the rope stowed under my bunk.

Moth interrupted from the bunk above. 'Are you doing both shifts tonight, sir?' he asked.

Jelly, about to get into position for his demonstration, halted and looked up.

'What? Oh . . . four four seven A. Yes. What business would that be of yours?'

That was Moth's number, the final 'A' meaning 'attendee'.

'It's just that . . . well, it's forecast to snow heavily tonight, sir. That means, if you don't leave until mid-morning, after a double shift, then the roads might be blocked. So you might have to sleep here in the staff accommodation unit.'

'So?' said Jelly. 'We do have facilities here for staff who are unable to return to their billets. What of it?'

'Well, I was just wondering if you had remembered to turn off the water in your flat at home, sir. If you end up trapped by the snow here for several days, your water pipes might freeze and your flat would flood,' Moth went on.

Jelly stared at Moth for several minutes, his face showing no sign of even having heard the boy. Finally, Jelly spoke. 'Excellent. You see, eight six five, that's the sort of forward thinking you need if you want to be in the special forces!' He stood up, walked out through the door and locked it behind him.

I collapsed back onto the bunk, drained. 'Moth . . . you are a . . . genius!' I croaked. 'He'll cancel his second shift!'

'We can't trust what he says,' Moth said. 'We still don't know if he's doing a single shift or a double.'

My sickness and depression dissolved, excitement flooded back, despite the near ruination of our plans. 'No falling asleep now,' I whispered to Moth.

'As if!' replied Moth. I heard him break wind noisily.

'Nervous?' I giggled. We lay awake, my heart clanging away under my ribs like all the cell doors of the Institute being synchronously opened and slammed.

Midnight came – we knew because there was an audible, albeit very brief, ring on the bell. This should have been the time for us to put on the layers that would have protected us from the cold and wet, but without our equipment we had little left to do. I kept an ear to the door, and Moth started to make up his pack. He placed his folded blanket on his foam mattress, rolled it into a tube, then wrapped the tube with layers of plastic sheeting. This he lashed around with lengths of electrical flex. Then he made my pack in the same way, remembering to leave out my blanket. He moved the table underneath the window. He took out my hacksaw blade and put it on the table with the soup can.

We got back into our bare beds, and waited. 'Please, please change shift,' I kept repeating, my insides bouncing.

Time seemed to have a different nature now, neither fast nor slow. My senses were super-tuned; it seemed as though I could hear every sneeze and groan and snore from every cell in the block. This huge influx of detail made it impossible for me to track the passing of the minutes.

Keys . . . chatter . . . a laugh . . . the scrape of a chair. Shift change! I closed my eyes and almost did that thing, that thing no one does any more. Not me, anyway.

'Go!' I whispered.

First, we moved Moth's lamp to the corner of the cell farthest from the door, behind the bunks, and switched it on. We placed the empty metal soup can so that it stood upright, resting on the bulb, and covered it all over with my blanket to stop the light from showing out through the door, and to suppress the smell. I stuffed our single remaining plastic bag into the tin – I'd wanted to use many more, but they'd all been taken – and waited. After a few minutes, the bag melted into a gloopy mess, which I stirred with the hacksaw blade. Then, wrapping the hot tin in a pillowcase so as not to burn my hands, I carried it to the door and used the blade to spoon the molten ooze into the door lock. With the plastic from only a single bag, I had no idea if it was sufficient to gunge-up the lock as I'd intended.

We flicked off the light. The empty can went out of the window, the hacksaw blade into my pack.

We made up our beds. We arranged Moth's books and anything else we could find on our beds so that they would look something like our sleeping bodies to anyone looking in through the peephole, at least in the dark.

I pushed out the window bars, against the direction of the angled cuts, then hopped onto the table and opened the window.

'Your mattress,' I said. Moth handed his bundle to me, and I squeezed it out of the window. It fell with a soft thud into the compound below. We did the same with mine.

Moth climbed onto the table. I took a deep breath and picked him up, hoisting him onto my shoulder, fireman-style. Using all my strength I fed him feet first through the open window, huffing and puffing and staggering precariously on the rickety little wooden table as I did so. It was like threading a giant needle.

He scraped down on the outside of the window, his feet resting on a little ledge there, his hands gripping the window opening.

We faced each other momentarily, him on the outside, me on the inside. His face was bleached with fear, a moon disk.

'Clockwise to Titan, Moth!' I said.

'Clockwise to Titan!' he replied.

Chapter 11

The Window

I passed Moth the two window bars, the rope and a fold of paper that contained a fresh mix of toothpaste and boot polish. He shuffled as far to my right as he dared.

Facing the window, I pushed my head, shoulders and arms out and jumped up as hard as I could. Beneath my feet, the table scraped noisily on the floor. After three goes, I had my upper body out of the opening. Resting on my outstretched arms, I tried repeatedly to raise and bend one leg so that it would pass through the open portion of the window. The gap was terribly small, and Moth was almost knocked off his ledge as I struggled and flailed, half in and half out.

'I can't do it!' I said in a panic. 'I'm stuck!' I whispered to Moth.

I truly was stuck. Any plan has parts that cannot be rehearsed, and this was one of them. I was too big for the narrow opening, and now I was wedged, my head and torso outside, one leg resting on the table, the other leg scrabbling for purchase against the inside wall as I tried to bring it up to the level of the gap.

In my maddening struggle, and being able only to look outwards, I could not see into the dark cell behind me. I suppose that was another part of the plan we'd failed to practise, the gluing-up of the door lock. It didn't work. Failure announced itself in the form of a single pull of huge force on my free leg. I was dragged down and back out of the window in one fell movement, my chin striking the table before I crashed onto the floor. I was stunned, doubly so when I recovered enough to open my eyes and saw Jelly's face staring into mine. He had switched on Moth's reading lamp and was holding the naked bulb close to my face.

I was expecting the usual scarlet face and boiled-egg eyes routine, but Jelly was totally professional – that's how serious this was. Saying absolutely nothing, he pulled me to my feet and thrust me in the direction of the cell door. I fell against it and struck it with my head. Striding to my side, he pressed me against the wall with a hand on my throat as he removed a special key from his breast pocket. The key I recognised even in my dazed state; it fitted into any of the emergency units that were sited along the corridors, and there was one just outside our cell. One twist of the key and the sleeping dormitory would shatter apart as alarms rang and every spare claviger in the Institute came clumping over.

Coldly, calmly, Jelly started to open the cell door. He peered into my face. I returned his stare.

Then I realised something. And so did he – his look showed me he did. It was the look of a man speared upon the tines of a dilemma.

To let us escape would be a gross dereliction of duty.

But if The Moth so much as set foot outside the gate it would be a cataclysm for the Director! Instant dismissal!

Jelly's brain was in the squeeze.

The muscles around his eyes puckered and fluttered, the instability soon extending to all the features on his face, as if they were staging a rebellion against their owner, or set in motion by the contradictory drives that snaked through him. He opened his mouth to say something, but all I received was a dry gurgle.

Something odd was happening to the light in the room. Fighting the force of Jelly's hand against my neck I swivelled to my right to see that The Moth had clambered halfway back into the cell. Dangling head first through the window over the table he was gently shaking his reading lamp, causing the bulb to vibrate in its loose fitting. The light flickered on and off, on and off, on and off.

Duty . . . or promotion? Duty . . . or promotion?

Jelly wobbled.

His eyes shut, both hands flopped to his sides, and he fell backwards against the bunks with a loud crash, striking his head first on the metal bedstead and then on the floor. A dark stain spread out over the crotch of his trousers.

'He's dead!' I heaved, pressing myself even harder against the wall, rejecting the reality of what I was seeing. 'We've killed a claviger!' Every organ in my body started to fragment.

'Grand mal seizure. He's epileptic, that's all,' came Moth's voice. With more grace than I'd imagined him capable of, he slid himself back into the cell completely and jumped down from the table. 'Episodes can be brought on by stress or flashing lights,' he continued. 'I had an uncle who was epileptic. Wonderful man, a scientist and a wrestler! It's just a condition, like diabetes or dandruff. Nothing to be scared of.'

These extraordinary reassurances complete, he moved over to Jelly and knelt over his body, putting his cheek against the man's face. 'Nasty knock to the head, mind you,' he said. Then, 'I think he's breathing. Yes . . . yes!'

Jelly's leg kicked out in confirmation of Moth's diagnosis, accompanied by a sound midway between a sigh and a groan.

'How long, Moth? How long before he recovers?' I gabbled.

Moth glared up at me, his eyes blank disks behind his spectacles. 'Minutes? Hours?' he said. 'Never?'

We looked at each other, we looked at Jelly. 'We must go, Moth! Now more than ever!'

Moth located Jelly's keys on their ring and used one to lock the cell door. Finding the keys caused a small bottle of pills to roll from the claviger's pocket onto the floor. I scooped up the bottle, thinking spitefully to delay the man's recovery. How I abhorred Jelly! The parasite had wrecked our chances at the last possible moment! Even his collapse would probably benefit him more than us!

Moth gave me a dirty look. 'Leave him some!' he said. I unscrewed the lid and reluctantly tipped a few of the pills onto the floor besides Jelly. Then I stuffed the bottle up my sleeve.

We chucked the keys out of the window after that, and turned off the still-flickering lamp. Moth moved to cover Jelly with my blanket, but I snatched it away. 'Throw it out,' I said, 'we leave nothing with our scent on.' It went the way of the keys, into the rubbish bins and skips below.

For the second time, I threaded Moth out through the window. Before I followed him, I had an idea, a weak one, but a way to wring hope from our devastated plan. What was that crumby saying of Harete's? 'When you fall into nettles, find a dock leaf.' In the dark cell, I scrabbled around for my dock leaf. A pencil stub and a crumpled piece of paper came to hand from the floor, Moth's centaur drawing. I smoothed out the sheet and wrote on the reverse, 'Thanks for all your help, Jelly, see you as arranged in –' and then I added the name of my home town, far away to the south. The paper was folded and slipped under the base of the lamp, certain to be found in even a cursory search. I thought about adding a confession too, words that would get Retread out of the bin, but I didn't know what to write and anyway, time was too short.

Then I followed The Moth, this time tipping the table onto its end, and using the extra height this afforded me to allow myself to drop feet first down the outside. Finally, the two of us stood side by side on the outside of the window.

'What did you do? Just then?' he hissed at me.

'Muddy the waters!' I replied. From inside the cell came a second faint groan.

I took the plastic rope from Moth, and hung it over the stout handle used to open and shut the window. Two nights ago I had bent the handle sharply upwards to transform it into a hook from which the rope would not slip. I tied the two ends of the rope together to make it into a loop. This was why I had needed a length twice the distance we needed to drop – so that I could make it into this loop. That way, once at the bottom, I could undo the loop and pull the rope free. Not only would that not leave an obvious clue as to our method of departure, it would enable us to reuse the rope.

'Hold both sides of the loop!' I reminded The Moth. He nodded, and taking a length of rope in both hands he pushed himself free from the window ledge. Slowly, gingerly, he walked down the wall, letting the knotted carrier-bag rope slip through his grip in measured intervals. I breathed a sigh of relief as I saw him spread his legs wide to pass either side of the windows directly beneath ours.

Once he was on the ground, he tugged the rope to signal me. Then I, too, was down the rope and into the waste compound. I undid the knot, and with a yank I retrieved it.

We had another surprise waiting for us in the compound, but this time a good one. On the ground, in a heap piled around a waste bin, were the bags of all the things confiscated from the cells. Prominent amongst them because of its size, and the strips of bubble wrap leaking out of it, was the sack with our own stuff in it. We could not believe the change in our fortune as we tipped out the sack. The compound was dark, but there was enough spillage from nearby security lights to see by. 'Sloppy of them!' I crowed. 'Too lazy even to take it to the boiler room for burning!'

Wasting no time, we did what we had originally intended to do in our cell. Moth stripped off to his shirt and shorts, ignoring the intense cold, and with well-practised movements he pulled over his limbs the tailored tubes of bubbled plastic we had so carefully made days before. He secured these with strips of tape, and did the same to the wide swathe of the same packaging material that went around his chest. Over this he put back his normal overalls, then the second, larger pair. On his feet he put three pairs of socks, then his shoes. Next came his waterproofs, the ones we had made from fused bags. He put on his mittens and balaclava, and pulled the waterproofing bags over his shoes. His food bag and water bottle were tucked in his overalls.

I used a shard of glass from my rediscovered tin to cut off long lengths of the adhesive tape and sealed his mittens to his sleeves, his foot bags to his legs, and the top half of his waterproofs to the bottom half. I then dressed the same, leaving off one mitten, and he assisted me in taping myself up. We gathered up our mattress rolls, I coiled the rope around my shoulders. I reflected that the clavigers' cell clearance had probably aided us, for had we dressed in the bulky layers inside, neither of us would have made it through the tiny window opening.

Snow was now falling, I was hugely relieved to note. We crept across the compound to the opposite side, sticking close to the wall. Moth crouched behind a pile of empty boxes, and I ventured out along the far wall to the large wooden double door. Set into this was a much smaller door, a door for people on foot. This was fastened with a padlock, as I knew from my observations from the cell window. From the tin, I produced one of my two remaining padlock-openers, just like the one I had given to Harete. The lock was large, weathered and rusty and it took several frustrating minutes of jiggling with the metal strip before the padlock clicked open. I slid it off the hasp and carefully pulled the creaking door open. I gestured for The Moth to come over. We slipped through the door, pulling it to behind us. I realised I now had the weighty padlock in my hand. For a second, I dithered. Which looked more suspicious? A missing padlock, or an unlocked padlock? As Moth hared across the courtyard to the far corner I stuffed the padlock into my mattress roll, and raced after him.

The Moth was hunched in the corner of the courtyard at the bottom of the outer perimeter wall. This was higher even than the compound wall, and was adorned along its length with a coil of barbed wire strung between regularly spaced metal bars. I knotted the rope into a loop and threw it, lasso-style, over one of these bars, catching it on my second attempt. I threw over our mattress rolls, and then heaved myself up the wall with the rope.

The rope had regular knots along it, formed where each bag had been joined to the next in the chain, and these helped me grip it as I climbed. Once on the top of the wall, I carefully positioned myself between two of the wire coils. *A shoddy job – typical of this place, typical of amateurs*, I thought to myself. The wire coils were so loosely wound that there was ample space to tread between them without getting caught. The wire was just a token effort. 'It's only kids inside, they can't do anything,' that's what the wire said. The Moth grabbed the rope and started to climb up after me, but with less success than I, as his feet kept slipping and scuffing on the wall. I pulled on my end of the rope to assist him, then grabbed his arm and dragged him up the rest of the way.

As he reached the top I freed the rope loop, tossed it down, and jumped onto the mud below. I retrieved the rope, and looked up at Moth, wobbling around like an idiot between the loose coils.

'Come on!' I rasped. 'They could catch us any second!'

We should have had several hours of safety, and a fine puzzle of intact bars and a locked cell door to cause further delay. That had been the intention.

But it was all now irrelevant, I reflected. Jelly changed everything. There he was above us, curled unconscious like an adder in torpor. His absence would be noticed long before ours. Would he live? How much time did we have before he recovered? What would he do when he did? By getting only as far as the perimeter wall we had surely already bought him his desire; from this point on he had as much incentive as anyone in seeing us recaptured.

The uncertainties grated worse than outright defeat. I raged at the undoing of my plans, at the cavity that lay where I'd prepared solid foundations. Our beautiful freedom was ten minutes old and already dying in our arms, thanks to that capricious man.

I could only hope my own diversionary note would cast doubt on Jelly's integrity and direct our seekers' attention to the south.

I've already related what happened next, how we met Harete and made our way to the river, drifted downstream to the pylons, and started our walk. Like my rope made of bags knotted together into a chain and then turned into a long loop, I've come round, back to the start.

Now I must describe how the loop unravelled.

Chapter 12

The Great Wheel

'Come alive! Come alive!' said a voice, and I woke up. Harete knelt over me, shaking my shoulders.

'Some guard you were!' she said scornfully. It was early morning, and we were still in the long grass under the pylon. Just us; no ring of guards with rifles and hot-fanged dogs.

'What happened?' I gasped.

'Nothing. You fell asleep,' she said, now shaking The Moth.

I sat up and looked around me. 'I remember just waiting and watching . . . but they never came. Those noises stopped, the voices, the lights, they all just stopped. I must have dozed off,' I said, sleepily.

'Guess so!' said Harete, clearly not impressed. I felt very ashamed. My steel had tarnished in the dawn's dew.

Moth woke up, and joined in the dreamy confusion.

'Why did they stop? They couldn't have been more than a field away,' he said.

I scratched my head. Everything felt peculiar. Another thin, freezing fog had dropped, scattering the dawn light into a shady, grey haze. The plastic sheet we had slept under was crisp with a hard frost. I was so thirsty I started licking it off the plastic.

'Dunno. Maybe the fog got too thick,' I suggested.

'What shall we do?' Moth asked, looking at me.

'Do? What do you think we're going to do? Sit here and have a sing-song? We carry on, of course! And look for water. We really, really need water,' I said.

The previous morning's surprise had been the footprints. That day's was even less explicable. Picking up the plastic top-sheet, something solid fell from it. Moth picked it up and turned it over in his hands.

'Chocolate,' he said.

Harete and I boggled. 'What? Let me see!' I said. He was right, though. It was three chunks of a chocolate bar, wrapped in silver foil. We looked at it in disbelief.

Harete frowned. 'A gift. Whoever tried and rejected our food the other night came back and took pity on us,' she ventured.

'Poisoned bait,' I said. 'Dropped by the helicopter, only we failed to notice it that night. It got caught in our bedding. Chuck it, Moth. It's Orion's cruel trick.'

'Is it *completely* impossible for you to believe that someone might be trying to help us?' said Harete. She turned to The Moth. 'Let me try it, please,' she said. 'I'll eat only a tiny piece. Worst case, I'll be sick and we'll know to suspect everything. But if I'm right, we've found an ally and maybe a shortcut to safety.'

'Don't let her, Moth!' I shouted. 'We can't know what poisons they've got or how strong they are. If someone wanted to help, why leave so little?'

'Because they don't have much themselves? Or to see if we can trust them, perhaps? You need to take risks to

250

earn trust. Whoever left it took a risk, we should do the same.'

I so wanted Harete to be right. Her willingness to chance everything for us and her faith in the existence of unseen help were qualities I knew were inaccessible to me. And for exactly that reason I could not bear the thought of them leading to her injury.

Between us, Moth weighed the two alternatives. 'I think . . . poison seems more likely than pity,' he concluded, and he hurled the chocolate away. Harete punched him.

We folded up the plastic sheet, I retrieved my glass shard, and we set off. The farmland was still undulating here; it dipped and rose in long, shallow waves that approximately matched the spacing of the pylons. Or rather, I reasoned, the pylons had been sited so that each one stood on a peak. We had to slip and stumble down the ploughed slopes, cross the flat bottom and then climb the rising slope on the other side. The troughs were sufficiently deep that when we were in them we could see nothing but our little valley. Even the pylons were hard to see in the streaky fog.

We each chewed on small blobs of fat as we walked. In the low night temperatures it had solidified somewhat, and was a touch more palatable for it. At each pylon we reached, Moth scanned the field edges for leftover crops, his idea to supplement our diet, but the ground was hard and difficult to dig into. Once we found something that might have been a carrot, but it was more black than orange and we threw it away. Doubtless we were all thinking of the chocolate, but no one mentioned it.

'So thirsty . . . won't the fog mean there will be moisture

on the pylons?' asked Harete. There was, but not much, and in our desperation we ended up licking beads of condensation straight off the cold metal.

BAROOOM!

We were midway between pylons, down in the trough between two crests, when we heard the noise. A huge throaty, roaring noise; the noise of a heavy-duty engine being woken up. The sound came from behind us, but from how far away we could not tell because the little valleys bounced the sound around.

Moth, Harete and I immediately broke out of our drowsiness and started to run up the slope to the next pylon. There, we looked backwards – but still nothing could be seen. The spluttering, rumbling growl became amplified and was joined by other sources, forming an advancing, accelerating flank of anger tearing at the air behind us. A clamour of other noises was audible now too, including jangling, rattling noises like fetters and keys being shaken in anticipation of our imminent re-capture.

We ran again, down the slope into the field beyond. My lungs burned with the effort, my hideous plastic waterproofs whipped and cracked, my pack bounced and joggled against my tired legs. Moth stumbled, and went rolling and tumbling down the slope. His mattress roll bounced free and tripped me over, and I too went sprawling and pitched head first into the frosty mud, landing artlessly besides him.

Harete tore over to us, every step she took with her bad leg making her howl out with pain. She bent, took hold of our arms and helped us both upright together. On our feet again, a screen of red-brown dust engulfed us. Instantly, the

252

dust invaded and overwhelmed our eyes and throats, stinging dust as dense as clinker. The turbulent cloud of grit and the deafening thunder told us that the vehicles must now be only just behind the closest peak. Sightless and suffocating, we gripped each other and tried to run on. As I struggled to move, I glanced behind me. There it was, coming over the crest, for a few seconds rising above its own cloud of pulverised soil, pumping chugs of black smoke out through an exhaust pipe as big as a factory chimney.

Not a tank, a tractor.

But not a normal tractor; a giant tractor. The machine was tremendous, the size of a house, with four colossal doubled-up wheels, each taller than a man and wider than a car. Way, way up in a glass-walled cabin atop the monster sat not a marshal with a troop of men, but a single driver, wearing headphones, grinning sideways, over to his left, towards another machine of equal power which tore down the slope slightly ahead of him.

That second massive machine slammed past us, spraying everything with chunks of mud ripped up by the cleats on its humungous tyres. The first machine drove straight ahead; we were pinned on its centre line. It was so wide and approaching so fast that I did not know which way to dodge. I split to the right, Moth spun to the left. The tractor bore forwards, its front wheels a solid, grinding wall of black rubber.

Directly in front of me, in the centre of the storm of churning mud and dust, stood Harete. She lowered her head. In comparison to the roar she gave out, the sound of the tractor was reduced to a prissy mewl. She folded her arms over her front and bull-charged us, smashing Moth and me across the path of the tractor. Then her arms sprang outwards from her chest, imparting to us a second push that propelled us, rolling, heels over head onto the dirt and into safety. In a fatal reaction to the final impact, she rebounded backwards, right into the path of the accelerating vehicle.

'HARETE!' yelled The Moth, lying right beside me yet almost inaudible. The tractor blasted by us, buffeting us with its sucking side draught.

But Harete was under it. I saw her go under; I watched the vast, black rubber tyre with treads deeper than a handspan roll over her, squash her down. For a tiny fraction of a second her body assumed the curved radius of the wheel and then she was gone under, and the tractor roared off, up the slope and away.

Moth and I stared, dumbfounded, disbelieving. A single thought came to me, one single, horrible word: *stomped.*

To our left and to our right, more tractors thundered past, many almost within touching distance. Some pulled trailers, some carried great rattling, spiked metal implements behind them, raised off the ground on hydraulic arms. Several had arrays of headlights mounted on their cab roofs, blazing away to help them see through the fog. But Moth and I remained where we lay, cleaved to each other, staring at a single patch of earth. Moth's breath came in short, hoarse pulses. He was beyond tears, I could see that. He was deep in shock. I held him close to me and noticed how cold he was.

Many minutes passed by. The fog lifted. Stillness returned, a calm that was unflinchingly resistant to our hopes. From where Harete had fallen came neither a scratch nor a whimper.

'We have to see her, Moth,' I whispered. 'We have to say goodbye. And say how much we loved her.'

We crawled the few paces that divided us from our friend.

There rested Harete's corpse, crushed lengthways into a plough's loamy furrow. The ruts here ran in the same direction the tractor had driven in. Harete lay pale in her clay grave, her body looking almost undamaged, arms by her side. Her face was neutral in expression; she looked calm.

I pulled off my mitten and worked my bare hand down inside her balaclava, wriggling my fingers until they were touching her neck under her many layers of clothing. I felt for a pulse, but found nothing. Hoping to detect a trace of breath, I borrowed Moth's spectacles and held one of the lenses under her nostrils. The lens clouded over, and Moth was on the cusp of fainting until I pointed out that the lens's breath-free twin had done the same. The condensation was only moisture from the damp air.

'My brave Demeter, my Ceres, my Harete,' sobbed The Moth. He succumbed completely to his grief and fell down, wailing. Few tears came to him or me, I noted, and I wondered if perhaps dehydration had robbed us even of those.

I mumbled only, 'Goodbye, Harete.' All I could manage. Saying those two words hurt like breaking teeth; I had wasted all chances to tell her of my feelings, or learn more about hers, and our last words had been wasted on a futile argument.

I knelt beside Moth and bent forwards to plant a kiss on her muddy forehead.

Inwardly, despite my immeasurable despair, I was relieved that the matter was complete. Even a broken leg would have been a disaster. We hadn't seen a tree for days; I couldn't even construct a crutch or a splint. And if she had been paralysed . . . that would have been worse than this. We would have had to leave her to die of exposure or to be clubbed to death. This way . . . this way, it was simply finished.

We sat by the furrow and waited for a long time. Nothing seemed real any more. 'She's dead, she's dead,' I repeated under my breath, but the truth had no salt to its taste. Rationally, I knew that without Harete we were reduced in strength by much more than a third. The verdant meadows of our destination receded, all my hopes for living a life worthy of the word imploded. The Other country reverted to being just another place.

Moth spoke first. 'Bury her, please.'

'Here will do,' I said, and I started to break up the furrow's lip and crumble the soil over her. Moth's hand lashed out and gripped mine.

'No it won't! She deserves a monument!' he snarled at me. 'She saved our lives, and died doing so!'

There was only one possible object that could serve in that role. We were crouching in its long shadow, and, as I hesitated, reluctant to waste time and expend energy, yet also greatly sharing Moth's desire, the shadow slipped over us, moving clockwise.

Slowly, with great effort, we raised Harete's body and half carried, half dragged it the short distance to the nearest pylon. Harete's obelisk looked like all its neighbours, of course, and it did not even carry a number. There was a natural dip in the ground between its feet, and we lowered Harete in and covered her completely over with dry, cold earth, saying nothing. I tamped down the soil with my fists and feet.

'We have to sail on. Harete wouldn't have wanted us to give up,' Moth choked when the job was done. I was taken aback at his composure. Until he uttered those words I had assumed that Moth was going to insist on maintaining a vigil and abandon the journey, as even I felt tempted to do. Then I recalled his attitude towards another death and remembered: this was the new, pitiless Moth.

'Are you sure you want to? Even now, after this?'

'Yes. Harete is on Olympus now. I hope she can look down and guide us, become our Hera. Besides, what else can we do?' asked Moth, and he looked me straight in the face. 'Death is death. It's final. Staying here won't help.'

He was correct, of course. To give up would have been to invalidate Harete's sacrifice.

'We need to crack on, then. The tanks we heard last night were nothing but those tractors, working late into the evening,' I said quietly, picking up my mitten and walking back to collect our mattress rolls. I took Harete's too, so as to leave no sign of us. 'But the marshals are still behind us. They're pushing us onwards, stopping us from turning back. They'll be hoping we get picked up at the border.'

I was right, too. Crawling briskly to the top of the incline we had rolled down and peering over, I could already see the distant blue figures pressing forwards and reformed into a neat, wide, disciplined line. They plodded inexorably, unstoppably, a blue bank of club-toting terror. Time was on their side; they had no need to hurry. Like me, but unlike The Moth, they knew what they were squeezing us up against. The line of marshals was like a piston moving along a cylinder in a car engine, compressing the fuel and air into a smaller and smaller volume until the spark licked it and made it explode.

How had they known so soon that we'd be going north? Still that made no sense to me. I was loath to credit the club-luggers with enough subtlety to see through even a single bluff.

'Do you think the men in the tractors saw us?' quizzed Moth when I had shuffled back to him.

I stopped and turned and placed a hand on Moth's shoulder. 'Moth, look at you. Look at me! We're covered from head to foot in tatty shreds of plastic, and bathed in mud. We're practically *invisible* out in these fields!'

Wearily, the two of us gathered our things and steeled ourselves to continue.

Before we had taken two steps Moth shouted, 'Wait!' and he dashed back to Harete's grave, with me in tow. Kneeling by it, he took off a mitten and out of his sleeve he pulled a square of folded paper. He poked it into the soil.

'What was that?' I asked, astounded.

'My drawing of Chiron, the centaur,' he said, his lip juddering. The grave thus consecrated, we turned towards the next slope.

This slope was the biggest we had encountered so far, and when we got to the top we could see the flat, brown, cold land smeared out all around us. Far, far ahead a row of red blobs receded underneath diffuse smudges of smoky exhaust, all that remained to be seen of the tractors. We were pressed between red earth and blue sky, between red tractors and blue marshals.

And ancient Chiron had the answer, I knew at last, Moth's words having taken the duration of the climb to work fully into my grief-dulled mind. My plan to muddy the waters in the cell with Jelly had backfired, for I realised then that the note I had written there, the one I had hoped would frame Jelly and divert the authorities, must have been written on the map, the other sheet of paper that had been on the cell floor. *I had personally handed the authorities our entire plan, our northbound intentions!* The single surviving spore of hope was that the map had drawn no special attention to the role of the pylons on our journey. But what of it? I was the world's greatest fool. I had killed Harete.

'Moth – please – I'm . . . it's my fault,' I said.

Moth cast his eyes down. 'We're both guilty,' he muttered.

We struggled back over to the pylons and walked on. I held onto Moth's hand for a long while, until he shook himself free. The winter sun shone and we warmed up a little, but this only made us thirstier. In another act of unforgivable stupidity, we had forgotten to remove Harete's food bag tucked inside her clothes when we buried her, so had failed to extract even an atom of advantage from the terrible situation. The loss of food did not seem to matter at that moment though; it was fluid we needed. Why had I misjudged the water so badly? Had I done nothing right? The breeze evaporated the moisture drops from the pylons, the ditches were dry, the few puddles too thick and muddy to even contemplate drinking from.

I found a smooth pebble and popped it under my tongue to suck. Moth did the same. 'Don't choke on it!' I warned him. Had I swallowed my pebble, the matter of the map was so tightly lodged in my own craw there wouldn't have been room for it to pass.

On we trudged, without complaint or conversation. We did not stop to rest under the pylons, we just carried on walking. A new momentum seized us, a cold, plodding impetus that knew no haste, yet knew no respite either. We were compelled to walk, we could not stop. We absolutely would not stop until we found water, or came to our destination, or died. If we had stopped then we would have had to think about Harete, and that was a prospect much worse than going thirsty.

Like broken robots we tottered on, insensate, incoherent. Our thirst became monumental, all-consuming. We felt no pain in our legs or feet, the cold did not concern us, the wind went unacknowledged. Feelings like that were for the living, and as the hours passed by I realised we were no longer in that category. We were something else now, something only half alive, something that just walked and thirsted and mourned. Harete's death ceased to trouble or shock me; it became just another fact: mud is brown, pylons are grey, Harete is dead, Harete who saved us is dead *because of me*!

My head buzzed and my vision faded, became black and white. The landscape droned on and on forever. There were no hedges now; only the pylons to my left broke the monotony. They were no longer guides and providers, I could see. They were iron-footed inquisitors, a line of jurymen linked by harp wire, cages welded to stilts.

A new torment arose within me, nourished by my delirium. Were we going in the right direction? I tried to see the sun, think what it meant. Why were the pylons to my left? Did it matter? For a while I became convinced that the pylons had to be to my right, so I turned around and started walking in the opposite direction. Some minutes later I became suspicious as to why the sun was shining in my face, something I had not experienced before whilst walking. I had to shield my eyes with my hand and squint into the light.

I turned around once more and retraced my steps, unaware that in doing so I had crossed underneath the line of the pylons. My confusion deepened. What was it I had taught the others? Pylons to the left? I *was* going in the wrong direction after all! We all were! Not *all*, couldn't say that any more. Only *both*. How long had this been going on? I spun around in utter disarrangement. No . . . no . . . it was sun *set* to the left. The pylons could be to the left or the right . . . and the sun had to be behind us. That was it. Follow The Moth, I thought; we can't both have become disoriented, surely?

My eyes found The Moth and I resumed my original course. The two of us had become spread out over quite a distance. The Moth and I were each shuffling along in our own private miseries, paying no heed to each other. Alarmed at how far apart we were, I forced myself to stop walking. Stopping was agony; I had almost to beat my legs with my fists to override their compulsion to continue.

I waved to The Moth and gestured for him to come to me. When I caught his eyes he turned his stiff head like a mannequin and lurched over.

I looked up, hoping to see some sign of rain or sleet in the clouds, but there was none. I did see the pylon's number, though – number one-three-zero.

'Moth,' I croaked, 'I've lost count. How many have we done?'

The Moth looked almost comatose. He had to flick his lolling head back to see me through half-shut eyes.

'About eighty,' came the husky reply.

We had only the strength to unwrap two crinkling plastic sheets and to lie down between them.

I shut my eyes and tried to sleep, may even have done so for a while, although it was not quite dark.

The Moth's wailing woke me up. I listened to him for a few minutes before cranking open my eyes. On and on and on he sobbed, but I couldn't hear him properly, he sounded a long way away. Drowsy, confused, I sat up to silence him. He was not by my side. He was a short distance away from the pylon, on his knees, begging at the feet of a tall, black horse.

The shock roused me like a dousing in ice water. I rolled away from the bedding and pressed myself tightly to the ground. Standing on a ridge, silhouetted by the orange furnace of the setting sun, were four black horses. Riding them were four horsemen in black uniforms with strange, square hats.

'Please! Take me, my time is up!' Moth was crying. 'I'm ready for the end! Take me to Harete!'

One of the horsemen dismounted. He sauntered over to The Moth and drew out a long baton from where it was hooked to his belt. The baton was telescopic; he tugged on the end to lengthen it still further. Holding my breath, I heard smooth metal glide over smooth metal. I watched as he placed the baton's tip on Moth's skull, and waited for him to lift it up and smash it down.

Instead, he shone a torch into Moth's face, and used the baton to flick Moth's greasy hair away from his forehead.

'No,' he shouted to his mounted colleagues, sounding disappointed. 'He's not got the mark. No sign.'

'Please!' cried Moth, prostrating himself.

'Go away!' said the man, sternly. He flicked all his fingers, as you would to dismiss an annoying infant who had toddled into a room where the grown-ups were talking. 'They must be coming up the drainage channels; most of the traps have rusted. But he's not one of them. Get lost! Scram!' he shouted again, these last words directed at Moth.

With professional ease, the man remounted his horse. 'Tell you what, though,' I heard him laugh to his companions, once he was back in the saddle, 'if we do find that piece of scum tonight, we'll have us one hell of a beating!' The four of them geed up their horses and cantered off over the fields towards the west.

Moth remained where he was for a long time, devastated by his rejection. When he trudged back to me, he tried to explain. 'I thought . . . I thought they were . . .' he started, but I put him back to bed and lay down next to him.

The day shrivelled to its termination and a cold, parched night followed.

Chapter 13

A Slip-Up

A woman – my mother, I think – was standing next to a high wall. I could not see her face, only her skirt and her legs. She was laughing and chatting with a friend. The wall was made of brick, a really warm, old, worn brick, the sort that soaks up the heat of a summer's day and re-radiates it in the evening. My dream-me – and I knew even then it was a dream – turned and walked to where there was a doorway in the wall.

My dream-self was perhaps three or four years old. He knew everything I knew, but did not let it bother him, and I knowingly shared in his unknowing. The young boy and me, we understood that our selves were layered like the leaves of puffed pastry, separate but part of the same, in some places touching and in others held apart by bubbles of time. Using his eyes I looked through the door and saw a dusty yard full of junk. A yellow hose lay coiled in a heap, the colour so vivid that I had to look away from it in case it left spots in my eyes. From the hose, a delicious trickle of fresh water gurgled into a glossy puddle. I merged back into the boy and together we shared the outrageous, unspeakable beauty of what we saw. The fact that this was a dream did not cause us any bitterness. When I felt sufficiently restored, I happily let go and wafted upwards, back to the real world.

I lay on the ground next to The Moth and basked in the intensity of my reverie. The dream had not cheated me; it had not fooled me into thinking it was real. My mind was not playing out a callous ambush; I felt sure it was treating me, rewarding or guiding me, even. I smiled and yawned.

A less sweet aftertaste percolated into my wakeful mind. How fine it had felt to be that young me, that child! Was adulthood so grand? Might not childhood be a better state? I chewed over this new thought, not ungrateful for it.

I wanted to tell Moth and Harete about my dream, and then I remembered that Harete was gone. The realisation was like suddenly finding a sharp flint under my tongue. How could I have forgotten? After the sweetness of the dream the memory of Harete's death was like swigging a draught of battery acid.

When we were both fully awake, we licked the dampness off the plastic sheets and then off the metal struts and beams of the pylons. We pulled up handfuls of the grass and weeds under the pylon and shook the dew from them onto the plastic sheet, and drank that too. We harvested beads of moisture from our rolled-up packs, and sucked on plant stems.

'Not enough,' choked Moth. 'We've had almost two days without a proper drink. We can't go on for much longer. We'll be joining poor Harete soon, but our end will be much more drawn out and painful than hers.'

'I know. Today will be different,' I told him. I made no mention of the nocturnal horsemen – already it seemed to belong to another lifetime. What *was* the mark they had looked for on Moth's head? Or had that belonged to another dream?

Beneath the unending zinc lid of clouds we set off again. There was no sleet, no snow, no rain and not even a breeze. The weather had been turned off.

We ambled across the fields from one pylon to the next. Every ditch was dry, or had just black ooze in it. For a long time now we had seen no hedges; the fields were separated from one another by raised earthen embankments.

Several pylons into the morning's journey, on a slight rise, we stopped.

Moth grabbed my arm roughly, pulled me to him and said, 'For pity's sake, we need water. You said today would be different. Why?'

I felt hugely calm, and protected as if in a bubble. I gave him a brief summary of my dream.

Moth blinked repeatedly. 'You've gone. You're mad. I thought you'd last longer than I . . . but you've gone first. A dream? Is that what you are telling me; you think we'll find water today because you had a nice dream?'

'I understand, Moth. Sounds mad . . . but I just know. Those things in the dream, they were . . . symbols. You should appreciate that. They were promising us something, something we want,' I said.

Moth's face boiled into a purple stew. Without any great interest I wondered if he was going to hit me. His breathing turned into very loud snorts, then slowly diminished in volume as his normal colour returned. 'Oh, I do appreciate your symbols. I appreciate them hugely. Please, do permit me to slake my raging thirst on your fabulous symbols. And whilst I'm doing that, perhaps you can dream up a five-course meal for me?' he sniped, and sat down with his head in his hands. 'That dream was not telling you anything!' he snivelled. 'All those colours and textures . . . it was most likely just your brain compensating for the lack of visual stimuli over the past few days.'

'I don't see why my dream is any less important than your blasted fables and myths. You're always banging on about those. They're no more true than my dream,' I said.

Moth sighed, as if having to explain something to a small child. 'But I don't use those legends as an excuse to lead my friends on wild adventures! Is this entire escape also based on some dream you had? Those fables are just for my inspiration. That's all. I don't believe they hold messages for me; that would be insanity!'

Moth's words failed to hurt me. Maybe it was insane to believe in a weird dream, to feel reassured by it, but I did not care. Scanning the landscape, I saw something, as I was convinced I must.

Saying nothing, I pointed with an outstretched arm at what I had seen. Moth ignored me, so I tapped his shoulder and nodded in the direction I was pointing. When he saw it too, he stood up and shielded his eyes.

'What is it?' he asked.

'Farm buildings of some sort, that's my guess,' I said.

We squinted at it some more. In a dip in the ground over to the west, to the left of the pylons, there stood a group of squat, regular shapes.

'Will they have . . . ?'

'I don't know. Seems likely though, wouldn't you say?'

We gathered up our things and changed course, cutting diagonally across the fields and moving cautiously downhill in the direction of the cluster of rectangular objects. It took probably another hour before we drew near enough to confirm that they were buildings. We moved forwards more slowly then, bending over and running before taking up position behind a low embankment a short distance from the farm. The sight of it triggered a terrible fretfulness in The Moth. He kept standing up and squatting down, he fidgeted and moaned, 'Please, please, please let them have water.'

'Calm down. We need to see if there are any people about first,' I hushed.

The buildings looked to be a mixture of tumbledown wrecks, large metal sheds and small brick or stone barns. We edged left and right along the embankment to try and see as much of it as we could without approaching any nearer. We saw no movement or other signs of people; we heard no sounds.

'Let's go. Carefully!' I instructed him. Bent double, we zigzagged like commandoes over the remaining field and into the farm. We climbed over a low wire fence and, for the first time in days, found something other than naked earth under our feet. The ground was made from knobbly-textured concrete slabs. It felt good to walk on something even and flat again.

We moved guardedly along the side of a huge modern-looking shed. It was the size of a small cathedral and made from concrete panels set into a metal frame. Opposite it stood the ruins of a small stone cottage, the roof slates missing, the doors and windows long gone. All around lay piles of farm-related waste: plastic barrels, metal drums, rusting barbed wire, sheets of corrugated metal, plastic sacks, fence posts, concrete blocks. More buildings came into view as we rounded the corner of the super-sized shed. There was a long row of what looked like dilapidated animal stalls and some small, lop-sided wooden and corrugated-iron buildings that were so stuffed full of rubbish it was impossible to tell where the walls ended and the contents began.

The silence was absolute. Only our own rustling clothes made any noise at all.

'Abandoned?' said Moth, the disappointment palpable in his quavering, throaty voice.

I pointed at the ground. On the dirty cement by my feet was a recent-looking cigarette end. A few paces farther on we saw boot prints where the concrete floor was coated in mud.

We pressed on, coming soon to a small door set into the side of the great shed. Pushing it open, we peered inside and let ourselves in. The shed was gloomy, admitting light only through small rectangular slits up where the roof met the walls. Through the murk I could see row upon row of wooden pallets stacked head-high with plastic sacks. Edging farther in, I examined the sacks. Fertiliser, chemicals to replenish the depleted soil. I thought of Harete, lying rotting in the soil. Would the rye grow richer where she lay? Would she have a crypt of tall barley? I rested against a pallet and tried to cry, but nothing came out. My tongue felt thick and swollen and my head felt painfully tight. Surely my own demise was not far off now? I felt sure I was close to collapsing, and no longer found the idea disturbing.

We skulked along the narrow aisles between the pallets towards the distant, darker end of the shed. The stacks of pallets ended and the space opened out.

Parked in that voluminous space was one of the massive tractors from the day before. The smell betrayed it before I comprehended its dark shape, a sweet smell of oil undercut with a sharper tang of metal. The dormant vehicle hulked in near total darkness facing me square-on, a slumbering sentry. Its huge front tyres stood out either side of it like obscenely over-developed rubbery biceps. Was this the one that had killed Harete? Had it come for us too? I swayed towards it, wanting to make sure.

A metal trough on wheels was parked up next to the tractor, surely a thing to be towed out to where animals needed feeding – or watering. We snaked eagerly towards it, hoping the hope of maniacs to find it full of fresh water.

From the bottom of the dry, half-cylindrical trough a woman's face looked up at us. The face and the body were like no others I had ever seen. Moth and I became screwed to the floor, mesmerised by the horror and the ruined beauty of what lay there. She was impossible to age. Small, but definitely not a child, with perfect brown skin and hair so long that it draped over the edge of the bowser. Even in the half-light of the shed, it was clear that she had been ruthlessly beaten. Her skull was lopsided, like a cracked egg, her jaw was . . . only one phrase came to mind, but it seemed inappropriate. *Out of whack.* The sight was repellent beyond anything I'd ever seen, even in the Institute. 'This must be what "one hell of a beating" looks like,' I whispered. Presumably, no handcuffs had been required. This would be my fate too, I told myself; perhaps Harete had been the luckier of the two of us.

On the woman's forehead was tattooed a single, stylised triangle.

Δ

'What does it mean, Moth?' I asked him. The woman's tight-fitting clothes were unfamiliar in design and feel, smooth and waxy and grey, halfway between oilskins and leather in texture, and vividly embroidered in golden thread with pictures of fish and birds and mermaids and seals. Her shoes were tiny. One arm was exposed where the jacket had been torn, and the skin underneath was drizzled with more tattoos, florid bands of complex symbols I could not name that twined around her limb like vines over a trellis. Amongst the symbols, a design like a three-pronged candelabra predominated. The style of the exquisite ink work reminded me of something, but I was too far gone to think what. I rested my hands on the iron side of the trough and peered in closer.

'What is this, Moth? Poetry? Music?' I whispered.

'Both. It's maths,' replied Moth, frowning. 'The equations of waves.'

To my surprise, Moth slipped a hand inside one of the jacket's pockets, seeing that it bulged slightly. What he pulled out hit me harder than a baton. It was a chocolate bar, wrapped in silver paper, missing three chunks.

'Pity,' he said.

I was disgusted by his indifference. 'A pity! Moth, is that all you can say, that it's a pity?' I gasped.

'I meant, the chocolate we found was left out of pity. For us. By her. It wasn't poisoned bait,' he explained. 'She must have been trying to help us, just like Harete guessed. I wonder why?'

'Put it back,' I croaked. The barn suddenly felt very, very cold and my thirst swooped back upon me, reawakened and intensified by the shock.

We left the shed by the same way we had entered. Moth lay against the wall in the sunshine, I tapped into the deepest lees of my strength and carried on walking. Bewildered, I tiptoed away from my friend and went around the next corner of the shed. The buildings opposite opened out into a small courtyard lined on one side by a brick wall. Not like the wall in my dream, I noted with some sadness, because it had been painted a nasty creamy-yellowy colour. The ground there was thick and slippery with black mud, and it smelled bad too. Halfway along the yellow wall a short pipe rose out of the ground, and on top of the pipe was a brass tap.

I walked over to the tap. My hand hesitated as it reached out. Could I take the disappointment if it was rusted up, if nothing but a faint hiss and a brown trickle were to dribble from it? I grabbed the tap and turned it. The tap did not budge. Again . . . still nothing, no movement. My chest deflated.

'Clockwise to Titan,' I mouthed bitterly to myself, and I turned to walk away. Then, I froze. Which way had I turned the tap? Had I made Moth's mistake, was my brain so addled from lack of fluid?

I spun around and gripped the tap again with my quaking hand. 'Think of a clock face!' I commanded myself. I pictured the big clock in the Institute's canteen, saw the hands moving down on the right-hand side and up on the left. That was clockwise . . . clockwise to tighten . . . so turn the opposite way to open!

I wrenched the tap hard and water exploded from it. The water gushed and splattered onto the ground, instantly washing a large semicircle under the tap clean from the smelly mud. I knelt down in the newly cleaned space and stuck my mouth under the tap, sucking hard on the brass teat, filling my desiccated mouth and stomach.

'MOTH!' I yelled, but I did not need to. The sound of the water crashing onto the floor in the otherwise silent farm was so loud and so distinctive that he had already started to race towards it.

He drank as I had, and soon we were soaking wet. We filled our water bottles, we tipped them over ourselves and refilled them, we danced and splashed in the water, we were heedless to the possibility of discovery. We cavorted and sang and hugged each other. What it was to be alive, to no longer thirst, to drink! Harete's death, the savaged corpse in the shed, nothing else mattered. We were intoxicated!

'To Harete!' I declaimed.

'To dear, departed Harete!' shouted Moth, and we toasted her with water, then finally allowed ourselves to cry real tears, weeping copiously for Harete and a little less for ourselves. I wept more than Moth, for I had also a burden of regrets for my lethal errors.

'She was the best of us, Moth,' I said. 'The bravest. She was the pylon-finder, the dogged dragon-fighter; she gave her life for ours!'

Moth nodded between sobs. 'She resisted the siren's lies,' he reminded me, 'and she told the best story.' We toasted that too.

'To the mermaid! To she who tried to help us!' I ventured, but it snuffed out the mood. We sobered up.

When the novelty of no longer being thirsty had worn off, we set about poking around for anything else in the farm which could be of use, but came up empty-handed. Even the old farmhouse had nothing in it but a table, some folding chairs, an ashtray.

'I don't think this is the real farm. It's just a . . . an outstation, some place where they keep machinery and stuff. The real farm must be elsewhere,' Moth reasoned.

Moth was reluctant to leave our little oasis, despite the sinister presence of the body and my reminding him that we had to return to the pylons and do much more walking before the day was out. I said he could have about ten more minutes to scout around, and I parked myself on the ground near the tap. Refreshment eclipsed remorse, and I decided to conjure up some reason to forgive myself over the map. The best I managed was the hope that they wouldn't think us that stupid.

Occupied by this exercise in self-exoneration, I barely glimpsed Moth race past the end of the courtyard at high speed, skidding in the slippery slime underfoot. Then something else went past, fast. I heard Moth's feet running on the concrete, and another sound too, an odd, fast-paced, tapping sound.

My brow furrowed – surely if he had seen a person he would have shouted out a warning? I stood up. Moth raced back across the end of the courtyard, froze, and bolted towards me.

'Hey! What's up?' I asked, swivelling my body towards Moth as he hared past.

Something huge and pale brown bolted past me from behind so fast that it spun me around and I splashed down into the foul mud on the concrete below. I flipped myself over in the dirt and saw Moth flattening himself against the wall at the far end. Ten paces in front of him stood a huge pig, almost the size of a pony. The pig stood with all four legs splayed slightly outwards, its head bowed, steam hosing in bursts from its nostrils. Incredibly, the beast charged Moth, like a bull, head down, squealing horrendously. Moth dashed out of the way. The pig yawed its massive bulk around and galloped after him, grunting furiously.

'Where's it from?' I yelled at Moth as he passed me by, utterly bamboozled, not yet sure if this was something funny or something serious.

'I opened a gate; it was under some straw. I kicked it; I didn't know it was there!' he shouted, running the words together into one long, breathless sentence.

From the ground, I grabbed a wooden stave. The animal must have been longer than a man was tall and probably would have reached to my chest, had I been brave enough to stand next to it. It was a mottled pink and brown and as fat as all the sins in the world. It must have weighed half as much as a small car.

Fixing Moth in its eyes once more, it charged him with another ear-rending squeal. Moth dodged and dived again.

'You must have kicked it somewhere very painful!' I cried, and I took a swipe at it with the plank as it clattered past. I missed, but the joust continued; the pig saw me and decided to give me a taste of the same. It came powering like a freight train, and I barely had time to fling myself out of its way before it wheeled around for another attempt.

I was right by the tap now, against the yellow wall. Reaching up from where I lay, I grasped the tap above me and turned it on, full blast. I jammed my thumb over the end of the tap and sent out a thin, fast jet of water from the small gap it made.

The water jet caught the creature on the side of its head. It skidded to a halt, slipping almost as much as I had, despite having four feet. It emitted a huge grunt, swivelled round and bounded towards the tap. I leapt from its path, but the pig did not continue to chase me. Instead, it twisted its head at an angle, opened its mouth and started to drink from the freely falling water.

'Get the stuff and let's run like fury!' I shouted, chucking Moth his gear from where I had gathered it up. As we pelted out of the courtyard, Moth tore at his food bag, snapping the carrier bag's handles where they were tied to his pack, and twirled the bag in the air like a slingshot. He aimed the bag straight at the pig, which had now slaked its thirst and was turning around once more towards us.

The bag landed well in front of it, and split open. The remaining slab of grain-and-sugar-encrusted lard inside slid out and whooshed over the ground, landing right under the pig's snout. It sniffed at the odorous offering, and started to enthusiastically lap up the slops.

We ran out of the farmyard, Moth hobbling.

'Do you think it will follow us? Across the fields?' Moth asked as we swapped the concrete for the familiar feel of rutted clay. He was winded, but not wounded.

'No idea! Good idea of yours, Moth, throwing the pig your food,' I said.

Winded he may have been, but The Moth was still The Moth. 'Not a pig, a sow – didn't you see the udders? Probably full of steroids, poor thing . . . maybe that was why it was so bad-tempered . . . anyway, I figured if it was thirsty, it was probably hungry too,' he mumbled, adding, 'Mind you, it does mean I have no food now.'

'It was almost inedible anyway. We've just enough to last if we share what remains between us,' I pointed out. In reality I knew that with the loss of The Moth's food, we were now on starvation rations.

I voiced my wider troubles. 'Why are all the animals in this land so wrong, Moth?' I said. 'Giant pigs! Sick cows! Rabid dogs! And yet everything gentle and good, like Icarus and Harete and the mermaid . . . everything good gets crushed.'

'You said it yourself,' Moth replied. 'This nation is the farm; we cultivate all the monsters ourselves. We pen them in and feed them the ground-up bodies of their own kind; we beat them and train them to kill.'

'Isn't there any hope? Can nothing good rise again from this country's soil?'

'No. Maybe. A hero . . .' he began, then halted. For the first time in many days, I saw a look enter Moth's eyes, the look he always had when he made a connection with his legends. 'The Crommyonian Sow,' he said. 'Slain by Theseus.'

'Thee-see-us?' I repeated, blankly. But Moth was lost to me. I ruminated on my own sins, for surely I too was a self-made, cell-farmed monster? And The Moth?

We scurried over the fields and back to the friendly pylons. The rest of the day passed in what was by now a routine fashion. Pushing against the cold, dry winds and occasional bursts of sleet we trudged on. Moth entertained me by talking about Odysseus, Theseus and Jason, his heroes from the land and time of never-was, of Heracles, who had to contend with birds, bulls, boars, dogs, deer and lions.

I only half-listened. I was paying more attention to our surroundings and keeping an eye out for the marshals. All I remember of his lessons was laughing when Moth told me about Jason losing a shoe as he crossed a river on his way to reclaim his kingdom ('Complain about my planning all you like, Moth, but at least we've both kept our footwear,' I joked) and that Theseus was raised in the land of his mother and had to journey over land to rejoin his father, fighting robbers and monsters on his way.

Our mood was more optimistic than it had been at any point since Harete's death. We had lost more food but had ample water and we were now well used to the walking. The loss of Harete was still uppermost in our minds, a savage, flaming burden, but a tolerable one. We had determined to continue, and had made an unspoken pact that we would mourn her properly only when the ordeal was over, whatever the outcome.

Three other facts served to improve our temperament. Firstly, late in the afternoon, we passed pylon one-zero-zero.

'If pylon number one is at the border, we have one hundred more pylons to pass,' Moth pointed out. We did not need to say what we both thought, that the end of our journey was in sight. We continued without ceremony, pondering the unknowable future.

The second reason for an improvement in morale was the transformation in the countryside. The farm station seemed to mark the beginning of a new topography. Rapidly, pylon by pylon, the landscape over which we crawled changed to become more human in scale. The fields became smaller and more irregular in shape. The boundaries between them started to be marked by hedges again, but hedges small enough to force our way through or climb over with relative ease. We began to notice clumps of bushes and trees in the corners of fields, and, most gloriously, saw and drank from a small, meandering stream which trickled out from the direction of some distant spinney. The stream's irregular course gave it the look of something that was simply there of its own will, not something that was directed by the hand of man.

The final reason was that, for the first point on the journey, we seemed to be alone. The force of marshals that had been steadily maintained at our backs across the open steppe had vanished. Part of me briefly dared to wonder if we might succeed after all, but I buried the thought under a pylon. The more I chewed it over, the more this new factor mutated from a joy into a worry. The marshals had not evaporated, I theorised. They had merely halted, for the new terrain lay under the jurisdiction of a different power. The piston under us had risen in the cylinder as far as it could go, and the squeeze was now to be applied from above . . . and then would come the spark.

Our final resting place came at pylon zero-seven-zero. 'Seventy more to go. One day's hard walking!' we cried together.

That night we made our proper bivouac, the first for three days. We shared out the last of our food between the two of us. It was indeed virtually impossible for us to eat our fare now. It was not the foul nature of the stuff so much as the tedium of it that made our bodies rebel. After days of cramming the noxious mush into our mouths we were mad for the taste and texture of something else. Only by stuffing the lard into our mouths, holding our breath and chewing and swallowing as fast as we could, was it possible to ingest it. We forced ourselves to eat almost all of what we had left, saving just a small portion for the next day's breakfast.

The night was the first truly cold night we had experienced on our travels. We had been very fortunate so far with the weather; it had probably not dipped much below freezing during the days, and the nights had all been mild under their lid of clouds. But that night was cloudless and the stars were blistered across the limitless black cupola of the sky.

'There's Orion,' said Moth without warning. I swore loudly and started to struggle to my feet, then noticed he was pointing upwards at the sky. The stars looked completely random to me. Moth picked out the constellation he said was named for a hunter, showed me the three stars that made his angled belt. Moth named them too, alien names that would have been outlandish even in the Institute, but I'd long ago decided what Orion wore on his belt: wire, pistol and handcuffs, one pair.

'The *consternation* of Orion, more like it,' I remarked. My hands automatically crossed over my crotch.

'A portent,' Moth said.

'I know, but it's the best I could do. The plastic's getting very ripped,' I answered. We both laughed at the jokes, and shuffled together under the blankets and covers. Moth was not sleepy; he seemed annoyingly fired up by the sight of the stars and the nearness of the end of our journey. What had happened to his normal nightly ritual of complaining about his feet and his other, innumerable maladies?

'I've been thinking again about Harete's story,' he chirped up. 'Remember, we asked why threats always seem to come in threes – like the giantess had to do battle with the lizard, the lyrebird and the double-threat of the vulture and the eagle?'

'Hmmm?' I replied, hoping The Moth would pipe down. I was tired.

'Well, since then we've had two threats – the tractor and the sow. So maybe we've a twin threat tomorrow!' He sounded like he was looking forward to it.

'It was only a story, Moth, not a prediction,' I said quietly.

Mention of Harete crippled me. The map. My fault we'd been chased by marshals, had met the tractors.

'Yes, yes, but stories can foreshadow the truth. Think about this as well. In her story, the giantess vanquished each enemy by turning its powers against itself. But that's what we did today!' he carried on. 'It's always the sweetest kind of victory.'

'What? Moth, belt up!' I snapped. 'What about the pig? We didn't use its size against it,' I countered.

'No, but you could argue that the essence of a pig is its greed. And we did distract it with water and food. So we used its greed against it.'

'Harete was killed, Moth, remember? She didn't defeat the tractor by using its power or its wheels against it, did she? She didn't beat it at all!'

Moth wriggled as he thought. 'I know,' he sighed, 'the story failed her.'

'Garbage! You told me this morning that you didn't think stories held messages,' I fumed. 'As for using your enemies' strengths against them, seems to me it was Harete's talents we relied on more, with little help from you,' I spat, feeling Moth was belittling Harete. I paused to muster my reserves of sarcasm for a new assault, but as I thought deeper, it occurred to me there was a certain truth to his theory.

'Jelly – I guess it was his condition we exploited . . .' I began. The dogs? Those poor cows? No . . . but Toffee's desire for the blade, that fitted the pattern. 'Maybe . . . maybe the essence of Sticky was eating things he stole, so I defeated him by feeding him glass from a bottle I'd stolen!' I prattled, weighing up my reinterpretation of the event as I spoke.

Silence. I winced, aware of what I'd just said. Inwardly I cursed myself. How could I have been so careless as to let that slip?

Moth spoke up, his voice now flat with disappointment. 'So it was you who did it, like the whispers said. And you promised us that you weren't involved.'

'Oh dry up! All right, I did do it. I crept into his cell and tipped some ground glass into his vile gob. Big deal, so what! I did it for you,' I yelled, my face aflame. 'He was sewage. A thuggish gangster who ruined life for everyone! He twisted the head off Harete's pet! It's people like him who make everything in life wretched and frightening! Who cares about him?' I blasted back.

'What about Retread? He's facing serious charges now. He may be hanged if Sticky dies.'

The mention of Retread made me blush even hotter. 'He won't die. He'll be fine,' I said, convincing not even myself, nor even certain who I was referring to.

Moth squirmed around. 'There's . . . something else, too. If our country provides convincing evidence you're a credible suspect, something more than rumours, well, that would complicate things,' he said. 'They might hand you back. They might hand us both back. Assuming we even make it there.'

We both retreated into a long silence. From the very first, I'd intended to use The Moth's glare to blind others to my sins, and I'd always known he would never consent.

Moth milked his new realisations of their inevitable conclusions. 'That's why you wanted to escape, wasn't it? To save yourself. Not to help me,' he said. 'Just as I said that first dawn, by the river.' He turned abruptly over on his side and in so doing whipped away the portion of blanket and plastic sheeting that had swaddled me. 'Of course, if you hadn't done it,' he pointed out, as I knew he would, 'Harete would still be alive.'

Cold air washed over me. I screwed myself into a ball and scrunched up my eyes and fists. Moth was right; everything was ruined because of me. I had promised Moth and Harete; why hadn't I kept my promise? The rage would have gone in time. I could have blinded myself to the nastiness and not let it abrade me to dust, could have fended off Sticky's attempts to condemn me to the Establishment.

Harete would still be alive, and Moth and I would not be starving and freezing in a field.

I'd known the truth from the start, of course, had tried to dab it away, but Moth's discovery of it reflected it back onto me, focused and intensified it, and left me no gaps to hide in.

I'd never be free of the Institute. Trying to use Moth for my own ends, attacking Sticky, forsaking Retread . . . I belonged in that place, it was all I was fit for. Had I ever believed otherwise? No, I realised. I'd only ever thought I was better than other people because I was smarter. The fiasco of my ruse with the note in our cell gave the lie to that last, ragged vestige of my worth.

'Too cunning for my own good,' I whispered to myself, 'and too stupid even to do it well.'

My stomach rumbled loudly and I curled up to obtain some warmth, but there was none to be had.

Chapter 14

The Vase

Even the fact that this might have been our last day on the walk was not enough to thaw the mood that had dropped like frost upon me. By early morning we had hacked past the first ten pylons and no word had been spoken between us. I held back and let The Moth press on ahead.

My night had not passed well. The cold had been intense; I was still shivering constantly. I felt colder than I had ever felt before. Even the river five days before had felt warmer than that morning. *Was the river really only five days ago?* I wondered in confused amazement. We seemed to have been on the walk forever. My skin felt pinched and drawn, my toes and fingers and nose throbbed with cold. I pictured scorpions crawling inside my clothes, jabbing me with icicle-tipped tails and freezing my blood. A good depth of snow had fallen in the early morning, and it was falling still. Maybe it would be better if I just died on the way, I snivelled, maybe that would be the fitting reward. I tallied up the people whose lives I had ended or damaged: Harete's, without doubt; Retread's; Sticky's; maybe even Jelly's, although I felt no sympathy for those final two. After all, Jelly might very well have profited from us.

My convictions had frozen solid during the night and would brook no warming current of hope. I was murderous crud, fit only for incarceration or even . . . something hard rattled down the inside of my sleeve to my cuff. Peeling away my mitten I saw the splintered plastic bottle of Jelly's tablets I had taken from his uniform. A scaly fish darted under the icy surface – would these be sufficient, if taken all at once, to prevent me from doing more damage?

Up ahead, I saw Moth suddenly drop to the ground behind a small hedge. He flapped his arm to tell me to lie flat, and put his finger to his lips. Complying felt burdensome. Why bother, when capture and punishment were both inevitable and warranted? I'd soon be in the warming hands of Capo-Colonel Orion, sampling his brief and barbaric hospitality. Orion troubled me in other ways; he steadfastly refused to be pictured. Composing his face was like chasing rubbery Institute beans around your plate with a fork; the features slid around and squidged into different shapes but rejected all efforts to pin them into place. He simply wasn't *gelling*. Unless . . . I squeezed the pill bottle tighter, my new escape plan.

Moth pointed through the hedge. Shifting my head about to get a view through the foliage I looked ahead. The field was small, maybe the smallest we had seen so far, no more than a couple of minutes' walk from side to side. Our next pylon stood on the far side of it. Between us and it, a man walked along the hedge on the opposite side of the snow-covered field and looked over in our direction. Squinting, I could see he was wearing dark blue overalls and big boots and some sort of hat. His hand kept moving up to his mouth and down again, and I decided he was speaking into a walkie-talkie. Or possibly eating a sandwich. We crouched low and watched him for several moments.

The man pocketed whatever was in his hand, walked along the hedge, then vanished though a gap in it. We heard an engine start up, and saw a glint of blue move along at speed.

'Must be a road there. We're getting dangerously near civilisation,' I mumbled, keeping my voice low. It was an effort to care.

'Was he a marshal?' asked Moth keenly.

I sighed heavily and rubbed my sleep-glued eyes. Cold and stiff, I felt three-parts dead. 'No, not a marshal,' I yawned. 'Yes, he had blue clothes and black boots, but they were more like rubber boots, loose and sloppy. And if my eyes didn't deceive me, his hat had ear flaps. Either that, or he had very long hair, but in neither case could that be a marshal. Just a farmer, I should think. Whatever.'

'*Whatever?*' Moth hissed angrily at me. 'What's wrong with you today?'

'Nothing,' I said. 'Look . . . we need to split. Stick with me and I'll only get you killed. And it's like you said, if we do make it over together, being with me will ruin your chances of staying.'

Moth's eyes displayed real horror. 'Don't forsake me!' he yelped, and he put out a hand towards me.

'Yes!' I shouted back, batting him away and no longer worried about keeping quiet. 'I'm contaminated! All my plans end up with people being poisoned or hanged or buried under a pile of mud. Get away from me! Find a

287

farmer and tell him your dad will pay twice any reward offered for your capture; they'll smuggle you over in a lorry load of turnips.'

A flock of birds flew out of the hedge some way from us.

The Moth's face blanched under its broad stripes of grease. 'We're so close, we can't quit now! Not you, not you of all people,' he squawked.

More birds flew out of the hedge, nearer this time. Sick of being the adult, the commander, his words prickled me more than I could tolerate. 'I can quit if I want!' I said, standing up. 'Are you too thick to save your own life? Damn you!'

As my head rose above the level of the hedge I found myself staring into the plump, ruddy, hatless face of a man on the other side.

'Temper. And mind your language, whatever you are. Making enough noise, wasn't you? I've been creeping along here for five minutes trying to get a look at you,' said the man. No, not a man – a boy. A very large boy, probably not much older than me but a head taller and built like an oak wardrobe. He wore the same sort of blue overalls and rubber boots as the man who had driven away, but carried a double-barrelled shotgun, which he now raised up and pointed at my face.

'I don't know what you are, but stand up, both of you,' he said. He did not seem the least bit excited or cross. Maybe this was an everyday occurrence for him.

The Moth stood up beside me, and we tentatively raised our arms. The huge youth laughed. 'I never said raise your

hands, but all right, let's have it! Like cops and robbers!'
He moved back from us and, clamping the shotgun
awkwardly under his right arm with a finger on the trigger,
he used his left hand to take a walkie-talkie from his breast
pocket.

'Da – I've got 'em. Two. No idea. Look like none we
ever had before, real freaks. Like scarecrows or . . . clowns.
White paint on their faces,' he said in response to the
indecipherable noises coming from the radio. Just before
he signed off he came forwards two paces, then stepped
briskly back again. 'Tell you what though, they stink like
you would not believe! Even the pigs would run away,' he
said, and laughed heartily again.

He switched his attention back to us. 'We're going to
wait here. Da's coming back with the pickup. No need to
worry now; we collect you lot all the time. Just stay where
you are, cos I will shoot if you run. Allowed to, up here,
this near the border. Different laws up here, see, special
zone!'

The boy seemed to be enjoying his work tremendously.
I could imagine him coping with hard farm work with ease.
He seemed to have been forged in the same foundry that
had made the behemoth pig and gigantic tractors.

His breath steamed in the cold air, but his thick, ungloved
fingers showed no signs of suffering from the cold, unlike
ours. His porky hands looked strong enough to plough a
field on their own. Even his unfamiliar accent was thick,
strong, cheery, and not at all like the one the clavigers
spoke with.

We waited; inert, defeated, crushed. The snow was

coming down harder now, settling on our unmoving heads and shoulders.

'Are we very near the border, then?' I ventured, my curiosity tickled.

'Oh, it speaks! And what a funny voice! Never you mind the border, think you know well enough anyhow. We get your lot over from time to time. Well, all kinds really . . . your sort, up from the delta, then townies who think they'll drive up and hold a protest, or . . . whatever it is they want, smuggling or daft things, throw themselves on the wire sometimes they do, or they hold up babies for them on the other side to see. Madness!' He laughed again, genuinely uproarious, happy laughter. I wondered furiously what it was exactly that he had seen.

His walkie-talkie burbled and he listened carefully to the instructions issuing from it, responding to each one, 'Right. Right. Yup. Will do.'

'Off we go then,' he said, and he waved the gun to show us which direction to walk in. He kept on his side of the hedge and we moved along on ours. 'You can put those arms down!' said our happy farmer's boy, 'I don't suppose you've got guns in those funny bags of yours.' We dropped our arms and lugged our mattress rolls and water bottles as normal. Soon we were directed through a break in the hedge, then we crossed the small field and through a metal gate and onto a road. A real road, narrow, but properly metalled! I could see the black surface peeping up through gaps in the compacted ice and snow.

A minute later, a battered blue pickup truck came slithering along the road. From the glimpse I got of him through the windscreen the driver did not look like he shared his son's love of laughter. He turned the noisy truck around in the mouth of the gate and reversed up to us. The boy dropped the tailgate and told us to hop in. He hoisted himself onto the truck bed and stretched out a beefy hand to yank us both up in turn, and the truck drove off through the snow.

The drive did not last long, but it was not without event. The narrow, twisty road was already becoming impassable with the snow and ice; the driver had to turn on his windscreen wipers and headlights and drive in low, grinding gears all the way.

'Big fall last night,' confirmed the boy, grinning as the three of us slid about crazily on the cold metal floor. 'Was you out in it? I bet you was, from the look of you. You're idiots, you know that? There's me in my bed with a belly full of roast pork, and there's you in some hole in the ground! And you go on about living the free life; that makes me laugh,' and he laughed uproariously again, to prove his word.

We heard a sharp bang and a grinding noise from somewhere underneath us. The truck slewed wildly, almost spinning around in a full circle, and the engine stalled. Laughing boy just gurgled even more, but did not take the gun off us.

The truck door burst open and the driver jumped out. 'That's had it. We jumped the road and the back axle's bust on a rock. Hang you scum! If it wasn't for you I wouldn't even be out today,' he shouted, white faced with anger, pointing a single finger at us. The one finger seemed more dangerous and scary than the two gun barrels. Da was, if anything, slightly smaller than his son, but a big man all the same. I dared not meet his gaze. He seemed to be the sort of man who was permanently in a rage. We were told to jump down from the truck and we plodded after him, his son bringing up the rear. We were frogmarched by the grumbling farmer and his good-natured offspring along the road for just a few minutes before the farmhouse appeared in view.

The house looked prosperous and well-cared for under its thickening duvet of snow. Moth and I glanced at one another. I knew what he was thinking, because I was thinking it myself. He was looking at the smoke coming from the chimney, and he was imagining the beds inside, the food, the soft sofas, the heat of the fire. The food . . . above all, the food. I felt renewed sorrow then for the pointless, lethal escapade we had set out on. The house looked perfect, a perfect place for a couple to make their living and raise a happy giant of a child. What more could a person want? We were being given a teasing, taunting glimpse of a life we would never know, and never did that unattainable life hold more simple or necessary pleasures than right there and then, as our adventure collapsed in supreme humiliation.

Da unlocked the front door and went inside, leaving the two of us and our guard stomping our feet in the cold. He stormed back out shortly afterwards and slammed the door behind him.

'Hell! Blast!' he shouted, and opened the front door again purely so that he could slam it once more to vent his annoyance. A wedge of snow slid off the porch roof and crumpled softly onto the ground behind him.

'What's the matter, Da? Phone lines down?' asked the son. Not knowing his name, I decided to call him 'Sonny' – it fitted his happy disposition.

'No, the phone's working. But they're not in! None of them! Only that halfwit helper of theirs, and he's no damn good. He says they've all gone over to the machine station; that blasted sow of theirs has got out and is running amok. There's no phone there; I'll take the little tractor,' Da replied, removing his hat with the ear flaps to scratch his bald head. 'Something else he mentioned too, I'll have to tell you later,' he grumbled hesitantly, and I took it he meant when Moth and I were not around.

'Just phone the marshals, then!' said Sonny.

'No! No, I'll tell you what we're going to do,' said Da, menacingly, and he walked over and examined Moth and me closely, shaking his head in incredulity as he did so. 'We're going to do what they did up at Top Farm last year. We're going to hold these . . . creatures . . . in one of the barns and get a message up to the delta. Their families will pay a good ransom for them, much better than the bounty the marshals pay for illegals. I need a new axle now, so I want a good amount. This lot,' he turned to his son and jabbed a thumb over his shoulder at us, 'they don't want to get involved in anything official, and their folks'll pay over the odds to keep 'em out of the clink.'

'Ooh, I dunno, Da . . . that's a bit . . . well, I suppose so! If you think it will be all right,' said Sonny, warming to the idea with a smile broad enough to fly a plane through.

Da clapped his son across his broad back and chuckled. 'Course it is! Top Farm made enough from theirs to build that glasshouse. I'll get a new pickup out of this lot. They're close knit, see, and they pay cash – or gold.'

He pulled his hat back on and set off across the farmyard, yelling over his shoulder as he went, 'Keep them covered, and blast 'em in the legs if they make any trouble! I'll be back in about an hour.'

'Shall I take them inside?' asked Sonny.

'Not in my house, not with them smelling like that,' came the answer.

Sonny dragged a wooden crate over near the front door and sat down on it, still holding the shotgun. Moth and I stood facing him, silent, confused, shivering. We exchanged small shrugs and quizzical looks to let each other knew that neither of us really understood what was going on. Now we were stationary we began to freeze. The Moth's face looked blue and he was shaking violently.

'Mister . . . can't we wait inside? We're freezing to death here!' I pleaded.

'You heard what Da said. That's a right stink you've got on you; we don't want that muck in our house.'

'But . . . he's sick,' I said, nodding towards Moth.

'He'll live!'

Desperation gave birth to a crazy lie. 'He's . . . uh, eliseptic!' I declaimed confidently. Moth's shivering ceased and he blinked up at me in astonishment.

'Epileptic!' he snarled from the corner of his mouth.

'Yeah, he gets them . . . seizures! Here! Look!' I said, and from the end of my cuff I shook free Jelly's cracked tablet bottle and tossed it over to Sonny. He caught it smartly in one of his meaty hands and peered at the worn label and the yellow pills inside.

'Blow me down! Same as my sister's. She gets the fits and faints an' all,' he gasped.

'I'm sorry to hear that,' said Moth sincerely.

'Huh?' said Sonny. 'It's nowt. She's tougher'n all of us,' he said, narrowing his eyes. The big hand clutching the pill bottle migrated north to scratch his forehead, 'Still, we don't want you . . . suffering, do we?' he mumbled.

I grinned at Sonny. I was warming to him. Despite the danger we were undoubtedly in, I relished a new chance to use my talents. With the pills I'd thrown away went a portion of the morning's depression.

Sonny thought for a moment more. On his face I could see him debating the pros and cons, balancing the greater price a well-looked-after captive might fetch against his father's instructions. At last, he said, 'Well . . . all right . . . we'll go round the back. But you'll have to wipe your feet! And I'm on you with the gun all the time, mind!'

Walking backwards with carefully measured and tested paces and occasional glimpses over his shoulder, he led us around the side of the house to a back door. He opened the door and stood to one side, motioning with the gun for us to walk in. We dropped our gear by the doorstep and trooped inside, making sure we wiped our feet thoroughly on the doormat. Sonny followed us in and pulled the door shut behind him.

We shuffled into the room. It was the kitchen, and no kitchen ever looked more inviting to any pair of foot-sore travellers than that one did to us. The floor was made of red tiles, the walls were painted white. A big pine table and chairs took up most of the space and a pine dresser stood against one wall, laden with decorative plates and knick-knacks. I noticed several pairs of rubber boots standing by the door like soldiers on parade, fishing rods propped up in a corner, a deep sink stacked high with plates. But although we saw these things, none of them was what really interested us.

We did not even pay much attention to the sturdy black-leaded range at the far end of the room, although we felt its warmth as soon as we crossed the threshold and appreciated it very much indeed. The loaf of freshly baked bread on the worktop must have been smelled if not seen by us both, and despite the fact that it made us cry and drool with want, even that gorgeous object was not the focus of our fascination. What drew us into the room and held us frozen was a mirror hanging on the wall opposite the door.

We stood together in front of the mirror and boggled at what we saw. We moved our heads from side to side and up and down, unable to believe that the bizarre animals we saw reflected in it, bobbing and weaving in synchrony, were really our own images. We touched our faces, and one another's too, to confirm this extraordinary truth.

I had grown used to the sight of The Moth as he doubtless had grown used to the sight of me, but somehow I had never expected that I would look as comical as he did.

Under my balaclava my naturally dark face was black and leathery with dirt and the effects of exposure to the winter winds. The lard I had rubbed onto it had not soaked into my skin but stood out in bright white bands like tribal warpaint. I had traces of a moustache and beard, and I rubbed my hand over these with a mixture of pride and astonishment. My balaclava was matted with soil and grass and had adopted a peculiar pair of pointy tips like joke ears.

I half-turned my body, first one way and then another, in order to better see how I appeared. My plastic waterproofs were far more ragged than I had realised; they were really nothing but a mass of peeling, curling black shreds. The bags over my shoes had disintegrated to nothing. Only the multicoloured rope made of the carrier bags still wound over my shoulder and the overalls under my waterproofs looked to have survived reasonably intact, albeit appallingly begrimed and squalid. Everything was splattered and caked with mud. Black mud, brown mud, grey mud, yellow mud, dry mud, wet mud; my body was a palette for an earth artist, a masterpiece in soils.

Moth took off his spectacles, themselves more mud than glass, and repeated my gawping motions as he studied his own clay-caked face and tattered clothes. Looking at him looking at his reflection, I started to convulse. I quaked and juddered and broke out into a gut-busting laugh. Soon Moth joined in and together we laughed and laughed and laughed. The warmth of the room and the laughter broke apart the last of the ice that had entombed me since the previous night.

Poor Sonny, who seemed to find just about any sentence he or anyone else uttered a source of infinite hilarity, seemed shocked and a little unnerved by our laughter.

'Hey . . . what's the matter . . . even you lot have mirrors . . . didn't you know what you looked like? Just as well you can't reflect the smell, you should be grateful for that!' he said, warily. Using his sock-clad foot – for he had removed his rubber boots and put them with their comrades lined up by the door – he scraped two pine chairs over from where they rested underneath the table and poked them towards us. Needing to put a third chair by the table for himself, he turned away from us for a few seconds. During that slim interval, Moth tugged off the remnants of his ragged balaclava. I assumed at first this was solely because the kitchen was so gorgeously warm, but his real motive became clear when he rapidly dabbed a crude triangle on his still relatively clean forehead with the dirt on his finger. I quickly copied him, but without understanding why.

'Come on then, sit down, if you can tear yourself away from that mirror,' Sonny said. 'We'll sit here nice and warm and wait for Da to return.'

We did as offered. Sonny sat in his chair at the end of the table, nearest to the blazing range. The warmth of the room was bliss beyond description to our iced-up bodies. The mere act of sitting on a chair seemed like a pleasure so great it should have been reserved for saints.

'Hey, we had another of your lot around here recently, a girl. Well, woman!' Sonny announced, sounding like he was sharing news with close friends in the pub. 'Only she got away, running about somewhere. You know her?'

'No!' we said together, almost too readily. A memory of the smashed-in face of the mermaid came to me. If that was who Sonny meant, Da had clearly not yet shared with him news of her fate.

'Hey!' shouted Sonny in alarm, whipping the barrels suddenly upwards again and this time cocking the gun for good measure. 'Wait a minute!' he went on, clearly agitated. 'Was you on a thieving trip? You lot's always on the steal! Was you casing this farm?'

We shook our heads vigorously.

'Sick of it we are!' bellowed Sonny, stamping his foot on the tiles. 'Diesel, seed, poultry, we're sick of spending our dough and seeing it go downriver.'

'Not us,' burst out Moth. 'Different . . . clan. Yes, clan! We're no thieves.'

'Oh!' came the startled reply. 'Well, you do look different, that's true. Never knew you lot was organised that way.' He relaxed and the gun drooped down.

A brief silence, then Sonny quizzed us some more. 'What was you here for then?' he asked, suspicion and barrels both rising again.

I'd been preparing for that one. 'We were on our way to town, to get a doctor to look at him,' I told Sonny, flicking my head towards Moth. 'We need more medicine. He's got *complications*.' The final word I mouthed, and juiced with a knowing nod. The idea bridged to another. 'In fact, he's really quite ill. If he doesn't get to hospital soon, he'll die.'

'Ooh, you . . . you can't try that on me . . .' Sonny said, but I could sense doubt in his voice. 'What town was you going to?' he asked. He named several places, none of which meant anything to me. I told him the name of the only town I knew in the area, the one nearest to the Institute.

'But that's well over four hours away, even by car! And you was going to walk there? Pull the other one!' he snorted.

'No, honestly. We have friends there. We had it all planned out. That's where we were headed. We were hoping to hitch a lift,' I assured him.

'What was you going to pay the doctors with?' Sonny asked. Once more, the gun barrels perked up, and I could see Sonny's finger tighten on the triggers.

I was one step ahead. 'This!' I said, and with a flourish I produced the ring I had taken from the truck in the slaughter yard. Jiggling around in my overalls, the dull ring had become cleaned and polished, and in the brightly lit kitchen it glowed and sparkled magnificently. Sonny and I both sighed admiringly and leant close in to look at it, although The Moth paid it only a perfunctory sideways glance before turning away again.

The weighty ring comprised a broad band of silver-coloured metal, decorated with tiny, immaculately made engravings – a goat, a horse, a man, a crown, a dagger, an eye – each shape filled in with minute red jewels. Cleaned, it was stunningly beautiful. Looking at it then, an understanding came to me: no one who had worn such a fantastical item would have parted with it for any reason other than to give it to someone they loved, or because they were facing their own imminent annihilation. Moth's pretended lack of interest infuriated me, but I determined not to let my anger show.

'Nice!' whistled Sonny. 'That would certainly pay the

300

bill. And then some!' he said, then, 'Hey, don't let Da see it. He'll have that off you.'

On hearing this, I popped the ring into my mouth and swallowed noisily.

'Madness!' gasped Sonny. Even The Moth pulled a face.

I renewed my plea. 'Well? Do you believe us now? That we need to get him to hospital?'

Sonny sucked in his cheeks, but I felt he at least partly believed me. 'Maybe . . . well, don't you worry. We'll contact your folks and they can pay to have you back. All be over in less than half a week. He can't be so ill a couple of days will matter!'

'You don't understand. We're running away!' I begged. Sonny squirmed a little, and shifted uneasily in his seat. 'Our people are suspicious of his illness. They think he's possessed,' I carried on.

Sonny baulked and whistled. 'You lot have odd customs . . . half savage, I've always been told that. That's not my business though. Maybe . . . maybe I'll have a word with my da. Perhaps we'll just hand you over to the marshals; they pay for captured illegals, and it'll all be above board too. They'll see him all right!' said Sonny, brightening. 'As long as the marshals get to you before the square-hats do. They really hate your sort. We farmers might try to put the wind up you, dangle some scarecrows, but the border guards, well . . .' He let the sentence hang like a body from the gallows.

I smiled weakly. The boy was kind-hearted, but he was not a simpleton, and my approach seemed destined to flop.

We sat in silence for some more minutes. The cosy, snug

301

room was starting to erode my reborn resolve to escape. I began to worry about The Moth; I did not want him also to be seduced by the warmth and comfort. We had to get away! Whoever it was that Sonny and his father thought we were, it could not be long before they discovered their mistake. One way or another, we were destined to end up in the custody of the marshals within days or perhaps just a few hours. Once that happened, it would only be a matter of our fingerprints being taken before they knew who we really were.

Moth spoke next. 'Excuse me please, might we have some of that bread?' he asked.

Sonny stared distrustfully at him, then at the loaf behind him, then back at The Moth. He hummed and hawed again. 'You do look pretty hungry . . . but . . . I can't be letting you have that. If I take my hands off the gun to slice the loaf, you'll be off! Everyone knows you're full of tricks like that,' he concluded, shaking his head.

'Can't you please give us the loaf and a knife, then?' asked The Moth.

'Give you a knife! You'd like that, wouldn't you? Not a chance!' said Sonny, flashing us a smile.

'What about if you just throw us the loaf and we use our hands? We can't harm you with a loaf of bread. Please, it's not a trick; we really are hungry. You don't want our people or the marshals to think you starved us, do you?' Moth said, snivelling piteously.

Sonny's jaw ground round and round as he thought. 'No . . . all right then . . . it's only bread, after all, one way or another we'll be getting our money's worth from you . . .'

He leaned back in his chair, grabbed the loaf and tossed it towards us. It fell on the floor at our feet and we set upon it with the same gusto and degree of decorum the pig had shown when presented with Moth's bag of lard.

I pulled off my mitten and sunk my fingers into one end of the loaf, and peeled back a rough hunk, which I stuffed into my mouth. Moth plunged a bare hand into the soft white interior which had been exposed where I had broken off the crust. He plucked out a fistful of the fluffy white bread and proceeded to devour it. Even before I had finished ripping off the crust, Moth had bent his head forwards and gripped a corner of the loaf in his teeth. He snarled and twisted his head from side to side to loosen the corner, and almost bayed with delight through his stuffed mouth when it broke loose. The two of us slobbered and grunted and groaned as we ate; tears filled our eyes. Bread! Something to eat that was not that dreadful gritty dripping! We choked as we swallowed too fast, and took it in turns to smack one another hard on our backs.

Together, we reduced the loaf to crumbed rubble in just a few short minutes. Sonny almost fell off his chair in revulsion as he observed the devastation.

'You . . . you're not human! You're animals! It's all true! My gran used to say you lot was primitives, like cavemen,' he gasped, scarcely able to credit what he was observing. He clutched the shotgun tighter and switched it from one of us to the other in rapid succession.

We slumped back with huge sighs of relief, moaning with delight and a growing awareness of pains in our stomachs as our bodies strained to digest the new food.

Without a word, Moth suddenly pitched forwards, blinking hard, his attention anchored onto something else in the room. Whatever it was, it held him transfixed. He strained to see better, and I could see his lips moving as if he were reading.

Sonny smiled again, and ran his tongue around his mouth as if the sight of us feasting had awoken his own substantial appetite. 'Liked that bread, didn't you? Never seen anyone enjoy food so much. You wait till you try some of this, then; you'll probably die of happiness,' He stood up and risked turning around to take something out of a cupboard.

Perhaps emboldened by his full stomach, Moth rose and took a step towards the large dresser on his right, towards the object he had spotted. It attracted him with greater force than even the bread had, maybe promising to sate a larger appetite. What he had seen was a red and black coloured vase. Plucked from its shelf, Moth held it up with shaking hands for me to look at. The symbols that were baked into the glaze I recognised at once, although I could not read them – they were the same as the ones on the dead mermaid's body. Triangles, tridents, squares, crossed-out circles . . .

I was still examining the vase when Sonny turned back to us, holding a plate covered with a tea towel in one hand. 'Hey, you put that down!' he boomed, clearly distressed. He plonked the plate on the table and snatched up the gun in both hands again.

Moth looked back at him, scared but also cross. 'I'm only looking. It's in-in-incredible!' he stammered. 'Half savage? Primitives? Don't you know what this is?' he continued, proffering the vase towards Sonny. He was trembling, as if he were holding the most important thing in the universe.

'Yes, that's valuable, that is! That's over a hundred and fifty years old,' Sonny replied, visibly sweating. I could see him twitch and blink as he realised that he'd said something he should not have. 'I mean, it's not really valuable, just to us, this family, sentimental value. Belonged to my great-great-grandmother, that did. Please put it down! It's fragile!' he begged. 'She was half . . . one of you lot, so Da reckons,' he whispered in a low voice, as if letting slip a shameful family secret. He darted me an imploring look, perhaps believing this news might incline me to assist.

'Valuable?' Moth yelled, like the word was an insult. 'This is . . . revelatory! This is beyond genius, this is . . .' he spluttered, groping for the words. The vase wobbled precariously in the grip of his sweaty hands. 'You don't understand, do you? Neither of you!' he shouted angrily, this directed as much at me as at Sonny.

'Please! My da will murder me if that gets busted,' pleaded Sonny, adding, 'and anyway, it's a nice thing, why break a nice thing? Put it down and we can all have a slice of what's under this towel . . . you'll like it! My nan baked it.'

I switched my open-mouthed gaze from Moth to Sonny and back again. What was The Moth doing? Was this an act? I was sure it was not. I already liked Sonny, and his last words made me like him even more. Why break a nice thing . . . he was not one of *them*, he was a decent lad. And I so wanted to see what was under the towel on the plate; something baked, he'd said! A pie? A cake?

'Moth, I think you should do what he –' I started, but

got no further. Moth sprang without warning towards Sonny, I am sure intending to explain his discovery, but his foot was hooked around his chair leg and he tripped. The vase fell from his hands.

'You dog!' Sonny screamed and he dropped the shotgun as he hurled himself forwards to catch the vase before it smashed on the stone floor. As he threw himself towards us, I launched myself at the dropped gun. We each made our targets at the same time. Sonny caught the vase in his huge hands and lurched heavily into the dresser, winding himself and sending several items of crockery spinning to their noisy destruction on the floor. I snatched the gun and staggered painfully into the table, sending the object on the plate under the towel plunging to its doom. As I whipped around to point the gun at Sonny, I saw a beautiful golden brown cake land with a splat on the tiles.

'What do we do? What do we do?' I yelled. I hadn't planned for this! Moth ran to my side, aghast. Sonny carefully put the vase on the dresser and turned to us, purple faced. 'You ungrateful pair of tramps! After I let you in here and gave you food! Look at my nan's cake! Look at it! You . . . vandals!' he yelled, and he took a step forwards to grab his gun back. Terrified, I squeezed one of the two triggers, deliberately pulling the gun to one side away from Sonny and closing my eyes as I did so.

The bang was so loud it stunned all of us. The recoil pushed me back and bent me double over the table. Sonny threw himself against the wall, and a dozen more plates and dishes on the dresser exploded into powdery smithereens as the shot blasted them.

I opened my eyes and pitched upright again, dazed. I was grateful I had removed my mitten to eat the loaf; had I been wearing it I would probably have accidentally pulled both triggers. 'Are you all right?' I shouted to Sonny, who had fallen into a heap on the floor and was shielding his head under his arm.

'Yes, yes, just don't fire again!' he cried. He removed his head from under his arm and looked at the dresser and the devastated porcelain. Fortunately, and to my own great relief, the vase stood undamaged where he had placed it. 'Oh no . . . no . . . no . . . Da will slaughter me!' he sobbed.

'Tie him up!' I shouted.

'What with?' said Moth, flapping around the kitchen like a pigeon. I was grateful that the urgency of our changed situation had swept away his academic fervour.

I thought. The rope? Too easy for a strong person to snap. 'The tape! The roll's in my pack outside the door!' I shouted. Moth opened the door and rummaged in my mattress. He came back with the roll of strong, silver tape. 'Cut it with the bread knife!' I told him, nodding at the breadboard and knife behind me.

'Sorry, mister, we really are,' I told Sonny. 'We like you; you're a good person. But we can't go back! We can't! Please co-operate, else I'll shoot the vase,' I said, thinking this was probably a more effective threat than the idea of shooting him, and certainly easier for me to contemplate doing. Sonny snivelled and nodded and carried on moaning about what his da was likely to do to him. He meekly held his hands behind his back and let Moth bind them with the tough tape, then let him do the same to his ankles. Moth wound a strip over his mouth too.

I beckoned Moth over and whispered instructions to him, out of earshot of the blubbing giant. My mind was clear and I knew what we had to do. 'Find the telephone, cut the wire. Find the bath and any sinks, put the plugs in and run the taps on full,' I told him.

He dashed around the house to carry out my orders. The Moth was gone for a worryingly long time, and my nerves were thoroughly shredded when he finally returned, holding the disconnected telephone in his hand for all the world as if it were a hunting trophy. He looked strangely pleased with himself.

'Hey . . . mister!' I yelled. 'We're off. We're going to that town, like I said. When we meet our friends, we'll get them to send money to pay for the damage, I promise!'

Sonny nodded, damp eyed. He looked like he no longer cared one way or the other. Before we ran out of the door and gathered up our packs, remembering to take our mittens and the roll of tape, I carefully moved the vase further back on the dresser top in case it wobbled off. Sonny blinked a tearful 'thank you' at me. On my way to the door I determined to get something that might be of use to us. Food? Clothes? I dithered. There was no time. I grabbed the first thing I saw, a spool of fishing line sitting on the worktop, and hurried out.

Outside, it was still snowing. I twirled the shotgun around by the barrel and flung it away, and repeated the performance with the bread knife and the severed telephone.

'Try to walk in our old footsteps!' I shouted. We loped

across the driveway trying not to make new tracks. In this lumbering style we soon made it back to the abandoned pickup truck. I hesitated as we ploughed on past it, again aware of the possibilities it held as a supply of useful tools, and already angry with myself for not taking more advantage of our stay in the farmhouse.

I prevaricated, torn painfully by competing desires. Memories of another vehicle haunted me, and I decided to leave it. 'Now walk in the tracks the truck made!' I said. The path cut through the snow by the vehicle's tyres on our previous journey were already filling up with new snow, but they were still easier to walk in than the untouched areas. We wheezed and puffed as we ran, well aware of the possibility of Da returning at any minute, probably with others, to find his son bound and his china smashed. Rather than going back all the way to where we had first been captured, we wormed our way through a hole in a fence off to the left. After perhaps an hour we were close to the pylons, and we took a breather.

'Why the business with running the bath?' croaked Moth, purple with exhaustion.

'To waste more time. When his old man gets home he'll have to delay hunting for us to untie junior and, with luck, he'll spend even more time stopping his house from flooding,' I panted back. 'Who did they think we were, Moth? What was all that about "you lot" and rewards?' I asked. 'And what was it with the vase?'

Moth shrugged and took a sip from his water bottle. 'At a guess, up here near the border, the marshals will pay people if they capture anyone snooping around.'

'But who are the people he thought we were? Have you got any idea where they come from?' I persisted.

'A notion,' said Moth enigmatically.

'An ocean, did you say?'

'Perhaps.'

Of the vase, he said nothing, but I knew from the frown on his face that the memory of it was drilling a hole in his brain.

We trekked carefully along field edges, parallel to the line of pylons, ducking low behind hedges and walls. Only much later in the day when we had put a good distance between us and the farm did we dare to go right under a pylon which stood, exposed, in the middle of a field.

'Zero-three-eight,' I read out. 'We could get to the border by sundown if we hurry.'

'And if those farmers don't get us, or don't call the marshals,' Moth pointed out, 'or the border guards he mentioned.'

'We've a good chance. Remember, they don't want the authorities involved,' I reasoned aloud.

'What is at the border?' asked Moth. 'Do you actually know?'

I ignored his question, as he had mine about the vase. I noted that he had made no further mention of the ring, the last remnant of his mother, and that some dirty old pottery had been of much greater interest to him. Sonny still had the pill bottle, I realised, but my mood had changed and I didn't miss it.

Chapter 15

The Final Pylon

How agonising was the rest of that day! We knew we were close to the border and the end of our long trek, but the closer we got to it, the farther away it appeared to recede. The space between each pair of pylons was the same, but the land around them seemed designed to deliberately frustrate us. The fields grew ever smaller and more irregular in shape, and signs of habitation proliferated.

We spent almost all our time running in a crouched pose, or crawling on all fours, or making quick dashes between hedges and trees and walls. We had to skirt farms and barns and houses, we needed to dart across tracks and small roads, or dive into ditches as tractors *putt-putted* along lanes within sight of us. These were not the vast tractors we had seen days before, just ordinary small ones, usually with a farmhand or two perched on top and a bale of straw balanced on prongs sticking out from the rear. Many of the fields had grass growing in them, under the snow. Once, we vaulted a dry stone wall and almost landed on top of a flock of sheep gathered against the other side of the wall. The flock broke apart and the bleating beasts streamed away from us in rays that tracked back to our guilt. We could not even walk particularly close to the pylons because many of them stood adjacent to farm buildings or were inaccessible within plots of woodland.

'Wonder why all the greenery and people seem to be up here, near the border?' asked Moth. I suspected I knew why, but kept quiet.

Occasionally we passed near enough to a pylon to risk one of us dashing to it and reading its number. Disappointingly deep into the afternoon we greeted zero-three-zero.

'We'll never make it by evening,' grumbled The Moth, 'which means a night without food.'

We wove and threaded our way tentatively across many more fields, over dozens of streams and through mossy bogs. Even without the snow, the land was definitely getting wetter and marshier as we progressed northwards.

We paused by pylon zero-two-zero, vexed at how low the sun was to our left. Moth raised himself under one of the pylon's cross-beams and tried to see what lay ahead.

'Just looks flat and very green,' he said. 'Wonder why it's not covered in snow?'

We squelched on. The ground became persistently wetter but at least the buildings and roads became scarcer, the fields bigger and more open again, the going easier. The snow stopped falling, the clouds began to thin; it grew lighter. The snow did not seem to have settled on the wet ground, and before long we were in amongst the greener fields Moth had spotted.

Pylon zero-zero-nine was the same as all the others, but it stood in the middle of a junkyard. A muddy track ran through a gate in a stone wall and into a sodden field. The track fizzled out at the pylon's feet. Heaped up all around the track's terminus were scrapped vehicles and farm machinery and agricultural debris. It looked almost as if the local people had made votive offerings of metal to their pylon deity. Decrepit cars and wasted tractors squatted unloved on tyre-less wheel rims, slowly decomposing into coarse flakes of brown-red rust and diamonds of smashed glass. Obsolete harrows and ploughs and rollers lurked in senile repose in the long grass, presumably dumped as being far too small to fit the gargantuan modern tractors the farmers now used on the arable steppe we had crossed.

The Moth paid no attention to the scrap and just picked his way around it and carried on up an incline on his way to the next pylon. I delayed, taking my time to look over some threadbare tyres stacked in a wobbly ziggurat beside one pylon leg. As I clambered over the grubby black rings, trying to find an example that still had an intact inner tube, I saw an old van lying at an angle next to a crumbling conveyor belt. I dropped down and ambled over to examine it more closely. It was my dad's van! Not the actual van, of course, but the same design as the one he used to drive.

The little old van was battered and engineless, no more than a crust of rotted iron, but I recognised the smiley configuration of the glassless headlights and radiator. There was no mistaking the type. Although made of metal, the upper section of the van's roof consisted of a sort of trough made from fibreglass, stained green and roughened by mould but intact and uncorrupted by rust. I ran my hand over it.

'You just unclip the bolts and lift it off,' I said, but it was Dad's gruff voice I could hear. A memory seeped back, him working on his van at the kerbside and me, about

313

eleven years old, desperately wanting to help. Vandals had heaved a chunk of paving slab from a walkway onto the van and shattered the roof, but Dad wasn't fussed. Together, we swapped the damaged top for a new one as the radio in the cab played pop tunes. Then . . . I swallowed hard, and raced away, trying not to look at the van's smiley face.

I caught up with The Moth, striding determinedly through long, wet grass. 'Nine more!' shouted Moth. 'Just nine more pylons! And then we're free!'

The fields petered out into wet grassland. The ground grew boggier and soggier, the grass grew greener and taller. We were running now, both of us desperate to reach the end of the trail by dusk. Moth gave out yelps of boyish delight as we passed pylons zero-zero-eight, zero-zero-seven and zero-zero-six in rapid succession.

The grass became dense, mixed thickly with reeds and rushes, and as tall as us. We scythed through, parting the thick, sharp stems with our mittens, getting all hot and testy. Another obstacle, another delay! Moth was almost in tears as he rested from swimming through the reed sea.

'Oh, why this! So close to the end now, why this?' he grumbled. We sat on the wet ground to recover our strength. I was amazed that The Moth had not yet worked it out. He was so keen to get to the end that he had become blind to the evidence of the land around him. I knew he would be angry and broken by what lay up ahead but I saw no point in telling him until he found out for himself.

The reeds and grass rustled, our ragged clothing rustled. We sat still, heads bowed, and let the gentle *shisshing*, swishing sounds and bright evening sky relax us. The swishing sounds grew louder. We heard the characteristic zipping sound of clothes brushing up against sharp reeds, then voices. We held very, very still, became the mummies of the marshes. All around us the tall grass waved and swayed as men swarmed past us. Where the reeds parted, I saw that some of these men were civilians, presumably farmers, wearing waders and carrying shotguns folded in the crooks of their arms; others wore black jackboots and square hats, and no guesses were needed as to their occupation.

Up close, those four-cornered hats put me in mind of upturned coal shovels. For both groups, there was an eagerness to their actions quite in contrast to the slow, grinding menace of our earlier pursuers. *The marshals' job had been to hem us in*, I thought grimly, *these men are aiming to pick us up.* The men smashed onwards, not seeing us.

Minutes after they had left we dared to raise our heads and look after them. A long line of men, maybe fifty or more, moved in a front from east to west through the waving grass.

'For us?' gulped The Moth, despairingly. We skulked on, always following the line of pylons.

Past went zero-zero-five, zero-zero-four, zero-zero-three.

The Moth was unstoppable now; I could barely keep up with him. My bowels loosened as I anticipated the bitter letdown he was about to experience. How had he not put it all together, with all his intelligence? How could he be so unthinking?

We went under zero-zero-two. The next pylon was ahead

of us and above us on the top of a long, raised, horizontal embankment.

'Last one! That's it! The border!' he squealed, and he squelched on ahead at a gallop, disappearing from my sight into the dense reeds. I sighed heavily and plodded on.

When I caught up with him, The Moth was sitting cross-legged under pylon zero-zero-one with his back to me, looking due north. The ground at that point was so wet and unstable that the pylon builders had made a concrete raft for it to stand on. I climbed onto the cement square and shuffled next to him. Snagged on one of the pylon's feet was a heap of greasy rags. It fluttered forlornly where the wind caught it, a suitably dismal flag to fly at the finishing post for the survivors.

'Sorry. I thought it was obvious. And when I realised you didn't know, I figured it was best to let you find it out for yourself,' I said tenderly.

'Yes. Yes, you did the right thing. I'd have given up days ago if I'd known,' he replied, his face streaming with tears. 'And you're right. It was obvious. The way the ground has got wetter and wetter, the reeds, the reason all the most fertile farmland is in a strip up here . . .'

'I thought you'd clicked from the start, back when I showed you that map. The way the border wasn't straight, the way it dipped up and down in a curvy line,' I continued.

Moth nodded and wiped his nose on his sleeve. 'Of course. Borders between countries often follow natural features, and if not, they're usually straight lines. What else could it have been?'

He stood up and swept his arm despondently from left

to right and we both looked out over the huge, wide river that filled our vision.

The river was in flood. Just like the much smaller river we had drifted down at the start of our travels, the waters of this river were swollen with autumn rains and winter snowmelt and the level was far above its summer low-point. The long bank on which we and pylon number one stood was an artificial levee made to contain the river in winter. Beneath us, the reed-covered bank sloped down to the water's surface. The river stretched from as far as we could see to the left to as far as we could see to the right. It was probably three times wider than the river near the Institute, but we could see plainly enough over to the other side, to the far bank and the Other country.

Moth could only whisper, 'This is the absolute end. We'll never escape.'

The heap of rags stirred and shifted as a gust of wind caught it.

'You took your time,' said a voice from the rags.

Chapter 16

The Serpent and the Tortoise

Harete came out from under her rags and joined us. Moth and I did not accept her at first; we shrank away from her and clutched at each other because we knew her to be dead, we knew we had been driven insane by our ordeal and by the unanswerable questions it had posed us at the end.

Harete wept and beat me hard on the chest with her fists. She clawed at my face with her fingernails until I sloughed off my husk of disbelief and took her for real.

Then she hugged me, and hugged The Moth, and she kissed us both. But only I returned her kisses, and I did not hurry myself about it. I'd never kissed a ghost before. Or a girl, for that matter.

None of us spoke for a long time, for on the banks of the impossible, impassable river the joy of our reunion was so great that we forgot words ever existed. The sight of Harete was bread for our eyes, the sweetest ever baked.

Gradually, we recovered and together, in the last hour of the day's sunlight, we pieced together her story.

'I remember the tractor, yes, and it coming towards us really fast, you pair running this way and that like two boozed-up baboons, and me pushing you.'

'Thanks for that, by the by!' I said, hoping to sound relaxed and casual. But my neck had constricted to the width of a straw and the words came out all squeaky and broken.

'I think that thing drove over me. Why did it do that?' she puzzled, sounding as if it had been an insult, rather than a near-fatal accident.

'I don't think the driver saw you. He was looking to his side, to the next tractor. I think they were racing each other,' I told her.

'Why didn't I die? It had enormous wheels!'

'That's why you weren't killed. We were lucky the furrows ran parallel to the direction the machine was driving in. It simply shoved you down into the deep furrow and ran over the top of you. You were just stunned! Those massive tyres spread the tractor's weight out and stopped it from flattening the ruts,' I explained, understanding now myself. Moth had been right – Harete had defeated the tractor by using its own essence against it, those huge tyres.

'But you thought I was dead?'

Moth and I looked sheepish and nodded. 'I saw you get run over, Harete. We both did. It was awful!' said Moth, looking sickly, and more than a little guilty too.

'Boys . . .' Harete said, a thin smile on her face, 'promise me one thing? Never, ever become doctors. Or undertakers.'

She carried on, 'All I remember after that is waking up in total darkness, screaming and choking. Something dreadfully heavy was pressing down on me, and there was a . . . creature . . . with its claws in my mouth and nose, scraping out soil.'

'A dog!' I gasped, but Harete glowered at me.

'A seal. My mute seal, I called her. She never spoke, not once. She was beautiful! Such clothes! I think it was she who'd saved us from the attack dogs that time, and she who gave us the chocolate.

'She uncovered me, peeled away the clods, blew air into my lungs. Just as well the mud you'd buried me in was thick and clumpy, boys, there was plenty of air in the gaps between the lumps. That's how I avoided suffocating.'

'And then? And then?' Moth butted in.

Harete shrugged. 'Once I'd recovered from the shock of being buried and of finding you'd left me, we walked. I walked – she seemed to dance over the land! She gave me water and food. She bandaged my leg. Look!' she cried, and she rolled up her trouser leg. Wrapped around the wound made by the trap's fangs was a tube of cloth made of a leathery, rubbery fabric. I knew it at once to be the mermaid's sleeve.

'She was hard, Moth. Hard!' Harete went on. 'And fierce. When we stumbled into a patrol, it was the marshals who ran away! Only horses scared her. We walked for . . . a day? I can't remember, it's like a dream now . . . And then horses came and she ran away to divert them from me. I never saw her again. So I just walked on, following the pylons. She'd given me enough food.'

The Moth and I sat, reeling. When we came to share our own story with Harete, I had intended to omit mention of the mermaid, the mute seal, but The Moth related it in detail.

Harete had a blissful calm to her, the serenity of those returned from a place none is supposed to speak of with experience. Without an iota of anger, she turned to me. 'I

320

knew she was dead, else she would have come back to me. Nothing could ever have captured her alive. Was it worth it? We owe her. You owe her. . . . because of this!' She pointed at the river, and what lay in it.

'We'll never get out! Look at it!' she commanded. 'I thought our suffering was going to be over . . . that there would be just a . . . checkpoint, and you'd already have a ploy to sneak us past. Why did we bother?' she sobbed. But still she took my hand and squeezed it.

The Moth took her in his arms. He looked at me through his filthy lenses and said calmly, 'For all that I concede it was sort of obvious there was going to be a river here, I agree with Harete. Why did you bother? This is un-crossable. I thought you believed in planning every detail, thinking everything through; I thought you laughed at people who made silly plans with great holes in them . . . why have you tricked us like this?'

I coughed and replied, 'There always has to be one final unknown, Moth. Always. No matter how hard you plan and prepare and consider every angle, no matter how hard you work . . . it's always the same. Every scheme ends with something . . . imponderable.' For the moment I glossed over the other chasms that had opened up in my plan on the way over, and was grateful that the others did not mention them.

Moth went back to consoling Harete. They both started crying again, and soon I joined in too. Soaring joy and wonderment, guilt, crushing disappointment, emotions of every hue and stripe flushed through us.

Dried out, I had my say. 'Did you never dream what

321

it would really have to be, the lid that locks the lies in, the crease that hides the crimes? Almost no one is allowed to leave this land! This is a country where the children of important people are locked up with criminals like me and Sticky to keep their parents from speaking out of turn. Where farmers are paid to shoot strangers who come to even look at the border; where people gather on this ridge and lift up babies to show to their relatives on the other side, because they are not allowed to visit or telephone or write to them. And sometimes, as our friendly farmer's boy told us, sometimes people actually throw themselves on that barbed wire, so keen are they to get out.'

Harete and Moth hung their heads, but I carried on. 'This is a land where border guards lay bear traps for people and chase strange, tattooed women and batter them to death. For sport! One where dissenters are treated like infected cattle, herded to places known to no maps and murdered without trial.' I looked over at The Moth, but he just stared impassively back at me.

I had more to say. 'This country is the Institute, just bigger. Everything that was rotten and sick and deceitful about that place is true of the entire nation. There was no way we would be allowed to stroll over the frontier, just like we were not allowed to saunter out of the Institute. Think about it!'

'We do understand that,' muttered Harete. 'I just wasn't expecting anything this formidable.' She waved a hand dismissively at the far bank. 'It doesn't even look any different over there.'

322

I laughed out loud. 'What did you expect? Waterfalls and unicorns and castles made of candy?'

I felt happy. The situation seemed right and proper to me. This was how things had to be. We were three again, and I had a puzzle to solve.

Wasting nothing of the remaining light, I examined everything there was to see from the top of the levee. I saw the wide, white river below me that flowed from west to east. I saw the top of the opposite bank, and a row of small boats nestling above the waterline at a point more or less directly across from us. I saw the barriers that had been erected to prevent anyone who made it this far from swimming or rowing across. The barriers were not like the crummy, amateurish wall and its loose coils of barbed wire that had formed the Institute's perimeter. No, whoever had designed these obstacles was an expert in the art of containing human beings.

The first barrier was a fence of closely packed barbed-wire strands. The top portion of the fence bent inwards, towards us. That proved beyond all doubt that its intention was to keep us in, rather than people from the Other country out. I could not judge how strong or well made this fence was because almost all of it stood underwater. Only the top edge of it poked above the level of the flooded river, at the bottom of the embankment. Scanning along the line of the fence I could see a region just to my left where this seemed to have been pulled down. Perhaps the flood water had eroded the foundations of the fence posts at that point and the whole thing was leaning over. But that fence did not really matter. It was just a line in the sand, a thing to say, 'You have reached as far as you are allowed to go.' It was not the real barrier, nor did it mark the line of the frontier between our nation and the Other country.

I allowed myself to picture a conference, a meeting of army officers and politicians and surveyors and lawyers. They had probably met many decades before I was even born in some completely different country, in a large hotel taken over especially for the occasion and swarming with armed guards. They had probably flown in from their own wrecked, smouldering nations in military aircraft, leaving their families and compatriots to carry on sweeping up the rubble and burying their dead. The generals and the politicians would have spread out maps and photographs on tables and brought in armfuls of ancient parchments recording deeds and treaties. And over many days they would have argued and thumped the table and turned puce with rage and threatened renewed war and then calmed down and made compromises, especially once reminded by their hosts that neither one side nor the other had anything like enough of an army to do anything much at all to the other side. Not now, not after the war they'd just fought. And eventually, late at night, long after the waiters had retired to bed and the last of the cigars had been smoked and the coffee had turned to stone-cold syrup, they would have agreed that the border between the two countries should run along the course of the river. But along which bank? Finally, some wizened politician sitting in a wing-backed chair would have come up with the last compromise: the border should run along the exact middle of the river. Everyone would have nodded, papers would have been signed, and all would have flown back claiming peace and victory.

And so, months later, engineers from our country – for this was, like its smaller, submerged friend, definitely a product of my nation – would have set about making a barrier along the exact, dead centre of the river. This was a fortification designed to stop anyone from my country experiencing what life was like in the land of our former enemies. Doubtless our leaders would say it was to stop an invasion from the north, to keep out their spies and saboteurs, but who believed what they said?

The engineers had done a good job. The fence must have been truly mighty, because even with the level of the river so far above its norm, a height at least twice that of myself still stood proudly, lethally, above the surface of the water. From where we stood on the summit of the high riverbank I could see over the top of the great fence, but not by much of a margin.

The fence was made from rolls and coils of shiny razor wire, so tightly packed that it was almost impossible to see through it. The razor coils snaked around a framework of concrete poles, which must have been sunk deep into the riverbed. I guessed the wire went all the way down to the riverbed too, maybe even deeper, otherwise people could have just swum underneath it. All in all, the fence was about twice as thick as my outstretched arms were wide. So there it was, snaking parallel to the bank along the dead centre of the river – a high, thick, dense wall made of a billion razor blades. Catching the setting sun, it looked like a beautiful, scaly, silver serpent.

The Moth came over to me again. 'Do you have a plan? Can we get over the wire like we got over the hedges, with the mattresses?' he asked.

'Not a chance.'

'Can we at least float over to the wire with our mattress rolls and take a look at it?'

'No. Look at our waterproofs. Shredded. We'd die in five minutes in that cold water.'

'Then it is hopeless. We have to give up and turn ourselves in,' he said.

'Don't be daft. I'll get us over.'

'But you have no plan! We have no way to get to the wire and no way to cross it or cut it or go under it!'

'I have no plan *yet*. I just need to think,' I said, sitting down on the concrete base under the pylon.

Pylon number one was not in fact the final pylon on our side of the river. There was one more. It was at the bottom of the embankment, just on our side of the first small wire fence. That pylon – pylon zero I supposed it was numbered – was different from every pylon we had seen so far. Number zero was much shorter, perhaps only half as tall as the others, and its stubby arms were positioned oddly, pointing at an angle over the river. The high-voltage power cables strung between the pylons had to drop at a steep angle down to that last pylon. The cables then passed over the river to a pylon on the far side, a pylon belonging to the Other country. It was of yet another design, and shorter even than our pylon zero. For this reason, the cables dropped lower still as they traversed the river. You could not have sailed a tall ship along this stretch of the river, especially with the water level raised up in flood; the mast would have struck the power cables and probably electrocuted everyone on board! But, even at their lowest point, the power cables were way higher than anyone could possibly leap or reach.

Whoever had engineered the pylons must have had a sneaky mind, I thought. I found myself admiring him, or her. The unknown designer must have considered the idea that someone from our side of the river might have tried to climb up pylon zero and slide along one of the sloping power cables and over the razor wire to the Other country. To prevent this, each power cable had a massive disk of jagged metal placed around it like a collar.

Beyond that first pylon on the far side of the river lay a rectangular area covered in massive transformers and peculiar-looking electrical equipment. I recognised the transformers as being the grey, house-sized cubes covered in ribbed cooling fins. Other devices there spouted great tapering horns made from stacks of insulating porcelain disks. Squinting, I could make out huge metal cabinets with ladders and cooling fans and control boxes, gantries and warning signs. And away on the other side of all that mysterious stuff, on the limit of my vision in the last minutes of the day's light, I could see the power cables rise up and be taken in hand by the first of a new chain of pylons that headed out north and west. Those looked as tall as the ones we had followed, but different in design. Having grown so familiar with the ones on our side of the border, I found them rather sinister in appearance.

Moth saw them too. 'A new race of titans,' he whispered.

The river, the razor wire, the transformer farm and the

distant pylons were interesting enough, but the thing that really engrossed my mind was the first, short pylon on the other side of the river. Looking at it intently, the word that came to my mind was *festive*. Had I not known better, I would have said that someone had decorated the pylon. There were white squares and banners dotted around the metal struts and even multi-coloured balloons and bunting tangled up in the pylon's lattice work.

Shielding my eyes against the horizontal rays of light that reflected from the pylon's metal body, I tried to make out the odd things dangling from it.

'Moth, what are those?' I asked. Moth wiped his spectacle lenses and squinted.

'Protest signs. Someone has hung signs from that pylon. Hand painted, on sheets and bits of cardboard.'

'What do they say?'

'I . . . I can hardly see them in this light, and at this distance. Oddly, some are written in our language, not theirs. So they're for us to read. The bigger ones are in their language.'

'What do they say, Moth?'

Moth read and translated. '"No to trade with murderers. Stop the smelter", "Free the people, stop the money" and "No volts until our brothers have votes!"'

Once I knew what I was looking at, I could just about read some of the amateurish placards too, the ones written in the language of my country. '"Peace!", "All Nations are an . . . abomina . . . abomination", "Brothers, Sisters, Unite", "We work for your freedom." Wonder what that's about?' I said.

'A protest. Someone, or some group protesting against

328

the deal. You know, the way in which our country sells theirs the cheap electricity and they sell us cheap aluminium.'

'Are they allowed to protest like that?'

'Over there, yes. Even if they were arrested for damaging the pylon, they'd only get a small punishment.'

I whistled softly in amazement. What a country! And Harete thought that place had looked no different! Try something like that in our land . . .

'Not much use to us, though,' said Moth, turning away.

The triplet of sky, pylon and river reminded me of that first dawn on the run. In sympathy, my hair started to bristle. *Look hard*, a voice inside me said. *Think.*

My eyes fell on the balloons.

There were dozens of them, tied on long threads to a high cross-beam of the remote pylon. They must have been filled with something other than air because they did not droop down and bat about limply at the whim of the wind. Rather, they stayed aloft and tugged on their strings and rattled against the power cables themselves. In fact, there was even one tied to an actual power cable! *Imagine that!* I thought. *Imagine scaling the climbing frame of a pylon, edging out over the glass insulator and onto the high-voltage cable itself just to tie on a balloon with a message!*

'Moth . . .' I croaked. 'Moth . . . they're dead.'

'Who are dead?'

'The pylons are dead. They're off. They're not carrying any electricity.'

Grabbing her under the armpit from where she lay on the ground, I yanked Harete to her feet.

I pointed out the balloons to her. 'You know about

electricity. Look at those balloons. The strings are tied to the pylon's frame, but the balloons are touching the actual cables. One balloon is even tied to a cable!'

Looking, then understanding, she nodded. 'If they were working at even a fraction of their full voltage, anything which touched the metal pylon and the cable together would be . . . vaporised!'

'Something else,' I added. 'No hum. Transformers hum, don't they, Harete? Moth?'

'Yes. The magnetic field causes the iron particles to oscillate and make a buzzing noise,' Moth confirmed.

'Look at those monster transformers over there! And no hum! No buzz!' I said, hopping from one leg to the other with undirected excitement.

Harete looked more dubious. 'Not sure we'd hear the hum over here. But the balloons . . . yes . . . I agree. Maybe there's some, some disagreement or something between our two countries and the power's been cut.'

We scratched our heads and wondered what this bizarre discovery might mean for us. For some reason, I felt a little cheated by the pylons. All the days we had followed them, slept under them, been guided by them, I had imagined them to be living, potent beings, carriers of a stupendous and vital energy. And now it transpired they were nothing but mute, useless towers, mere ornaments.

My world was inverted, my mind spun anticlockwise as I unwound the deceptions we had endured. The power lines were powerless; Harete was alive; the chocolate had not been poisoned; the vacant landscape I had spied from the pylon had been teeming with people. There was a

330

corollary to all this deceit, and I hastened greedily towards it: maybe the insurmountable barrier was conquerable too, maybe it held the key to its own undoing.

Harete changed the subject. 'Where are we sleeping tonight?'

We busied ourselves with preparing for the night. Fearing the return of the men, I suggested we made a sort of nest farther down the embankment, deep in the tall weeds and reeds. We slipped down the bank and moved away upstream from the pylon in case it was used by our hunters as a sort of meeting point. On a spot where the ground levelled out slightly, just a short distance higher than the lapping water, we spread out some plastic sheets and blankets from our mattress rolls and made ourselves as comfortable as we could, despite our renewed and voracious hunger.

Not long after we had made the little camp, a boat came motoring along the river. The boat sounded powerful; we heard its throbbing, pulsating motor growing louder and louder many minutes before it *swooshed* by us. As it did so, the boat's wake sloshed water high up the bank and almost swamped our nest. We peered above the weeds to look. The boat was black hulled, lit by small lamps dotted over its hull. The large cabin was lit up too, and we could see the silhouettes of people in square caps moving about inside it, long, whip-like aerials which stuck up from the superstructure, a turret with a machine gun mounted on the prow.

'Square hats. Border guards,' said Moth. He and Harete turned away, but I watched for a few seconds more. One man standing on the boat's prow was not wearing a square hat. His was round, peaked, and jammed tightly onto his head. Light from the cabin showed it to be lavishly iced with gold braid, with more braid stitched on his epaulettes. To complete the garb, he wore a webbing strap diagonally across his chest. Someone in the cabin adjusted a window, and the man's face was lit from below. I nodded with satisfaction. *My Orion!* Doubtless working with the border guards, he had come in person to apply the final pinch. *It had to be him*, I told myself, I'd felt it all along.

The boat gunned its engine and slid off, gathering speed. A searchlight mounted on the cabin roof flicked on and we could see the whole of the river in front of the boat illuminated as it vanished downstream.

I did not sleep. Moth and Harete lay in each other's arms; I lay beside them and thought. I gathered in my mind everything I knew and I churned it around and around, synthesising a brand-new and brilliant thing. Deep into the night, about the time I began to feel satisfied with my creation, the patrol boat slewed menacingly past again, this time travelling upstream.

A while later, I shook The Moth awake.

'Moth, I'm going to get something. Remember that scrapyard we passed? At pylon nine?'

'Mmmm?' Moth woke up and blinked at me. 'Are you coming back?'

'Of course I am! Unless I get caught or break a leg or something,' I said, not fully able to believe what Moth had just asked. Did he really think I might just scarper? 'Listen! I should be back by dawn. Stay right here, in this very spot, as quiet as spiders. If I am not back by midday tomorrow, make your way to the scrapyard to look for me. If I'm not there . . . hand yourselves in. Promise me you won't try to swim across the river. And that you and Harete will look after each other!'

'I promise,' yawned Moth. 'Goodbye then.'

'You mean "good luck"! Moth, I am coming back!'

I packed one bottle of water and the hacksaw blade into my overalls, shouldered the rope, and started to climb up the slippery bank to the top of the levee and pylon number one. The night was clear, cloudless and cold, but a half-moon was up and loaned me a little light. My expedition was much scarier than I had thought it would be. The light was much too poor for me to be able to see where I was putting my feet, and I was terrified of losing count of the pylons, so I stuck my head up above the grass stalks, fixed my eyes on the distant form of the next pylon and just walked in as straight a line as possible towards it. But I kept stumbling and tripping over, and the journey through the black, wet forest became a suffocating, blind torment. When I reached pylon number nine I was in a state of hot panic, convinced I had lost count and would have to return empty-handed. Thrashing out of the grass, I saw the pylon in front of me and the dark shadows of the slumbering metal waste beneath it. In my haste, I forgot about the steep incline. I lost my balance, smacked onto my belly and skidded painfully down the slope, crashing into the stack of tyres at the pylon's feet.

Dusting myself down I worked my way across the junkyard to the smiley-faced van. Falling over in that place would have meant gashing my head on some sharp chunk of festering steel, so I moved very slowly, probing ahead of me with one foot. On reaching the van, I set to work liberating the fibreglass roof with the aid of my hacksaw, cutting around the corroded clips.

Every juddering draw of the blade in the dark took me back to the kerbside in the shadow of the tower block. We'd needed to saw through some rusted bolts that day too.

'It was you who chucked the rock, wasn't it?' Dad's rumble again. Home, the job done and the tools carefully cleaned and packed away, he bundled me into the single bedroom of the tiny flat we rented and slammed the door. I'd known a massive walloping was due, but I couldn't have expected it to be like it was.

Moving to the opposite side of the van to work there, I took a much-needed breather. I looked for the moon, hoping its brightness would purge the memory of the thrashing and, more, of Dad crying afterwards and stabbing himself in the back of his hand with a screwdriver as I looked on in pained confusion from the corner of the room. I guess he'd understood I'd damaged the van because I wanted him to stay home from work with me, but why that mutilation? Had it been to punish me or him? Like me, I suppose he understood *things* well, but people very little, and himself not at all.

Some hours later, with my fingers bruised and sliced, the roof slid off the top of the van and crashed to the ground.

I tipped the roof upside down so that it resembled a flat-bottomed, high-sided sled, and anchored the rope to a point on the front where one of the fastening bolts stuck

334

out. With all my strength I then started to haul the object out of the scrapyard and up the incline. Over the course of the night the soaking wet ground had frozen, and the slope was now covered in thin sheets of ice. Every time I managed to lug the van roof-sled halfway up the slope, I would slip over and the weight of the thing would drag me all the way down to the bottom again. Time and time again I tried to drag my load up that slope, and every attempt ended up with me tumbling back to the start.

'Get up! Try again, chovy!' I goaded myself. Moth's story of Sisyphus, condemned for eternity to push a boulder up a hill, came back to haunt me. Was this my destiny, too? 'It was a myth! A myth!' I shouted. Holding onto the truth, I redoubled my straining and finally succeeded.

'Thanks, Dad. Sorry!' I wearily shouted back at the scrapyard as it disappeared slowly into the gloom behind me.

The roof was heavy and its blunt end made it hard to pull through the towering grass, but I was able to make slow, withering progress. I was gravely aware of my lack of food – nothing since yesterday's bread – and began to doubt that my energy would endure.

Now that I had my plan, and all the things I required to make it happen, there was one last matter for me to decide as I slogged painfully back through the night. My plan was workable, I was confident of that, but flawed in one respect. Only two of us could make the crossing. No matter how I reimagined my scheme, there was no outcome that allowed all three of us to get across the river and over the razor wire. Since The Moth had to cross, the choice was between myself and Harete, and that meant she and I could never be together.

The night dragged on, and I dragged the roof and my thoughts. An age ago, a different me had thought that Harete had the least to lose by staying. Now I knew differently. Why should I give up my own desires so easily, and destroy her hopes too, her chance to bloom in the land of mint and sugar? Wasn't it Moth who had the least to lose? Then again, without him there could be no safety for me.

In the half-light of the half-moon I rested my sore back against pylon seven and thought penitently about my own half-truths. Turning, I pressed my lips against the pylon's metal leg and kissed it, because the pylon was my brother, all the pylons were my brothers. We all stood together, capable and ready, but denied the thing that gave us reason.

Hours later, in the dawn's testing light, I scraped the roof past pylon three. By pylon two, the day had begun, and with it returned our pursuers. Just like the day before, I had to stop stock-still and wait whilst a group of them flailed about noisily in the reeds. They were close! Panicking, I flipped the roof over and wriggled underneath it. My decision was wise, because seconds later I heard the squelch of waders as a man walked right past me. He kicked the upturned roof and walked on.

Fear worked its way rapidly through my body as an alternating series of cramps and convulsions and I barely had time to prepare. That cursed piece of jewellery worked its way out with everything else – even nine-parts buried, the shine of the ring was visible. I wiped it clean on the wet grass.

The return of the ring brought me nothing but sadness. Although I was now able to cross Harete's name off the list of deaths caused by our misadventure, that of The Mother Moth remained, and with it all my doubts about the boy I had thought to be my friend, but who was really just another stone-cold zealot. How casually he had received the news of her destruction! Alive, she'd been to him a pure-white sculpture basking on a plinth. Dead, she was another cold legend, the woman who had given her life for her son and his ideals.

Once more I reviewed my escape plan and shuffled the pieces around. Any two from three . . .

Lying under the roof, holding my breath, I realised that I now faced the twin problems of avoiding our hunters and getting to The Moth and Harete before they gave me up as having abandoned them. And so, for the last stretch, constantly alert to the men all around me, I adopted a new mode of travel. I positioned myself within the roof, held onto its sides with my arms stretched out behind me, and scuttled along low on the ground, wearing it on my back like a tortoise wears its shell. Whenever I heard a suspicious sound I dropped to the floor and hoped no one would think to look underneath the discarded junk.

Tortoise-style, I blundered past pylon one, peering out from under my shell so that I could estimate where it was down the embankment that I had left the others in their nest.

'Moth!' I hissed, unable to pinpoint the location. 'Moth!'

Was I too late? Had they now set off to find me, or been caught, or handed themselves in?

Minutes passed. 'Moth! Harete! It's me!' I called again, as loudly as I dared.

I saw a pool of reeds shimmy over to my right, lower down the embankment. Immensely relieved, I came out from under the shell, inverted it once more, and dragged it on its smooth bottom down to the spot. The two of them were there, huddled together in the nest of plastic sheets.

'Oh, hullo!' said Moth. 'You're back. Have you brought something?'

By that point my mind and body were far beyond ordinary fatigue. All I could manage was to wave a hand in the direction of the van roof that lay in the reeds beside them.

'What's *that*?' asked Moth, contemptuously.

'Our boat,' I said, and fell asleep.

Chapter 17

All Over

Harete and Moth woke me up close to midday. I felt groggy and weak and very, very hungry. They told me how they had waited and grown worried when I had not returned at dawn as I had promised, but had lain still and not panicked. They had heard the hunters that morning, and observed the patrol boat pass by three more times since I had left for the junkyard. Moth had even had the good sense to make an estimate of the boat's timings, and concluded that it passed by once every four hours, the most recent passage being about two hours previously, whilst I had been asleep.

Together we looked at the van roof. Upside down, it looked to my eyes like a fine little boat.

'More like a punt, actually,' said Moth, 'because it has a flat base.'

'Can you get us over the wire, too?' asked Harete, looking more tired and greyer and colder than I had ever seen her looking before.

'Yes, I believe so,' I answered. 'But I will need help, and not just from you.'

I had to work now. My preparations began by unwinding several very long lengths of the fishing line I had stolen from the farmhouse and tying them in parallel to one end of our carrier-bag rope, so that they would share the load between them. To the other end of the fishing line strands I tied the padlock liberated from the door of the waste compound back at the Institute. How our time there seemed like another life now, an impossibly ancient fable!

The opposite end of the bag-rope I formed into a loop about the size of my head, and to that loop I tied a single length of the fishing line. The line was heavy-duty, I noted with satisfaction, but it cut easily with a glass sliver.

Our boat still lacked one critical component until, near to us in the reeds, Harete tripped over a rotting wooden sign. Most of the letters had worn away, but the red skull and crossbones were still visible. We guessed it had been a warning sign that had fallen off the first, small fence. I immediately set Harete to work sawing the sign into three short planks with the hacksaw blade. 'Paddles,' I explained, and I mimed how she and Moth would sit in the boat and use them, like in a canoe. This would be much more effective than using our bare hands as I had been resigned to doing.

One job remained.

'Your father's,' I said. Into The Moth's hand I pressed the ring. He studied it carefully this time, turning it around and around, before handing it back to me.

'Yes,' he said flatly, 'as I thought.'

'Then your mother was . . .'

'Oh, she's fine,' interrupted The Moth breezily, 'I telephoned her neighbours yesterday.'

My jaw hinged open as Moth continued. 'From the farmhouse, before I disconnected the phone. That's what kept me. I had to pretend to be from the gas company, and I spoke in a code, but they understood. They're sympathisers. With luck, they'll have spirited her away to safety already.'

'But the ring!' Harete burst in. She knew; I had shared my worries with her as we made the paddles.

The Moth sighed and rested his head sideways against his folded knees. 'It was my father's. And he did give it to my mother. But the last time I saw *that* –' he nodded at the ring in my hand – 'it was on the Director's finger.' He shut his eyes and his voice crumbled to a mumble as he continued. 'The Director visited her in secret at home. She paid him . . . bribes, and . . . so I could receive those food parcels and letters.'

My gawping face asked my questions for me. Moth went on. 'Shameful – that brutal creep demanding things from a judge's wife, a professor, my mum! I can hardly bear to think . . . even now. You can keep it; it's tainted for me,' he said.

Harete read Moth's quivering antennae better than I could. Like an idiot, I was still thinking that a beautiful ring was a stupendous price to pay for a few bags of sweets.

'Whatever went on between them,' Harete reassured him, 'I'm sure she did it for you. These things are, you know, um, *complicated*.'

A dejected Moth finally turned his face towards us. 'Maybe so. But they executed him in that dreadful place. I'd wanted it to end, but not for him to be killed! That was my fault, don't you see?' he said. 'I should have seen it might happen, if we escaped. Worse, I think I actually did!'

A salvo of doubts rocketed from me, and in reaction I

341

collapsed backwards into the reeds in stunned relief. The Moth was no flint-heart. His reticence had not been indifference towards his mother, but huge concern for her, and unwarranted guilt about the fate of the Director.

'You're not to blame,' I told him. 'Not for anything, and certainly not that. Now, let's open the window and get you flying towards the light!'

We carried the boat further down the embankment to the water's edge. Not very far away was the top of the submerged first fence. We located the spot I had seen the day before, where the top of the fence had become broken down, so that there would be a clear run from the point where we stood straight over it and out into the river. The Moth and Harete knelt side by side in the front of the boat, holding a paddle each. I threw in our mattress rolls and my carefully prepared rope-line-padlock combination and the third paddle.

'Back in a minute,' I said. 'Whilst I'm gone, think of a name.'

'A name?'

'For the boat! All boats have names!'

I set off up the embankment. At the top I took the little tobacco tin that held my glass shards and emptied them out. I opened the tin wide and held it out in front of me, angling it so that it caught the sun. The sun was not ideally placed, it was too far to the south by then, thanks to my oversleeping, but I was able to make the polished brass flash in such a way that anyone looking from the other side of the river should have been able to see it.

From up there, near pylon one, I could see the men on

the far side, in the Other country. They were working on their boats at the top of their embankment. I flashed my tin. It was time to break one of the Institute's hard-learned rules, to take a risk and trust someone else.

Flash! Flash! Flash! Three in quick succession.

Then a pause.

Flash! . . . a long pause . . . *Flash!* . . . a long pause . . . *Flash!* . . . a long pause. Then three quick ones, and three slow ones, and so on. SOS. SOS. SOS.

I saw the men from the other side stop to watch. I waited until they cried out and started to drag their boats down the steep bank and into the water, out of my sight behind the wire coils. I gave them enough time to row to their side of the razor serpent, the barrier they did not make or want or need, and then I headed back to our boat.

Splashing past the little nest of flattened reeds and plastic sheets we had slept in, I did not notice the man lying in wait for me. He was wearing a dark green jacket and green waders and a green hat. He jumped up and grabbed me around the waist.

'Got ya!' he cried.

I screamed and fell over into the waterlogged mud; my tobacco tin spun out from my right hand and the man collapsed heavily on top of me, pinning me down.

'No!' I shouted. 'NO!'

The green man's head was on my chest, his arms were holding down my arms. I bent my head forwards, took his ear in my teeth and bit down as hard as I could, until his blood filled my mouth.

'Animal!' he roared, leaping up from me. I rolled out

from under him and jumped clumsily away from the solid fist he swung at me. As he spun around under the momentum of his own missed punch, I grabbed one of our plastic sheets from where it lay in the remains of our nest and tossed it over him. He floundered under the flapping wet thing and toppled over, letting me spring away again. I sprinted blindly through the reeds, almost missing our boat. I jumped into it with such force that the boat dislodged itself from its resting place and slid down into the water. The Moth and Harete began to row with the little signboard paddles.

Green Man came ripping out of the undergrowth and threw himself forwards. He plunged face down into the water behind us but his outstretched hands grabbed hold of the back of the fibreglass boat, stopping us dead in the shallows. I picked up the heavy padlock, attached to the fishing line, and started to beat his fingers viciously with it, mashing them with an atrocious force dredged up by my fear and desperation. He let go with a scream and retreated, soaked, to the bank. We paddled out, with me using the third board on alternate sides with alternate stokes. We made it to the submerged fence and the little boat shot across the top of the sunken barrier, and then grated to a halt.

I plunged my head into the freezing, clear water to take a look. The top of the fence had indeed been bent down, but it was only a tiny distance beneath the surface of the water. We had run aground on it. Just at the moment I lifted my face out of the river there was a *BANG!* and I felt a cloud of sizzling objects rip through the air above my head and spatter into the water, creating dozens of overlapping ripples where they landed. Green Man had made it up the embankment and had fired at me with a single-barrelled shotgun. Kneeling in the boat, facing backwards, I shoved my hands into the water and gripped the rusty barbed wire. I pressed down hard with my hands, lifting the boat a fraction, and told the others to rock from side to side. We ducked down as the second shot sprayed over us. With a lurch, the boat scraped and scratched over the wire and out into the river. All three of us paddled fanatically, keeping our heads low. Shot number three missed by a good way, and number four showered our backs with dozens of pellets, but by that time we had put such distance between us and Green Man that they lacked enough impetus to hurt.

'Paddle to that point,' I instructed them, indicating a place against the razor-wire coils just slightly upstream of the overhead power cables that sloped down across the river. Harete and The Moth were able to steer the boat by varying the relative force with which they paddled. Turning around, I could see about two dozen men gathered on top of the embankment. They could not harm us, I reasoned, we were out of range of their shotguns. We had only to hope that none of them had a hunting rifle. The men started to jeer and make gestures at us, and I took that as a sign that they had nothing more to threaten us with.

The razor-wire coils looked magnificent as we drew near them. They caught the sunlight and scattered and reflected it like a tray of diamonds in a jeweller's shop window. Every lethal silver blade and every silver coil glittered and sparkled and shone with a baleful brilliance. We had to look away from the blinding, dazzling wall and focus instead on the water.

From the other side of the coils we heard voices.

'Hullo! Hullo! Are you all right?' came a man's voice. It had a strange foreign accent and sounded friendly, the voice of quite an old man I guessed.

'Yes, yes, we are safe,' I shouted back.

'Are you coming over?' called the man.

'Yes, can you help us?' I cried.

'Yes! If we can! But I do not know what you want us to do.'

'Get boats here, as many as you have, draw them alongside the wire,' I told him.

'We have them already,' came the reply.

'What is your name?' said the man, after a pause.

I told him my name. My real name, not my Institute name. The Other country, it seemed to me, was a place where things and people could be called by their proper names. The man laughed. 'Oh, my friend, you are a long way from home. Does your boat have a name too?'

'Psst, what's it called, Moth?' I asked.

'*The Anti-Charon*,' said Moth, breathlessly. He spelled it out for me and told me how to say it properly.

I laughed. 'Moth! Even now, even now . . . Hey, mister! It's called *The Anti-Ka-Ron*.'

'*The Antique Iron*? Very appropriate!' he yelled back.

'What's your name?' I shouted out.

'Peter! I am here with my friends to go fishing.'

'Peter, I need to ask you a question. The cables up above us . . . they are not working, is that true?'

346

'I have no idea, my friend. But I know that the factory where we used to work has no power, and that the power comes from these cables. That is why we are fishing today, and all days; we have no work whilst our countries bicker,' said Peter.

Our boat barged into the wire barrier, causing it to shiver and shimmy slightly. We used the paddles to manoeuvre the boat so that it lay parallel to the wire, nestling against it. As we faced downstream, the Other country and Peter and the fishermen in their boats lay to our left, completely invisible through the mass of razor wire. Our own country and the gang of loudly jeering men were to our right. High above us, and perhaps two boat lengths downstream, stretched the thick metal power cables, sloping gently down from right to left. Looking up at them, I noticed that the cables too were made of many thin, weak strands of narrower wire braided together.

Wobbling, I stood up in the little boat, and told Harete and The Moth to do all they could to keep it steady. I rearranged the rope and its attached fishing line into a loose coil, free from knots, well away from my own feet and other obstructions. I picked up a length of the line (in fact, several lines in a loose bunch) with the heavy padlock at the end and started to slowly twirl it around.

I whirled the line in a vertical circle, playing out more and more line until the spinning padlock only just avoided hitting the surface of the water when it reached the bottom of the circle. My arm sang with pain, but I was determined to get it right on the first shot, doubting I had the energy or the nerve to make more than one attempt.

'Please,' I said. 'Please!'

With a huge cry, I let go of the line on the up-swing. The padlock with its trailing lengths of fishing line arced up high into the air. As I let go I jumped up to boost my throw, and when I landed back down into the little boat with a thump I almost caused a disaster: the boat rocked wildly, and it was only because The Moth reacted quickly and pressed his wooden paddle against the razor wire to stabilise us that we did not capsize, and that he was not thrown onto the horrible barbs. At the time, though, I was not aware of these things. My eyes locked onto the padlock and its payload of line as it traced a parabola through the air. Up, up, up it went, and I almost toppled out of the boat as I tilted back my head to watch it. The jeering men on the embankment fell silent. The padlock clipped one of the power cables. I knew that if I was wrong, if there was current flowing through those thick cables, then that would be the instant we would all die. Nothing would be left of us but three charred bodies floating out to sea.

The padlock appeared to actually skitter for a second on top of the power cable, then wobble, and then start to descend. But had it gone over the cable, or was it falling back on the same side as I had thrown it? I could not tell, could not make out what was happening up above me, but I knew that everything depended on what happened in the following second.

The coils of fishing line and the carrier-bag rope in the boat beside me suddenly raced upwards. I had done it! The padlock and attached line had crossed over the power cable, and as it was falling down on one side it was pulling

348

up the rest of the line on the other! I howled with triumph, then immediately had to duck low as the descending padlock swung past my head at great speed. Again the boat wobbled crazily, and again Moth saved us from turning over or from being tipped into the silvery razors.

The padlock and line swung past my head two or three more times before I was able to catch hold of it.

'Moth,' I said, 'you first.'

Moth stood up. Harete held the boat steady as I showed him what to do. He put one foot into the loop I had made at the bottom of the carrier-bag rope, the rope which was now dangling vertically attached to the fishing line that went up and over the power cable and down on the other side. He grasped the rope with both hands, still not understanding what was about to happen. I used some more of our tape to bind the third wooden paddle to his free foot, taping it along the sole of his shoe.

Harete understood. She knelt down and wound the other end of the line, the one with the padlock on, around her arms, ready to pull on it. I crouched beside her and grabbed the line slightly higher up. We both had on our mittens now so that we could hook the taut line around our hands without it cutting into them too much.

'Pull!' I shouted.

Harete and I both pulled down on the line. Moth rose up, his feet now just slightly above the bottom of the boat. As Harete and I strained and pulled down on our side of the line, his side moved up. We tugged and heaved together on the taut strands of fishing line. I would take hold of the line and use my arms and my body weight to pull it down towards Harete. She would then reach up and pull down the next length, and then we would swap over again, making sure that one of us was holding the line at all times. Moth continued to rise, standing with one foot in the loop at the bottom of the rope and using the other foot to push himself away from the razor wire every time he swung near it. A few times he unwisely put out a hand to hold the wire in an effort to stop the rope spinning, but each time he instantly withdrew it, badly cut.

Hauling down on the thin fishing line was torture. Every time one of us let go, the other was taking the whole of The Moth's weight in their hands. Moth could see the strain on our faces and he now understood what I had wanted him to do. Rather than trying to swing away from the coils, he used his foot with the wooden plank strapped to it to stand on them, letting them take some of his weight. The coils buckled but supported him well enough that we could substantially relax our grips between pulls. I realised then that there was no way Harete would be able to lift me. The choice of who went and who stayed had been made for me, even though I had already made that same selection whilst returning from the scrapyard.

We manoeuvred The Moth up the wall of razor wire, one tug at a time. The coils were stacked at an angle, wider at the base, so he moved up and across slightly on each pull. The boat rocked and swayed but kept in place. Eventually, Moth was dangling from the rope right at the apex of the razor wire. Harete and I were sweating and groaning as we kept the line taut to keep Moth raised up. Suddenly, the line slipped slightly and ran through our fingers and Moth dipped down with a pained squawk into the wire. He yanked up his legs, but one foot, the one in the loop at the bottom of the rope, touched a curl of razors. We pulled down harder on the line and hoisted him back up, but his foot was caught. One of the terrible blades had dug into the shoe leather. Moth could see this, and screwing his eyes against the pain he pulled his leg up with all his failing strength. His foot ripped out of the shoe, leaving it impaled on the wire coils. We could see his ankle bleeding where he had torn it past the blade. I could see Moth's blood, and at the same time tasted Green Man's blood in my mouth, mixed with a memory of the taste of bread.

The invisible Peter and the fishermen now set to work, needing no encouragement or instructions from me. One used a boat hook to reach out and grab The Moth and drag him, another used a long, flexing fishing rod to pass around his back and nudge him forwards. Because of the way the power cables sloped down slightly towards their side, they were able to edge The Moth towards them, over the top of the wire coils. He now had only to pass over the sloping flank of coils on their side before we could let go.

'Let down the wire slowly, very slowly, just a bit at a time,' called Peter. Almost at the limit of our stamina, Harete and I let the line pass through our hands in short jerks. We lowered Moth down and Peter and his friends pulled him across to them with the boat hooks. Moth kept up a running commentary, for we could not see him now. Suddenly, the line went slack.

'We have him! We have him in the boat!' said Peter, and a huge, joyful cheer went up from the fishermen.

Astonishingly, even the farmers on the embankment on our side cheered and waved and clapped and fired off their guns into the air in celebration.

Harete and I collapsed into heaps in the bottom of our boat, all strength wrung out of our starved bodies.

'Now you,' I said to her, but we both knew that I would never be able to lift her on my own.

I grabbed the slack line and rapidly pulled it, arm over arm, to retrieve the rope on the other end of it from Moth's side of the razor wire. Once it was high above the wire coils, I pulled it back across to me using the single strand of fishing line that had been tied to the bottom of the loop. This needed some jiggling to work the point where the fishing line hooked over the power cable back 'uphill' and onto our side of the razor wire.

'You'll never do it,' said Harete. I knew she was right.

Then Harete must stay with me! The thought crackled deliciously. I squinted up at the configuration of the wire and the cables and paid a long look at Harete, recovering on the floor of the boat. Then I made a last-minute adjustment to my plan.

'Peter,' I said, 'are you there?'

'Of course! We will all be here for as long as you need us. But please hurry now, because friends have told us on the radio that the patrol boat on your side has turned around and is heading very fast back downstream.'

'Peter, I am going to throw you the other end of this line. When you have it, on my signal, get your friends to pull on it and raise up my friend. We're both totally done in over here.'

352

When Peter acknowledged my request, I repeated my earlier throw. I twirled the padlock on a length of fishing line into a rapidly spinning circle, let go, and watched it curve high over the razor wire. This was a much easier throw than the first one because the wire coils were only about one half of the height of the power cables. I heard the padlock splash into the river on the far side. The line was still looped over the power cables above us, but now we had the end with the rope attached, and Peter and The Moth and the fishermen had the other end.

Harete needed me to help her stand, so drained of energy was she. I made sure she had a foot in the loop and was holding onto the rope tightly.

'Now!' I called out.

Harete shot into the air like a gymnast on a trampoline. With no more than two or three heaves, the strong men on the other side had raised her high above the wire coils. They had already developed a new trick. I saw a weighted fishing line fly out and wrap itself around Harete's legs, binding them tightly. The men now pulled on that line to slide Harete sideways over the top of the razor wire, then they lowered her slowly down by playing out my fishing line. I guessed fewer than three minutes elapsed between the time she had put her foot in the loop in our boat to the time she was lowered into Peter's boat next to Moth.

I slapped my forehead in disbelief. Why hadn't we done that for The Moth? Laughing, delighted for my friends, I joined in the whooping celebrations I could hear coming from over the impenetrable barrier and from the embankment too.

My little boat heaved and rocked and I was hurled down into its bottom. Its noise masked by our celebrations, the border patrol vessel had slunk up on us like a crocodile. The great black boat sliced through the water with terrific haste and drew alongside my pathetic shell. It was all I could do to lie flat and cling onto the punt's sides as it was bucked violently up and down by the larger boat's wake.

The patrol boat revved its motors. In shape, it resembled an inverted clothes iron, with a sharp prow and a blunt stern. Underneath it, the deep waters foamed and the boat turned around to present me with its stern. Then it began to reverse straight at me. If there were screams from The Moth and Harete and Peter, I did not hear them. I was totally absorbed by the flat slab of the boat's rear, as high as a house, surging towards me on the one side, and the mountain of razors on the other. The gap between the two narrowed, then the ramming boat slowed. Over the boat's guardrail there appeared a familiar face. The lines of gold braid on his cap and his epaulettes looked like scrolls of butter. They, and the white webbing strap over his puffed-out chest were doubtless all marks of his elevated rank. In his hands was a long pole with a hook on the end. What had Tulips told me? *Orion was a legend.* Monsters I had always believed in, but never legends.

'Hold steady, eight six five! I'll soon have you out of this squeeze,' Jelly shouted down at me with repellent zest.

The pole clonked into the bottom of my tiny boat and scraped around, groping for me. I grasped it and pushed it away, preferring to be sliced on the razor wire. *The squeeze,*

I thought. I'd dropped my guard and been caught. And this time, there would be no angel to rescue me.

Above, Jelly made to lunge again with the pole. 'Don't fight me!' he barked, scowling with frustration. 'If it wasn't for me being here, you'd have already been shot. Let me get you.' The patrol boat bashed into mine, scrunching it into the wire with a noise like the tines of a fork being scraped over a china plate.

'They made me the new Director,' Jelly yelled down at me. 'And nine five two recovered! Said he'd tried to kill himself. Lies, but it got that other boy off the hook.' His own hook swung low over my head, brushing through my hair. *I wasn't a murderer! And Retread was safe!* The news was scant comfort right then, my little craft starting to groan, the fibreglass hull threatening to shatter like an egg.

Jelly grunted and swore as I dodged the pole again. 'Co-operate, boy! There are things you don't know. You can do great things for me, and I can help you. I told you I had connections with a higher power.'

The patrol boat was too close now for Jelly to manoeuvre the pole comfortably, so he gestured angrily to the bridge and it backed away slightly with a growl of its motors. Jelly juggled with the long pole, sliding it backwards and upwards under his arm like a pool player adjusting his cue for a shot in a room too small for the table. He licked his lips and corrected his grip once more before the final spearing thrust.

An incandescent pulse of yellow light burst out above me. Looking up I saw a hoop of fire in the air, and heard screams from over the razor wire and from the boat. I

355

smelled burning plastic, and felt shrivelled, blackened embers pattering onto my clothes. The fishing line and my carrier-bag rope were gone, atomised.

Jelly had vanished, too, the pole splashed into the water, flaring orange flames at one end. The patrol boat's engine's stalled, a horn hooted, smoke gusted from the bridge and from the deck. It took all my concentration to steady my fragile craft as the other boat lit up its spluttering motors again and retreated, lurching at speed towards the far bank. It ground noisily over something, and came to rest at an angle. Square-hatted crew members began to dive overboard and swim to shore, helped up by the farmers, as the boat caught alight.

'Are you there? Are you safe?' I shouted out over the wire.

'Yes, everyone is fine! We are all fine; your friends are fine,' shouted several voices all at once.

'They switched on the current! The power lines are live again,' I yelled. 'He must have brushed a cable with the end of that rod.'

'We are lucky no one was touching the fishing line. Even the water was electrified there for an instant,' said Peter. A pause, and then he added, 'But we . . . we cannot now rescue you, my friend. We have rope and wire, but we cannot use the power lines as a hoist.'

Through the wire I heard Harete and The Moth burst into tears.

'I know!' I said. 'That's fine, because I wasn't intending to come anyway,' I added, speaking the truth.

'Oh!' said Peter, sounding very surprised, 'were you really not?' From Harete and Moth came more howls of anguish.

'No. I'm not . . . I'm not ready to come.' Then I asked him, 'Can you help me escape? I certainly can't go back now, look at that boat burn! They'll send another very soon.'

There were shouts and many other sounds from the far side. Then a paddle, a proper canoe paddle, came twirling over the wire like a gigantic sycamore leaf. It splashed in the river next to me, and I pulled it into my boat. Then came another one, then lunchboxes and haversacks and fruit, rubber boots and sweaters and hats and gloves and a clasp-knife and a box of fishing tackle and a pair of binoculars and a sleeping bag and flasks of drink and a radio and many, many more items. Some things dropped right into my boat, some into the water around me, some came loose and some were stuffed into bags.

'Enough! Enough!' I shouted. What people! What people to throw such things to someone they did not even know, could not even see! I piled all these wondrous goods into one end of the boat and started to use one of the paddles to row gently downstream. Peter and The Moth and Harete followed me in their boat on the other side of the wire.

'Paddle downstream for about thirty minutes. Then you will start to enter the delta,' advised Peter.

'The delta? What's that?' I asked.

'The river delta! Where the river spreads out wide, splits into many channels and goes into the sea. Like a crow's foot, or a triangle.'

'I had no idea we were so close to the sea.'

'Listen. In thirty minutes, you will start to enter the

delta. The river splits into many streams, separated by mud banks. Keep taking the smallest channels, the patrol boats are too big to follow you into them. Wherever the river forks, always take the narrowest route.'

'Understood! What then? Shall I go out to sea?'

'In that thing? No, go deep into the delta, and let the delta gypsies find you. They are strange people, but noble ones; they look after themselves and each other. As long as you are not a police – what do you call them? Marshals? – then they will welcome you as they welcome all who drift.'

'Delta gypsies? Who are they?'

Moth's jubilant voice floated over to me, saying, 'Of course! The gypsies of the delta. The mermaid!'

'They are people who live on the delta, in houseboats and in camps on stilts. They do not care about nations or passports or barriers –' at this point I heard Peter whack the wire coils contemptuously with an oar – 'they work illegally, harvesting the delta, collecting cockles and other shellfish.

'Some call them savages, thieves. But fables say they have composed symphonies from the equations of creation, that they are the sages of the sea. There are stories that their prophets are blind and their warriors are mute, that they once lived everywhere but jealousy consigned them to the margins and the marshes.'

Moth's voice bubbled over. 'Remember the vase! Their wisdom must be . . . the stuff of legends,' he said.

Peter spoke again, 'Stay the winter with them, and then they can take you anywhere you want to go.'

'Even to Canada? Maybe I could go and see if Topsy-Turvy really does exist!' I joked.

'Yes, even Canada!' chuckled Peter.

I started to row a little faster. Moth spoke, sounding serious and excited. 'My father will be able to speak now, and when he does, his words will crack the world. The government over there will fall. My father may return as a new leader, an elected one. All these barriers will come down, our nations will be one, and all shall have law.'

'I'm delighted to hear it, Moth,' I said, unsure if I believed him or not, and not caring either way.

'Come over to us; get the delta gypsies to bring you to us,' he shouted back.

'No, my mind is made up. I've used you and sheltered behind you for too long! Moth . . . your myths and legends, the ones you live by . . . they're all made up, there's no truth in any of them, is there?'

'There's lots of truth in them. Not historic truth, not scientific truth, no . . . but there are things there to inspire and guide and warn and amuse; stories can do that.'

'Yes, I understand, Moth. But I want to make my own legends now, not live by your old ones. I want to find my father, now that you've found yours, and maybe my mother too. And have adventures and do more bad things and eventually learn not to do bad things.'

'Do all that! Then come to us!'

'I will!'

Peter spoke, saying rapidly, 'We need to go back. We will delay any new patrol boats; we will show them who we have here with us and they will probably not even bother with you. And we will call out our own river police to perform a stand-off across the border. We will buy you lots of time.'

He stopped his rowing boat and started to turn it about. I pushed away from the fence with my new paddle and began to row harder and faster. We shouted out our final farewells using all the names we knew for each other.

'Goodbye, Harete. I mean, Arete. Goodbye, beautiful excellence!'

'Goodbye! Goodbye!'

'Goodbye, Moses!'

'Goodbye, Mohammed!'

'Goodbye! Goodbye!'

'Goodbye, my Hermes! Most cunning of thieves, traverser of boundaries, messenger, inventor, friend of travellers,' cried Moth, his voice growing fainter and fainter.

I ceased to listen. I picked up an apple from the bottom of the boat and clamped it between my teeth. Turning once, I gave the distant line of brother pylons a sly wink, pleased that they were restored to their proper role as bearers of a dangerous cargo.

The river grew wide and the kind winter sun warmed my back as I struck out for the delta. I bit into the crisp apple, and thought of new names to call myself.